Laiden's Daughter

Book One of

The Clan MacDougall Series

By

Suzan Tisdale

Prologue

Northern England, late winter, 1329

The wee bairn wept as bitter winds whipped down from the hills thrashing whirlwinds of snow around the feet of those gathered to pay their last respects. They were there to say goodbye to Laiden, the bairn's mum.

The little girl clung to Moirra; her tiny face buried in the auld woman's wool skirts. Moirra had been her mother's best friend until the day she died. Now, she was the only good thing the child had left in the world and the only person who remained who would protect her from her father.

The bairn tried to be brave, as Moirra had told her she needed to be, but it wasn't easy for someone so young. When Laiden died, Moirra had made the sign of the cross, wiped tears from her wrinkled face, and told the bairn that her mother was in a much better place. Young though she was, the bairn wondered what better place could there be than here with her daughter?

The priest spoke in strange words the little girl did not understand. The tone of his voice and the lead colored sky matched the heaviness in her heart. He didn't seem to be reading from the book he held in his claw-like hands; he seemed instead to have memorized the words. There was no sadness or feeling to his scratchy voice. The bairn did not care for the skinny man with the dull brown eyes and wished he would go away.

Perhaps, the bairn thought if she could just lie down next to her mum and warm her, then her mum could come back from the better place Moirra had told her of. Earlier that morning, she had shared her idea with Moirra. Tears had welled in the auld woman's brown eyes before she gave the little girl a hug and told her, "'Twere it that simple lass, I woulda done it meself."

They had been by Laiden's side for days, had placed cold rags on her forehead, and covered her with blankets. They offered her warm broths and had prayed over her. None of the herbs the healer provided had worked. In the end, nothing had worked.

On the morning of her passing, Laiden must have known she was not long for this world. She begged and pleaded with Moirra to take care of her daughter. Moirra made the promise, a promise the bairn wished desperately the auld woman could keep. She did not want to stay with her father and brothers. The three older brothers were mean to her, especially when no one was looking. They thought it quite funny to leave spiders in her pallet or to pull at her braids.

As a light snow began to fall, the bairn's thoughts turned to the morrow, and all the morrows that would follow without her mum. Who would sing to her at night or comfort her when she was frightened? Who would tell her stories or care for her when she was ill? Who would teach her to weave or sew? Who would protect her from her father and brothers? She could only pray that it would be Moirra.

When the priest had finished speaking, the people gathered around her father. They gave him their condolences and offers of help should he need it. Broc stood somberly, nodding his head, but said nothing. He was a tall man and strong, but somehow he seemed small this day, and his skin looked nearly as ashen as Laiden's had been when she died.

Long after the men had covered her mum's body with stones, the bairn remained at her side. Her stomach hurt from missing her so much. The only thing that kept her from screaming out was the fear that even on this day, her father would send her to cut a switch with which to beat her. Such an outburst would not be tolerated, no matter the reasons behind it.

After a time, Moirra came and took her back to the bairn's own cottage. Perhaps they were going to pack up what few belongings she had before they would go to Moirra's home. She had, after all, made a promise.

The pain in the auld woman's eyes when she asked her of it was quite evident. Moirra explained that first she must speak to Broc and together they would make the decision as to where she would live and who would care for her.

Moirra tucked the bairn into her pallet by the fire and pulled the blankets snuggly under her chin. Had this been a normal day, the bairn would have pleaded for permission to forgo her afternoon rest. Today however, was not a normal day. Moirra told her not to worry, that all would be well. The bairn wanted very much to believe her.

After night had fallen and the candles were lit, the bairn feigned sleep. She stayed quiet and hidden under her blankets as she listened to Broc and Moirra argue over what was to become of her.

"How are you goanna teach her about things when she's no longer a bairn but a full grown lass? Have you thought of that Broc?" Moirra asked, frustrated with his obstinacy.

Broc would not listen. He would not let anyone take Laiden's daughter. It wasn't out of devotion to his dead wife that he kept the child, there were other reasons; reasons he could not share. While it was true that he had loved Laiden, loved her with all that he was, she had not been able to return those feelings. After all these years, after all he had done for her, he could not lay claim to that which he wanted most -- her love. Her heart, right up until the end, had always belonged to another.

The bairn could not understand why this cold, distant man refused to let her live with Moirra. She had known her whole life, short as it was to this point, that the man held no good feelings towards her. She was always in the way and stealing her mother's affections from him. He never hid his resentment toward her for it.

Had the bairn been blessed with the ability to read minds, she would have known that it was guilt and fear that drove Broc. Guilt for a lie he had told long ago in order to keep Laiden for himself and the fear of being found out that kept him from letting the child go.

"Nay!" Broc's voice rose with anger. "I'll not hear of it!"

The next words that Moirra spoke were words that would change the little girl's life forever. "I promised Laiden on her death bed that I would take care of her daughter! Why do you want the child, when you be not her real father?"

The child froze with uncertainty, fear, and dread. Surely she must have misunderstood.

A low growl came from Broc's throat. "I be more of a da to her than her own woulda been! I be the only da she knows and that is how it shall remain. I'll not hear anymore of the matter. Now be gone with ye auld woman!"

When Moirra left the cottage she took the bairn's heart with her. Only five summers old, she was bright enough to figure out that her life would never be the same. The grief and anguish she felt at losing her mother increased a hundredfold the moment she realized she would never be allowed to live with Moirra.

As she lay hidden under the blankets, her mind asked questions her heart could not answer. Sadness, blended with the dread in her heart, formed into quiet tears that spilled down her small cheeks. She prayed that God would keep her safe and would protect her from her father's wrath. God would have to, for He was the only one left who could.

One

Northern England, 1343

Hot searing pain burned Aishlinn's face and throughout her body, yet she remained firm in her resolve not to succumb to the demands the earl was making. She'd not bed this smelly and repulsive man, no matter how badly he beat her.

With all the strength she could muster Aishlinn stood firm. On legs weak from fear, she teetered for a moment and tried to stare him down. "Nay," her voice was but a mere whisper.

Intense anger and fury filled the man's eyes as he threw another blow to her face. Her mouth filled with more blood and sparks of white light burst before her eyes as she fell to the floor.

"How dare you!" he yelled as he towered over her. "I am your lord. I am the Earl of Penrith and you shall give me what I demand!"

Her breathing was labored, her heart filled with fear and hatred. Wiping her bloodied lips on the torn sleeve of her dress, she took a deep breath. Through eyes so swollen she could barely see she looked up at the earl and told him once again, "Nay."

A loud growl escaped the earl's throat. An impatient man to begin with, he was furious with her stubbornness. He had bed countless women over the years. Many had been willing partners while others had to be persuaded a bit more firmly to give in to his demands. But this wench was different. For some reason she would rather be beaten to death than simply give him what he wanted. He was an Earl after all, and no one denied him anything. Ever. He was a man of privilege.

Appointed to this God-forsaken land by the King of England, the earl was accustomed to having anything he wanted. It mattered not to him if this wench surrendered willingly or fought him every step of the way. He would have what he wanted.

He stared down at the trembling heap lying on the floor. When she had first arrived in his room, he had tried to be gentle, yet firm. When words had not worked to convince her to warm his bed, he had gone with a much sterner approach. Still, she refused him, even after several slaps to her face and some well-chosen blows to her body. And the leather strap he'd taken to her back and legs had done nothing to change her mind.

It had been her willful disobedience that had angered him more than anything else. Now she lay upon the floor before him, battered to the point he no longer recognized the beauty that had caused him to want her in the first place. Her face black and blue, her dress torn and bloodied, and still, she refused him. Who on earth did this young whore think she was?

She tried to steady her breathing to keep from passing out. Every inch of her body hurt and she was exhausted beyond measure. But she simply could not give in, could not submit to his demands.

She had no idea how long she had been in the earl's room. It had been very late when Baltair, one of the guards, had come to her room. When he had told her the earl wished to see her, fear shot through her veins for she was certain there could only be one reason why she would be summoned to his room.

Baltair had respectfully turned his back while she slipped back into her dress before escorting her to the earl's room. "I'm sorry, lass," he had whispered before opening the door to the earl's chambers. Aishlinn was certain she had seen a glimpse of genuine sadness in his eyes when he had closed the door behind her.

She had heard many a story about the earl and his lust for women. She also knew that he was a ruthless man who would inflict instant punishment on anyone, regardless of age or gender, who had either defied or displeased him. The earl was merciless.

Aishlinn now lay upon the floor of the earl's chambers and prayed. She prayed that he would grow weary and give up or that God would strike one of them dead, preferably the earl. She was saving her purity for a husband she knew she would probably never have, but saving it nonetheless. As far as she was concerned, the earl could shove hot coals up his arse; she would not bed him.

It was no longer important to him to hear her utter the word "yes". He bent down and grabbed Aishlinn by her arms. His eyes were filled with rage as he lifted her and threw her upon his bed.

Her heart shattered into a thousand pieces as she flew through the air. No matter how hard she fought, no matter what she did, he would have what he wanted.

The next moment he was straddling her and she felt the cold hard blade of a dagger against her throat. A repulsive smile had formed across the earl's face when he saw the first hint of fear in her eyes. Grabbing the top of her dress, he began to cut it from bodice to hem. His movements were careful and slow and he would pause frequently to glance at her face. The fear flashing behind her green eyes excited him more.

She could no longer fight him. In the recesses of her mind, she heard a small voice tell her that if perhaps she gave in to his demands, then afterwards she could flee this place. Perhaps she could find safe passage to London and start her life over. No one would ever have to know what the earl had done to her this night.

As the last bit of her dress gave way to his knife the earl angrily tugged at her sleeves. Rolling her out of her dress, she landed face down on the mattress. She gasped when she felt his knee in her back and his hand grab her hair. Violently he jerked her head back and she could feel his hot breath on her ear. Droplets of blood from her cut lips ran down her chin. Angrily he whispered in her ear, "You have a decision to make whore. Do you choose life or do you choose death?"

Aishlinn had no fight left in her. Let him have his way and then she could be gone. If she had to walk all the way to London she would. Surviving the night was all that mattered now.

Nearly retching on her own words, her throat and mouth dry, she answered, "I choose life."

Though she could not see the earl's face she knew the evil smile remained upon it. Victory was his; defeat hers. When he rolled her over onto her back the sordidness in his smile terrified her.

With the dagger still in his hand, he grabbed her dress and wiped the blood from her mouth. It mattered not to him that her lips were cut and swollen and still bleeding, he kissed her anyway. Harshly and savagely his tongue found its way into her mouth. His breath smelled of whiskey and onions. The vileness of it caused her to gag. Her stomach churned with disgust and shame. She had never been kissed before and this was not how she imagined her first kiss would be.

He stopped for a moment still displaying that same nasty smile, "You'll be choking on more than my tongue momentarily dear."

Aishlinn had no idea what he meant and dreaded the thought of finding out.

More revolting kisses came as he began grabbing at her shift, tugging at the sleeves. Trepidation, fear and disgust washed over her. Thoughts and images of her family came rushing into her mind. She saw her father's face, shaking his head and telling her he had known all along that she was no good. Then her three brothers appeared, laughing and taunting her. "'Tis what you get for thinking yer better than ye really are! Yer worth nothin'."

Then she saw her mum, beautiful, strong Laiden, and she held such a curious look upon her face. 'Twas her mum who said "Nay! Do not give in!"

Aishlinn's heart sank when she felt the earl pulling her shift down, his hot hands upon her small breasts, squeezing them forcefully. 'Twas then that Aishlinn realized he had made his first mistake. He had both hands upon her breasts. Where was the dagger? She turned her head and saw it lying upon the mattress and realized it was within her reach. She could still fight! Perhaps if she could grab the knife, she could threaten him with it. She could threaten to cut off his manly parts or stab him in the heart if he did not stop.

Slowly, she reached for the dagger. She would pretend for a moment, repulsive as the thought was, to enjoy what the earl was doing. Pretend just long enough to grab the dagger. When she feigned a soft moan of pleasure the earl mushed his face into her neck and bit her. She could feel his manhood growing as she carefully wrapped her fingers around the hilt of the knife.

'Twas then that the earl made is second mistake; he believed she was truly enjoying his hands and mouth upon her. With his face still buried in her neck he said, "I told you that you would enjoy this." 'Twas then that he moved his mouth to her breast and bit.

The pain was unbearable. A low growl escaped her throat and without thinking, she plunged the dagger into his back, pulled it out and thrust it in a second time. She had not intended to harm him but she could take no more. The earl lifted his head and looked at her. The victorious grin had been replaced with a look of complete bewilderment.

"You whore!" he muttered as he let out a long, slow breath then collapsed upon her.

Two

It took every ounce of strength Aishlinn had left to wriggle out from under the earl. Blood oozed from his back and soaked into his shirt. Her stomach churned violently as the coppery smell of blood and sweat assaulted her senses. Her hands trembled while her mind raced, fighting hard to regain her wits. She needed to flee this room and this castle and she needed to flee it quickly.

With trembling fingers she unbarred the door as quietly as she could. Taking a deep breath, she pulled it open just a crack, enough to peer into the hallway. 'Twas empty and dark, save for the few lit torches that lined the walls. She tried not to look at the dead man in the bed as she grabbed her dress and hurried out of the room. Blood rushed in her ears and her heart pounded as she tiptoed down the dark hallway.

As she rounded a corner, she caught sight of a guard slumped over in a chair. She prayed for him to be either passed out from too much drink or a sound sleeper, she cared not which. A jolt of pain shot through her chest as she took a deep breath. Clutching her dress to her chest as if it were a shield, she dared not breathe as she held herself close to the wall and tiptoed past the guard. She prayed God would show her some mercy and would not let her encounter anyone else this night.

Through the semi-darkness, she crept quietly down the three levels of stairs as quickly as she could. She paused at the last step to listen for sounds of life and tried to think the best way of escape. To her left was the large gathering room that led to the kitchens. She knew that area well, for that had been the portion of the castle where she had worked since arriving less than a month ago. To her right was the earl's library and an area of the castle she was not at all familiar with.

The gathering room was filled with sleeping men, passed out from drinking too much wine consumed throughout the night. Some of the men lay upon the massive tables while others slept on the cold stone floor. A few of them snored heavily, while others ground their teeth or mumbled in their drunken sleep. If she took the route she knew best, she risked stumbling over one of the drunkards and waking them. If she went in the opposite direction, she risked getting lost in parts of the castle she did not know.

She decided the best route to freedom was the one she knew. But before her foot could touch the floor, a large hand suddenly clamped around her mouth while an arm grabbed her around her waist. She was lifted off the ground and whisked down the hallway.

Besieged with fear and pain, she could not cry out or struggle against the firm hold he had on her body. She could hear nothing but the blood rushing in her ears and the pounding of her heart. Freedom would not be hers this night. She could only pray that the person who held her would be merciful and kill her quickly.

It was a familiar voice whispering in her ear as she was taken into the earl's library.

"Aishlinn! Please do not scream, do not let out a sound!" The voice was firm yet pleading. "I'm going to set you down but do not utter a word. If you scream out I'll not be able to help you escape. Do you understand?"

She thought she detected a slight note of fear in the man's voice. She nodded her head in agreement as she tried to tamp down the wave of fear that was all consuming.

Very slowly he set her on the floor and loosened his hold. She spun around to see who had grabbed her, but it was far too dark to see anything more than the black shadow. Aishlinn heard him step across the room and a moment later the sound of a candle being lit. Moments later the room was bathed in the soft light.

It was Baltair who stood before her. But why? Why had he brought her here and why was he helping her? Uncertain if she should be fearful or relieved to see him, she stood still, holding her dress to her bosom, as she searched his eyes for any sign as to what his intentions might be.

He looked clearly sorrowful, but Aishlinn could not begin to fathom why.

"I am so sorry for what he has done to you," he whispered. "I should never have taken you to him. It was fear for my own well-being that made me do it."

Baltair had not expected Aishlinn to fight as fiercely as she had. Baltair had remained outside the earl's chamber room door after he had brought Aishlinn to him. He had worked for the earl for many years and knew all too well how he treated young women. When he realized that Aishlinn was not going to give in to the earl's demands, no matter how harshly the earl made them, Baltair knew in his heart what he must do. He could not bear the thought of another young girl being killed.

As fast as he could, he had left Aishlinn alone with the earl long enough to saddle a horse for her potential escape. He was both surprised and relieved to see her standing on the stairs when he returned. Baltair had grabbed her when he realized she was going to attempt to escape through the kitchens where people were still awake.

"No one deserved what he did to you and it is my fault for it," he told her, his voice solemn yet anxious. "I've a daughter about your age, Aishlinn. I'd never want her to go through what you did."

Seeing the guilt and sorrow in Baltair's eyes, Aishlinn was fully prepared to thank him for helping her. He grabbed her hand and led her to the large fireplace before she could utter a word.

"We must move quickly before anyone wakes," he whispered. He drew back a large tapestry that hung on the wall next to the fireplace.

"Say nothing," he told her as he pulled her through a hidden doorway. "The sounds carry here."

Aishlinn had no choice but to follow him into the darkness. She stayed close, with one hand clinging to his, the other grasping firmly to the back of his coat.

With each step, the pain in her ribs seemed to intensify, making it quite difficult to breathe. She pushed through the pain, for now she must concentrate on escape.

Baltair led the way through a maze of corridors and tunnels that seemed to snake along endlessly. Aishlinn had no idea where he was leading her. She hoped the sound of her pounding heart would not echo through the hidden corridors. An eternity seemed to pass before they came upon a very narrow passage. It led through the thick walls of the castle and spilled out into the courtyard.

Creeping quietly in the darkness, Baltair held a firm grip on Aishlinn's hand. She wondered how Baltair was able to see in the darkness, for she could barely see the back of his head.

The night air was frigid and brought goose bumps to her bare skin for she still wore only her shift. She did not complain of the cold or the stones and sticks that pricked at her bare feet. Freedom was too close at hand for complaint.

They hugged the castle wall and walked a good distance before Baltair led her toward the large arched entranceway of Castle Firth. Soon they passed through a small wooden door hidden by heavy vines and before she knew it they were walking along the dirt road that led away from the castle.

She could smell and hear the horse before she could see it.

"Aishlinn," Baltair whispered, "this will be a good mare for you. Stay upon this road until the sun breaks at your back."

Before she realized what was happening Baltair grabbed her about the waist and set her upon the saddle. An unbelievable amount of pain shot through her ribs and back when he lifted her. She nearly tumbled off the other side of the horse before taking a firm hold of the saddle.

"When the sun breaks, leave the road and head north and west!" He tucked the reins into her hands.

Aishlinn had planned to flee to London, which was to the south and east. "But London does not lie in that direction, Baltair!" she argued.

"You'll not want to go to London, Aishlinn," he told her. "I'm sending you to Scotland. They won't think to look for you there." His voice was anxious as he led her and her horse down the road. "If you want freedom Aishlinn, you must go to the Highlands. Trust me!" There was more than a hint of fear and desperation in his voice.

"Remember! Stay on this road until the sun breaks at your back, then head into the forests and keep going north and west. You'll find your people there, Aishlinn!" He gave her no chance to respond before he slapped the mare's rump hard with the palm of his hand.

Aishlinn did not have time to ask Baltair what he meant by *her people* for the mare had taken off the moment his hand came down upon it. She was nearly tossed again from the saddle and clung on to it for dear life. Why on earth he was sending her to Scotland, she had no clear idea. She could only pray that Baltair was right in his decision.

A sudden surge of hope washed over her as she flew down the road and thought of Scotland. Her mother had died long ago when she was just a little girl. Aishlinn knew very little of her mother's life before she had married Broc, but she did know that her mother had come from the Highlands. It had been Moirra who had told her. She had promised to tell Aishlinn more when she was older. Unfortunately, Moirra had died before she could keep her word.

If Moirra was correct, then there was a small chance that Aishlinn could find her mother's clan. Perhaps she could even learn who her blood father had been. Perhaps her mother's family or her father's might be willing to take her in, offer her a home.

With no idea just how far away Scotland might be, Aishlinn kept the horse at a full run. She prayed for God's speed and His mercy. She would need His divine intervention in finding her mother's clan, for she hadn't a clue how to do it on her own.

Three

Duncan McEwan and his men had been riding for days, searching for the reivers who had taken some thirty head of cattle from their clan more than a sennight ago. Their mission was simple; find the thieves, inflict a swift and befitting punishment and bring back that which belonged to them.

Duncan had been convinced the thieves had belonged to a clan with which his own feuded. However, the tracks they had been following, did not lead in the direction of the Buchannans. Instead, they led away and toward land the English had taken from Scotland decades ago. Duncan could not imagine why reivers would travel such a distance to steal cattle. None of it made much sense.

He and his men were stopped near a wide stream as they allowed their horses to drink and rest before heading out again to points uncertain. 'Twas growing late in the day and the sun shone brightly as it cast dappled shadows across their bare chests and the cold ground. 'Twas early spring now and he was glad the days were growing longer and warmer.

Duncan was dressed only in his leather trews and boots with his sword hanging at his side and his broadsword strapped to his back. 'Twas warm for this time of year and he knew all too well the weather could change quickly and without notice.

He thought back to something his father had been fond of saying: "Welcome to Scotland lads. Don't like the weather? Wait a few minutes fer it will surely change."

His father had been such a good and honorable man and his death, even after these many years, still tore at Duncan's heart. Someday Duncan hoped to exact his vengeance on the man who had killed every man and woman, and nearly every child from his village.

Duncan looked around at the six men he traveled with. On or off the battlefield, these were men he could depend on. Hellions, aye, but fierce, loyal and honorable warriors each.

He smiled as his cousin Rowan entertained them with the stories of lasses he had conquered. They'd all heard the same stories before, many more than once. A few of the events they had personally witnessed or had been a party to. But after these many days away from the clan and their families any story was better than none.

Rowan was going on about one particular lass he had had the fine pleasure of knowing in Inverness last fall.

"Aye!" he said with a mischievous grin. "She appeared to be a very fine bar wench! Her hair as soft as a new bairn's bottom and her eyes the brightest blue I'd ever seen!"

Findley and Richard McKenna tried to hide their knowing smiles. Though three years separated them in age they looked very much like twins with their matching brown hair and eyes. They were of the same height and build, and whether frowning or smiling, it was often difficult to tell them apart. Though not quite as tall as Duncan or Rowan, what they lacked in height they well made up for in strength and agility.

They had been with Rowan in Inverness and knew the story he now told very well. However, Tall Thomas, Gowan and Manghus had not taken that particular trip. They had been at home with their wives.

The two brothers let Rowan ramble on for a while longer about the pleasures the woman had brought him that night. Finally, Richard broke in. "Aye, Rowan! She did show ye a few things that night!" he said, trying to stifle his laughter.

"Aye!" Findley chuckled. "You were certain she be the love of yer life. If memory serves me, ye demanded someone find a priest so ye could marry the fine lass that night!"

Rowan was not happy about being interrupted. Before he could tell the brothers to shove sticks up their arses, Richard said, "But when ye woke the next day, no longer so into yer cups ye could no' find yer arse with both hands, ye let out a bloody yell!" He could no longer contain his laughter. "Ran like yer arse was on fire! Out of the inn half naked! Ye swore that God had somehow replaced yer fine maiden with a very plump auld woman missing most of her teeth!"

"And she had more hair upon her face than Rowan!" Findley was laughing so hard that tears formed and filled his eyes.

Everyone laughed, save for Rowan. He glared angrily at each of them. While his fierce scowl would make most men back down, his friends knew him too well to be worried. "I was getting to that part, Findley!"

Duncan laughed with his men, as Rowan's face had turned crimson. Duncan wasn't sure if Rowan was more embarrassed than angry. Laughing, he left his friends to needle each other while he went back to study the tracks that had led them to their current location.

Something had been gnawing at Duncan's thoughts throughout much of the day. These tracks they followed and the direction in which they led were troublesome. He could not imagine why reivers would travel so far to steal cattle. Duncan's own clan MacDougall held decent enough relations with most of the neighboring clans. Still, there were others who they had been feuding with for as long as anyone could remember. However none of those feuding clans were this far to the east.

Who would travel this far to steal their cattle? They had traveled by several glens filled with cattle that were more easily taken than Clan MacDougall cattle. Were they being led on a wild goose chase for some unknown reason?

He pondered the many possibilities for several minutes before sharing his opinion with the others. "Rowan," he began. "Do ye think it odd we've ridden after the reivers for these many days now?"

Rowan was working the knots out of his back and neck. He stretched his arms out wide and yawned before answering. "Aye, Duncan, I do."

Duncan's eyes scanned their surroundings. The land before them was thick with trees and brush. Rocks and pebbles lined both sides of a wide, meandering stream. It made no sense to him why the reivers brought the cattle this way. "It be an odd route to bring cattle through, do ye no' think?"

Gowan agreed. "Who do ye suppose traveled so far to reive cattle?"

Duncan could see the wheels turning in the minds of his men. Their faces told him that none of them thought they were dealing with simple-minded reivers. Something more was afoot but exactly what they were not certain.

"Mayhap it be a trap by the English to draw us into battle," Gowan said. "Or, things are far worse to the southeast than we ken."

Neither option was good. Both meant trouble.

Four

Aishlinn could not begin to guess how far she had traveled, only that she had been riding nearly non-stop for two days. Or had it been three? She had no clear idea.

She had remained hidden in the forests and trees, just as Baltair had told her to do. Occasionally she would be forced to travel across open fields and wide streams for there had been no alternative. Thus far, the only signs of life she had seen were birds, deer and the occasional tree frog. Had she a weapon with which to hunt she would have killed any one of them in order to eat.

In the wee hours of yestermorn she had come quite close to a small cottage. Not knowing if she was still on dreaded English soil or that of Scotland, she had been too afraid to stop and ask for help. Hungry, tired and in an ungodly amount of pain this day, she was beginning to regret that decision.

The land before her had turned greener and more lush the further north and west she traveled. It was far different than the browns and grays of the English soil she had grown up on. Having never traveled more than a few miles from her home before, she knew not what to look for. She searched her memory for any description of Scottish lands that Moirra might have mentioned but none came to mind. All of Moirra's stories had been about the Highlanders, not the Highlands.

She wondered if she would she even recognize a Highlander if she saw one. Her only frame of reference on the matter came from Moirra's faerie tales. According to Moirra, they were all big, tall and quite hairy. She was not sure if she should risk her freedom or her life based on the stories told by an auld woman.

Sometime late yesterday her saddle had become loose and fallen from the mare's back, taking Aishlinn along with it. In too much pain, and exhausted from lack of sleep, she hadn't the strength to lift it let alone enough to return it to the mare's back. She abandoned it and now rode bareback.

She had dismounted only long enough to relieve her bladder. Fearful that if she remained on foot too long the horse would wander away she stayed upon the mare as much as possible. The thought of having to walk to wherever the good Lord was taking her was far too frightening.

When the exhaustion became too much to bear, she slept slumped over with her head resting upon the mare's neck. If ever she were forced again to make a decision between saving her own life and traveling alone, with no weapons, blankets or the means to start a fire, she might be tempted to choose death. The longer and further she rode, death became the more amiable option.

It was too late now to change her mind. Nay, death from exposure was more desirable than death at the hands of the earl's soldiers. She trusted that Baltair would be able to buy her some amount of time, but how much she did not know. As exhausted, cold and hungry as she was, she could not give up. If the guards ever found her it would be a most certain and painful death.

She was thankful that her stepfather had taught her to hunt and fish and to find her way about. Growing up she had resented the man for not allowing her to be like the other young girls in their nearby village. Many a time he had told her she was plain and no husband lay in her future so he taught her to take care of herself. Now that she was far from the only home she had ever known and in very unfamiliar territory, she was glad for what he had taught her.

As she coaxed her mare along, images of her family kept flashing through her mind. Her mother had been gone so long that Aishlinn no longer remembered what she looked like. She could however, remember her mother's gentle strength. Often she would hear Laiden's voice as it offered words of encouragement that urged her on and begged her to not give up.

She would catch glimpses of Moirra's smiling auld face as well. Her heart ached from missing both women. There were a few times when she could have sworn she saw the two women riding along with her. It was those images from which she drew the strength to continue.

More often than not however it would be images of her father's face that would come crashing in. He always looked so disappointed. Aishlinn felt as though she had somehow let the man down. It was true that Broc had never been much of a father to her. Aishlinn was certain her mother had married him only to save her from being born a bastard.

The man had not one redeeming quality that Aishlinn had ever witnessed. Cold and hard, he never had a kind word to say to her. Why he had chosen to keep and raise her, Aishlinn supposed would always be a mystery. He had made it abundantly clear over the years that she had not been wanted.

Visions of her brothers would come to visit her as well. Just as in real life, her visions were filled with them taunting and laughing at her. They had never been particularly kind to her growing up. And their contempt of her grew even greater after Broc's death. It had gotten to the point where Aishlinn could do nothing right. No matter how hard she worked in the fields or in the home it was never good enough. They would always find something to chastise her for.

Then nearly a month ago they came to her and informed her that she would leave that day for Castle Firth. Horace, the oldest brother, was going to marry a young woman from the village. He wanted the cottage they had grown up in for his own. He felt the home not big enough for all of them, especially two women. So it was done; Aishlinn was sent to Castle Firth.

Admittedly, Aishlinn had felt a great sense of relief at the news. She would be away from her cruel brothers forever. Certainly life as a scullery maid or chambermaid had to be better than the life she had been enduring. Had she known then what fate had in store for her, she would have fled to London the moment they told her the news.

She fought hard to push their faces and voices from her mind and tried instead to focus on freedom and her future. She would daydream of a cottage by the sea. Maybe she would marry a decent man who would not beat her or insult her. Maybe God would bless her with many children. She would plant gardens and learn to weave. Her home would be filled with much love and laughter. But she had better chances of sprouting wings and flying to the moon than someday having a husband and children of her own.

Her mind wandered back and forth from future to present making it increasingly difficult to concentrate. Now was the time for focus, not silly daydreams. She had to keep her mind and wits sharp about her.

Aishlinn had slowed her mare to walking pace again. It would do no good to have the mare collapse dead from exhaustion and leave her stranded on foot.

As her thoughts turned to a soft pallet and a warm meal, she thought she heard the sound of voices. She pulled the mare to a stop in a band of tall trees and strained her ears to listen. It was men's voices she heard coming from behind her.

Fearful that the voices belonged to English soldiers sent to find her, her mind raced while her heart pounded. For a fleeting moment she thought of simply giving herself over to them. But the thought of being hung, disemboweled and tortured to death was far too terrifying.

She grabbed tightly onto the reins, kicked the mare's flanks and flew into a full run. As she went crashing through the trees, the branches and limbs re-opened the cuts that had only begun to heal. As fast as the mare ran, Aishlinn prayed.

Had God merely been tempting her with freedom? Was He now ready to punish her for taking a man's life? Surely He had not let her come this far simply to have her caught now. She kicked the horse again and held tightly to the reins.

The moment she caught sight of the men standing in the clearing she knew it was over. The soldiers were not behind her but in front of her. Instinct told her to run and to run quickly. She kicked at her horse again and prayed that the mare would somehow sprout wings and fly her away to safety.

She had paid no attention to the ground under the horse's feet. Her only thought was of escape. She was horrified when she felt the horse stumble, and then rear its head. Unsuccessfully she tried to settle the mare, holding on as long as she could. When the horse reared again, Aishlinn knew instantly that all was lost. She was sent flying from the horse's back. Agonizing pain enveloped her the moment she hit the ground and bright dots of light flickered in front of her eyes before everything went black.

Duncan and his men had heard the rider coming toward them at a full run. They barely had time to draw swords and step out of the way before the rider came crashing through the trees. They caught only a glimpse of a lass atop a gray horse as she raced toward them.

Before Duncan could warn her that she was running too fast on the rocks, the mare stumbled and reared. He could see the lass was holding on for dear life as she tried to settle the spooked animal. Before she could gain control, the horse reared a second time, pitching its rider. The lass fell and fell hard. Momentum worked against her as she rolled a few times before coming to a stop face down in the frigid water of the stream.

Duncan reached the stream first and hurried in after the lass. The icy water rose above his ankles. He scooped her limp body into his arms and was surprised at how slight she felt. As he carried her to a small clearing, Tall Thomas and Rowan pulled plaids from their packs. The men moved on instinct for there was no time to do much thinking on the matter. Duncan held the lass in his arms while his men covered her with the plaids and blankets.

Her clothes were soaked and clung to her skin and her hair was plastered to her face. When Duncan brushed aside her hair, each man gasped with surprise. Swollen black eyes and bruises covered most of her face and there were many small cuts on her swollen cheeks and lips. Duncan wondered who could have done such a thing to someone so young and small. It set his teeth on edge as anger and disgust blended together deep in his gut. He'd seen soldiers wounded in battle that had looked better than this wee lass lying limp in his arms.

Aishlinn dreamt she was covered in deep snow, hiding from the earl and her brothers. She could not remember ever being so cold or frightened. The earl cursed while he made promises that once he found her he would have what he had wanted. Then he would kill her. Her brothers urged him on, cursing, mocking, and making threats of their own.

The cold snow and fear of the earl brought violent shivers to her body. She wished her mum and Moirra would come and take her away to somewhere safe and warm. Her heart broke when they did not answer her pleas for help.

Suddenly there were hundreds of soldiers surrounding her. They pulled her from her hiding place. She tried to explain to them that she had only been defending herself; she had not meant to kill the earl, only to frighten him. Her pleas went unanswered as they lifted her from the snow and began stabbing her with their swords. The earl and her brothers were laughing. The more the soldiers stabbed her, the more they laughed. Bile rose in her stomach but she could not retch; she could only beg and plead for mercy.

Duncan gently rubbed her arms and legs in an attempt to warm the battered young girl while he looked for signs of broken bones. After several long and tense moments, her small body began to shiver fiercely. He could not make out the mumbled words that were coming through her chattering teeth and was relieved that she wasn't dead. He heard Tall Thomas say he would start a fire.

With her head resting upon Duncan's shoulder, she slowly began to move her arms as if fending off something only she could see. Duncan began to whisper soothingly to her that all was well, that she was safe, and no more harm would come to her.

Tears flowed from her swollen eyes and she looked such a sad sight that it nearly made the Highlander want to cry. "Ye be fine now, lass," he whispered to her.

Her eyes began to flutter open. Through small slits she stared at him blankly, still foggy, not yet seeing. "I'm sorry," she said weakly.

"She be English, Duncan," Findley said in his native Gaelic. "Try the English."

Duncan nodded and began speaking to her in English. "Sorry for what, lass?"

Mumbling through chattering teeth, she answered him. "I did n-not mean to kill him."

Duncan smiled at her, certain it was the fall and bump on her head talking. "'Tis all right lass, ye be safe now." He knew not what else to say.

Five

Something was pulling her from her dream. Low, muffled voices that she could not understand. As the heavy fog began to lift, she slowly became aware that she was not alone. She tried to focus her eyes as well as her mind, both requiring a good deal more energy than she had. Where was she and who was speaking to her? Why was she so cold and wet? It was then that the memories came flooding through and fear took its ugly hold again.

The soldiers had found her! Terrified, she tried to move, to stand and run, but every muscle in her body ached and her ribs screamed at her to remain still. Her arms and legs felt as though they were made of lead and no matter how hard she wished it, she simply could not move.

Someone was holding her, speaking to her. Her eyes began to focus and a man's face began to come into focus. He had long brown hair and blue eyes and he was smiling at her. Her heart sank and her stomach reeled with the realization that she would not be getting away. She had been captured and knew that very soon she would be back in Penrith. Her life was over.

The cuts stung from the tears that streamed down her face. She pleaded aloud for mercy, not certain she recognized the sound of her own voice; it sounded so weak and dry. She heard another man's voice but she could not understand what he was saying.

"Please," she begged him, "I meant not to kill him."

Duncan looked up at his men. They appeared as befuddled as he was. "Now what be this about killin' someone?" he asked as he tried to keep his voice soft and reassuring.

Still struggling to move, she said, "The earl," She muttered. "I m-meant only t-to f-frighten him." She took a deep breath, still shaking. "He would not s-stop and it h-hurt so m-much."

From the bruises and cuts Duncan and his men could surmise she had taken one hell of a skelping. Could what she was telling them be true? Could something so small as the lass before them have taken someone's life?

"Please. Let me g-go. I p-promise not to t-tell you found m-me."

"I'm afraid we canna do that, lass." Duncan knew she was afraid of something, but the possibility of leaving such a young girl alone out here was not an option.

"Please, I beg of you. Leave me." More tears fell as she continued to plead with them. She would rather die here alone and freezing than to be returned to Penrith.

Duncan and his men exchanged confused glances. There was no way they would leave her here. He tried to lighten the moment by saying, "But lass, some of us have mothers."

Aishlinn was dumbfounded for she could not imagine what having a mother had to do with anything. Her head was pounding and she could not make sense of what he was trying to tell her.

Duncan smiled to his men. They knew what he meant and knowing smiles formed on their own faces. "Our mothers would skin us alive if we left a distressed lass stranded and alone out here in the middle of nowhere," Duncan told her.

Rowan added, "Aye. Me own mum would skin me, then reattach me skin so she could do it again." The men nodded their heads in agreement. Rowan's mum was a fierce woman and it would have mattered not who this lass was nor the circumstances surrounding why she was here. Had the men left her and anyone found out, it would be a most certain death for each of them.

Aishlinn was too tired and cold to care if these men had mothers or not. Visions of what they were going to do to her raced through her mind. "P-please do n-not take me back."

"Back where lass?" Duncan asked.

Aishlinn looked at the men who surrounded her. Perhaps they were cruel men, wanting only to toy with her before they would shackle her and take her back to Penrith.

"Are you not K-king Edward's s-soldiers?" Aishlinn asked breathlessly. It was near agony to speak. She wanted only to sleep and to be warm and to be away from them.

The men looked insulted by her question. "Och!" they protested in unison, apparently quite appalled by such an accusation.

A wry smile formed on Duncan's mouth. "Now lass, do we look like the king's soldiers?"

She stared at each of them for several long moments. They certainly did not wear the uniforms of soldiers. Bare-chested each of them was, with scabbards at their sides and long flowing hair and braids on either side of their temples. Nay, the English did not dress in such a manner. As she lay there terrified and freezing, she searched the cloudy regions of her mind for a few moments before it finally dawned on her. These men were Scots!

But that meant little to her at the moment. She could not be certain as to their intentions. They could be mercenaries hired by the king or the earl's own men sent to find her.

"Nay," she said. "Ye d-do n-not."

They seemed quite pleased with her answer as a broad, proud smile came to each of them.

"I be Duncan McEwan," the one whose bare shoulder her head rested upon said. "And that be me cousin, Rowan Graham and that be Richard and Findley McKenna, and that be Manghus Williams." Each man bowed at the waist in acknowledgement of his name.

"Tall Thomas be buildin' us a nice fire." Duncan gave Aishlinn's arm a gentle pat. "Now," he began. "Tell us what be yer name lass?"

Wanting nothing more at the moment than to be free and warm, she gave up attempting to make sense of anything or to fight. Perhaps, if they were mercenaries, she could buy herself some time and escape the moment the opportunity arose. Weakly she answered him. "Aishlinn."

Duncan thought it a fine name and repeated it. "Aishlinn. We be pleased to make yer acquaintance." Her body still shook from cold and he knew he needed to get her to the fire quickly. He held her tighter and stood.

He had moved so quickly that it frightened her. Afraid he was going to toss her to the ground, she reflexively wrapped an arm around his neck. Her body tensed from fear and the pain in her ribs intensified. The doubt and despair were overwhelming.

Standing still for a moment, Duncan smiled and said, "Now let's see how Tall Thomas be doin' with that fire."

With his men following, Duncan carried the lass to a spot by the fire. He held her close to his chest as he sat down upon a plaid. Aishlinn remained fearful but was glad for the warmth his body was providing. She wondered if she would ever be warm again. Her wet shift and dress clung to her body and chilled her to the bone. Someone gave Duncan another plaid and he carefully wrapped it around her.

Embarrassed, humiliated and terrified, she remained rigid, ready for whatever onslaught, abuse or treachery these men might inflict upon her. She wondered if she would ever be able to get free and make it to her mother's clan.

Duncan sat holding Aishlinn close to his chest as the others helped collect more wood for the fire. Aishlinn was afraid to speak and could not find the strength to ask what they planned on doing with her.

It did not take long before a blazing fire flickered before them. Tall flames crackled and licked up towards the sky, the heat a welcome relief from the bone-chilling cold.

It was Rowan who finally broke the long silence. His low deep voice startled her. "Lass," he began. "Who did this to ye?" He was sitting very near her and stared at her face. Humiliated at what the earl had done she cast her eyes to the ground. Aishlinn hoped that if she were honest with them, then they might show her some kind of mercy. "'Twas the earl."

"Was that why ye killed him?" asked Duncan, not looking at her but at the fire before them. She noticed that his nose appeared to have been broken at least once. But it did not look ghastly or out of place on his bearded face.

Swallowing hard she nodded slightly. She did not want to think back to that night in the earl's chambers. She wanted to forget how it felt when she plunged the dagger into his back. The memories brought an instant wave of nausea to her stomach.

Looking up at the man called Duncan, she searched his face for some sign that would tell her what his intentions might be. She could see the muscles in his jaws clench and what appeared to be anger in his eyes. The intensity of it alarmed her.

"I meant not to do it." She was deathly afraid of these men. "He was hurting me and I felt the dagger in my hand…" her voice trailed off as she thought back to that moment.

"I can't say that I blame ye," Duncan said through clenched teeth. Knowing any man could do this to such a small girl brought forth much anger.

"What be the earl's name?" Gowan asked.

Aishlinn swallowed hard again and braced her body for the beating she was sure would come with her confession. "The Earl of Penrith," she whispered.

Instantly all eyes were upon her as bewildered expressions came to each of their faces.

"Ye killed the Earl of Penrith?" Rowan asked, astonished by the notion. Aishlinn tensed more and began to pray that God would grant her enough strength to run, though she knew it would be impossible to defend herself against seven men.

"Aye, I did," she answered warily.

She noticed then that the men stared at Duncan. He had not taken his eyes from the fire and he was working his jaw back and forth. Ever so gently he sat her on the ground and stood while his men gathered around him.

She wanted to crawl backward and run away, but the fear that filled her to her marrow froze her in place. She knew it would not be long now; she had confessed. She wondered if they would kill her here or take her back to Penrith. It mattered not anymore.

After several long moments of silence, Duncan turned back to her. His piercing blue eyes seemed to search hers for something. "Yer certain ye killed the Earl of Penrith?" he asked.

Unable to find her voice she nodded her head.

Suddenly, an odd and curious smile came to his face. Why were they toying with her? Why didn't they just pull their swords from their scabbards and kill her and be done with it?

"Then lass," Duncan began, "We be forever in yer debt."

Aishlinn stared at him in stunned silence. She had anticipated a beating or torture. Not a smile and certainly not gratitude.

"'Twould be our honor to see ye to safe lands, to see ye to yer people and yer family," he said.

Perhaps she had injured her head when she fell. Perhaps she was hallucinating from lack of sleep and food. Or perhaps she had lost her mind. This was a very confusing turn and it was probably too much to hope that he was not lying to her. Confused and leery she asked him, "You'll not take me back to Penrith?"

"Nay!" Each man said, aghast at the notion.

"I don't understand. Are you not mercenaries?" She was growing more confused with each passing moment.

"Mercenaries?" They all laughed at her. "Nay!" Duncan smiled proudly as he looked at his men. "We be Highlanders!"

She had never seen a Highlander before this day. Moirra had told her many stories of Highlanders being big strong men with great senses of honor and pride about them.

These men were enormous! Each wore his hair long, well past his shoulders; some had two braids at their temples, others only one. Their breeches were made of leather and were tucked into leather boots. Three of them were bare-chested, exposing well-defined and almost unbelievable muscles, as well as scars that were more likely than not earned in battle. Arms as big as tree roots, massive legs, and shoulders broader than Aishlinn had ever seen on any man before. They simply did not seem real.

In Moirra's faerie tales, the Highlanders were big, hairy and beastly looking men. While Aishlinn would agree they were all very big men, she could not necessarily say they were beastly looking. Moirra also warned that Highlander men liked their drink strong and their women ready. As a bairn

Aishlinn had not understood the auld woman's words. Older now and alone in the forest with seven of them, she prayed quietly that there was no truth to the stories.

Duncan stepped toward her and bent on one knee. "We be grateful to ye lass. 'Twould be our great privilege to see ye to yer destination. We will defend yer life and yer honor to our deaths." His expression was quite serious.

Years of experience with cruel and harsh men, warned her not to trust the ones standing before her. "What do you know of my honor," Aishlinn asked. Why would they make such a pledge?

Duncan studied her for a moment. "Ye killed the Earl of Penrith, did ye not." It was statement, not a question.

"Aye, I did," she answered attempting to sound stronger than she actually felt at the moment.

"Then lass," Duncan said, "I owe ye a lifetime debt of gratitude for what ye've done."

He could sense that she was quite perplexed. He raised an eyebrow, then with a wry smile and a wink he said, "Ye see, lass, ye saved me from havin' to kill the whoreson meself!"

The fire burned steadily as they all huddled around it. Aishlinn was wrapped in several plaids and Duncan sat uncomfortably close to her. The tears had stopped, but the shivers and doubt running through her mind had not. She was still very leery of these men.

The day was growing darker and the fire cast flickering shadows upon the group. They had sat for some time in quiet reverie, each of them lost in private thoughts. It was Manghus' deep voice that finally broke the silence. Quietly he began to explain why they were so glad to hear of the untimely passing of the Earl of Penrith. Duncan remained quiet as he absentmindedly poked a long stick at the fire.

Manghus explained that some ten and seven years ago the Earl of Penrith had ordered the destruction of a village. The earl had been convinced that someone in that village had stolen several pigs from his lands. Instead of searching out the reivers individually, the bastard had ordered the destruction of the entire village. The earl meant it a lesson to anyone who would steal from him or would offer refuge to those who hid from him.

"Duncan was just a lad at the time," Manghus told her, his voice laced with sadness. "Only eight when it happened." He paused for a moment as he stared blankly at the fire. Aishlinn wondered if he wasn't staring at something from his own past. "Twas Duncan's village. Only three lads survived it. Duncan be one of them."

From the angry and pained expressions on the faces of the men around her, Aishlinn knew the story had to be true. No one could have feigned the pain, sadness and regret she saw in their eyes. Her heart broke for the men. She knew their pain well. An odd sense of relief washed over her for now she could understand why they had made their pledge to protect her.

"Aye," Duncan said, growing disgusted at the flood of memories. Angrily he tossed the stick into the fire. "And Findley and Richard be the others." He was done reliving it. Not a day had passed since the murders of his family and friends that he did not think of killing the man responsible. Many nights he had lain awake thinking of all the different ways he could kill the Earl of Penrith. Although he was glad to hear of the earl's death a very large part of him wished it had been at his own hands.

He looked at Aishlinn and tried to guess her age. She looked to be around ten and five or six at the most. He could not get over how wee and tiny she appeared. Yet she had somehow managed to kill the man who had left him an orphan so many years ago. He felt an overwhelming sense of gratitude towards her as well as a bit of admiration.

He wondered what else the earl had done to her besides the severe beating. Knowing the earl's reputation, Duncan was certain the bastard had raped her. He imagined it would take a very long time for her to recover from such a thing, if recovery were even possible.

Huddled under the several plaids they had wrapped her in she still shivered. Duncan could see she fought against sleep for every few moments her head would list to the side before she would jerk and try to right herself. He knew she must be terrified and why shouldn't she be? She had been through a hellish ordeal and was now alone in the forest with seven strange men. He wondered how long it would be before she could trust anyone again.

He slapped his forehead with his hand as it dawned on him that she was still in her wet clothes! She would certainly catch her death of cold.

"Lass! Me apologies for being a thoughtless man." He went to his pack and pulled out a tunic, trews and wool leggings and brought them to her. "Ye be still wearin' yer wet things. Let me help ye get out of them and into somethin' dry."

How dare he suggest such a thing! Moirra was right. Highlanders may have a strong sense of honor, but they were beastly men just the same.

Sensing her mortification, Duncan did his best not to laugh out loud.

"Lass! I be promisin' I'll not take advantage of the situation. I mean only to help ye. Me intentions be honorable."

It took some convincing and only after each man took an oath to impale himself on his own sword should he so much as think of catching a glimpse of her whilst she changed, she finally relented. Duncan carried her to a large pine tree where he took great care in setting her upon her feet. He promised to stand guard, not to peek, and not to abandon her.

With aching muscles she slowly removed her wet dress and shift. They were soaked and landed on the ground with a wet thud. The cool early evening air instantly brought chill bumps to her bare skin. She wished she could move more quickly, but her aching bones and unrelenting shivers made moving at anything other than a snail's pace nearly impossible.

She donned the linen tunic, its hem landing just past her knees. She knew she looked ridiculous. The course linen scratched at the welts and cuts on her back but at least it was dry clothing. The trews were just as enormous! The legs were far too long even after rolling them up a few times. She imagined she could have fit both her legs into just one of the legs of the trews. And they would not stay put! Frustrated she huffed and grabbed the waist of the trews with both hands. With the leggings in one hand she stepped from behind the tree, kicking her wet clothing with her bare toes.

The laugh escaped Duncan's mouth before he had a chance to stifle it. "Ya've been swallowed whole by a beast made of cloth!"

Honorable men, my foot! Aishlinn thought to herself. An honorable man would not laugh at a young woman in distress! Had she not been so tired and cold and had not every inch of her body hurt beyond measure she most assuredly would have kicked him in his knee.

Still laughing he apologized for he knew he had embarrassed her but he could not help it. He carried her back to the fire and shot a look at his men that warned them not to laugh as he did his best to stifle another chuckle.

Rather gently he put her down and bade her stand still while he went to his pack and drew out a belt. She teetered and struggled not to keel over. Before she realized it, Rowan stood next to her and offered his hands for support so that she would not fall. She was in the process of thanking him when she caught sight of the belt in Duncan's hands. Duncan could see the fear rising up in her as she lowered her head and began to shrink away.

"'Tis only to hold the trews up lass, nothing more." He spoke softly and was sorry that he had frightened her. He carefully drew the belt around her small waist and cinched it as taut as he could. 'Twasn't perfect and the trews did slip a bit, but at least it kept them from falling off completely.

Quietly she thanked him as he and Rowan led her back to the fire.

After settling her in and covering her with plaids, they shared their evening meal with her. She was famished but her stomach felt uneasy and she was able to eat only a little. The oatcakes were nearly as chewy as the dried beef, but she was very grateful to have something in her stomach.

The exhaustion was overwhelming, and her eyelids grew heavier. Unable to fight the weariness any longer, she lay down upon the plaid. With no strength left to cover her own tired and cold body, she kept still as Duncan pulled the plaids over her shoulders. His lips curved into a warm smile as he tucked the blankets under her chin. "Are ye warm lass?" She could hear the genuine concern in his voice and it surprised her. Not since her mother and Moirra had passed had anyone shown her any kind of concern, save for Baltair who had helped her escape. She was used to harsh words and criticisms, not kind gestures. She nodded her head and closed her eyes.

Her body wanted desperately to sleep but her mind would not surrender to it. Soft quiet tears came again. She could do nothing to stop them any more than the memories that brought them. She did not want the men to think her weak or foolish so she pulled the plaid over her head to cry unnoticed.

She tried to unfurl her fingers to wipe away the tears, but they seemed frozen now after riding for Heaven-only-knew how many days with a death grip upon the reins of her mare. The cuts in her back stung, her face and eyes throbbed obstinately. She tried to take in a deep breath, but the action caused pain to shoot through her ribs and down her spine.

She longed for her mum, for Moirra and for a quiet, simple life. She wanted a home of her own where she would always be and feel safe. Why could she not be more like her mum, strong and beautiful? Perhaps if she had been either of those things her life would have been so different.

Shivering, she thought back to the day the brothers had told her she would be going to work in Castle Firth. They had not allowed her to take anything with her save for the clothes on her back and the blanket her mother had made for her when she was born. Had she not been so relieved to leave her brothers, she would have protested more adamantly about taking more of her mother's things with her. The blanket had been the only thing from her childhood she had left to remind her of her mother. Now it was gone forever, tucked under the pallet at Castle Firth.

Aishlinn had learned a few short days after arriving at Firth that her brothers had traded her to work there. They had traded her for two sheep. That was all she had been worth to them. The thought pricked at her heart now, though she should not have been surprised by it. They had never been fond of her to begin with. Still, it stung at her pride to think she was of so little value to them. Would anyone ever think her worth more than two sheep?

Pulling the plaid tighter, she tried to will her mind to stop wandering. What made her think she had worth or value? Hadn't she nearly been born out of wedlock? She had never learned the true identity of the man who had fathered her. Had her mother loved him and did he love her? Was he a good man? And what had caused his death?

Had Broc not married the pregnant Laiden who knows how Aishlinn's life could have turned out? Would it have been possible to be worse than it was?

Aishlinn knew that Broc had loved her mother, had loved her dearly. But looking back, she knew that although her mother had been warm towards Broc, it was more likely than not out of a sense of gratitude. She didn't think it possible that her mum could have truly loved the cold and distant man.

She had another go at taking a deep breath, a bit more slowly this time. Another jolt of pain shot through her ribs. Perhaps if she quit breathing altogether the pain would eventually subside. At the rate she was going, she thought she might have to be dead a good sennight or two before the pain would ever leave her body.

She tried to focus on something other than the agony and tried to concentrate instead on the few good memories she had left of her mum and her childhood. She vividly remembered having laughed often as a child. Never in the presence of Broc or her brothers however, for it was quite evident that none of them enjoyed laughter. Unless it was at Aishlinn's expense. Nay, the laughter never subsided then!

Was there a chance that she could leave her past behind and start anew? If she could find an inner strength, find some part of her mother inside her soul, then maybe she could. Perhaps she could be strong and take control of her own life from this point forward. She was, after all, Laiden's daughter.

Six

They waited for the lass to fall asleep before Duncan, Rowan and Findley broke away from the fire. They left the others behind to watch over the lass. They had much to discuss amongst themselves and did not want her to overhear their conversation. Duncan grabbed Aishlinn's dress and shift that had been drying on a branch near the fire and they walked back towards the stream. Not one man spoke until they were certain their voices would not carry.

"Why," Rowan began, slipping back into the Gaelic. "Why would the earl skelp a wee lass so?" He had a good idea as to why, but did not want to say it aloud.

"We ken the earl well Rowan. Evil needs no reason to skelp or to kill," Duncan told him. None of them doubted the earl's cruelty as they had witnessed it themselves at very young ages.

Rowan took the dress from Duncan and studied it. "'Tis been cut clean from top to bottom." Duncan thought of it and an image of the earl standing over a terrified Aishlinn came to his mind. As clearly as he stood there now, he could see the earl draw the dagger and cut her dress. How terrified she must have been! He did his best to quash the anger and disgust that swelled in his stomach.

Aishlinn was no kin to him, as complete a stranger as any, but that mattered naught. He could not think of one thing that would cause a lass or a woman to deserve such treatment. He thought of Aishlinn and how light her body had felt when he pulled her from the water. He could not imagine a man going after one so young and the thought sickened him.

"Do ye really believe that wee lass could have killed the earl?" Findley asked, motioning his head back in the direction of their camp.

"Aye, I do," Duncan said. One look at her battered body was all he needed to be convinced she had done it and that it had been self-defense. He imagined he would have done the same had he been in her position.

"Her dress be threadbare and worn," Rowan said. "Many a time it's been patched and sewn together." He paused for a moment. "And no shoes upon her feet!" He was appalled.

The same thoughts bothered Duncan as well. Another wave of anger began to wash over him as he stood with his men trying to sort it all out.

"And her hair!" Findley said. "'Tis cut short!" He shook his head, disgusted with the notion.

Duncan knew plenty a Highlander woman who would rather have her eyes pulled clean from their sockets by ravens than to have her hair cut. Aishlinn's blonde locks barely went past her shoulders. It was difficult for him to shake the images of her battered body from his mind. She was defending herself, he was certain, but the English did not put much stock in self-defense. And apparently, they had also gotten to the point of savagery where they cared not about beating and raping a small, young girl.

"If she did kill him," Rowan began, "then surely the English will be after her." He looked at Duncan. "They probably be no' far behind."

They had to agree with him. If the lass spoke the truth, then the English would definitely be looking for her. They would want to bring her back to Penrith to mete out unthinkable punishments. Duncan vowed he would not let that happen. Kin or not, stranger or no, this lass had suffered enough. No matter who she was, he knew two things: they could not leave her here, and they would not allow her to be captured by the English.

Duncan looked into the faces of the men standing before him. They had pledged their fealty to her for killing the man who had haunted each of them for so many years. They would die before they'd allow the English to get their hands on her.

"We take her back with us. The reivers can have the cattle," Duncan said, pulling himself straight and tall. The lass was worth far more than the thirty cattle. He found himself suddenly thankful for the thieves. Had they not stolen the cattle then Duncan and his men would not have been here this day and Aishlinn most certainly would have drowned in the stream. He knew as well that if by some miracle she had managed to survive her fall she would either die from starvation or at the hands of the English when they caught up with her.

"The English will not get their hands on the lass. The earl deserved what he received," Duncan said. 'Twas settled and they made plans on what to do next. Duncan would send Tall Thomas, Findley, Gowan and Richard back in the direction the lass had come to scout for any soldiers that may be looking for her. Duncan and the others would take the lass the fastest route possible back to Dunshire, to Castle Gregor.

With no idea how many soldiers might be looking for her, they thought it best to return as quickly as possible. They would be safe within the walls of their home surrounded by hundreds of able-bodied warriors. Duncan had great faith in his men, knowing that if there were soldiers out looking for the lass, they would be able to assess the situation quickly and return unscathed.

If it were just Duncan and his men, they could make it to the safety of their castle within four days, five if the weather turned against them. He knew the lass needed rest and proper attention for her injuries, but what she needed most was the safety his home offered. They would allow her to rest for a short while before heading out to Dunshire.

They returned to the fire some time later and Rowan filled the others in on their decision. As expected, the men readily agreed. No more harm would befall this lass, not while they still had a breath left in them. Each man was certain as well that once they arrived safely at Castle Gregor, their clansmen would show her nothing but kindness.

The men let Aishlinn sleep while they hurried to pack the camp. It would be a long and arduous ride back to Dunshire. Duncan prayed it would be an uneventful trip for the lass' sake.

When they were ready and dared not wait any longer, Duncan gently touched Aishlinn's shoulder. She woke with a jolt and sat up, disoriented, afraid and in a good deal of pain. "Haud yer wheesht!" he whispered to her. "'Tis me, Duncan." He gave her a moment to wake more fully before he spoke again. "We need to away this place, lass."

It took a few moments to remember where she was and what had happened. She tried to stretch her tired bones, but her body screamed in opposition to that idea. She winced as she tried to stand; the pain was unbearable. Duncan helped her to her feet and waited patiently as she tried to steady herself.

The trews were still giving her trouble, and her fingers grasped tightly around the waist. She looked about her surroundings as she shifted her weight from one leg to the other. "What be it ye need lass?" Duncan asked. She was thankful at the moment that it was still quite dark for he could not see her face turn red. He repeated the question, a little more impatiently this time.

"I need a moment alone," she whispered to him.

He was ready to ask her why when he realized what she meant. Seeing she could barely stand he knew walking on her own wasn't a possibility. He lifted her into his arms and carried her to a large pine tree. He waited as patiently as he could to let her tend to nature's call.

Holding on to the tree for balance, Aishlinn finally came around it, still unable to hold her balance. At the rate they were going it would be a month before they made it back to Castle Gregor. Duncan let out a quick sigh before scooping her up again and carrying her to where his men waited.

Manghus was already mounted, anxious to put as much ground between them and the English as possible. Duncan handed the lass to Rowan so that he could mount his own steed. All this being passed back and forth as if she were a bairn was quite humiliating for Aishlinn and she looked forward to the day when she could walk on her own accord.

She took notice that only three men and three horses remained. "Where is my horse? And where have your other men gone?" she asked.

Before she could gain an answer from any of them, Rowan was lifting her up to Duncan. She was readying herself to protest when she felt Duncan's hands gently take hold of her waist. He lifted her as if she weighed no more than a feather and sat her upon his lap. Speechless, she sat rigid and had to remind herself to breathe, though that action brought forth great pain. They were tall, enormous and frightening men. Although they had shown her nothing but kindness, they were still a terrifying lot!

"We be sendin' yer horse back, lass," Duncan told her. She could feel his breath on her ear as he wrapped a plaid around her shoulders, then his arms to hold the reins. She started to object, but he stopped her before she could utter a word. "We be hopin' that if they find the horse without ye upon it, they may think ye fell from it. And if they think ye be out in the forests on foot, they might give ye up for dead."

Although she did not like the thought of not having her own horse to ride, the idea did make sense. Too tired to protest let alone ride on her own, she simply nodded her head in agreement.

"And I've sent me men to scout for soldiers," Duncan told her as he gave a gentle tap of his heels to move the horse forward. "We ken ye be needin' rest lass," he whispered. "And I promise there be a nice hot bath and a soft bed waitin' for ye at Castle Gregor. But for now, me chest will have to do." He gently pressed her head to his chest.

Aishlinn had never been this close to a man before, save for the earl. And that experience was not nearly as nice as this one. She was still befuddled at the entire situation. Not since her mum's and Moirra's deaths had she felt much kindness from anyone. Now here she was, in the middle of God-only-knew where, with complete strangers and they were treating her as if she were their own kin. She wondered why. Why would they go out of their way to keep her safe and warm?

A thought suddenly dawned upon her that she had no idea where they were going. She wondered if they were attempting to keep her calm and quiet while they secretly returned her to the English. The prospect was quite frightening. She grew tense and fearful and sat upright. She wished the sun were up so she could gain a better sense of direction.

"What be the matter, lass?" Duncan whispered as he nudged his horse along.

"Where are we going?"

"We be taking ye to Dunshire," he told her. "Don't worry lass. We'll make arrangements to get ye back to yer family."

The thought of being returned to her family was more frightening than being handed over to English soldiers. Either prospect was a death sentence to be sure. "I have no family," she told him. For the most part, that was true.

"No family?" Duncan asked.

"Nay. My mum died when I was five." She fought the urge to jump from the horse and run away. "My father died some two years ago."

Learning that she had no family began to shed some light on how she ended up here. Had she a family, Duncan was certain they would have done better to protect her from the earl. "No family at all?" he asked her.

Aishlinn shook her head. She wanted to be as honest as she could with them and debated on how much she should tell them. She figured honesty was the best course to follow at the moment. "No real family. I have three brothers, but they're the one's that sent me to work and live at Castle Firth. If you send me back to them, you might as well just give me to the soldiers. 'Twould be the same thing."

"But surely yer brothers would protect ye," Rowan said. He couldn't imagine not doing so himself.

Aishlinn laughed out loud at the thought. "They traded me to Castle Firth. They traded me for two sheep." She let that sink in for a moment before going forward. "I imagine now I might be worth at least a keg of ale to them. They'd think naught about turning me over to the soldiers."

Duncan was stunned and thought mayhap she was exaggerating. He knew that he would rather die a hundred deaths than turn a sister over to anyone who would do her harm. He could not fathom what she said to be true. "But lass, why would yer brothers do such a thing?"

Aishlinn let out a heavy sigh. "They be not my real brothers. My real father died before I was born. 'Twas their father that married my mum." She decided to leave out the part of being conceived out of wedlock, as it had always been a sense of shame for her. "I'm not their real kin. They are selfish and lazy men who care for nothing but their own comforts."

Duncan had known a few men like that, but none so selfish they'd treat a sister, real blooded or not, in such a manner. He could not blame her for not wanting to return. "Then ye not be wanting to return to them?"

"Nay, I want not to go back." Going back meant death, there was no doubt of it.

Several long moments passed before Manghus asked, "What about yer mum's family? Or yer real father's?"

Tears welled in her eyes. "I know not of any family." She didn't even know her real father's name, let alone any family he may have had. And the only thing she knew of her mother was that she had been from the Highlands. It hurt to think she knew nothing of her own history or who her family might be, and anyone who could tell her was now long dead.

"Ye've never met any of yer own kin?" Duncan could not imagine growing up without any family. While it was true that he had lost his parents and many of his kin a long time past, he had been fortunate enough to have many aunts and uncles. After his parents died, he had been blessed with being raised by his father's best friend, Angus McKenna, who also happened to be Findley and Richard's uncle. After the raid on their village, the three of them went to live at Castle Gregor and were raised as brothers and to this day, they considered themselves as such.

"Nay. I have never met any." She was growing weary and truly wanted to sleep but there were too many questions, too many uncertainties racing through her mind.

Duncan had felt sorry for the lass before, for what she had endured at the hands of the earl. His heart had sunk more at learning 'twas her own brothers who had sent her to live with him. But on learning the lass knew naught of any of her own people brought a greater sense of sadness and pity to his heart.

"I do know that my mum was from the Highlands," Aishlinn told him. Oddly enough it felt good to say it aloud.

Duncan raised an eyebrow. "A Highlander ye say?" That was promising news. "Ya no' be English then?"

"Nay!" Aishlinn shuddered at the thought. She despised the English for what they had done to her people.

"Ye be one of us then!" Duncan said happily. He knew his people would welcome her with open arms, especially once they learned she had killed the earl. Having learned what he had of the lass and her life thus far, the possibility of helping her find her real family delighted him.

"We will help ye find yer people then, lass," he told her.

His next thought worried him. "I just hope it not be any we have feuds with!" He would push that thought aside for now and concentrate on getting her to the safety of his castle.

Aishlinn had long ago given up hope of ever finding her blood family or the truth of her own existence. The prospect of finally finding the family she had dreamt of since her mother's death brought an overwhelming sense of joy to her heart. There was however, a part of her that remained fearful. What if they were all gone and that was the reason her mother had ended up in the England? Or what if they did not want her?

Knowing nothing of the inner workings of Highlander clans, it mattered not to Aishlinn if her own clan feuded with Duncan's. After all, these men had saved her life. Feud or no, she would always be grateful to them for that. It was strange for her to think there was the chance of finally finding her real family. As she lay her head upon Duncan's chest, she prayed they would be as nice as these men.

Seven

They rode hard and fast for Dunshire, with Aishlinn sleeping atop Duncan's lap. He held her closely, wrapped in plaids with her head in the crook of his arm. After several hours of holding her so tightly, his arm began to ache. When he thought of all the lass had gone through, he decided he could put up with a little pain.

It was becoming increasingly difficult for Aishlinn to breathe or to remain awake. Duncan repeatedly apologized for the fast pace at which they rode but he knew that the sooner they reached his home, the better her chances of surviving. Pausing only long enough to eat, stretch their legs, and rest their horses, they raced toward Dunshire.

It was difficult to sleep being jostled about like a sack of leeks, riding along at a full run. Sleep did not come any easier at night when they stopped to rest, for that was when the nightmares came. In them she was always hiding; in the snow, a tree, or a grotto -- it mattered naught. Each time she was found by the king's soldiers and carried back to Penrith. She would wake frequently, fighting for air and with a churning stomach. The dreams were telling her no matter where she hid the soldiers would find her.

Even though she was covered in plaids and slept as near to the fire as she could, it was still difficult to become warm. When the dreams frightened her to the point of waking, she would find that Duncan and Rowan were sleeping very close to her. They guarded her as if she were the Queen of Scotland and had forgone their own warmth and comfort by covering her with their own blankets.

They would not stop for long for they did not know how close the English might be. The pace was brutal, but necessary if they were to get the lass to the safety of their clan. Duncan and his men were used to sleeping little and riding hard for they were warriors. But the lass, he was certain, was not trained for such things.

They would sleep for only a few hours before Duncan would startle her awake. She knew he was not doing it purposefully; it was the dreams, the pain and the fear that rippled through her body each time she woke. "Haud yer wheesht!" he would quietly say to her. She did not know what those words meant but assumed it to be some kind of Celtic or Scottish greeting for good morning.

Aishlinn had no idea how far they had traveled for she was in and out of awareness far too many times to count. She longed for a hot bath and a soft pallet to collapse onto. She yearned to sleep peacefully, without the terrifying dreams that haunted her each time she closed her eyes.

Duncan was growing fearful that the lass would not survive the ride back to Dunshire. The longer they rode the more she slept and the more he worried over her. When he would feel her body fall limp in his arms he would explain to her the need for her to remain awake. Doing what he could to keep her from falling into a sleep she might not wake from, he told her stories. He would describe the lands that surrounded his castle and tell her tales of his childhood, his clan, and the family that would welcome her with open arms.

They had been riding nearly nonstop for two days when Duncan realized he had to get her off the horse and into a bed. "Manghus," Duncan said, "We be no' far from Aric McDonald's cottage. I fear the lass will no' make it the full trip to Dunshire."

Manghus and Rowan nodded their heads in agreement as they began to veer their horses northward. Duncan's clan held good relations with the clan McDunnah of which Aric was a member. They knew Aric would offer them shelter, food and protection if needed. His wife Rebecca would tend to Aishlinn's injuries without question.

Arriving late in the morning, Duncan and his men bounded down a small hill that led to Aric's cottage. Aric's sons had been playing out of doors when they caught sight of Duncan and his men. The boys raced into the cottage to announce that riders approached.

Aric McDonald came rushing outside as Duncan and his men stopped in front of the cottage. He was a mountain of a man, with light coloring and arms as big as tree trunks. Aric took one look at the lass sleeping in Duncan's arms and began belting out orders for the boys to fetch water and then tend to the horses.

"What the bloody hell happened to her?" Aric barked as Rowan took the lass from Duncan. She lay limp in his arms while Duncan dismounted then took her from him.

Aric led the way into his cottage where his wife Rebecca was in their small kitchen with their young daughter preparing the mid day meal. "What is all the commotion, Aric?" Rebecca asked as she turned to see the group of tall MacDougalls walking into her home. Her eyes grew wide at the sight of the lass lying in Duncan's arms.

"Och!" Rebecca said. "What the bloody hell happened to her?" She quickly went across the room to draw open a curtain that hid a bed. Duncan gently laid Aishlinn upon it while Rebecca went about examining the wounds. She told her daughter to fetch bandages and warm water.

"Again, I ask what the bloody hell happened to her," Aric said, a bit more quietly this time.

"It's a story best not told in front of yer little ones." Duncan said as he stood staring down at Aishlinn who was still and limp upon the bed.

"This is at a man's hands," Rebecca whispered through angry teeth. She could see the faint markings left by fingers around Aishlinn's neck.

"Aye," Rowan said. "And again, not to be told in front of yer bairns," he warned.

Duncan spoke up. "Can we talk outside Aric, away from yer children?"

With a quick nod of his head, Aric led the MacDougall men out of doors and to a spot behind the barn. "Who is that lass and who the hell did such a thing to her?" There could be no doubt the man was angry.

"Her name be Aishlinn," Duncan said as he dusted the dirt from his trews. "And 'twas the Earl of Penrith that did it to her." Aric's eyes turned to dark slits at the mention of the earl's name.

"What in God's name for? What could such a wee lass as that done to him?" Aric knew the answer before he finished asking the question. "The whoreson!" he said as he ran a hand through his hair. "She be a Sassenach?"

"Nay," Rowan offered. "She be a Highlander, or at least her mum was. Her mum died when the lass was but a bairn and she be raised by a stepfather and three brothers. The stepfather now be dead. 'Twas her brothers that sent her into the hands of the earl."

Aric listened intently, his face growing redder as his anger increased. "What of her father then? Her blood father?" he asked.

Manghus shook his head. "She says he died before she was born."

"A Highlander orphan, then she be?" Aric asked. "What clan?"

"She ken no'. I think her stepfather kept it from her," Duncan said.

"It gets better," Manghus said as he crossed his arms over his chest and hung his head.

"Better?" Aric asked. "What do ye mean?"

Duncan had to tell Aric the truth for a band of English soldiers could be fast approaching. "The lass laying in yer bed, Aric?" Duncan said. "She killed the Earl of Penrith."

Aric attempted to speak but could not get the shock dislodged from his throat and 'twas nearly all he could do to keep his chin from falling to the ground. "She killed him?" he whispered. "How in the hell did such a wee thing as that kill the earl?"

"Stabbed him," Manghus said. "With his own dagger. We ken no' much else of it."

"We be fairly certain she stabbed him because he was rapin' her," Rowan said angrily.

Aric glared at the men before him. "So someone finally gave that bastard what he deserved?" There was not a clan in all of Scotland who did not despise the Earl of Penrith. Once word spread of his death, great celebrations would most likely take place.

"Aye," the MacDougall men said in unison.

Aric's chest puffed out as he crossed his arms. "Then she must be a McDunnah, with courage like that to no' only take such a beating from the earl, but to kill him as well!" A sly smile came to his face.

"That is a possibility, Aric," Duncan replied. He was not ready yet for anyone to lay claim to the lass. "We've sworn our allegiance to the lass and will be taking her to Castle Gregor with us. We'll sort out who she belongs to later. Right now, we have to get her healed enough to ride. The English could be closer than we realize. I've sent Richard and Findley to scout nearly three days ago. We've no' heard from them since."

With a band of English soldiers possibly descending upon his home at any moment, Aric decided it best not to argue to whom the lass might belong. The McDunnah clan was small in comparison to the MacDougalls and he knew theirs would be a better match against the English than his own would be.

"Well then," Aric said as he led the men around the barn, signaling the conversation was done. "We best see to it that the lass is well cared for." He turned and looked at the travel worn MacDougalls before him. "I'll make haste and warn Caelen that there might be trouble a comin'. While I'm sure we'd do well against the English lads, I think it might take more than the four of us to do it." Caelen was the chief of the Clan McDunnah, a good friend of Angus', and hated the Earl of Penrith as much as any other Scot.

While Duncan did not want word to spread that they now protected the young lass who had killed the earl, he did not relish in the thought of only the four of them against the English. "Aric," Duncan said as he followed him into the barn. "I fear if word gets out what happened, then it could spread to the ears of the English."

"Aye," Aric said as he began to saddle a horse. "That's why I'll be speaking to Caelen and Caelen alone. If word gets to the English that we have her here..." his voice trailed off for he did not want to think of the battle that most assuredly would ensue. "We'll come up with a different story of how the lass came to be in yer hands. Dunna worry of it."

Within minutes Aric was mounted and leaving to meet with Caelen. As he rode away from his home, he sent a silent prayer up that the good Lord would keep his family as well as the MacDougalls safe until his return.

Eight

Beams of light streamed down through the trees and cast brilliant threads of gold onto the fresh spring grass and blooming flowers. A tall, strong man stood in the center of the trees. Light glimmered and danced all around him. It glanced off his fine clothes, his hair and the sword that hung at his side. Though she did not know his name, could not see his face, she knew the man standing before her was her father, her real father.

Warmth radiated from a smile she could not see but could only feel. With open arms he stood waiting for his little girl. He scooped her up and squeezed her so tightly that she struggled to breathe. He was whispering to her that she was bonny and sweet, and he was here to protect her. She need not worry or be frightened ever again.

In that place between dreaming and waking, a small voice spoke her name. It was whisper soft, as if it were being carried on the wings of a butterfly. Something warm and soft caressed her cheek. Weakly, she batted her hand at it, demanded it go and leave her to the dream. It ignored her quiet order and continued its soft assault. She attempted to curse at the offender, but her mouth was so unbearably void of moisture, her curse sounded more like a dry and husky grunt.

When her eyes fluttered open, the bright sunlight burned at them. She squeezed them shut, attempted to mutter another curse, and buried her head into the pillow. When the fog finally lifted, she realized she was in a bed and lying on her stomach. There was something damp and cold upon her back. She tried to lift her head to catch a glimpse at whatever it was, but the movement caused her head to throb.

When she made another futile attempt to lift it again, she heard a very soft voice speaking in her ear. She managed to turn her head, and saw that the voice belonged to a little girl. The child possessed cherubic, rosy cheeks and bright blue eyes that sparkled in the sunlight.

It was a little girl, no more than eight, who had been whispering Aishlinn's name. She smiled sweetly before disappearing. Aishlinn wondered for a moment if she was still dreaming or had finally succumbed to death and now awaited entrance into heaven. With another move of her head, the relentless pounding proved she was not in heaven. Hell perhaps, for the pounding had a decidedly hell-like quality to it.

She had only closed her eyes for a moment when she heard Duncan's voice. "Lass! Yer awake!" He was crouched beside her and looked quite relieved, if not downright happy, to see her. It was as if they were long lost friends who had not seen each other in months. She thought it was quite odd.

Aishlinn tried to speak. Her mouth and throat were as dry as sand, and she couldn't manage a whisper. She tried to roll over to sit but was immediately stopped by Duncan. "Nay, lass! Lay still, now."

She was thirsty beyond all measure. She raised her hand and pointed to her open mouth.

"Be ye hungry?" she heard Rowan ask from behind her. She cringed and shook her head and realized instantly she should not have done that. The throbbing had turned into an all out assault, as if someone were hitting her with a large tree limb.

"Thirsty, then?" Duncan asked. She nodded her head yes and knew that should she move it again, her head would definitely explode.

Within moments someone had handed Duncan a tankard of water. Aishlinn pushed up to rest on her forearms as Duncan carefully held the tankard to her lips. The water was as cold as the winter snow and it made her teeth hurt, but it felt magnificent as it hit her tongue and traveled happily down her throat. With her thirst finally quenched she collapsed back into the bed. "Are we at your castle?" she managed to ask.

Duncan smiled at her. "Nay, lass, we're at the home of friends. I swear ye were near death when we arrived!" he told her. "Rebecca and Mary have been taking good care of ye."

Without a clue as to who Rebecca and Mary might be, she lifted her torso and rested on her arms again to look about the room. A draft was floating in from somewhere and when she lowered her head to stretch her neck, she noticed she was completely naked from the waist up! Only the bottom half of her body was covered with a blanket. If it were possible to die from embarrassment she very well could have when she felt cold air dancing gingerly across her naked bosom. Aishlinn gasped, covered her bare chest with her arms and plopped face down into the pillow.

Duncan and his men were doing their best not to laugh. Aishlinn spoke into her pillow, demanding to know where her clothes were, but the men could not understand her muffled words. She kept her face buried and thought death from suffocation might not be a particularly bad way to die. It most assuredly would be better to die that way than from the embarrassment that flooded throughout her weary body.

Several agonizingly long moments passed when she heard a woman's voice and the woman did not sound particularly happy. The woman was yelling something in Gaelic to which Duncan responded in kind, but he was not nearly as loud or angry sounding as the woman. His voice resembled that of a child who had just been chastised by his mum. Moments later Aishlinn could hear the sounds of boots as they scurried across the floor, quickly followed by the sound of a slamming door.

"The eejits be gone now, lass." The woman's voice was softer now and very near Aishlinn's ear. "I booted their arses out the door, and they'll not be comin' back 'til we've got ye properly covered."

Aishlinn took a chance and rolled her head to the side to see who was speaking to her. The air cooled her burning cheeks and it felt good to take fresh air into her lungs. A very beautiful woman with dark blonde hair and blue eyes was crouched next to the bed and she was smiling at Aishlinn. "I be Rebecca, lass. I had to put salves and bandages on yer back. The cuts were starting to get infected, but I believe I've managed to stop the worst of it for ye." She brushed hair from Aishlinn's eyes. "How do ye feel lass?"

"Besides mortified?" she whispered.

"Och! Dunna worry over it, lass. The hellions didn't see as much as they could have!"

Somehow that did nothing to make Aishlinn feel better. The simple fact that they had seen her naked back and portions of her naked bosom was enough to make her skin burn red again. She didn't know which hurt more at the moment, her back or her pride.

"Let me take a look at those cuts of yers, lass."

Aishlinn remained as still as she could whilst Rebecca tenderly lifted the bandages and examined the cuts. "They be healin' quite nicely! I'll need to be puttin' on fresh bandages. I imagine ye'll be wantin' to move those achin' bones a bit fer ye been on yer belly for two days now."

"Two days!" Aishlinn was shocked.

"Aye. Ye were in a verra sorry state when the MacDougalls brought ye here. Ye'll be needing plenty more rest lass, before yer healed proper."

Aishlinn sighed for she could not remember a time in her life when she had slept for so long. Unsuccessfully she had tried to count the days since she had fled Castle Firth, but too much of it was tangled and blurred. It was like trying to catch a clear glimpse of the roots of a gnarled auld tree whilst staring at it through a piece of linen. 'Twas impossible as well as a bit maddening.

Rebecca took her time to remove the old bandages, careful to cause as little discomfort for Aishlinn as possible. Once the bandages were removed, she carefully cleaned the cuts with warm water before she applied the salve.

The salve more than stung, it downright burned. Aishlinn hissed softly and dug her fingers into the mattress. She tried to relax, for when she tensed, her muscles were quick to remind her why she was here. When she took a deep breath, while still painful, her ribs no longer screamed in agony. It was quite a relief to be able to take in a breath and not wish for instant death.

"I'm sorry for being such an inconvenience to you, Rebecca." She was trying to think of something, anything other than the burning in her back.

"Och! 'Tis not an inconvenience to me, lass," Rebecca said as she began to apply fresh bandages. "May the bastard that done this to ye rot in hell for all eternity!"

Aishlinn was certain the bastard in question was doing just that, and for a moment wondered if she should share that fact with Rebecca. Not knowing what Rebecca's opinion of her was at the moment, she decided against it.

Rebecca applied the last of the bandages and began to wrap long strips around Aishlinn's torso to hold them into place. It wasn't easy for Aishlinn to suffer such an indignity as having a complete stranger care for her in this manner, nor to be seen naked. Aishlinn held her breath and tried to remind herself that she had suffered other mortifications, many far worse than her current predicament, and she should be well used to them by now.

When she was finished, Rebecca patted her shoulder. "'Tis the best I can do for now, lass. I'm afraid I dunna have a gown small enough for ye. Why, I'd have to cut me own in half for it to fit ye!"

It was impossible from her current position to judge Rebecca's size. There was no doubt however, that the woman had been blessed with a very ample bosom. 'Twas a blessing Aishlinn was certain she would never be bestowed with.

"I've a nightdress that'll do fer now," Rebecca told her as she helped Aishlinn to roll over and sit up. It was a struggle, for her muscles ached from the beating and lack of use, but they finally managed. "Should be plenty of room in it so it willna rub."

Rebecca had been right. There was room enough in the nightdress to hold two of Aishlinn but at least she was no longer naked. When she attempted to lie back in the bed, her cuts insisted 'twas not the best of ideas. She lay instead on her side and found she was growing quite sleepy again.

Rebecca stepped away and returned a few moments later. "I've broth and warm bread for ye, lass. Ye'll be needin' yer strength about ye, for 'tis another two days to Castle Gregor."

Aishlinn drank and ate as much as her stomach would tolerate. She repeatedly thanked Rebecca for the kindness she and her family were showing her, to which Rebecca repeatedly told her 'twas not a bother and to quit worrying so. It did not take long for her to fall asleep after eating, but not before she sent a silent prayer of thanks to the Good Lord for putting her in the care of such kind and good people.

Night had fallen before Aishlinn woke again. Although she had never been drunk before, Aishlinn imagined her current state might closely resemble the after effects of being in one's cups far too long. She blinked a few times, rubbed her eyes and winced for they were still quite swollen and sore.

The little girl was sitting on the edge of the bed and looking quite concerned. Aishlinn could not help but smile at her. "Who are you?" she asked.

"I be Mary," the child answered quietly. "Does it hurt much, Lady Aishlinn?"

"Aye, but only a bit, thanks to the good care you and your mother have shown me." Her little face beamed at Aishlinn's compliment. "Mamma says I'm a very good helper. And I'm smart too." She continued to stare at Aishlinn's face. "Mamma says a very bad man did that to ye," she said. "Was it him that cut yer hair too?"

"Nay. My brothers did that. As a punishment." Regrettably the words were out of her mouth before she could stop them.

Mary's look of concern turned instantly to one of anger. "That's mean! Did ye beat them up for it?" she asked as she thrust her tiny hands to her hips. Aishlinn could only wish she had possessed the nerve at the time to have beaten them senseless. She noticed that Mary was casting a deathly glare at someone. Aishlinn turned to see that Mary was staring at two boys, most likely her older brothers. They had the same dark blonde hair and blue eyes that Mary possessed.

"We'd never do that to ye, Mary," the oldest boy said sternly.

"Aye. Papa would beat ye dead if ye did!" She stuck her tongue out at the two of them.

"Aye. But only a coward would do such a thing." With heads held high, both boys left the room.

Very soon Duncan appeared with Rowan and Manghus behind him. Duncan looked relieved to see Aishlinn awake.

"Mary," Duncan said. "Could ye leave us be for a moment, lass? I've a need to speak to Aishlinn privately."

The little girl crawled down from the bed and returned her hands to her hips. "Ye'll take care of her well, won't ye?"

"I do so promise, Mary," Duncan said with a warm smile. Mary studied the men for a moment. Apparently convinced they would take proper care of her charge, she disappeared behind the curtain.

"How be ye, lass?" Duncan asked.

"Better than when you found me," Aishlinn told him.

"Good," Duncan said as he put a hand to her forehead. Although it was the simplest of gestures, Aishlinn was not prepared for the way his hand felt upon her skin. Men never touched her that way. Tears welled and she fought hard to hold them back.

"What be the matter lass?" Duncan asked. "Are ye in pain? Do ye need Rebecca?"

Aishlinn shook her head. "Then why do ye cry?" he asked.

How does one explain to a complete stranger that his simple touch brought back a flood of memories and feelings she had not experienced since she was a bairn? She did not have the words to express how she felt at that moment. "I know not why you're all being so kind to me!" she blurted out. "You know me not and yet you all watch over me as if I were one of your own."

"We be Highlanders, lass!" he said as if that was all the explanation necessary. He gently brushed the tears from her cheek. "We help those who need it." For Duncan, it was simply how things were done. You helped those who needed it.

He gave her a few moments to compose herself. "Do ye think ye might be able to travel in the morning lass?" he asked her. "We dunna ken how close the English be. We'll be much safer at Castle Gregor," he told her. "But if ye feel not up to it yet--" Aishlinn stopped him with a wave of her hand.

"I want to waste no more time lying abed," Aishlinn said. "I could ride now if we needed." It was a little lie, but one she felt necessary. She knew the longer they lingered here, the closer the English might be nearing. "I want no harm to fall on this family."

Duncan was touched by the lass' concern. She had heart and worried more over others than she did of her own safety. "We can wait a little longer lass. Ye'll eat and rest and we'll leave before first light." He said as he lifted her hand into his giving it a slight squeeze. "Do ye think ye stand to eat a bit?"

"Aye, I do," she answered as she struggled to move. Duncan helped her to sit and carefully propped pillows behind her back. It was too painful to lean against the pillows so she sat tilted sideways.

Rowan appeared moments later carrying a trencher piled high with enough food she thought for three people. She thanked him kindly before digging in. Duncan and his men stood towering over her and it seemed they watched every bite she took. "Why aren't you eating?" she asked them.

"We've already eaten, lass," Rowan said.

None of them moved, their eyes planted on her. An uneasiness began to spread over her for she could not figure out why they stared at her so. "Is there something the matter?" She asked. They remained silent.

Rebecca walked in, shaking her head and rolling her eyes. "They just want to be sure ye eat, lass. Hellions though they are, they've great concern over ye. They worry ye be too small and frail. I told them ye only appear so, because they're all so big and tall. But they dunna believe me!" She shook her head at them. "Will ye quit starin' at the lass so queerly, lads? How's she supposed to eat with ye sitting around watchin' her every move?" Playfully, she punched Rowan in the arm and he feigned great pain, rubbing the spot as if he had been shot with an arrow.

Before Aishlinn realized it, the small area was filled with people. She was formally introduced to Aric and she thanked him for giving them all safe refuge. "No worries, lass!" he said, his voice deep and booming.

She was next introduced to Robert, who was thirteen and the oldest of their sons, followed by Bruce who was eleven. Mary had climbed into the bed and sat next to Aishlinn. "'Tis our honor to protect ye, Lady Aishlinn," Robert told her with a bow. Bruce, not wanting to be outdone, gave a bow and a wave of his arm. Aishlinn smiled as she thanked them for their allegiance. "Such braw young men you are!" Aishlinn said. "I feel safer knowing you are both here to protect me."

Both boys stood straighter and Robert blushed at her compliment. "It's what we warriors do, Lady Aishlinn."

Aishlinn felt it odd to be addressed as Lady. By English standards, she was nothing more than a peasant. Having no royal blood running through her veins and being raised as she had, being referred to as Lady was odd indeed. "Do ye like the bread, Lady Aishlinn?" Mary asked. "I helped mamma bake it today."

"Aye, Mary. It's the best I've ever eaten." And it was not a lie for it was soft and warm with just the right amount of crunchiness to the crust. "Perhaps you'll share your recipe with me some day?" Aishlinn asked.

Robert stood with his arms crossed, looking every bit the image of his father, Aric, who stood in the same manner at the foot of the bed. "Lady Aishlinn, how old be ye?" Robert asked.

"I turned ten and nine this past winter," she told him. He looked rather deflated by her answer, and she did not know why. Aric grunted. "I took ye for not much past ten and five!"

"Ya daft men! I told ye she be older but ye dunna listen," Rebecca said, rolling her eyes at her husband. "Forgive the hellions, lass. Warriors they well may be, but they're eejits as well."

"Are ye married?" Robert asked her.

Aishlinn cringed. "Nay, Robert. I am not."

"Is there a suitor then ye have?" The question of having a suitor was just as ridiculous as the notion of having a husband. Neither suitor nor husband lay in her future.

"Nay," she told him as she turned her focus to her trencher. Aishlinn knew that most women her age were already married with a bairn or two. She had long ago resolved herself to being an auld maid, for she knew she was a quite plain young woman. Her stepfather had always been quite honest with her in that regard and that was the reason why he raised her in the manner he had.

With a chuckle, Aric slapped his eldest son on the back. "Lad, take yer brother and sister out and tend the animals." Robert looked decidedly displeased but did as his father had told him.

Aric waited for the children to leave. "Forgive me son, lass, but he's taken quite a fancy to ye." He smiled as he gave her a wink.

She shook her head, not believing that anyone, least of all a thirteen-year-old boy would take a fancy to her. She was certain they were merely being polite. With her appetite now satisfied, she handed the trencher to Rebecca.

With a simple nod and a warm smile from Aric, Rebecca left the room. The men stood motionless as each studied Aishlinn very closely. The silence was deafening. "Why do you all stare at me so?" Aishlinn asked her voice tinged with worry.

"Forgive us, lass. We've simply so many questions," Manghus apologized.

Certain she would get no rest this night unless she quelled their curiosity. Aishlinn inhaled slowly before speaking. "Well, then ask them." Thrusting her chin upward, she squared her shoulders and hoped she looked far stronger than she felt.

Duncan took a deep breath. "Can ye search yer memory, Aishlinn, for just a moment?" he asked softly. "Ya said ye ken no' of yer mother's or father's clan. Are ye sure, lass? Ye've no names, no recollection of anything that may have been told to ye?"

Aishlinn thought hard for a long moment. "There is nothing. I did not learn that Broc was not my real father until the day they buried my mother. All I know is what her friend Moirra told me long ago; that my mother was a Highlander. She promised to tell me more when I was older, but she died not long after."

Pity-filled faces looked at her. She did not want their pity, only their help in finding her family, if indeed there were any left.

Duncan did not want to push, but he had to. "Nothing at all then? No stories, no slips of the tongue? Please think, Aishlinn."

"Moirra told me faerie tales, nothing more, just faerie tales of big, strong Highlander men. But none in those stories were as kind as all of you."

Duncan was puzzled. "What do ye mean, lass?"

Would it be considered un-lady like or unkind to share what Moirra had told her? Their continued stares of curiosity told her she could, as long as she was careful not to insult any of them. "She said Highlander men liked their drink strong," she stopped, trying to find the best way to phrase what Moirra had said.

"Go on, lass," Aric encouraged her, a most serious expression on his face.

She threw all caution to the wind and blurted it out. "Moirra said Highlander men liked their drink strong and their women ready." She held her breath, anticipating they would be insulted by what she had just said.

Laughter filled the room. They certainly did not appear insulted. Proud was a more apt description. "What is so funny?" Aishlinn asked.

"Those be not faerie tales she told ye, lass!" Rowan said as he slapped a hand to his knee. "They be the God's honest truth!"

Aishlinn's face burned red as a jolt of fear rushed up from her belly. For a moment she worried they might expect her to "be ready". Then she remembered her plain, homely face and felt better. She was too plain to be wanted by any man, let alone one of these braw Highlanders. For the first time in her life she felt glad for being ugly.

When she asked if they were quite done laughing, it only brought forth more of it. They may be brave and honorable warriors, but she suspected they were more hellion than anything else. She waited patiently for the laughter to cease. "Do you have more questions of me?"

Rowan stepped close to her, the smile gone from his face, replaced with a look of concern. "Lass, why did they cut yer hair?" he asked. "Ya told

Mary it was a punishment. What could ye have done so terrible as to deserve that?"

Shamed, her hand went to her hair as she tried to smooth it. She imagined she must look a fright to them and did not blame them for their curiosity. Oh, how she wished they had cut it for some untold brazen act she had committed. Alas, she had no exciting or adventurous story to tell.

Duncan made a mental note to admonish Rowan later for his blatant disrespect at having asked the question. Though he was as curious as the rest of them as to why she had been punished in such a manner, he still felt it an insensitive question.

"For burning the evening meal," she told them quietly. "'Twas about this time last year. I had been working in the fields all the day, plowing them to ready for the spring planting. I put a stew on the fire and fell asleep. They were angry the stew had boiled dry and was ruined."

She left out the part of how she had been awakened by a strong slap to her face that had knocked her clean from her chair. It was Horace, her oldest brother who had slapped her awake. He cursed at her for quite some time before the other two had grabbed her and slammed her face into the table, whilst Horace grabbed her long braid and cut it. Later he had fastened the braid to the tail of one of their plow horses. He had derived great pleasure from being so cruel. She had cried nearly nonstop for days after. Finally, she had convinced herself that plain girls didn't need long locks and it would eventually grow back.

"I canna imagine doing such a thing to a sister," Rowan said. Hatred and disgust flickered across his face. Similar expressions could be seen on the faces of the other men as well.

"I canna believe they made her work the fields like a man!" Aric huffed. "'Tis an atrocity is what it is." The others nodded their heads in agreement. "We don't treat our women that way here lassie, ye can be assured of it!" With his massive arms crossed over an even larger chest, Aishlinn felt relieved to know he was on her side. "We'd rather be hung by our shorthairs than to let such a thing happen!" Duncan shot a look of warning at Aric that said to watch his language in front of the lady before them.

While she thought it admirable that they were appalled at how her family had treated her, there were reasons for their behavior. Aishlinn had not realized she had been talking out loud. "What were the reasons for treating ye in such a manner?" Duncan asked. She could not tell if he was appalled or bilious for his expression could have explained either condition.

She flushed again, humiliated and ashamed. Perhaps she could pretend to be in pain, or needing rest and bid them to leave. She knew there was no sense in prolonging the inevitable for eventually they would figure it out. It was probably best to warn them now. "You think my face looks frightful now?" she said quietly. "Wait until the bruises fade and the swelling leaves it." She twisted the edge of her coverlet between trembling fingers. "My stepfather taught me to work in the fields, to build things, and to hunt, knowing I would never be blessed with a husband. You see, even without the bruises and cuts, I am a quite plain and ugly young woman."

Loud protests filled the room as if she had just insulted the King of Scotland. Duncan shot to his feet, his face marked with anger and disbelief, unable to speak. Aric however, had readily found his voice. "What father would tell a lass such a thing?" he demanded. 'Twas a good thing Broc already lay dead in the ground, for Aishlinn was certain these men would seek him out and kill him for such an injustice. While noble, she thought, it was highly unnecessary.

Rebecca rushed in, her brow creased, and ready to yell at the men for yelling in the direct vicinity of her patient. When Aric relayed what Aishlinn had told them, Rebecca flew into a rage of her own. The profanities -- some in the English but many in the Gaelic -- which Rebecca slung in the direction of Aishlinn's dead stepfather, were enough to make most grown men blush.

The men in this room were apparently unfazed by such talk coming from a woman. Secretly, Aishlinn wished she had just an ounce of Rebecca's tenacity. Perhaps if she had known some of the words Rebecca knew, she could have used them as weapons against her brothers. Maybe then, they wouldn't have mistreated her or cut her hair. They would have been downright fearful of her.

Taken aback by the spectacle, Aishlinn lay still and bewildered in the bed. Tears threatened and she was not certain what to make of the outrage before her.

The look on Duncan's face said enough. He was utterly appalled by what she had just told them. He crouched on one knee before her and took her hand in his. "Lass, such a thing is not true. Yer stepfather be an evil whoreson of a man to have told ye such a such lies!"

"Duncan, really. You needn't be so kind. He did it only to protect me," she told him. Really, such a fuss they were making and over what? The truth of the plainness of one young woman?

Duncan shook his head. "Protect ye from what, lass?" He simply could not fathom it.

"He knew I be plain and would never find a husband to take care of me, Duncan," she said bluntly. Aishlinn had had her entire life to get used to the face that would garner her no husband or bairns. Once her face healed and these men had time to get used to it, then they would understand. "Isn't that what fathers do? Protect their children?"

"Aye," Aric said, stepping to her side. "A father protects his children from all manner of evil, lass," he told her. "But a father never tells his daughter such lies!"

"Even if it be the truth Aric?" Aishlinn gritted. She was growing weary of the topic. "Certainly a good father would always be truthful with his children, even if the truth hurt."

Aric pursed his lips together. "If ye be ugly and plain, then I be King David!" His scowl deepened and he looked quite menacing.

Duncan squeezed her hand again. "'Tis the truth, lass. Ye be no' plain nor ugly."

Aishlinn quietly searched for a memory or a time in her life when Broc or her brothers had said anything to the contrary. She could find none. Her entire life and everything she knew had been built around the premise that she was not only plain but ugly as well. Now here she was, surrounded by complete strangers who were insisting none of it was true. Although she would have loved to believe them, her heart insisted they were only being kind.

While everyone else in the room was lost in their own conversation regarding the outlandish and cruel behavior bestowed upon their new charge, Duncan's focus remained on Aishlinn. When a tear trailed down her cheek, he quietly suggested they take their conversation elsewhere and allow the lass to rest. After the last wish of a good sleep was made, and the curtain closed, Duncan remained at her side.

Crouching beside her, he lightly brushed a loose bit of hair from her forehead with his fingertips. A surge of something quite unfamiliar rushed through Aishlinn, and she knew not what to make of it.

"I ken ye be frightened, lass," he told her. His voice was soft and reassuring. "I ken we must appear to be a strange lot to ye, all big and loud and speakin' our minds. Och! We may stretch the truth a wee bit on occasion, but when it comes down to the very important things in life, we never lie."

Duncan knew that her current predicament could not be an easy one. He could only hope that someday she would realize he was being truthful with her.

"When we make a pledge or a promise, we keep it 'til our dyin' breath. When we swore to protect ye and yer honor, we meant it." Smoothing her hair he smiled at her. "And when I tell ye that ye be no' plain, ye can believe that I tell no lie." He squeezed her hand again, smiled and left the room.

While Duncan had been speaking, Aishlinn had been holding her breath. But the moment he stepped behind the curtain, she released it and with it came more than a decade's worth of tears.

Nine

Duncan came to her, as promised, before the sun had risen. He gently touched Aishlinn's shoulder and she awoke startled and frightened. "Haud yer wheesht, lass!" he whispered.

When she tried to stand, she found her legs wobbly and weak. They were not going to cooperate with her this day. She was tempted to use some of the words she had heard Rebecca using last night. Perhaps if she cursed her legs enough, she could scare them into functioning properly.

Duncan helped her to her feet and waited patiently for her to get her bearings. Rebecca soon joined them to help her out of the nightdress and into the trews and tunic. Duncan had been proper by leaving the women alone while Aishlinn dressed, but returned the moment Rebecca was done with tying the laces on the trews. She helped to put woolens over Aishlinn's feet before handing the lass over to Duncan.

As Duncan carried her out of doors, the cold morning air brought chill bumps to Aishlinn's skin. Stars dotted the clear night sky and a sliver of a moon hung high in the east. It would be hours before the sun would be up.

Duncan handed Aishlinn to Manghus while he mounted his horse. Aric had one hand on the bridle of Duncan's mount, his other resting on the shoulder of his wife. Rebecca had packed food for their journey to Castle Gregor as well as an extra blanket with which to keep Aishlinn warm.

"I've put fresh bandages and more salve in the bundle for ye," Rebecca told Rowan as she handed the bundle up to him. "Keep the wounds clean. Change them at mid-day, then at night and she should be well."

"Thank ye, Rebecca," Rowan told her as he tied the bundle to the back of his saddle. "Yer a good woman. Too bad yer already married!"

Rebecca shushed him. "Ye'll no' want Aric to hear ye say that!" She gave him a smile as she wrapped her shawl around her shoulders. They had all been friends for many years and she knew Rowan meant nothing by it.

Aishlinn thanked both Aric and Rebecca. "I fear I'll never be able to repay your kindness," she told them. Rebecca reached up and squeezed her hand. "'Tis nothin', lass. Return the favor by showing kindness to another when they need it." Aishlinn felt a twinge in her heart. Growing up she had been kept away from most people and had never been afforded the opportunity to make friends. Rebecca had been the first person that Aishlinn could consider as such, though their time together had been short. She could only hope that they would have the opportunity to meet again someday, and hopefully under far better circumstances.

"Remember," Aric said to Duncan, "tell Angus that Caelen offers our support against the English should ye need it. We'll be at Gregor in a fortnight, maybe two, to meet with him and his council."

Duncan nodded his head as Manghus lifted Aishlinn up to him. He wrapped a plaid around Aishlinn, then the blanket from Rebecca, tucking both securely under her chin. "I be sure Angus will appreciate yer support," Duncan said to Aric. "Express me gratitude to Caelen for us."

"I will," Aric said as he handed the reins to Duncan. "Keep the lassie safe." Aric gave a soft slap to the horse's rump. "Godspeed."

As the horses began to trot down the road towards Dunshire, Duncan gently laid Aishlinn's head upon his chest. "I still promise ye a hot bath and a warm bed when we get to Castle Gregor, lass."

Duncan's chest was warm and made her feel safe and protected. As she lay against him, she thought of how these men had behaved towards her. They fussed over and guarded her as if she were as precious as gold. And for reasons she could not fathom, they had sworn their unyielding allegiance. It was difficult to understand why these men were so intent on protecting her. As her eyelids grew heavier and her body warmer, she decided the reasons why did not matter. Far too tired to think further on it, let alone to will her mouth to speak, she promised to swear her own allegiance to them very soon. For now, all she could do was snuggle into Duncan's chest and sleep.

The sun had risen long before Aishlinn woke again. She lifted her head to catch a glimpse of where they might be, the movement bringing a twinge of pain in her ribs that she would not admit to and her bladder begged for relief. Not wanting to be a burden or appear weak in the eyes of Duncan or his men, she remained quiet and hoped that they would soon stop for a rest.

Duncan bade her good morning with a smile; his blue eyes twinkled in the morning light. Aishlinn yawned as she tried to stretch her weary muscles. 'Twas not an easy task when one is atop someone's lap and on a horse no less. Perhaps they would stop soon and once dismounted, she could stand, stretch and move her muscles a bit and find a good tree. Or a rock. Or a bush. Anything behind which to hide so she might give some relief to her bladder.

They rode in silence for a while longer. Aishlinn tried to gain a more comfortable position; one that would take some of the pressure off her bladder that was threatening to empty its contents upon Duncan's lap. After a while longer, she decided she could no longer remain quiet on the matter. "Duncan, I do need to stop for a moment."

"Are ye in pain lass?" he asked with much concern in his voice.

"Aye," she told him.

Duncan immediately pulled rein and brought his horse to an abrupt stop. Rowan and Manghus pulled up beside them. "What be the matter, lass?" Duncan asked, very concerned for her. He began to wonder if they'd left Aric's too soon and were pushing her too hard.

Aishlinn squirmed as she tried to right herself, praying that the Lord would allow her to hold herself a bit longer, at least until she could get behind a tree. "Duncan, I really must get down straight away." The urgency in her voice told them what they needed to know. Duncan handed her to Rowan who sat her upon the ground. She cursed under her breath when her legs nearly gave out. Duncan dismounted and waited to see if she could walk on her own. When she continued to teeter, holding on to Rowan with one hand and the horse with the other, Duncan sighed. He scooped her up and headed toward a tree with Rowan following behind them.

"I can walk, Duncan," she said with an irritated sigh. She was frustrated that her body wasn't healing as quickly as she would have liked.

"Aye, I'm sure ye can, lass," he told her before setting her down. Holding on to the tree for dear life, she prayed that they would both go away. She would pee down her own leg before she'd allow either of them to help her with such a delicate matter. A great breath of relief escaped her when they stepped away to give her some privacy.

After several long minutes, and only because she had to struggle with the blasted trews, she finally hobbled from behind the tree. She appeared delightfully relieved and was smiling. Duncan stifled a chuckle as he looked down at her. The lass' head barely reached the middle of his chest, her hair was mussed and the clothes hung so loosely upon her, that she had the appearance of a child playing dress up.

Whilst she had been otherwise detained, Duncan and Rowan had spread a plaid on the ground and opened the bundle Rebecca had given them. Her smile disappeared in the blink of an eye when she caught sight of the items spread out on the plaid. There was no way to change the dressings on her wounds without removing the tunic. She went red from head to toe at the thought.

"We need to change yer bandages, lass," Duncan told her as he slid an arm around her waist to lead her to the plaid. Roots grew instantly in her feet and refused to proceed forward.

There had been many times in her life where she had wished she'd been born a lad and this was one of those moments. If she had been born the opposite sex, she would have been better suited to work in the fields and hauling rocks. There would have been no braid to cut and no trading her for sheep. There would have been no beatings or attempt at rape. And if she were a man right this very moment, she wouldn't be trembling with embarrassment and fear at the prospect of baring her back to anyone.

Duncan could see the nervousness in her eyes. "What be the matter, lass?" he asked.

What be that matter? Where Aishlinn came from, young ladies did not bare their skin to men they were not married to! Well, a harlot or a bar wench might, but Aishlinn was neither of those things.

Thinking she might be worried that they would not be as gentle as Rebecca had been, Duncan attempted to sooth her worries. "Lass, I promise we'll do our best to be gentle and not harm ye."

The only harm she was worried about at the moment was to her reputation. What if word got out that she had removed her clothing in front of a man? Two men to be exact! "You'll be seeing my back," she whispered.

Rowan coughed lightly and turned his back to her while Duncan let loose with an exasperated sigh. "Aye, lass, we will be needin' to see yer back fer that's where yer cuts are." He could understand the lass' reluctance but now was not the time to stand on proper social protocol. "If we dunna change yer bandages, they could grow infected." He hoped she would listen to reason.

While the thought of infection did not please her, perhaps it would be worth the risk. "But what would people think?" she asked as her knees began to knock together.

Duncan threw back his head and laughed heartily. Aishlinn's eyes blazed with anger. He was a man, a blasted fool, who could not appreciate the fallout of a sullied reputation. "I am glad, Laird McEwan, that I'm able to bring such amusement to you," she gritted her teeth at him. She noticed Rowan had remained with his back turned and his body shook with laughter. "And you as well Laird Graham." They could both take a leap from the nearest cliff as far as she was concerned. Men set the rules in this world, and then laughed at you when you followed them.

"Lass, there be no one here but us," Duncan said through smiling lips.

"Yer reputation will remain in tact." He shook his head as his laughter began to subside.

Rowan had managed to take a deep breath and turned back to them. He was doing his best to remain composed as well as thoughtful. "Lass, we really must change the bandages. We'll only be lookin' after ye like a brother would towards a sister who is ill or injured."

Her own brothers would have poured salt into her wounds and laughed while she cried in pain. Neither Rowan nor Duncan appeared to be anything like her brothers. Aishlinn knew they meant well and she began to relax a bit towards the idea. She couldn't very well change her own bandages. And as long as they behaved as a good brother might, then perhaps she would be able to suffer through the embarrassment.

The sun had risen long before Aishlinn woke again. She lifted her head to catch a glimpse of where they might be, the movement bringing a twinge of pain in her ribs that she would not admit to and her bladder begged for relief. Not wanting to be a burden or appear weak in the eyes of Duncan or his men, she remained quiet and hoped that they would soon stop for a rest.

Duncan bade her good morning with a smile; his blue eyes twinkled in the morning light. Aishlinn yawned as she tried to stretch her weary muscles. 'Twas not an easy task when one is atop someone's lap and on a horse no less. Perhaps they would stop soon and once dismounted, she could stand, stretch and move her muscles a bit and find a good tree. Or a rock. Or a bush. Anything behind which to hide so she might give some relief to her bladder.

They rode in silence for a while longer. Aishlinn tried to gain a more comfortable position; one that would take some of the pressure off her bladder that was threatening to empty its contents upon Duncan's lap. After a while longer, she decided she could no longer remain quiet on the matter. "Duncan, I do need to stop for a moment."

"Are ye in pain lass?" he asked with much concern in his voice.

"Aye," she told him.

Duncan immediately pulled rein and brought his horse to an abrupt stop. Rowan and Manghus pulled up beside them. "What be the matter, lass?" Duncan asked, very concerned for her. He began to wonder if they'd left Aric's too soon and were pushing her too hard.

Aishlinn squirmed as she tried to right herself, praying that the Lord would allow her to hold herself a bit longer, at least until she could get behind a tree. "Duncan, I really must get down straight away." The urgency in her voice told them what they needed to know. Duncan handed her to Rowan who sat her upon the ground. She cursed under her breath when her legs nearly gave out. Duncan dismounted and waited to see if she could walk on her own. When she continued to teeter, holding on to Rowan with one hand and the horse with the other, Duncan sighed. He scooped her up and headed toward a tree with Rowan following behind them.

"I can walk, Duncan," she said with an irritated sigh. She was frustrated that her body wasn't healing as quickly as she would have liked.

"Aye, I'm sure ye can, lass," he told her before setting her down. Holding on to the tree for dear life, she prayed that they would both go away. She would pee down her own leg before she'd allow either of them to help her with such a delicate matter. A great breath of relief escaped her when they stepped away to give her some privacy.

After several long minutes, and only because she had to struggle with the blasted trews, she finally hobbled from behind the tree. She appeared delightfully relieved and was smiling. Duncan stifled a chuckle as he looked down at her. The lass' head barely reached the middle of his chest, her hair was mussed and the clothes hung so loosely upon her, that she had the appearance of a child playing dress up.

Whilst she had been otherwise detained, Duncan and Rowan had spread a plaid on the ground and opened the bundle Rebecca had given them. Her smile disappeared in the blink of an eye when she caught sight of the items spread out on the plaid. There was no way to change the dressings on her wounds without removing the tunic. She went red from head to toe at the thought.

"We need to change yer bandages, lass," Duncan told her as he slid an arm around her waist to lead her to the plaid. Roots grew instantly in her feet and refused to proceed forward.

There had been many times in her life where she had wished she'd been born a lad and this was one of those moments. If she had been born the opposite sex, she would have been better suited to work in the fields and hauling rocks. There would have been no braid to cut and no trading her for sheep. There would have been no beatings or attempt at rape. And if she were a man right this very moment, she wouldn't be trembling with embarrassment and fear at the prospect of baring her back to anyone.

Duncan could see the nervousness in her eyes. "What be the matter, lass?" he asked.

What be that matter? Where Aishlinn came from, young ladies did not bare their skin to men they were not married to! Well, a harlot or a bar wench might, but Aishlinn was neither of those things.

Thinking she might be worried that they would not be as gentle as Rebecca had been, Duncan attempted to sooth her worries. "Lass, I promise we'll do our best to be gentle and not harm ye."

The only harm she was worried about at the moment was to her reputation. What if word got out that she had removed her clothing in front of a man? Two men to be exact! "You'll be seeing my back," she whispered.

Rowan coughed lightly and turned his back to her while Duncan let loose with an exasperated sigh. "Aye, lass, we will be needin' to see yer back fer that's where yer cuts are." He could understand the lass' reluctance but now was not the time to stand on proper social protocol. "If we dunna change yer bandages, they could grow infected." He hoped she would listen to reason.

While the thought of infection did not please her, perhaps it would be worth the risk. "But what would people think?" she asked as her knees began to knock together.

Duncan threw back his head and laughed heartily. Aishlinn's eyes blazed with anger. He was a man, a blasted fool, who could not appreciate the fallout of a sullied reputation. "I am glad, Laird McEwan, that I'm able to bring such amusement to you," she gritted her teeth at him. She noticed Rowan had remained with his back turned and his body shook with laughter. "And you as well Laird Graham." They could both take a leap from the nearest cliff as far as she was concerned. Men set the rules in this world, and then laughed at you when you followed them.

"Lass, there be no one here but us," Duncan said through smiling lips. "Yer reputation will remain in tact." He shook his head as his laughter began to subside.

Rowan had managed to take a deep breath and turned back to them. He was doing his best to remain composed as well as thoughtful. "Lass, we really must change the bandages. We'll only be lookin' after ye like a brother would towards a sister who is ill or injured."

Her own brothers would have poured salt into her wounds and laughed while she cried in pain. Neither Rowan nor Duncan appeared to be anything like her brothers. Aishlinn knew they meant well and she began to relax a bit towards the idea. She couldn't very well change her own bandages. And as long as they behaved as a good brother might, then perhaps she would be able to suffer through the embarrassment.

Thankfully, the men had allowed her to keep her tunic on while she lay face down on the plaid. Manghus had brought water to clean her wounds with and apologized repeatedly for it being so cold. The tunic was so big that Duncan had no troubles pushing it up towards her neck so that he could get to the bandages.

Although the cuts were healing nicely, her back was a ghastly sight. A dark bruise, looking very much like the bottom of a man's boot, could be seen quite clearly just under her left shoulder blade. There were five deep cuts across her back, left by a man's belt. Not just any man's belt; these were left behind by the same bastard who had killed his family. If the man had not already been dead, Duncan would be on his way to Penrith to slice his blade across the man's throat.

By the time he was finished cleaning the wounds, applying fresh salve and bandages, his jaw ached from clenching his teeth. He could not comprehend how a man could do such a thing. Duncan was also baffled by the fact that not once in the past days had Aishlinn complained of being in pain. She had only winced twice when he had applied the salve, but spoke not a word. Duncan knew from his own experience how badly the salve stung when first applied to a cut or open wound. But the lass had only balled her hands into fists and said nothing.

Duncan had carefully lowered the tunic and patted the back of her head. "We be done now, lass." His throat had gone terribly dry and left his voice sounding husky.

Aishlinn quietly thanked him as she pushed herself to sit. His stomach seized when he saw her face and the tears that had fallen from her eyes. She wiped her cheeks with the sleeves of the tunic but said nothing.

"Lass, I ken it hurts like the devil. 'Tis right fer ye to say it does," Duncan told her.

Aishlinn forced a smile to her face. Yes, it did hurt like the devil, but she had learned at a young age that the only thing complaining got you was a slap to the back of your head. Or worse. "Aye." It was all she could think to say as she tried to stand.

He studied her closely for a moment and realized she was quite a remarkable young woman. She complained not of anything and did her best to behave bravely. There was not one woman who came to his mind, who could have endured what this lass had, and still manage to hold on to her composure and pride. He also took note that she was doing her best to not be a bother to them. He tried to give her a moment or two to walk on her own. He saw no sense in allowing Aishlinn to try to force her body to do something it was not quite capable of doing just yet. Duncan scooped her up in his arms and headed towards the horses. There would be time, soon enough, when she wouldn't need to be carried to and fro. Today wasn't that time.

"Really, Duncan," she told him. "I do know how to walk. I believe I mastered that task right around the age of one!" If they would only give her but a minute, she would be able to convince her legs to move on their own accord.

"Aye. I'm sure ye did lass. But I'd rather not wait while ye relearn it! We need to ride away from this place and get to Dunshire quickly." He quashed a smile that had formed when she began to protest again. "Lass, I'll damn well carry ye if I damn well choose. Ye be in no condition to argue the point." He handed her to Rowan and mounted his horse.

"How long do you plan on carrying me wherever I need or wish to go?" she asked him. Rowan handed her up to Duncan who sat her gently upon his lap before wrapping the blankets around her. "Until I grow weary of it." He cast her a look, that had she known him better, would have warned her not to argue the point.

"I'm not quite as helpless as you might think, Duncan McEwan," she huffed at him, refusing to allow him to place her head upon his chest. Although she did rather enjoy that spot, she was growing quite frustrated. Not with Duncan or his men, but with her own inability to walk unassisted.

Duncan nudged his horse along. "Yer not?" he said. "Then do ye care to find yer way to Dunshire alone?" He was not about to abandon her, but she didn't need to know that at the moment.

Her eyes flew open and her mouth clamped shut. He could see the fire begin to rise in her eyes; deep dark green eyes the color of heather right before it bloomed. "If you did choose to leave me here, I can assure you I am quite capable of finding my way about. My father did not raise me to be an addle-headed woman, incapable of finding her way to the end of the road and back." She crossed her arms and scowled at him. He returned her scowl with one of his own and she had to admit, his was far more intimidating.

"Lass, I'll thank ye no' to try my patience this day." He was not used to people questioning him. But he had to admit he did admire her tenacity.

'Twas then that Aishlinn noticed he had a very handsome face. He had full lips that she imagined might be quite warm and soft. Her wandering mind had caught her completely off guard when she thought of how those lips might feel if they were to touch her own. She was never one to daydream of such things! Well, at least not very often. Disheartened, she shrank from the realization that plain women such as she did not receive kisses from men like him.

When she noticed Duncan smiling at her apparent submissiveness, she sat upright. 'Twas agony to do it, for her ribs and back still ached. But she did not want him to think she would cower every time he might cast a scowl her way. "What about tomorrow?" she asked as she forced a sweet smile to her lips. "Would that be more to your liking m'laird?"

He nearly burst out laughing when she batted her eyelashes at him. He somehow managed to maintain his composure as well as his scowl. There was no doubt in his mind that if he had abandoned her here she would find her way to Dunshire. "Do no' try my patience this day, or any other," he warned her, knowing she had no idea whose lap she sat upon. Had she been aware of the fact that he would someday be the chief of Clan MacDougall, she would hold an entirely different attitude towards him.

She did not know why tears welled in her eyes. It could have been from the way he growled his warning or his scowl or from embarrassment. Her attempts at levity had failed and she felt like a fool.

His heart lurched when he saw the tears. He nudged his horse to go faster for he did not want his men hear what he was about to say. "Lass, I'm sorry." He was the leader of hundreds of men. It would not do to have them question his authority or might if he melted every time the lass looked at him. "People do no' normally question me when I give an order. I dunna want my men thinking I'd be swayed by a bonny lass," he whispered to her.

Had her face not been black and blue then he would have been able to see the blush come to her cheeks. She dared not ask the question that popped into her mind. Do you really think me bonny? She knew what he meant, that he was a leader of men and he had a certain appearance that he must maintain at all times. Thinking it best to ignore the question burning in her mind, she chose instead to apologize. "I'm sorry."

Rowan and Manghus caught up to them. Duncan gave her a slight hug. 'Twas just a little hug, a nudge really and there was no hidden meaning to it. Still, it sent shockwaves spiraling down her spine. "No worries, lass," he whispered to her.

"We must hurry if we wish to reach Dunshire before winter," he told his men as he tapped the flanks of his horse. For a brief moment, Aishlinn wished they would not hurry. She knew that once they arrived at the castle, there would be no other opportunities to have Duncan's arms wrapped around her.

In those rare moments when she was awake, she would listen to the men as they spoke in their native Gaelic. Aishlinn felt the language had a rough and powerful quality to it and somehow it made her feel closer to her mother. She wished she had been blessed with learning it, but where she grew up people were not allowed to use anything but the English. The king's edict had been passed not long after Aishlinn had been born. Its simple goal was to squash anything Scottish. Whether it was their language, customs or traditions he'd not allow the lowlanders any of it. They were now part of England and English they were expected to behave.

They did camp that night, but not for long for they had lost two days by seeking shelter at Aric's home. After only a few hours of sleep, Duncan gently nudged her awake. It startled her and she let out a slight squeal. "Haud yer wheesht!" Duncan whispered and smiled as he helped her to her feet. He debated whether he should carry her or allow her to walk on her own. He watched her closely for a moment and when he saw she did not teeter to the point of falling, he decided the latter.

As they walked in the dark, Duncan at the ready should she need his assistance, Aishlinn whispered to him. "Thank you for allowing me to walk." Although she would never admit to it, she rather liked being carried by the tall Highlander. Duncan noted a tinge of pride in her voice and he was about to whisper "you're welcome" when she tripped on a rock and nearly fell flat on her face. He caught hold of the back of her tunic, and pulled her upright. Letting out a heavy sigh, he scooped her up and carried her to the horses.

Aishlinn bit her lower lip to keep from protesting, although she was quite glad to have him hold her. Eejit! She thought of herself. Men like him do not care for lasses like you. Quit acting a fool.

Rowan bid her good morning in English when Duncan handed her to him. He mounted his horse and readied the plaids. Still embarrassed over tripping and wanting to impress the men with the fact that she was learning some of their Gaelic words, she smiled sweetly, and with a good deal of pride said to Rowan, "Haud yer wheesht!" The men remained quite still for a moment before Duncan burst out laughing. Aishlinn face burned crimson. "Did I not say it correctly?" she asked him as Rowan handed her up.

"Nay," Duncan laughed as he set her upon his lap. "Ye said it correctly, lass."

"Then why are you all laughing?" she asked, rather puzzled. "I merely bid him good morning in your own language." She could feel Duncan shake with laughter.

"Nay, ye didn't, lassie." Duncan said shaking his head as he tapped the horse's belly.

"Does haud yer wheesht not mean good morning?" Confusion and embarrassment began to flood over her.

"Nay lass, it does no'."

Aishlinn waited impatiently for an explanation. When she saw none was forthcoming she said, "But you've said it to me each time you wake me." She was quite confused and growing more perturbed the more they laughed.

"Aye, I have," he said. "But only because when I wake ye, ye let out a bit of a scream."

She had not realized it and she felt humiliated.

"Ya were scarin' poor Rowan with it!" Duncan's laughter was building up again.

She folded her arms across her chest and huffed. They may have saved her life, but they could be as rude as the day was long when they wanted to be.

Biting his lip to help squelch his laughter, Duncan explained it. "In yer English it means for ye to be quiet, to hold yer tongue."

If there was something beyond embarrassment she most assuredly felt it. She wanted to jump from the horse and hide somewhere until the feeling went away. She supposed she would only need a fortnight or two. She felt an apology to Rowan was in order, in spite of the fact they were all having a grand time at her expense. "I am sorry, Rowan," she murmured.

Manghus said, "No worries there, lass. We've been tellin' him that for years!" The men burst into another fit of laughter and she decided then that she would not try to speak their language again. And if they didn't stop laughing, she might not speak to them again in any language.

Ten

They had ridden through a dense forest for several hours before spilling out onto what could only be described as the most beautiful glen Aishlinn had ever seen. Majestic mountains rose before them as they crossed a very wide meandering stream. Rich, lush grass, interspersed with all manner of flowers, blanketed the hilly landscape. Sheep could be heard in the distance and sounded as though they were answering to the calls of the birds and insects that chattered all around them.

As Duncan led the way towards the mountains, an overwhelming sense of awe flooded over Aishlinn, before the dread set in. If the English ever found her, she hoped they would be merciful and kill her swiftly so that she might be buried on this land. Dead or alive, she never wanted to leave.

"Is it no' as beautiful as we told ye lass?" Duncan asked.

"Nay," she smiled. "It is even more so."

Picking up the pace, they rode in silence for a long while as they headed west. Aishlinn could not shake the fear that was building in her stomach. Fearful that if the English did find her she would be forced to leave. And if they didn't, what kind of life was in store for her? Would she find her family? And if she did, would they accept her as one of their own? There were too many unanswered questions rolling around in her head, making her feel uneasy and frightened.

Unable to hold in all the questions she had, she looked up at Duncan. "Are you sure Duncan, that your chief will not care that you've brought me with you?"

"Now lass, we've told ye before he'll no' mind." He could understand her worry and could not fault her for it.

He studied her face more closely. The swelling had gone done a good amount, but still had far to go. He found himself looking forward to seeing what her face would look like without the welts and bruises.

"Do you think Duncan," Aishlinn said as she looked out at the land before them, "that if we can't find my own people, that your chief would allow me to stay with yours?"

"Aye, I do." He had no doubt of that. Angus was a good man and he'd not turn someone away who needed help. And if anyone needed help it was this young lass.

Aishlinn's brow furrowed as her mind raced. She wasn't really listening to him as she chewed on her bottom lip. "I'm a good worker. Perhaps he'd allow me to stay if I promised to work hard. I can do many things. I could tend the animals or work in the kitchens. I could even work the fields." Her voice trailed off as she thought of all the things she was quite capable of doing.

"Do you suppose he'd allow me to stay if I promised to do those things?" she glanced up at him, looking for reassurance.

"Nay," he told her.

Her eyes grew wide with apprehension. "But you just said he would let me stay."

"Aye, I did." He was being playful with her.

"But-" she began before he cut her off.

"I said he'd let ye stay, Aishlinn. But he'll no' be putting ye to work in the fields. Mayhap the kitchens, but no' the fields, or with the animals, or building things." He let the words sink in for a moment. "He'll let ye stay Aishlinn, that I promise. But no one will be expecting ye to work like a man."

Her first instinct was to protest. Why on earth were these men so insistent that there were certain things that only a man could do? She thought about it for a moment and then realized perhaps it wasn't that only a man could do them, but that he should do them.

Her mind went back to the night with the earl. He had told her that she had to bed him as payment for him allowing her to live and work in his castle. The earl expected it from all the women who lived there. It was payment for the enjoyment they had in living such a fine life behind his castle walls. If one could call working from sun up to sun down for no coin and a thin pallet upon the floor an enjoyment or a fine life. Fear began to rise in her at the possibility that Duncan's chief might expect the same things from her.

Very quietly she asked, "Duncan? Will your chief be expecting certain things from me?" She was afraid of what his answer might be.

Duncan smiled, knowing full well what she meant but deciding to be mischievous about it. "Aye, lass, I'm afraid he will."

He felt her shrink with dread the moment the words left his mouth. He had expected she'd protest and become angry, but instead tears welled and he immediately regretted toying with her. Mayhap there were some things that a man should not jest about. "Lass, 'tis no' what ye think."

She looked up at him and the tears intensified the dark green of her eyes. He felt like a toad and told himself he would never do that to her again. He would not jest of such things and he would never bring tears to her eyes.

"He'll only be asking for yer respect and honesty and nothing more." He wasn't sure if she believed him and his guilt grew with each tear that fell down her cheek.

"The chief be a happily married man." He hoped that knowledge might quell the fear he was now certain filled her heart.

"I promise lass. I'd no' let another man do to ye what the earl did." He searched her eyes for some sort of acknowledgement to his promise. "I'd kill any man who tried."

Aishlinn did not know at first that Duncan had been toying with her. But when she looked into his face she could see the sincere guilt he had felt. When he looked into her eyes, and promised he'd never allow anyone to hurt her again, she knew he spoke the truth.

She felt thankful and relieved to know that someone cared enough to keep her safe. She knew it be a common, brotherly sort of promise he had made her and nothing more than that. But she was glad for it all the same.

None of them slept well that night as they camped hidden in a very small grotto at the base of the mountain. They had built a fire, but it did nothing to help warm Aishlinn's aching and tired bones. The cave was damp and frigid. Mists of gray formed with each breath they took. No matter how many plaids she had upon her, the cold from the damp floor wicked up through her skin and caused her teeth to chatter. When Duncan woke her a few hours later, he had a look of great worry upon his face. "Have ye a fever, lass?" he asked as he placed his hand upon her forehead. Her skin was cold and clammy.

"Nay," she told him through chattering teeth. "The ground is so cold."

Duncan immediately scooped her up and carried her to where his men waited. 'Twas Manghus he handed her to today while he mounted his horse. Once Duncan had her upon his lap, he wrapped two plaids and a blanket around her shivering body. "It won't be long now Aishlinn, and we'll have ye a warm bath and a soft bed." She fell asleep almost immediately, glad again for his warm chest and arms.

They rode hard and fast. Duncan's only concern was getting Aishlinn to the safety of his people and the castle walls. The sun was high to the west when they made their way through the valley that opened up to the land belonging to Clan MacDougall. Aishlinn woke when she felt the horses come to a stop at the top of a large hill.

The grandeur of Castle Gregor was more beautiful than she could ever have imagined. An enormous thick wall made from large gray stones that seemed to stretch on forever surrounded the keep. Within that was another equally imposing wall of stone that encircled the immense castle, its stables, courtyards and various small buildings. Five square towers stretched tall above the four-story castle. It all lay sprawled near a very large loch that glistened gold in the afternoon sun. The sight was as beautiful as it was imposing.

Numerous cottages spread throughout the rolling lands as light smoke billowed from their chimneys. Heather and gorse dotted the land and grew thicker as it traveled up the mountainside, seeming to fight for space among the trees. Tears came to her eyes as she looked upon the majesty of it all.

Excited to be home, Duncan gave her a slight hug. The gesture, she was certain, meant nothing to him, but it sent another curious shiver up her spine when he had hugged her. She was not used to being hugged by anyone, let alone a man. She shook the feeling aside and convinced herself that he was simply glad to be home.

The men let out loud cries that announced their return. Aishlinn held on tightly to Duncan as their small group raced down the hillside and in through the wooden gates that had been thrown open. They came to a stop on the west side of the castle and within moments they were surrounded by dozens of very happy people. Shouts of glee went up through the crowd and although she could not understand the language they spoke, their smiles and cheerful faces told her they were glad for the return of their men.

Duncan leapt from his horse and was immediately pounced upon by children and people of all ages. They were drowned in a flood of hugs, kisses and pats on their backs. Aishlinn remained on the horse, smiling nervously at the sight before her.

After allowing his people time to welcome him home, Duncan turned to Aishlinn with a broad and beaming smile. He reached up, grabbed her by her waist and carefully lifted her down. But instead of immediately placing her upon the ground, he held her for a very long moment as he looked into her eyes. The sunlight glinted off his chestnut colored hair and beard and she thought he looked quite handsome. If the strange feeling in her stomach did not cease and desist immediately she thought she might faint. Still holding her, a curious smile had formed on his face before he spoke. "Welcome home, Aishlinn."

Home. 'Twas a simple word that held so much meaning and heart to it.

The sound of his voice when he said it, with such genuine tenderness, brought tears to her eyes. Could she really be home?

Duncan decided he rather enjoyed holding her and chose not put her down. He liked the way she felt in his arms when he held her. Within moments they were swept away into the sea of excited people who shouted at them. Who be the lass? Why is she wearing trews? What is her name? Is she yer bride? Duncan understood the questions but would not answer them now for he had to get Aishlinn into the castle so that she could be tended to.

Manghus bid them good day, anxious he was to return to his wife. Rowan led Duncan around the castle to the doors of the kitchen. He threw open the heavy wooden door as Duncan whisked her inside. They stood in a very large kitchen that was alive with all manner of people who had stopped to see what the commotion was about.

A rather stout and auld woman let out a gasp when she saw the lass in Duncan's arms. Wiping her hands upon her apron, she walked quickly to them. "Duncan McEwan! What happened to her and why be she wearin' yer trews and tunic?"

Although the woman spoke in the Gaelic, the look on her face said enough; she looked a frightful mess! Duncan told the auld woman that Aishlinn spoke no Gaelic and to please if she could, use the English.

"Ye be English?" The auld woman asked, looking quite horrified. Rowan chuckled and shook his head. "Nay!" he told her.

"She be a fine Highlander!" Duncan said. He bent low and spoke in a hushed tone so that only the auld woman could hear. "She be an orphan, raised in the lowlands, no' blessed with being raised to ken her own language." He shook his head as if terribly saddened by it. "'Tis a sad story indeed Mary. One I hope to one day share with ye. But for now, could we no' have a hot bath for the poor lass?"

Mary studied Aishlinn, her face holding a sad and pitiful expression. "Ya poor thing!" Shaking her head she began racing about with the speed and command of someone half her age. She grabbed a young boy and told him to fetch someone named Bree. She told another to grab more young lads and tote tubs upstairs. While she belted out orders and rushed about the kitchen, Duncan looked at Aishlinn with a smile upon his face.

"Aishlinn, that be our Mary. She be in charge of the kitchens. And anything else she's a mind to take over!"

The auld woman stopped and gave him a stern look. "I'll have none of yer lip this day lad! Just because ye be a man now does no' mean I can't still give ye a skelpin'!"

Duncan laughed at her, before he turned to look at Aishlinn. "Mary helped to raise me. She's probably the only woman in the world I be truly afraid of!" Aishlinn turned her lips inward to keep from giggling. The thought of Duncan afraid of anyone, let alone this sweet auld woman was laughable.

"Well don't stand there like an eejit!" Mary scolded him. "Take the lass up to Bridget's auld room. I'll have baths and a hot meal ready shortly."

Duncan gave Mary a wink before he raced from the kitchens and carried Aishlinn up three flights of stairs.

Rowan led the way to a bedroom at the end of a very large open hallway and opened the door for them to enter. The room was large and well lit by two very tall windows. A large fireplace stood to their right while a beautiful bed sat to their left. The bed was adorned with luxurious looking blankets and pillows and a large wooden trunk sat at the foot of it.

A small table that held a brush, combs, and tiny glass bottles rested between the tall windows. Ornate tapestries hung on the walls and thick rugs lay upon the floor. Aishlinn had never seen such a beautiful room before.

"Duncan could you please put me down now?" she whispered. "I am feeling better and I see no rocks on which I could trip."

Duncan carefully set her down and stayed near in case she was not as well as she said. "This'll be yer room, lass," he smiled at her.

"Who else stays here?" she whispered. She was wondering who her roommates might be and would they mind sharing their room with her.

"None. Ye'll have it all to yerself," he replied.

There was no hiding her surprise. She had never had a room all to her own before.

"Be there a problem lass?" Duncan asked.

"Nay," she told him breathlessly. "It's a grand room." Inwardly, she thought, far too grand for someone such as me.

Duncan enjoyed the look upon her face. "Ya even have yer own privy!" he said, as he walked to a door near the bed and opened it. "Ya won't have to scurry about in the middle of the night to find one."

Aishlinn was stunned for she had never enjoyed such comforts before.

"Rowan!" Duncan barked. "Let Angus know we've returned and that I need to speak with him immediately."

Rowan nodded, bid Aishlinn good day and left the room quickly.

Duncan stood with his arms crossed over his chest as he watched Aishlinn look about the room. As her eyes fell from one object to another, he found himself wishing he knew what she might be thinking. He was about to ask her that very question when a very beautiful young woman with long black hair and green eyes walked into the room.

"Duncan!" she exclaimed as she ran up to hug him. Aishlinn remained standing near the fireplace and suddenly felt quite uncomfortable. The young woman was dressed in a very fine green gown. Her thick black braid reached to her very tiny waist. Aishlinn was surprised when she felt a tad jealous of not only the young girl's beauty but of the big hug she was now receiving from Duncan.

"Bree," he said as he finally let go and turned her to face Aishlinn. "I would like ye to meet Aishlinn. Aishlinn, this is me sister, Bree." He introduced them with a broad smile.

"Bree, she speaks only the English." Aishlinn was slightly confused for she thought all of Duncan's family had been killed long ago. Perhaps the lass was not a blood sister, but instead a foster sister. She would ask Duncan of it later.

The young woman's smile had quickly disappeared when she saw Aishlinn's face. "Lass! Ye do look a fright!" Bree said. Her honesty made Aishlinn want to crawl away and hide.

"But no worries! Yer bath will be here soon. We'll take good care of ye." The girl was a whirlwind of movements as she rushed out of the room and yelled at someone in the hallway.

Soon the room was a flurry of men who brought a tub and sat it before the fireplace. Young boys rushed in carrying buckets of hot water and poured them into the tub. Someone set a dressing screen in the corner as more and more water was brought in. A fire was lit while Bree rushed from the room only to return a moment later. "Duncan, yer bath be ready now! Be gone and let us have some privacy."

As the last of the hot water was poured into the tub Bree took Aishlinn's hand and led her behind the screen. Not knowing of the injuries to Aishlinn's back, Bree quickly began tugging at the belt and tunic.

"Bree," Aishlinn began, "I knew you mean well, but I've bandages on my back."

A puzzled look formed on Bree's face as she let go of the tunic. Aishlinn turned and carefully pulled the tunic over her head. She winced when she heard Bree gasp.

"Lass! What happened to ye?" she asked. She was appalled at what she saw.

"'Tis a long story, Bree," Aishlinn told her as she quickly removed the trews and woolens and left them lying on the floor. She grabbed a linen that hung on the screen, and wrapped it around her waist and chest, and left her back exposed. "Could you undo the bandages for me?" Aishlinn asked, keeping her back to Bree.

Bree gave a quick nod of her head and untied the long strips. She could not hold in her surprise when she began lifting the bandages from the cuts. "Och!" She shook her head repeatedly as she removed each bandage and tossed it to the floor with Aishlinn's clothes.

"A man did this to ye, dinna he?" Bree was smart enough to figure out the cuts were made by a belt or strap of some sort. What she couldn't figure out was why she had been beaten.

"Aye," Aishlinn said through gritted teeth. She took a deep breath as she felt the last of the bandages tug away.

The scent of lavender wafted through the air as it clung to the steam rising up from the wooden tub. Aishlinn had never taken a lavender scented bath before! Had never taken a scented bath of any kind before, for that matter.

Bree led her around the screen and to the tub. Aishlinn held on to Bree's hand for balance as she slowly stepped into the gloriously hot water and carefully sat down. She let out a long, steady, blissful sigh. 'Twas heaven.

Bree brought the stool from the table and sat down next to the tub. The puzzled look was still painted across her face. Aishlinn knew she probably had a hundred questions, but was too polite to ask them.

"How old are you Bree?" Aishlinn finally asked.

"I'm ten and six." Bree told her as she dipped a cloth into the water. Aishlinn took a deep breath, dunked her head under the steaming water for a few moments before coming back up. Aishlinn decided that Bree was old enough to hear most of her story. There were, of course, certain parts she couldn't have shared with an adult woman, let alone someone as young as Bree. Aishlinn would carefully walk around those bits and pieces of her life's story. She'd lie if she needed to.

While Bree lathered the cloth with soap, Aishlinn began her story, starting first with her mother's death and then Moirra's. Bree listened intently as Aishlinn told of how she had ended up at Castle Firth. She decided to leave out the part of the earl's death, instead telling the young girl that he had had been so drunk from whiskey that he passed out before he could complete the reprehensible deed.

The water was tepid and Aishlinn had been scrubbed from head to toe twice and her hair washed three times before she ended with their arrival today. Bree helped her from the tub and carefully wrapped the linen around Aishlinn's shoulders.

"Ya poor thing!" Bree said shaking her head as she led Aishlinn to sit near the fire. "What ordeals and trials ye've been through!"

Aishlinn wanted no one's pity, only help in finding her family. Deep down there was a part of her that hoped that day would not come too soon. She had grown quite fond of Duncan, Rowan and Manghus, and had quickly come to think of them as the brothers she had always prayed for.

"Have they brought yer things up yet?" Bree asked as she began to rub a drying cloth over Aishlinn's hair.

Aishlinn cringed inwardly, for she did not have things. "My dress was cut. 'Twas in Duncan's pack the last I saw it. Perhaps you could find it for me, along with a needle and thread and I could mend it."

Bree clucked her tongue at the notion. "Nay! We've plenty of things for ye to wear!" she said, shaking her head as if Aishlinn was daft. "I'll fetch ye a shift and then we'll take care of yer back and comb out yer hair."

When Bree returned a short time later, Aishlinn had begun to nod off near the fire. "Lass, ye dunna want to fall asleep before we comb out yer hair and put fresh bandages on ye. Lay upon the bed and I'll take care of yer back for ye."

Bree took great care at applying salve and fresh bandages to Aishlinn's back. While it stung considerably, it did not burn with the ferocity that it had this morning.

When she was finished wrapping the long strips around Aishlinn's torso, Bree gently tugged the shift over Aishlinn's head. Aishlinn had never seen such fine fabric before. She was certain it was too fine and rich a fabric for someone of her station to wear. But seeing that her alternatives were limited -- return to wearing Duncan's tunic and trews or wander about naked until her own clothing could be washed and repaired, she chose to remain quiet.

Sitting in front of the fire, with Aishlinn resting at her feet, Bree carefully ran the comb through the tangled mess of hair. Tears threatened, for the last person to comb her locks had been Moirra. And Aishlinn could not think of Moirra without her thoughts turning to her mother.

Aishlinn held her breath and tried to convince herself that her tears were the result of being weary and travel worn and not from the longing of missing Moirra and her mother. All that she needed was a nap and a hot meal and she'd be able to control her emotions much better afterwards.

"Och! Lass!" Bree whispered sweetly. "Ya be safe now." Bree gave her a slight hug around her shoulders. "And ye must be quite tired from yer journey."

"Yes I am. But I'm afraid all I've done these past days is sleep."

"Who could blame ye?" Bree said paying particular attention to a rather large knot of hair. "Ye'll no' have to worry about the English while yer here, lass. Angus will see to it that ye're safe, as will Duncan and the men."

"When will I meet Angus?" Aishlinn asked unable to suppress a yawn.

"Och! It will be at least a month. He was called to the high north for talks, just a day or two after Duncan left in search of the reivers."

Reivers? Aishlinn did not know what the young girl spoke of. "What reivers?" she asked.

"The reivers that took the cattle. Thirty head of cattle they took in the dead of night. That's why Duncan and the others were in the lowlands, to find the reivers that took 'em," Bree said.

Aishlinn felt ashamed knowing that Duncan and his men had given up a search for the cattle that were meant to feed their people. Visions of starving men, women and children leapt into her mind. "Why would they do that?" she thought out loud.

"Do what, lass?" Bree asked finally winning the battle with the knot of hair.

Aishlinn sighed heavily. "Why would they give up the search for the cattle to help me? You're people will go hungry because of it!"

"Och! Don't be silly, lass!" Bree patted her on her shoulders. "Our people will no' go hungry. We've been blessed with more than most and we've plenty more cattle to feed us!"

Although relieved to know the clan would not go hungry, she still felt quite guilty. These men had given up the search for their cattle and had taken great risks to bring her here. She worried that she would never be able to repay them for their kindness.

"All done!" Bree happily announced before standing. "Now ye get yerself into bed and I will look in on ye later." She smiled sweetly before leaving Aishlinn alone.

For as long she could remember, she had always slept upon a pallet, even after moving into Castle Firth for the servants' rooms had no beds. The bed at Aric and Rebecca's had been quite nice but she had only slept in it to heal her battered body.

Peasants and scullery maids were not meant to enjoy such luxuries. If she began to sleep in a bed now, it would be the same as telling a lie; she'd be pretending she was something she wasn't.

She could not deny that it looked to be a magnificent bed but she also could not deny her true station in life. Wrapping the linen tightly around herself, she chose instead to sleep on the floor by the fire. Yawning again, she tucked her head into the crook of her arm and within moments fell asleep.

While Duncan bathed, his thoughts turned to Aishlinn, who he knew at that moment to be completely naked, soaking in a warm bath of her own in the room right next to his. He was quite shocked by the mental image that came to his mind and gave himself a good chastisement for it. The lass was far too young, and had gone through far too much to have a big lumbering Highlander chasing her about!

He lathered up his face and shaved off the nearly month old beard that had sprouted upon his face. His mind continued to wander to thoughts of Aishlinn and he knew not from where those thoughts came. He nicked his face several times while shaving, unable to concentrate on the task at hand.

Blotting up the tiny droplets of blood, he cursed himself repeatedly. Mayhap it was the long journey or his gratitude towards her for killing the earl that affected his mind and led it to images he should not have.

The bath had left him feeling refreshed and invigorated. He donned a clean tunic and plaid before pulling on his leather boots. There had still been no word of Tall Thomas, Findley, Richard or Gowan and he hoped they would be returning soon. Word that the English had fallen for the trick of sending back the riderless horse would indeed be welcome news.

He assumed Manghus was now happily at home with his wife and regaling her with the story of their recent adventure. Rowan had by now partaken of a warm bath and was more likely than not seeking out the friendship and comfort of any available young lass.

Standing near the fireplace he wished that Angus were here now to seek his counsel on the matter of Aishlinn. Learning earlier from Rowan that Angus had been called to talks in the far north and that it would be at least a month before he would return did not help the matter. With Angus gone, Duncan was left as acting chief.

Rowan had also informed him that Isobel was off helping Brown Robert's wife deliver her first bairn, therefore he could not seek her counsel. Customarily he would have sought out Angus' advisors, but unfortunately they were all with Angus. If only he knew for certain what the English were doing he would feel much better about the entire situation.

Duncan ran his hands through his damp hair and began to pace. If he were to ever become chief of his clan, he would need a team of advisors of his own. Half the men he would have chosen for that position were busy at the moment, scouting the territory for English soldiers who could at this very moment be ready to descend upon his castle in search of Aishlinn. He would not allow that to happen.

Curious feelings had begun to creep into his chest as he thought of her. He felt quite protective of her as well as beholden, for she had killed the man who had murdered his family. But there was something more. 'Twas something that he could not quite put his finger on. Taking a deep breath, he decided to seek out Rowan and a few other good men he felt he could trust. Together they would make a plan of action in case the English attacked. But first, he should check on his guest.

Aishlinn's room was next to his own, just a few steps away. He knocked quietly but heard no reply. Had Bree still been in the room she undoubtedly would have bid him to enter. He knocked again and still received no response. Had she taken ill he wondered? Or had she fallen getting out of the tub and now lay unconscious upon the floor?

Quietly he opened the door and peered inside. He found her curled up like a kitten in front of the fireplace. The poor thing had been so exhausted from her recent trials and journey that she had fallen asleep by the fire.

Duncan entered the room quietly and crouched beside her. There was a hidden beauty to the lass, and not one simply masked by bruises and welts. Aishlinn's beauty ran deeper than skin. For reasons he could not explain he felt drawn to her in a way he had never experienced before. He wanted to know her better, to learn all he could of her. He was also anxious to see what her face looked like when it was free of the marks left behind by a cruel and evil man. She looked so peaceful -- nearly angelic as she slept on the floor by the fire. He resisted the urge to reach out to touch her cheek.

For days she had been sleeping on the cold ground. She'd not complained once of being cold, even when her teeth chattered and her body shivered. There had also been no complaints about the pain he knew she must have suffered. He could not leave her to sleep here on the cold hard floor even if she were by a warm fire. Gently he reached his hands under her tiny frame and scooped her into his arms.

She had been sound asleep when she suddenly felt her body being lifted into the air. She let out a loud gasp before she realized Duncan was lifting her into his arms.

"Haud yer wheesht, lass!" he smiled.

"What are you doing?" she demanded. "Put me down, Duncan!" She had no idea what he wanted or why he was here.

"Lass, ye fell asleep on the floor. I was merely putting ye in yer bed so ye could rest more comfortably," he told her. "Ye've spent enough time of late sleeping upon the cold hard ground." He remembered how cold she had been that morning, chilled to the bone with her teeth chattering.

"I'm used to sleeping on a pallet, Duncan," she protested.

Duncan wondered then if she was afraid of the bed after what the earl had done. Silently he sent a slew of blasphemies down to the bastard in hell. Mayhap a bed brought back too many painful and frightening memories. "Lass, the bed will no' hurt ye," he whispered trying to reassure her.

"I know that!" she said indignantly and let out and exasperated sigh. She knew he would not leave her alone about it. "I'm used to sleeping upon a pallet." She hoped she would not be forced to explain it further.

So that was it. The lass had never slept in a bed before. She was probably embarrassed and wanted not to admit it aloud. He decided to take a softer approach.

"Now, lass. What happens when ye find a nice young lad to marry? Do ye expect yer husband to be sleepin' upon a pallet or in a nice warm bed with ye?"

She went red with embarrassment. She knew that more likely than not she would never marry. And if she did it would be no business of Duncan's where she and her husband might sleep! She began to protest when she suddenly noticed his smooth face. He had shaved his beard and he looked even more handsome without it. "You shaved your beard," she said.

"Aye, I did," he said as he began carrying her towards the bed. "I find the lasses complain far less when I kiss 'em with a smooth face!" he said with a smile and a wink.

A momentary sensation of sadness, blended with a tint of jealousy, ran over her skin. Other women, women far more beautiful and buxom than she, would be given the honor of those kisses. She cursed herself for thinking such things.

As he stood holding her beside the bed she noticed an odd expression had come to his face. "Are you going to put me down?"

For an uncomfortably long moment, he did not move. His eyes seemed to be glued to hers. With a slight nod of his head he said "Aye" before he carefully laid her upon the bed.

It was as she had thought it would be, soft, warm, and quite luxurious. Taking a deep breath, she caught the faint scent of thrushes and lavender, as the bed seemed to wrap around and hug her tenderly. 'Twas an exquisite feeling of comfort, warmth and safety. 'Twas nearly as good as having Duncan's arms wrapped around her. Not quite as good, but close enough.

"Now," Duncan said. "Be that better than the cold floor?"

Aishlinn closed her eyes as he drew the blankets around her "Aye," she whispered softly.

He brushed a loose strand of hair from her forehead and wished he could crawl into the bed with her. He cursed himself for thinking it. "Good rest to ye, Aishlinn," he said and quickly left the room.

Aishlinn did not respond for she was lost in the tingling sensation she felt the moment he touched her forehead. She was not sure what that sensation was for she had absolutely no romantic experiences in her past to refer to. She only knew that when he was near her, when he touched her, she lost all sense of reality.

She would have to get these sensations and thoughts under control, reminding herself again, that men like Duncan could never be interested in someone like her. He was merely being kind, like a good brother would be and there would never be anything more to their relationship than that.

She also warned her heart against getting used to luxurious beds and hot, lavender scented baths. Soon, she was certain, she would be healed enough to begin to earn her keep here, and she would be living below stairs with the rest of the servants. But for now she would sleep in the bed, only because she did not want to catch a chill and risk getting the fevers. It had nothing to do with the luxuriousness that she was swathed in at the moment. It was for practical reasons alone and nothing more. But goodness, it did feel good.

Duncan did not breathe again until he closed the door behind him. *Wretched man!* He cursed to himself. It had taken every ounce of willpower he owned to not kiss her then and there as he held her in his arms. A scowl came to his face as he wondered where in the hell these beastly thoughts of his were coming from. Pushing them aside, he went in search of Rowan and cared not if he interrupted anyone his friend might be in the middle of.

Isobel had finally returned from helping Brown Robert's wife deliver her first bairn, a healthy baby boy. It had been an exhausting event that lasted well into the evening. Mary happily informed Isobel of Duncan's safe return and the fact he had brought a guest with him.

Isobel went in search of Duncan but found her daughter, Bree, instead. Bree excitedly shared the story of the orphaned Highlander lass. Isobel was certain her daughter was making things seem far more dramatic than they actually were. But when she finally found Duncan and discussed the matter with him, she knew her daughter had not been exaggerating.

There were only a few differences between Bree's version and Duncan's. According to Bree, the earl had passed out before being able to go through with his devious intentions. Isobel was certain Duncan's version was more in line with the truth. They could only assume that Aishlinn had lied either because she thought Bree too young or the truth was too painful for her to discuss out loud.

Isobel peeked into Aishlinn's room but was unable to get a good look at the lass for she had the covers pulled tightly about her head. She thought it best to allow the poor thing to sleep as much as possible.

Isobel returned to the kitchens and left instructions with Mary that the lass was to be left alone for now in order to rest. Mary promised she would have someone look in on on her periodically then quickly ordered Isobel to her own bed. Isobel may very well have been the chief's wife and the mistress of this castle but even she knew better than to argue with Mary. She went to her own room where she fell into her bed and slept until morning.

Eleven

Uninterrupted by the nightmares she had been having for many days, Aishlinn slept. She did not wake until well after the midday meal the following day. When Bree informed her of that fact, Aishlinn was appalled. She wasn't one to lie about in such a lazy manner. Very much ashamed of herself, she apologized to Bree repeatedly.

"'Tis all right, lass!" Bree told her as she brought a tray of warm broth and fresh bread and sat it upon the bed. "Ye've been through a trial, that is certain. No one holds it against ye fer sleeping!"

Bree was insistent that Aishlinn stay in bed while she ate. Too tired to fight, Aishlinn acquiesced but not before making certain the young girl knew she was not a slothful person.

"I'm not a princess who takes her meals in bed whilst others wait on her hand and foot!"

Bree giggled and shook her head. "But isn't it nice to be treated as one on occasion?"

Aishlinn had no good response for she had never really thought of it before. She had been kept far too busy over her years to have time to waste on such frivolous thoughts and daydreams. Well, perhaps she did daydream, but only on the rarest and most special of occasions. Such as when her brothers were being particularly cruel and she thought of very clever ways to get even with them. Or when she would fall into bed at the end of a bone-tiring day of working in the fields.

Only then would she lie awake and think of a knight in shining plate who would come to rescue her. Of course the knight in her dreams had always been blind and therefore cared not if her face was plain. The knight had only cared for her inner beauty. A regal knight with perfect vision would have taken one look at her extremely plain face and run away.

She let out a long sigh and turned her attention to the broth and warm bread dripping with butter. The meal left her feeling warm and content, but nature called and would not allow her to sleep again just yet.

When Aishlinn struggled to leave the bed Bree said, "Lass! Ye need yer rest!"

Aishlinn laughed at her. "Aye, I do. But if I don't get to the privy soon, you'll have a mess to clean!" Bree chuckled and helped her to the privy. Aishlinn thought it all ridiculous, the way everyone fawned over her, treating her like a bairn. When she was finished, Bree happily helped her back to the bed where she snuggled again into the pillows. The bed was luxurious Aishlinn thought, and prayed her body would not get used to it.

"Yer face looks much better this day, Aishlinn!" Bree told her as she grabbed the mirror from the table. "Look! Ye can see fer yerself!"

"Thank you, but nay." Looking at her own reflection was something Aishlinn never did.

"Och! But lass ye must!" Bree was an insistent.

After a few moments Aishlinn's curiosity got the better of her, and she took the risk to glance at her reflection. If what Bree said was true, that she looked better this day than last, then she could only imagine how terrible she must have looked in the beginning. Why on earth Duncan and his men had not fled in fear at the sight of her, she could not begin to guess.

Purple patches surrounded her eyes and dotted her still swollen cheeks and chin. The cuts on her lips remained but were barely noticeable. How anyone could tell her she was not plain she couldn't fathom. Tears welled as she slumped into her pillow.

Bree smoothed her hair and spoke to her soothingly, as she might do to a child with a bruised knee. "'Tis all right, Aishlinn," she whispered. "Ye'll be completely healed soon enough. Yer face is truly bonny, even with the bruises."

Aishlinn knew better. Bruises or no, it was still the same plain face her stepfather had warned her of. Not wanting to argue the point, Aishlinn closed her eyes and took deep breaths. "Thank you, Bree."

Bree stayed quietly at her side until Aishlinn fell back to sleep. Bree may have been young but not so young that she couldn't recognize a broken heart when she saw it. She felt sorry for Aishlinn and the life she had led.

Over the next few days the ritual of bringing meals to Aishlinn only to have her fall asleep soon after eating was repeated. Frequently Bree would give her updates on the color of her bruises and would try to offer reassurance that she was healing quite nicely. Aishlinn refused to look into the mirror again and was thankful that Bree did not push the matter further.

Duncan had been very busy those first few days after their return to Castle Gregor. Training would take up most of his mornings while the duties of acting chief took up his afternoons. Bree and Mary would update him on Aishlinn's progress several times throughout the day.

As he began to wonder if he should not send a search party for his search party, his men finally returned. Gowan, Tall Thomas, Findley and Richard rode through the gates late in the afternoon. Oddly enough they had returned with the missing cattle.

"What the bloody hell?" Duncan exclaimed as he bounded down the steps and into the courtyard. Gowan dismounted and handed his horse off to a young lad. "We came across the reivers on our return home, Duncan!" he said rather proudly. "They were camped to the north and west of the McDunnah's lands.

"What of the English?" Duncan asked, for that had been his main worry these many days.

"Now that is an odd story!" Gowan said as they waited for Tall Thomas, Richard and Findley to join them. A group of men came to lead the cattle to the pasture just beyond the keep.

As the group entered the castle, Duncan told a young lad to have food and drink brought to his men straight away. Though his men were travel worn, covered in dust and grime, they appeared peculiarly excited. For his men to return unscathed and apparently happy made Duncan assume they had good news. However he would not breathe a sigh of relief until he learned what had happened.

"We rode all the way back to Penrith and kept a watch outside Castle Firth," Findley told him as they sat down at a table. "There were no' a sign of any soldiers about. We watched for an entire day. 'Twas as if nothing had happened there at all."

Duncan found that quite strange. The bruises and welts across Aishlinn's body were evidence enough that something bad had happened to her. Had she been truthful when she said she stabbed the earl? A scowl came to his face as he wondered if there was more to her story than she had told them.

While he pondered the new information, food and ale were brought in. His men quickly downed a tankard of ale each before filling their trenchers with food. "We went north, south and east Duncan. We found nothin'," Richard told him before filling his hungry mouth with venison.

Duncan could make no sense of it. If what Aishlinn said were true, that she had in fact killed the Earl of Penrith, then most assuredly the English would be looking for her. That is, unless they knew not who to look for. Many questions raced through his mind and he needed answers.

"I'll need to speak to the lass," he told them as he stood to leave.

Gowan smiled up from his trencher. "Would ye like to know more of the cattle reivers, Duncan?" he asked.

Duncan had completely forgotten about the reivers. He was more concerned with what the English were doing. He sat back down. "Tell me."

"We headed north from Penrith and having found no sign of English soldiers, we decided to head home," Gowan said before taking a pull of ale. Wiping his mouth on his dirty sleeve he continued. "As we crossed over McDunnah land, through their northern territories, we came upon the reivers." He paused long enough to belch. "They were a fierce lot!" he smiled. "'Twas nearly all we could do to fend them off!"

Findley and Richard laughed raucously. Duncan cast each of them a puzzled look. He asked why they found a fierce lot of reivers humorous.

"They were children Duncan. The oldest a whopping ten and three!" Gowan said.

"Aye," Richard wiped a tear from his face for he had been laughing so hard. "And they were fierce. Good rock throwers!" he chuckled again. "Anyway, 'twas only five of them, all lads. They had gotten lost on their return home and that's why 'twas such a curious route we followed," he explained. "They had taken the cattle it seems for two reasons. One," he began as he held up a finger, "to prove to their chief that they were indeed fierce and able warriors." He took another drink of his ale.

"And two?" Duncan asked rather impatiently.

"And two," Findley interjected. "They were starving."

The scowl returned to Duncan's face. He was not sure if he would like where this story might lead.

"There canna be more than twenty in their entire clan, Duncan. Mostly auld men and women and a couple of men near Angus' age. Though I would no' give ye a groat for any of them." The smile had left his face.

"The lad's mother -- a bonny thing she is by the way," Richard added, "Och! She was mad at the lot of them! I thought she'd skelp them all for what they'd done."

"Her husband died three years ago," Findley said. "He was the last of their warriors. They'd been wiped out by a pox. How the auld survived it, I dunna ken. They've no homes save for a few tents and a hut they all sleep in for the winter. The lad's mum it appears is their chief of sorts." A rather pitiful look had come to all of their faces.

Duncan waited to see if they would offer more. "And?" he finally asked.

Findley stood and looked at him with a most serious expression painted on his face. "I'd like permission to bring them here, Duncan."

Though it was true they had room for them, and plenty of good fortune to share, Duncan wondered what he would do with the lot of them. He could not in good conscience ignore those in need. And the thought of a mother with five young lads to feed and no husband to help tugged at his heart. There was no reason for him to take time pondering what Angus might do. They would take them in. "I give it. Go get yer band of fierce reiver warriors, Findley. We'll take them in."

A broad smile came to Findley's face causing Duncan to wonder if mayhap his friend had not taken a fancy to the mother of the lads. "How bonny is she?" he asked.

Findley raised his eyebrows and smiled. "Bonny enough that I'd ride for days to get her."

Duncan chuckled as he stood and smacked Findley upon the back. "Be sure to explain to the lads though, that we dunna take too kindly to reivers. And if they ever think of stealing again, 'twill no' be their mum that'll skelp 'em, 'twill be me."

Duncan had tried that day to speak with Aishlinn. But when he entered her room, he found that she was asleep. It had been like that for days now and he was beginning to wonder if her injuries weren't worse than he realized.

The following day he decided he would try again. If he found she was still sleeping he would send for the healers. He was quite surprised to hear Bree's cheerful voice bid him entry when he knocked upon Aishlinn's door.

He was also surprised to find Aishlinn awake. But he was even more surprised to find a very beautiful lass sitting near the open windows -- one whose bright smile was enough to light even the darkest of nights.

Aishlinn sat with a shawl draped around her shoulders while Bree ran a comb through her golden blonde hair. Duncan wished for a brief moment to be the comb so that he might have a chance to feel her smooth, silky tresses. As he cursed his wicked thoughts, he promised himself he would attend two masses this week as well as confession and beg the Lord to forgive him these wicked thoughts.

Nearly gone were the bruises and he could see clearly that she did in fact have a most beautiful face. She had magnificent features -- an angular jaw and a perfectly proportioned nose. Her lips were full and pink and he imagined they would taste as sweet as honey if he were to kiss them. She had a long slender neck and dainty ears that he would not mind at all brushing his fingers against until he brought chill bumps to her creamy skin. By the time he got his sinful thoughts back in control, he was up to mass every day for the next sixty years and confession twice daily through eternity.

His thoughts had turned to Aishlinn's stepfather and the fine manner in which he managed to convince the lass that she had no beauty. Only a truly evil son of a whore would do such a thing. Duncan had not realized his face held a deep scowl until Bree brought it to his attention.

"What be the matter, Duncan?" Bree asked. "Ye look angry."

Duncan shook away the thoughts along with the scowl. "Sorry lasses! I was thinking of something else." He came into the room and stood near Aishlinn. "I am glad to see ye awake. How be ye this day, Aishlinn?"

"So much better, thank you, Laird McEwan." Her smile was sweet and appreciative.

Duncan chuckled as he reached out to put a hand upon her shoulder and he felt his own skin begin to sizzle when he touched her. He withdrew it quickly. "Ye may call me Duncan, lass," he told her, doing his best not to appear as addle-headed as he felt. There was a reason why he was here and it took him a moment to remember it. "Bree, I've need to speak to Aishlinn privately," he said, never taking his eyes from Aishlinn's.

"I'll come back soon, Aishlinn," Bree assured her before leaving the room.

Duncan pulled the stool from the fireplace and sat in front of Aishlinn so that he could read her face while he questioned her. Unease began to build in his stomach for he truly did not want to cause her any discomfort. But it was important that he have as many details as possible.

"Aishlinn, I've questions I need to ask ye," he told her. "I'll need ye to answer them honestly."

Puzzled by his statement, her brow creased. She had been completely honest with him from the start and had only held back the most embarrassing of moments. "Aye, I will, as I have done since we first met, m'laird."

Duncan nodded his head and he crossed his arms over his chest. "Tell me about the night ye stabbed the earl."

Aishlinn could live her entire life ten times over and it would not be enough time to forget that night. Memories of what had happened and what almost happened, would be forever burned into her soul. They would more likely than not, haunt her all the rest of her days. She took a deep breath before answering him. "I stabbed him."

"Aye, I ken that, lass. Tell me what happened before ye stabbed him." Duncan needed to make sense of why the English had not yet stormed his castle.

"All of it?" she asked, hoping he would at least allow her the decency to leave out the most painful and embarrassing parts.

"Aye, lass. All of it."

Collecting her nerve through another deep breath she began again. "I was asleep in my room when Baltair, one of the guards, came to me. He said the earl wanted to see me in his chambers immediately." A shudder came over her at remembering the sad look upon Baltair's face. "He took me to the earl's room."

"Ye were asleep? Was it late at night then?"

She thought it odd to ask what time it might have been. "Yes. It was long after the evening meal had been cleared and the kitchen put back into order."

"Did ye know why the earl asked for ye?" Duncan asked.

"Fairly certain." Her stomach felt heavy, as if she had swallowed a bucketful of rocks. "The earl had a reputation about him." She cast her eyes to the floor. "But I truly hoped it would be for another reason. Though I could not think of one."

He gave her a moment to gather her thoughts. It wasn't any easier for him to ask for the details of that night than it was for her to give them. The only comfort he had was in his firm belief that the earl now burned in hell.

A long moment passed before Aishlinn could lift her eyes to him again. "I would not bed him," she said firmly. "That is why he hit me. Again and again and again he hit me. Every time I told him 'nay', he would slap me. When I lay on the floor he kicked me. When I still said nay, he beat me about my back and legs with his belt." Her back and legs began to ache at the memory and caused her to shift uncomfortably in her chair. She swallowed hard to keep the tears from coming, deciding she had cried far too many tears of late.

"I have never been with a man that way and I was not going to do such a thing with the likes of him!" Her voice was beginning to grow angry. "I swore that I would die first before I let him do such a thing. But when he pulled the dagger out and held it to my throat, I could no longer fight. I hurt so badly, Duncan. I could barely see and it was painful to breathe."

The tears she had tried valiantly to hold back finally escaped. They traveled down her cheeks and fell from her chin. "I have never been more frightened in my life, Duncan. He cut my dress and pulled it from me." More tears fell. "He stank of wine and onions and he had not bathed. He was forcing himself upon me, tearing at my shift." The rocks in her stomach had turned to boulders.

Duncan's scowl deepened as she recounted what had happened. He swore that had she not killed the earl he would have an army of men swarming Firth at this very moment. "I'm sorry, Aishlinn." He couldn't find the right words to express what he truly thought at the moment.

Using the end of her shawl she wiped the tears from her face. "He was grabbing at me, pulling my shift up. That's when I saw the dagger."

Duncan raised a curious brow. Was there a possibility that she had stabbed him before he had time to rape her?

"I could not let him do that which he wanted, Duncan. He was so angry and I feared that when he was finished, because I had put up such a fight, he would kill me. So I picked up the dagger and I plunged it into his back. He had been biting me and would not let go, so I pulled the dagger out and stabbed him again." She was far too embarrassed to tell him exactly where the earl's teeth had been when she stabbed him. It was far too vulgar a thing to say out loud.

The anguish in her eyes was more than he could stand. He stood and pulled her into his arms while her body shook from crying. Duncan felt helpless and angry. Helpless because that was often how he felt when in the presence of a crying lass, and angry because he could not take the pain from her heart or the memories from her mind.

"I'm sorry to make ye relive it, lass. There are many questions that have gone unanswered." He smoothed his hands over her hair.

He let her cry it out for a while before finally setting her back upon the chair. "Lass, how did ye escape Castle Firth?"

"Baltair helped me. After I stabbed the earl, I crawled from under him and fled the room. There was a guard in the hallway, but he was asleep. I think from too much ale. When I came to the bottom of the stairs, Baltair took hold of me. He led me through secret corridors and to a horse. He told me he was sorry for taking me to the earl. Said he had a daughter my age." She wiped her face again.

"He's the one that told me to come to the Highlands. He said the Highlanders would help me. I wanted to flee to London because I felt it was bigger and would be easier to hide. But Baltair said nay, go to Scotland."

Duncan felt a sense of hope come to him then. If this Baltair was truly remorseful for taking Aishlinn to the earl, and then to help her escape, there was a possibility he lied to keep the English from looking for her. He felt he would owe a lifetime of debt and gratitude to the man.

"Aishlinn," he said, "the scouts have returned, lass."

"Are they well?" she asked with much concern in her voice. "They've not been injured have they?" While she had not had the opportunity to get to know those men who had gone in search of the English, she still felt a great sense of gratitude towards them.

Her next thought was that the English had followed them and were now waiting outside the castle walls for her head. "Are the English here?"

Duncan held his hands up to stop her. "Lass, the men are well. No one has been injured and the English are no' here."

He smiled as she sank into the chair relieved with his news. "'Tis why I had to ask ye of that night, lass. Gowan, Tall Thomas, Findley and Richard scouted all the territory. It seems the English do no' look for ye." He let the news sink in.

"I believe we may owe it to Baltair that we do no' have a swarm of English soldiers ready to ram the walls for ye," Duncan said with a smile. "How well did ye know the man?" he asked.

"Only by his name. We never spent much time together. I only saw him when he came to the kitchens for a meal." Her brow creased, as she thought of it further. Why had Baltair risked his own life to save hers?

Duncan had no idea why Baltair had helped Aishlinn and he doubted he would ever learn the reason. "Now," Duncan said slapping his hands upon his knees before standing. "I've work to see to," he told her. "I am glad that ye're doing well, Aishlinn."

Aishlinn stood and from the expression on her face, he could tell there was something on her mind. "What is it, lass?" he asked.

"What of me now?" she said quietly. "If the English are not looking for me, what shall I do? Where do I go?" She felt completely lost. Terrified of the English soldiers all these many days, she had made no plans for her future other than surviving it.

Duncan smiled. "This is yer home lass, at least as far as I am concerned. We'll no' worry over anythin' else until Angus returns. For now, I wish ye to consider this," he said spreading his arms out wide, "yer home."

He suppressed the urge to pull her into his arms again.

"Thank you Duncan," she whispered softly. "Shall I move to the maids chambers?" she asked him, "I'm ready to begin earning my keep."

Duncan needed no time to think on it. "Ye are a guest in this castle until Angus says otherwise. When he returns, he'll decide what tasks to give to ye. For now, ye'll stay here, in this room."

Had he admitted to it, which he would not do unless under direct threat of death, he enjoyed knowing she was but a few steps from his own room.

When he had seen her face for the first time, free of the bruises, his heart had skipped a beat or two or ten. For the life of him he could not figure out where these blasted thoughts were coming from. He did not like the idea of her moving below stairs and sleeping in the solar with the other women. He liked the idea of having her near.

"Aishlinn, will ye sit with me at the evening meal this night?" The words rolled off his tongue before he could stop them. Although he would very much enjoy having her sitting next to him at the evening meal, he was not sure if he would be able to keep his hands to himself.

"In the gathering room? With everyone?" she asked. She had never attended an evening meal as a guest before. A servant she was and nothing more. Her meals were always eaten in the kitchens, never with the powerful or privileged.

Duncan laughed at her. "Of course, in the gatherin' room with everyone," he said. She was a perplexing thing.

Aishlinn attempted to speak, stopped and tried again with no success. She searched for a way to word her question without appearing daft. "As a guest?" she asked him.

"Aye. As my guest." He was puzzled by her question. "What be the matter lass?" he asked her.

She blew out the deep breath she had been holding. "Please do not think me ungrateful Duncan, for you know that I truly am," she began. "But I've never been a guest to an evening meal. I'm a servant, a scullery maid. I'm not used to such things." A wave of red came to her skin and Duncan found that he rather liked the fact that she was painfully innocent.

"And?" he said, as he crossed his arms over his chest and silently cursed the English. The manner in which they treated the poor was shameful.

Her skin grew more crimson as she shifted her weight from one foot to the other. "I've no clothes!" she blurted out. "I have the shift Bree has given me and nothing else. I know not what happened to my dress, the one I was wearing when you found me. Do you have it? Please say you do so that I can mend it before the evening meal!"

More embarrassment came to her when she saw his scowl deepen as his eyes turned to black slits. She took the scowl to mean that her worn and tattered dress was not the proper thing to wear for such an occasion. She felt her heart fall to her toes.

"I'm sorry Duncan," she said, staring at her bare feet that instantly reminded her that she did not even own a pair of shoes. "I'll eat in the kitchens. It would probably be more proper for me to do so anyway."

She cursed her own heart for allowing it to let her think for even the briefest of moments that she was worthy of dining in the gathering room as a guest.

Damn! She had a way of pulling at his heart! She'd lived a life he could not imagine and had been through one hellish ordeal the past weeks.

Duncan knew all too well how she must be feeling at the moment. When he had come here as a boy, he had been in the same predicament. Not a damn thing to her name. Not even a stitch of clothing to call her own.

He pulled her chin up with his fingertips, forcing her to look at him. He had to tamp down the lust that shot up in his belly when he looked into those deep green eyes.

"Lass, yer dress was too ruined to be saved and it was thrown away." He could see a fire begin to form in her eyes as she began to protest. "Ye've a new life here, Aishlinn. One I'm sure will take some gettin' used to. I'll see to it that ye have a suitable dress to wear. And I'll no' have ye argue that ye'll no' go."

Aishlinn began to protest but stopped when the scowl came back to his face. She was prepared to absolutely insist that she knew her true station in life and it did not involve grand meals in the gathering room.

"I'll no' hear anymore on the matter," he told her firmly. 'Twas then that her deep green eyes, brimming with tears, melted his heart like butter left in the sun. "'Twould be my great honor and privilege to have ye sit with me this night, Aishlinn."

She could only nod her head, for his blue eyes were quite penetrating. And the way her skin felt, as if it were on fire, was the most peculiar sensation she had ever felt. She supposed it would do her no good to argue. But tomorrow she would insist that things be put to normal, with her below stairs where she belonged.

"I'll send Bree in to help ye, lass," he said before turning and leaving the room. For the life of her she could not figure out why her legs shook and her heart skipped several beats as she watched him leave.

Bree returned to Aishlinn's room as she had promised, her arms heavy with many dresses. She laid them upon the bed and began to hold each one up, twisting her lips, studying each one closely.

"These are some of Bridget's old dresses," she said, tossing aside a beautiful red gown. "Bridget is me older sister, well one of my foster sisters. Mum and dad have helped to raise many. She's married now and has a bairn. Bridgett lives in Ireland -- she married an Irishman! I ken she'll not mind ye wearing them!" She was prattling on so quickly that Aishlinn was having a difficult time keeping up and wondered from where on earth this girl drew her energy!

Aishlinn came to stand beside the bed and looked at the dresses. They were indeed fine and magnificent gowns of all colors and styles. Bree cried with glee when she found the one she'd been searching for.

"'Tis the one ye should wear!" she said as she pulled a spectacular deep purple gown from the pile. Made of very expensive silk with fine gold braiding around the collar and the sleeves, Aishlinn thought it far too grand and she could not imagine wearing it.

Holding up the dress next to Aishlinn, Bree said, "Aye, this is definitely the one. It brings out the green of yer eyes!" Bree was far more excited about the notion than Aishlinn happened to be.

"I could not wear something so fine Bree!" Aishlinn protested. "Perhaps you have something a little more plain?" Plain girls, she thought to herself, do not wear such things and only the well-to-do and royalty wore silk! Peasants were relegated to wool or linen.

"Don't be silly lass! Of course ye can wear it. Ye must wear it!" she smiled brightly. "The lads will be tripping over their tongues when they catch site of ye in this!" she giggled.

Back and forth they went with Bree insisting she wear the gown and Aishlinn insisting she shouldn't. Bree finally gave up and with a heavy sigh laid the dress upon the bed and walked out of the room. Aishlinn sank onto the stool relieved that Bree was gone. She hoped that she would return with a dress more fitting of Aishlinn's standing in life.

Moments later Aishlinn looked up to find Duncan standing in the doorway. "What's this I hear about ye no' wantin' to wear a beautiful gown?" He was smiling. Aishlinn was trying to catch her breath as she sat frozen on the stool. His smile had effect on her that she could not understand.

Duncan walked to the bed, picked up the purple gown and examined it closely. "Is the dress no' to yer likin'?" he asked.

"Nay! It's a fine dress. I've never seen one more beautiful," she told him.

"Then what be the problem?" he asked as he walked towards her. Aishlinn stood, wishing she could run and hide, but he was blocking the door. Why must he have that infernal smile upon his face?

When she did not answer, he walked closer to her. "Why will ye no' wear it?"

Aishlinn swallowed hard and took a deep breath. "It is a fine dress."

"Aye, that it is." He took another step closer as Aishlinn took another back.

"It is a fine dress." She knew not what else to say at the moment. There was something about his smile that made her insides feel as though she had cat o'mountains wrestling inside it. It apparently had an effect on her mouth as well, for she was unable to form a coherent thought, let alone a sentence that would make any sense.

"Ya said that." He was still smiling and continued to step towards her. Soon, she felt the wall against her back; she was trapped.

"Duncan," she managed to whisper. Her mouth had gone completely dry.

"Aye?" he said as he cocked an eyebrow. He stood so close that she could feel his warm breath upon her face.

While she rather enjoyed having him so near, there was a large part of her that wished he wasn't. His deep blue eyes and smile made it nearly impossible to breathe. "I'd not be deserving of wearing such a fine gown."

His brow furrowed. "What do ye mean no' deservin'?"

"I'm not meant to wear such grand things, Duncan." She took a very deep breath. "I'm a plain girl and I would look silly wearing such a thing."

His scowl deepened. "Ye be far from plain lass. And I'll no' have ye saying yer plain again."

The lass had no idea just how beautiful she truly was. He cursed the fool that had convinced her otherwise. His voice and stance softened when he saw the fearful look in her eyes. "I think ye'd look beautiful in such a gown."

Aishlinn shook her head. She knew he was just being kind and meant not what he was saying. She began to protest further when he came so close to her that he was close enough to kiss. She pushed the thought away as far as she could. It was a ridiculous notion.

"It would make me very happy to see ye in it," he told her as he brushed a loose strand of hair from her cheek. "Would ye wear it for me, lass?"

His voice was as smooth as the silk dress he wanted her to wear. "I believe it would also make the chief's daughter happy as well."

She could not think with him this close. What had he said? "Chief's daughter?" She hadn't a clue what he spoke of.

"Bree. She be the chief's daughter," he told her.

"She's the chief's daughter?" Aishlinn repeated before it finally sunk in. "Bree is the chief's daughter?" She was shocked to hear it. Never in the past days had Bree mentioned who her father was.

"Aye, that she is." He had not moved and his smile had grown brighter. He put his hand on the wall over her head as he stared down at her.

She wanted to crawl away. As far as Aishlinn could tell, the chief and his family were the equivalent of English royalty! And she had allowed the chief's daughter to see her unclothed and had even allowed her to wash her hair, to feed her and help her to the privy! Aishlinn felt humiliated and embarrassed.

"What be the matter, lass?" Duncan asked, still holding that wry smile upon those full lips.

"She helped me to bathe!" His blank stare told her he did not comprehend the significance of the matter. "She's the chief's daughter and she helped me to bathe! She combed my hair! She brought me meals! I should be the one tending to her!" She felt like such a fool.

"And if she be the chief's daughter and your sister, that makes you the chief's son!"

"Aye, it does. He be my foster father. I'm one among many the man has helped to raise."

Aishlinn was horrified and embarrassed. She had nearly kissed the chief's son! Foster or not, it would have been a most terrible temptation to succumb to.

Duncan laughed at her. "Lass, we hold no pretenses here like the English do!" he said. "Why, Isobel, the chief's wife," he said with mock horror in his voice, "actually helps to deliver bairns!"

Aishlinn wanted very much at that moment to kick him square in his knee. She did not like being mocked any more than she liked being laughed at. "It isn't funny, Duncan McEwan!"

It took several moments before he stopped laughing. "I am sorry, lass. But ye have to understand. None of us here sits atop high horses like the English do and pretend we be better than anyone else. We leave those notions to the English." His eyes seemed to twinkle even brighter.

"Lass," he said lowering his voice and moving in close to her again. "Ya be no' plain. And it truly would bring me great pleasure to see ye in the purple gown."

He inched closer, his lips nearly touching hers. Aishlinn felt herself going weak in the knees again. "Would ye please wear it? For me?" he whispered.

Every part of her wanted to say "Yes, I'll wear it for you, but only if you kiss me." She did not have the nerve to say it aloud. "I'll wear it," she whispered, wishing she could take it back the moment the words passed over her lips. "But only to not insult Bree." She swallowed hard again. "The chief's daughter."

"For the chief's daughter then," he said and after what seemed like an eternity he straightened himself and backed away. Aishlinn let out a sigh of relief.

Duncan laid the dress back upon the bed. He smiled as he turned to look at her. "And ye no' be plain, lass," he said before he left the room.

She stood on quivering knees and her heart felt as though it would leap from her chest and go bouncing out of the room to follow him. She tried to convince herself that she was coming down with some illness, the fevers perhaps. There was no other explanation for these odd feelings and sensations she was beginning to have, at least none that she felt brave enough to admit to.

It was quite difficult to speak with Bree after learning of her stature and standing among the clan. Aishlinn felt overwhelmingly uneasy with allowing the chief's daughter to braid her hair or to assist with getting into the purple gown. And Aishlinn felt close to fainting when the girl put magnificent slippers upon her feet!

Bree sensed that something was amiss. It took some prodding but she was finally able to pry from Aishlinn exactly what was the matter.

"What silly notions ye have, lass!" Bree told her as she grabbed a mirror from the table and handed it to Aishlinn.

"I've told ye before that we hold no false pretenses here. I have many friends but I find I can always use another!"

Aishlinn had been raised so differently from these people. The more she learned, the more out of place she felt. She was also beginning to wonder if it was a mistake not to have fled to London. At least there she knew what the rules were and how to behave. In London, she'd not be forced to look a fool wearing such a fine gown and slippers. No matter how they tried to convince her otherwise, she simply did not feel right or proper dressing in such a manner.

"Aishlinn," Bree said taking her hand. "I know ye were raised differently, with different ideas and notions and such. But ye be here now. We're a good people, lass, and no one here would ever harm ye in any manner."

Aishlinn knew that Bree and Duncan and the others meant no ill will towards her. They were merely being kind. It was their way. They couldn't change that any more than Aishlinn could change the color of her eyes.

It certainly could not be said that Aishlinn was ungrateful. She had prayed her entire life for the comforts of a loving and kind family. But now that it was being offered to her, free and clear with no strings attached, she found that she was frightened by it.

Bree had finished braiding Aishlinn's hair as best she could and tied a fine deep purple ribbon around the ends. She handed the mirror to Aishlinn and said, "Have a look lass. I think ye look beautiful."

Over the past many days Aishlinn had learned that Bree was as unrelenting as she was good-natured. Knowing it would do her no good to argue, she took in a deep breath and accepted the mirror. She was astonished to find the bruises nearly gone, save for the slight green and yellow around her eyes, and one mark left on her jaw. Though the bruises may be gone, she still found it difficult to believe herself anything but plain. Frustrated, she put the mirror back on the table.

Bree rolled her eyes, smiled and retrieved the mirror. "Look beyond the bruises, lass. I'd not lie to ye. Ye really are quite beautiful." She held out the mirror with a look of dogged determination across her face.

Plain girls do not need a mirror to know they are plain. Plainness needs no affirmation. In an attempt to have Bree drop the subject all together, Aishlinn relented and took another look.

Doing something she'd never done before she studied her own face. I suppose my jaw is average, as is my nose. There be nothing special about them. Perhaps her nose was not quite as big as her brothers had told her it was. Still it was just a nose.

My lips. Maybe my lips are not too thin, nor are they too full, but they are still just plain lips. And my cheeks. Perhaps they'd look better with a bit of pink pinched into them instead of the green blotches they currently held.

Perhaps I am not hideous, she thought. But I am definitely no beauty like Bree. Plain yes, but maybe not quite as hideous as my brothers had told me. That was a thought she could live with.

There was a knock at her door and she embarrassedly put the mirror down. She assumed it was Duncan and she felt a momentary sensation of what could only be described as excitement. Reminding herself to stop acting like a foolish twit, she pushed the feelings aside.

Bree cheerfully bid whomever it was to enter. A moment later the most beautiful woman Aishlinn had ever seen entered the room. Her hair was so black that the candlelight cast streaks of blue to the braid that cascaded over her shoulder and landed at her narrow waist. Her slender neck held up the most exquisite and soft face. Her full pink lips sat under a perfectly proportioned nose and dark eyelashes surrounded beautiful dark green eyes.

She possessed the kind of beauty and grace that would make other women jealous and men daft for her. There was something quite familiar about her as if they had met before. Aishlinn supposed the familiarity was because she looked so much like Bree.

"Mum!" Bree said before going to hug her. As the woman held her daughter's embrace her eyes fell upon Aishlinn. For a fleeting moment the woman's face held the oddest of expressions, one that made Aishlinn's heart fall to her feet.

"Aishlinn! This is me mum, Isobel," Bree said excitedly. "Mum, this is the orphan we told ye of."

Aishlinn quickly stood and curtsied the most elegant curtsey she could manage. "My lady," she said, averting her eyes to the floor as she had been taught to do.

The woman remained quiet. Aishlinn wondered if perhaps she was upset with her for wearing her daughter Bridget's clothes or for taking up residence in her room. The longer Isobel remained quiet and staring the more uncomfortable Aishlinn became. After several agonizingly long moments of silence Aishlinn began to wish she could shrink to the size of a mouse and scurry away. The longer they were silent the more her shoulders began to shrink with fear.

"Aishlinn," Isobel whispered her name.

"Yes, my lady," Aishlinn said as she felt her knees begin to quake.

"Bree, dear, please leave us," Isobel said without taking her gaze from Aishlinn.

Bree looked rather confused but nodded her head slightly before leaving the room. Isobel came and sat upon the bed, her eyes still glued to Aishlinn. "Aishlinn dear, come," she said as she patted the bed with her hand.

Aishlinn swallowed hard and found it quite difficult at the moment to will her feet to move. Isobel patted the bed again. "I won't bite ye, I promise."

Finally finding the nerve to move, Aishlinn went and sat beside her. Knowing it an insult to look royalty in the eye she kept her gaze firmly planted on the leg of the table in front of her.

Isobel let out a small sigh, "Aishlinn? Why do ye not look at me?"

Aishlinn continued to stare at the table leg. "'Twould be an insult to do so, my lady," she whispered.

She took Aishlinn's chin into very fine and soft hands and lifted it. "That is an obnoxious English custom, lass. We do no' hold such customs here."

Aishlinn could not move and knew not what to say or do. Isobel studied Aishlinn's face for a few moments. "My, but yer a beautiful young lady," she said. Aishlinn wondered if the woman had suffered some horrible accident that had caused her to lose her vision or her mind. Or both. Aishlinn began to feel pity towards her. To possess that kind of beauty only to be blind and witless; it was a shame.

"What be the matter, dear?" Isobel asked her.

Aishlinn shook her head. How did one address a lady such as this in her current predicament?

"Ye act as though no one has ever told ye that before!" her voice was laced with wonder. She stared into Aishlinn's eyes. "Ah," she said. "Ya dunna believe me." She put her arm around Aishlinn's shoulder. "All is right, lass. I've not lost my mind as yer thinking."

Aishlinn's eyes flew open. The woman must be bewitched! How could she have known what Aishlinn be thinking if she were not bewitched?

"No worries lass. I've not lost my mind and I canna read yers." Aishlinn started to speak when Isobel held her hand up. "I was a young girl once and 'twasn't so long ago that I dunna remember it. And I've two daughters of me own. I ken what it's like to think ye be too plain or too tall or too this or too that." Her expression had turned warm and soft.

"I ken ye dunna believe me now, but someday ye'll see that I've not lied to ye." She patted Aishlinn on her knee. "I've spoken with Duncan about ye," she said. "He speaks very highly of ye." Aishlinn felt her face flush again as a rush of excitement washed over her. She wondered what Duncan may have said about her but dared not ask.

"I've heard from Duncan and Bree. Now, I'd like to hear yer trials from ye."

There was a warmth and familiarity about the woman that somehow made Aishlinn feel safe. Reluctantly at first, Aishlinn began to tell the story of her life and how she had come to be at Castle Gregor.

By the time she was done her eyes were swollen and red from crying. There were parts of her life she had no difficulty telling. Others, such as what the earl had done, were heartbreakingly painful for her. She left out no details other than the feelings she found she was having for Duncan. When she finished, Isobel gave her a kerchief to wipe her tears and held her for a long time.

"Have ye told anyone else the details that ye've just shared with me?" she asked.

"Duncan, Rowan, Gowan and the others know nearly most of it. Bree knows a little, although I did not tell her exactly what the earl had done or that I stabbed him."

"Good, lass. We'll not tell the whole story to anyone for now. If anyone asks, yer simply our guest. A Highlander girl who had been sent to live in the lowlands for a time and now yer back. They dunna need to ken anything else."

Aishlinn had no desire to share her life's story with anyone for she felt out of place enough as it was. These people had opened their hearts and homes to her the moment she had stepped through the castle gates. She could live with them thinking she was simply an orphan for that was a pity she could readily handle.

"We will have to tell Angus of it when he returns. But for now, we'll remain silent on the matter," Isobel told her as she gave her another hug. "Ye'll find Angus a tall, braw man." Isobel smiled. "His heart be even bigger than he is. I think ye shall like him and he ye."

Aishlinn prayed that Isobel was right. Although she did not like having her entire future hanging in the balance, part of her was glad the chief was not here. His absence would allow her to spend more time with these people that she was quickly beginning to care a great deal for.

Twelve

The moment she laid eyes on Aishlinn, Isobel's heart shattered into a thousand pieces. It was a moment in her life that she could not have predicted and one that would soon have a very profound effect on many people. It was Aishlinn's deep green eyes that had nearly done her in. Those eyes should have held happiness, promise and hope; instead they held fear and sorrow.

The only explanation for the young woman, who had stood before her so shy, fearful and awkward, was that a lie had been told long ago. When the truth would finally be set free Isobel pitied anyone who had been a part of its telling, if in fact any of them still lived. When her husband would learn of the lass' existence, not only would his heart break as her own had, but the sheer and utter rage that would come to him, would put fear into the heart of any man.

She would keep her knowledge secret for now, for she had no other choice.

Thirteen

Isobel had left to make certain the kitchens ran smoothly and Bree returned to Aishlinn's room to escort her to the evening meal. Arm in arm they descended the stairs and entered the large gathering room. Long trestle tables lined the center of the vast space while smaller ones sat against the walls. A high table with eight chairs stood near the grand fireplace. The room was filled with people of all ages chattering, laughing, and enjoying one another's company.

The tables were set with all manner of foods. Warm and inviting scents wafted through the air. Aishlinn could smell roast beef and venison, leeks, and fresh bread. Her mouth began to water and her stomach growled with hunger.

As they stopped just inside the doorway, Bree searched the room with her eyes. Soon a group of smiling young lads approached them. "Bree! Will ye sit with me this night?" The tallest of the group asked.

"Depends, Young Thomas. How much ale have ye had?" Bree asked as she studied him closely.

"Only two mugs, I swear it!" he said, holding his hands up in defense of her question.

"And will ye be promisin' to keep yer hands to yerself?" she asked sternly.

"Only if ye want me to!" The young man and his group broke into a fit of laughter. Aishlinn observed quietly with her hands folded together. They spoke in Gaelic and she knew not a word they had said to each other.

"And what of yer friend here?" Young Thomas asked while he smiled broadly at Aishlinn. Although she could not understand the language, Aishlinn knew he was speaking either to her or of her. She grew quite uncomfortable and made a promise to learn the language as soon as possible.

"What do ye think, Aishlinn? Do ye want to take yer chances with these young beasties?" Bree asked, nodding her head towards the young men.

Aishlinn wasn't sure what to think of the question. "Do you mean to sit with them?"

Young Thomas looked at her curiously. "Ye be English?" he asked.

"Nay," said Bree. "She be a Highlander. She was raised in the lowlands and has returned to be with her family."

Young Thomas eyed Aishlinn suspiciously. With a raised brow he asked, "Who do ye belong to?"

"Me."

The sound of Duncan's voice as he stood behind her, nearly scared her out of her slippers. He looked so handsome in his tunic and plaids. Why must his eyes twinkle so, she wondered as she swallowed hard and tried to tamp down the excitement rushing through her veins at the sight of him.

"She'll not be joining ye lads this night." His smile seemed to hold a warning of some sort, but Aishlinn wasn't sure of what.

Aishlinn was as relieved as she was nervous. Relieved that Duncan was there for she didn't feel quite ready yet to answer the endless questions she was certain they would have for her. The nervousness shooting down to her toes came from the way her hand felt in his when he wrapped his fingers through hers.

Bree smiled and bid them good evening while she left to sit with the lads at a table across the room. Duncan did not let go of Aishlinn's hand as he escorted her to a center table where many large men were already seated. They were drinking ale and laughing loudly. As Duncan pulled a chair out for her, the men began elbowing one another to stand because a lady was to be seated.

As she stood by her chair, the largest, tallest man she had ever laid eyes upon stood and bowed his head at her as the others followed suit. She didn't mean to stare, but it was impossible not to. His immense size and girth was astonishing. At least two heads taller than any other man in the room, he made Duncan look like a bairn in comparison. He had long, light brown hair and hazel colored eyes and sported a full beard that ended in a point in the center of his large chest. Like Duncan's, his nose appeared to have been broken at least once. The only thing small on him was the faint scar over his left eyebrow. Aishlinn thought that perhaps he could be considered a handsome man, if one could get beyond the fear of his gigantic build.

"Lads!" Duncan began in English. "This be our guest. Her name be Aishlinn. She is no' English," he told them, for he knew that would be their first question. "She is a Highlander who unfortunately was raised in the lowlands and no' taught her own language."

The men remained standing and stared at her with pity in their eyes, as if not learning the Gaelic was the worst thing that could have happened to her. Such expressions on such big, tall men made her want to burst into laughter. She bit her tongue as she took her seat.

"This here be Kenneth the Red." Duncan said as he went down the line from left to right. As each man was introduced they would give a nod of their head before taking their seats. "Callum MacFarland, William McKenna, Daniel McAllister, Fearghus Campbell, Black Richard, and Tall Daniel." Aishlinn doubted she'd ever remember any of the names. "Of course, ye remember Rowan, Richard and Findley." Aishlinn was glad to see them and was about to thank them for all they had done for her, when the living mountain cleared his throat rather loudly. He was rolling his eyes and rocking back and forth on his feet rather impatiently.

"Och!" Duncan said with a wry smile. "This be Wee William."

Aishlinn wondered how a man so tall could be referred to as "wee". She turned to whisper in Duncan's ear. "If he is 'wee' I would hate to see 'tall' William."

Duncan chuckled and shared what she had said with the others and they all began to laugh rather loudly. She went red with embarrassment at the uproar she had caused.

Daniel McAllister spoke up. "He is called 'Wee' William, lass because he has a weeee," he was holding his thumb and index finger together as if measuring something quite small. More laughter erupted before he could finish and Duncan held up his hand to stop him. "Daniel! She be a lady, no' a bar wench!"

Aishlinn had no idea what they were talking about and could not resist the urge to ask. She leaned closer to Duncan and whispered, "A wee what?" she put her hand on his arm to stop him before he repeated her question to the others.

"Wee feet, lass," Black Richard offered from his seat next to hers. Men were confusing animals and it made no sense why they laughed at Black Richard's answer. She decided she probably did not want to know why they called the man "wee" or why they found his small feet so amusing.

Large platters and bowls of hot food were soon passed around the table. Her stomach growled as the delightful scents passed through her nostrils. While she had been quite grateful for the broths and bread she had been eating lately, she was thrilled to see roast venison and leeks, two of her favorite foods.

Someone filled her mug with ale for which she offered a polite thank you. Aishlinn had never cared much for the drink, but had to admit this was far better than the ale she was used to.

When her stomach was full and her heart content, she took a deep breath and pushed her plate away, certain she had no room left for another bite of anything. That was until someone offered her a small sweet-cake. It wouldn't do to offend the baker. It was warm and rich and she would have sworn she had never had one better.

During most of the meal, Duncan's focus had been on Aishlinn. Other men had been paying close attention to her as well. Had she been paying attention to anything other than the food, she might well have noticed it.

Content and full near to bursting, her eyes had grown heavy, but she wanted to stay and enjoy the evening. It was the first time she had ever attended an evening meal as a guest and she did not want to miss out on anything.

Listening for the first time that evening to the conversation taking place at her table, she realized the men had lapsed back into Gaelic. From the tones of their hushed voices the conversation appeared to be quite serious. She had caught a few of the men as they cast curious glances her way. Uncertain if the men stared because she was the only woman at the table or if perhaps they spoke of her, Aishlinn began to grow uneasy.

She waited for a lull in the conversation before asking Duncan if something was the matter. "Nay," he said. "Just a discussion of a clan we feud with." While his voice sounded reassuring, there was something in his eyes that told her he might be holding something back. She decided not to push the issue and turned her attention to others in the room.

Isobel sat at the high table with a group of women and most appeared to be close to Isobel's age, which Aishlinn estimated to be late thirties. The group of women was in a deep and seemingly serious conversation of their own, huddled together and speaking in hushed tones. Perhaps they spoke of the same feud as the men at her table.

Across the room, Bree and her tablemates seemed to be completely oblivious to anything else taking place around them. They laughed loudly, giggled frequently and the lads seemed quite fond of slapping each other upon their backs. Aishlinn could not help but notice that Bree and a rather handsome young man kept staring at each other from across their table. Aishlinn smiled inwardly, for the two of them looked as though they had a lovely secret between them.

After a while, it grew increasingly difficult for her to keep her eyes open. More than once she had nearly nodded off to sleep. There was a small group of young children playing in the corner and they appeared to have much more energy than Aishlinn. She envied them and looked forward to the day when she could stay awake past dark.

Duncan had taken notice of her sleepy eyes. "Och, Aishlinn!" he said smiling. "Are ye tired?"

"Aye, I am," she answered, returning his smile.

Duncan stood and pulled Aishlinn's chair out for her. To his friends he said, "We'll be leaving ye hellions now. I've a bonny lass to escort back to her room."

Aishlinn felt her face grow red at his compliment. Though she knew he was merely being polite, hearing him refer to her as bonny had caused that odd sensation in her belly and toes to return.

As the men bid them both a good sleep, Duncan took her hand, placed it upon his arm and led her up the stairs to her room. The odd sensations refused to yield no matter how hard she tried to wish them away.

"Thank ye for sittin' with me this night, Aishlinn," Duncan whispered as they stood outside her chamber door. "I hope ye enjoyed yer meal and the company."

Aishlinn smiled. "Yes, Duncan. I had a very nice evening. Your men seem very," she searched for a proper description. "Fierce," she said with a smile. "Thank you."

He seemed to look even more handsome as the glow of the torchlight washed over him. Wanting to rid herself of the thoughts she knew she should not have, lest she make a complete fool of herself, she turned to open her door. It would be best to remove herself from the situation altogether, and as quickly as possible.

Duncan put his hand upon her shoulder to stop her. "I am right next door if ye need me."

"I know. And thank you," she said knowing the sooner she got a closed door between the two of them the better. She pulled on the latch and opened the door.

"Have ye enough blankets?" he asked.

She looked at him curiously. "Aye, I do," she said as she stepped inside her room.

"Would ye like help with yer fire?"

"Nay. Thank you, but I do know how to stoke a fire." She thought he was acting a bit peculiar and wondered if perhaps he had not partaken of too much ale.

"Well, if ye've need of me, I be next door."

"I know and thank you again." When he made no effort to leave she asked, "Is that all Duncan?"

He let out a heavy sigh. "Aye."

"Well then, I shall bid ye good night." She closed her door and let out the breath she had been holding. It was going to take monumental efforts to keep her mind from wandering whenever she was near him. The bigger trick would be in trying to figure out how to keep her palms from sweating and her knees from knocking together at the mere sight of him.

I'm an eejit! Duncan cursed as he plodded to his room. A daft, foolish eejit! I have got to get these thoughts and feelings under control or I'm going to make a complete fool of myself. He removed his tunic and plaids and tossed them onto the chair by his bed. It was becoming increasingly difficult to be near her without grabbing the lass and kissing her full on the lips.

Naked, he paced back and forth in front of the fireplace. His mind wandered from thoughts of what he wanted to do to thoughts of what he should do. He wanted to tell her he was growing more and more fond of her as each hour of each day passed. He wanted to hold her and whisper in her ear how beautiful he thought she be. He wanted to take her in his arms and begin a kiss that would last for a lifetime.

But he knew that what he should do was leave her alone. He should step away and allow her to make an abundant amount of friends and have a good life. But his heart grew heavy at the thought of her finding a man who would woo her and earn the heart he wanted desperately to have as his own. He had noticed the number of eyes that had stared at her through most of the night and he had not liked it.

She was a beautiful young woman and Duncan knew she'd not have any problems with finding a suitor. Trouble was, he did not think he could stand the thought of anyone but himself in that position. He prayed that Angus would be home soon before he lost his mind completely.

Frustrated, he climbed into his bed and tried to sleep, but sleep would evade him this night. Each time he closed his eyes her sweet smiling face and dark green eyes stared back at him.

He tried to concentrate on things he needed to do on the morrow, such as sparring with his men. But when he thought of that, he thought of Gowan and Manghus who were by now in their cottages and in bed with their wives. Duncan wanted what they had; a wife, bairns, and a life filled with much love and laughter.

These thoughts and desires were completely foreign to him. Until the last several days he had always fancied himself a free spirit. He had never wanted to be tied down with the responsibilities of a wife or bairns. He had always enjoyed being able to come and go as he pleased. The lasses he had shared his bed with were too numerous to count, but there had been not one who held his attention for more than a few hours. And there had not been one who had made him want anything from them beyond meeting his physical needs.

Now he lay here in the late hours of the night unable to think of anyone but Aishlinn and he felt like a damned fool. She was nothing like any woman he had ever known. She was innocent and pure but with a fire and a spirit that the foolish men in her life had nearly destroyed. She was not afraid to speak her mind but was ever mindful not to insult anyone.

And the way she flushed red from head to toe whenever a compliment was given to her! Och! Such sweetness!

More than bonny, the girl was damned beautiful. She was not like the buxom and curvaceous women he had preferred in the past. Nay, she was slender and slight, a wee thing really, with fine, delicate features.

The deepest of green eyes she had. There was much pain and fear in them, too much he supposed. But there was something else that lingered just behind the surface, something that begged to be set free. Passion and desire, aye, but not in the romantic or physical sense. Nay, 'twas something deeper and more precious than that. There was something in her that wanted to be more than what people demanded her to be and that was what he wanted to give her. The freedom to be who she really was.

Though her hair was shorter than even his own it was the color of spun gold, soft and thick. He imagined running his hands through it while he kissed her delicate lips. He wanted to touch every inch of her creamy skin while leaving behind a trail of kisses with his lips. His body ached with wanting to press her close to his chest and to hear her soft, tender sighs of contentment. He wanted her to want him as much as he wanted her.

He tried to think of all the other women he knew and not one who came to mind filled his heart with the kind of feelings he held for Aishlinn. Aye, they were fine women and they would make any man a good wife. But they were not Aishlinn.

Duncan very much wanted to take away all her bad memories and replace them with happy ones. He wanted to protect her and keep her safe. He wanted to prove to her that not all men were evil whoresons. He wanted to give her a life that his heart knew she deserved.

Aye, those were the things he wanted to give to her, but how? Did he step aside and allow someone else, some other man, to give her those things she deserved? Or did he remain selfish and insist upon doing it himself? He did not know if he could live without her if he let her be. And he did not know if he could live with himself if he didn't.

Fourteen

Duncan had made the only decision he felt as right and honorable. He would stay away from Aishlinn as much as possible, letting Bree and Isobel take her under their wings. He would, however, maintain a very watchful eye over her. The moment it appeared anyone else might step into the shoes he wanted to fill, he would act.

For more than a sennight, he had spent his days with his men, sparring and practicing more zealously than normal, even for him, and his afternoons tending to the responsibilities of acting chief. He would pretend to be busier than he actually was, thereby conveniently missing the evening meals in the gathering room, which in turn kept him away from Aishlinn.

On several occasions, he had seen her walking the grounds with Bree and Isobel. She had smiled and waved at him, apparently pleased to see him. Duncan however had given her only a cursory nod of his head and had immediately fled in the opposite direction. While his heart ached at the sight of her, he had convinced himself 'twas the right and proper thing to do.

As the days grew longer and warmer he saw less and less of her wandering the grounds. Seeing Bree walking alone one afternoon he stopped to speak with her. He could tell something was the matter for the normally happy and energetic Bree was not smiling at him. In fact, she looked down right angry the moment she laid eyes on him.

"What be the matter, lass?" he asked.

Her pursed lips and furrowed brow were good indicators as to how angry she was. "As if ye dunna ken!" she said. For a moment he thought he might need to run or take cover, for she was certainly displeased with him. He had not a clue what he had done to make her angry. "But I do no' ken, 'tis why I asked."

Lowering her voice she said, "Ye've broken Aishlinn's heart is what ye've done ye daft eejit!" she said, poking his chest with her finger.

Duncan was stunned for he could not imagine what he'd done to cause her to say such a thing. The opposite sex, though quite intriguing, beguiling and wondrous, often left him in a state of utter confusion.

Bree could tell from his confounded expression that he did not understand. "Ya fool! Ye bring the lass here and then abandon her. Ye dunna speak to her. Ye dunna ask her how she gets along or what she does with her days. Ye avoid her at every turn. How do ye suppose that makes her feel?" She put her hands on her hips and looked thoroughly disappointed in him.

Duncan had not intended to hurt Aishlinn's feelings. He had merely been stepping out of her way to allow her time and to give her room to grow. He had been protecting her. "I meant no' to do that." He could not explain to Bree the reasons behind his decision.

"Well, whether ye meant to or no' 'tis what has happened. The poor girl thinks she's done something to offend or anger ye."

"Tisn't true!" Duncan protested. "She's done nothing." His stomach began to fill with intense guilt.

"Matters no' Duncan. How do ye think she should feel when ye dunna say even so much as 'good day' to her?"

"I meant only to give her time to make friends, to allow her to heal." That much was true.

"And why can't she still have ye as a friend while she makes new ones?"

He knew the real reasons why that would not work. When he was near her it was all he could do to hold himself in. It was for her own good he had avoided her.

"Ya need to go and tell her that she's done nothing wrong and that yer just an eejit fool of a man," Bree told him.

A look that resembled horror washed over Duncan's face. He did not know how he could apologize without explaining the reasons for what he had done. No good could come of it, he was certain.

"Duncan, she thinks ye've only brotherly affections for her," Bree said, though she knew better. "And I've said nothin' to the contrary." Bree had her suspicions about Duncan's true feelings, but they were just that, suspicions. She had kept them to herself until now.

"I dunna ken what ye speak of," he scowled at her. He would admit nothing, at least not now and not to Bree. His feelings were his own and he'd deal with them the best way he could.

Bree softened, not wanting to make matters worse between Duncan and Aishlinn. "Duncan, go to the lass. Tell her yer sorry and that she's done nothing wrong. She stays in her room now and does no' leave. She says she feels no' well,"

His protective instincts took hold of him. "No' well?" he asked. "Does she have the fevers?" If she were ill, he would make certain that great care was given to her.

Bree suppressed the urge to smile and instead chose to put a look of deep concern on her face. Aishlinn had fevers all right, but not the kind Duncan was thinking.

"I dunna ken, just that she has no' left her room since two days past. She stays in her bed and does not eat." She knew Duncan would go to her straight away if he thought Aishlinn ill. She was right for he dashed away without so much as a "good day" as he ran to the castle. Bree knew 'twas, perhaps, a devilish thing to have done, lying to Duncan as she had. But she had good intentions and knew in her heart 'twas the right thing. She tried to hide her smile as she went in search of Findley.

Duncan raced to the castle entrance, through the large gathering room and bounded up the stairs two at a time. He had made a terrible mistake by removing himself so completely from Aishlinn's life. Now she lay in her bed ill and 'twas all his fault. If anything happened to her, he would never forgive himself.

Not bothering to knock, he flung the door open, scaring the devil out of Aishlinn. He stood in the doorway, out of breath, his forehead covered with sweat. It wasn't the run that had done him in; it was his worry over Aishlinn.

The most confounded expression came to his face when he saw that she wasn't lying in her bed at death's door. She had been sitting in a chair near the open windows, but when he came crashing through the door he had startled her so much that she jumped up and knocked the chair over.

"Duncan!" she yelled at him. "What on earth is the matter?" Her first thought was that perhaps the castle was under attack and he was here to take her to safety. Her second thought, when she saw the confused look he held, was that he had lost his mind.

"Yer no' ill." He was surprised and relieved. He also realized he had been lied to. Bree had tricked him. He made a silent promise to remember to repay her some day.

"Nay! I'm not ill. Who told you that I was?" Confused and slightly perturbed, she straightened the chair and placed it back near the window.

"I'm sorry. I was misinformed."

"Is that why you came bursting in here? Because you thought I was ill?" she asked him.

"Aye, I did." He was trying to steady his breathing as well as his anger at Bree for lying to him.

Aishlinn studied him for a brief moment before she pursed her lips together and put her fists on her hips. God, how he had missed her, had missed that fire in her eyes. She shook her head and turned away from him and mumbled something under her breath.

"What was that, lass?"

"I said, a lot you care!" she shot at him from over her shoulder. She couldn't look at him at the moment and kept her eyes glued to the land outside her windows. If she looked at him now, he might see the heartbreak hidden beneath her anger. She'd not give him that satisfaction.

"But I do care." More than she knew.

"Is that why," she said, finally turning to look at him, "you have avoided me at all costs for the past sennight? Is it because you care that you turn and run the other way when you see me? Is it because you care that you do not even say 'good day' to me?" She was angry and not afraid to let him know it.

"I've have been busy with me duties and responsibilities." He was flustered and knew the conversation they were about to have would not end well for him.

"Well then, I would not want to keep you from all those important duties and responsibilities. With whom do I speak, Laird McEwan, about making an appointment with you? There is something important I wish to discuss with you," she seethed. Duncan was certain he detected a bit of hurt to her voice. "At your convenience Laird McEwan," she said as she curtsied elegantly before him.

He crossed his arms over his chest and scowled at her. Normally that would have been enough to cause her to back down from him. This day it did not work for she stood resolutely before him determined to hold her ground. "I have time now. What is it you wish to speak to me about?" he asked.

Cupping her hands together, she stood her ground as firmly as she could. "I wish to leave the comforts of your castle." In all reality it was the last thing she wanted to do, but Duncan had left her no choice.

She could have stripped herself naked and begun flying about the room and he would not have been nearly as shocked as he was at the news that she wished to leave.

"What? Leave here? Why? Where will ye go?" He did not like the idea of her leaving and he would not allow it.

"I do not know. I am told I might be able to acquire a position as a scullery maid at another castle with another clan. I have worn out my welcome with you, therefore I wish to leave."

"Who told ye that ye've worn out yer welcome with me?" he demanded. He would knock the fool right on his arse for spreading such lies.

She cocked her head slightly and looked at him as if he were daft. "You."

"Me?" he asked quite dumbfounded before the truth of the matter dawned in his rather thick skull. It wasn't what he had said; it was what he had done.

He ran his hands through his hair and tried to calm himself. "Ya've no' worn out yer welcome here. I'm quite glad to have ye here, Aishlinn, and I'll no' allow ye to leave."

If she could have picked up something and thrown it at him she would have. At the moment she was far too stunned and far too angry to do anything but stand with her mouth agape. "What do you mean you'll not allow me to leave? Am I your prisoner?"

Perhaps he could have chosen a better way to put it but it was too late now. "Nay, yer no' my prisoner, yer me guest, and ye'll remain my guest until Angus returns. Now I'll hear no more of ye leavin'." He started to walk away but she stopped him.

"Pardon me, m'laird, but if this is how you treat your guests, then I'd prefer not to have that privilege thrust upon me. I wish to leave."

If he had to put her in shackles and throw her in the oubliette to keep her from leaving, he would. "Nay. Ye'll no' be leavin'."

Aishlinn took a very deep breath in through her nose and counted to ten before letting it out very slowly. It was all she could do to keep from throwing the chair at him. "Then I'm your prisoner, and not your guest."

"Nay, yer me guest."

Aishlinn held up her hand to stop him for it was getting all too ridiculous. "No matter what you prefer to call me, m'laird, the fact is I want to leave and you say you'll not allow it!" She was growing increasingly frustrated with him. "I would like to know why."

"Why what?" he asked. He'd been momentarily distracted by the way the sunlight that streamed in through the window glanced off her lovely golden hair.

Were all men this daft, she wondered? "Why will you not allow me to leave?" she demanded to know.

He had been in more battles than he could count and he had the scars on his body to prove it. He had been with many women, most whose names he could not remember. He had traveled far and wide, and had seen things that most people never knew existed. He had scaled tall mountains, sailed across the ocean during a storm that had nearly taken his life and had even survived hand-to-claw battle with a cat o'mountain that had wanted to eat him for a midday meal. He had braved it all, relished in the glory and excitement that was his life. But somehow, he could not muster the courage to tell this slip of a girl the truth.

Warriors were trained to never succumb to desperation. If you were distracted or too flustered, you could lose your life. It was vitally important to stay focused at all times. If you kept your focus and your wits about you, chances were you could survive any battle. The same however, could not be said for love.

"What kind of brother would I be if I let ye leave, to just wander the countryside trying to find a new home? I swore me allegiance to ye, Aishlinn." For the first time in his life, Duncan had succumbed to desperation. He had blurted his answer and could only pray it would work. He simply could not tell her how he felt, at least not yet. He wasn't sure himself just what all these feelings were that were bouncing around inside his heart and interfering with the logical part of his mind.

"Then why," she asked, her voice soft and low, "do you ignore me? Have I done something to offend you?" She had been trying to figure out for days now, just what she had done to make him avoid her.

He let out a heavy sigh. "Nay. Ye've done nothing wrong. I've been busy." It wasn't an out and out lie. "And, I was tryin' to give ye room to find yer own way, to make new friends."

"I do not understand. Can I not make friends and have you for one as well?" she asked. "Or am I allotted only so many?"

His scowl softened as he chuckled. "Nay," he said knowing full well she could have as many female friends as she wanted. 'Twas the men that bothered him.

"Aishlinn, I am sincerely sorry that I hurt yer feelings. I'm a daft fool of a man and I beg ye forgive me for it."

It was quite difficult for her to stay angry with him -- she felt so beholden to him for all he had done for her. He did appear sincere and perhaps he had been quite busy with his duties. She searched his face and felt he told her the truth.

"I'll forgive you, Duncan. I know you are a very busy man and I'll not take up anymore of your time. But," she said, hoping that she might not sound weak or foolish when she asked her next question.

"But what, lass?"

"But could you, at least on occasion when you see me, could you not run in the other direction?" She could not admit that the first time he had done that it had nearly ripped her heart from her chest. She had to bite her tongue to keep from crying over it now.

The hurt in her voice brought a tremendous amount of guilt to his stomach. Though his intentions had been to protect her, he had in fact, ended up hurting her. "I do so promise." He thought about taking her in his arms then, and kissing her from the top of her head to the tips of her toes. Holding himself in, he righted his shoulders and bowed to her. He had to leave the room before he did just that.

Fifteen

Though it was rather difficult for Duncan to hold his tongue and say nothing of his feelings for Aishlinn, he did make a concentrated effort to spend more time with her. It was both a pleasure and an agony to be so near her and not touch or kiss her. But if having some of his time meant that much to her, 'twas the least he could do.

Aishlinn had finally convinced Isobel to allow her to work in order to earn her keep. Though Isobel would have chosen more refined duties, she had relented and allowed Aishlinn to help in the kitchens. It was a job that brought great joy to Aishlinn's heart, but none to Isobel's. The only condition put upon the agreement was that she could work only in the mornings. Isobel did not want to risk the young woman overdoing it to the point of exhaustion. When Aishlinn had asked to move from the room next to Duncan's, and into the solar with the other non-married women, Isobel had adamantly refused.

Aishlinn enjoyed working among the other clansmen and women because it afforded her the opportunity make friends and a chance to learn the Gaelic. She found it difficult to roll her *r*'s but refused to give up. Within a few days however she was picking up a few useful phrases and words.

She would often see Rowan and Findley about the castle grounds. She thought them both fine men and was glad to have them for her foster brothers. They made Aishlinn feel quite welcome and on a few occasions, they had even helped with bringing in supplies and stocking the larders.

Manghus was staying close to his own cottage because his wife was due to have their first bairn and he wanted not to be far from her. On occasion Gowan would bring his daughters to the castle when he had business to discuss with Duncan. Aishlinn would volunteer to keep the four little girls company while the men discussed whatever it was that men of their ilk were fond of discussing. Aishlinn truly enjoyed the time she was able to spend with the little girls, for it was the closest thing to having her own children that she would ever get.

Nearly every day she would see Black Richard, Tall Thomas, Daniel and Wee William. When they weren't practicing, they could often be found huddled together in some deep, manly sort of conversation. Black Richard appeared to be more refined and better educated than the other men he referred to as the best of his friends, but still, he was just as fierce as the rest of them.

There were many times when Aishlinn would find a dozen children surrounding Wee William, clamoring for his attention or a ride upon his back. The man looked positively silly as he walked across the grounds with a child clinging to each leg and an arm while another rode on his back. The little ones would squeal with delight as they rode along on the gentle giant or when he would chase after them pretending to be a ferocious monster.

Duncan would escort Aishlinn and Bree to dinner each night but he would encourage them to sit with those lads and lasses closer to their own ages. Aishlinn conceded, although she would have preferred to have her meals with Duncan and his men. While she was making new friends, and gaining more brothers than she knew what to do with, she still found herself daydreaming of Duncan.

Often times when her work in the kitchens was complete, she would sneak away to help the other young women clean various rooms of the castle. Although she knew Isobel would be displeased with her if she learned she was doing far more than working in the kitchens, Aishlinn was not one to sit about with idle hands.

On one particularly splendid afternoon, Aishlinn went outside to catch a bit of fresh air and to see if anyone wanted help tending the gardens. Having found she was not needed she decided to enjoy a walk around the castle grounds. They seemed to stretch on forever with all the hills and small glens. There were large stables and barns as well as little cottages scattered here and there. Just to the west of the castle, the tiny village seemed to be undergoing an expansion and its residents were in the process of building a kirk.

She stood at the crest of a hill and watched a group of children playing on the training field. They were pretending to be fierce warriors and play fought with sticks. The sight of them made her heart ache for bairns and a family of her own.

She had been watching them for a while when Black Richard approached her. He wore dark trews and a blue tunic and looked rather handsome with his black hair waving in the breeze.

"Good day, Aishlinn!" he said with a smile upon his face. "Yer looking well this day."

"Tapadh leat." She thanked him in Gaelic, quite pleased with her use of the language.

He returned with "Se do bheatha," raising a brow, impressed with her

Gaelic.

Aishlinn smiled and returned to the English. "I'm afraid I don't know enough yet to hold a conversation, Black Richard."

"'Tis all right lass. Ye be catchin' on quite well!"

He bent and plucked a long blade of grass from the ground. "How are ye liking Castle Gregor thus far?" he asked.

Her face beamed. "Oh, I like it very much! 'Tis a grand place and everyone has been so kind to me."

"Aye, we are a kind lot of people!" Black Richard chuckled. He rubbed the piece of grass between his fingers as he looked off into the distance. "Are ye making many friends as well?"

"Aye, I am," she answered. "Everyone has been go kind. And I've got more brothers now than I know what to do with!"

He turned to her, looking rather puzzled. "What do ye mean, lass?"

Smiling, she told him, "When I mentioned Duncan, Rowan, Gowan and the others were my brothers, the other lads and men asked could they be as well." She smiled at him innocently. "I grew up with three brothers who were not at all kind to me. Growing up I wished for kinder brothers and now I have so many!"

Richard tried not to laugh at her. He knew the lads here were enamored with Aishlinn. "Are ye sure of that, lass?"

Confused, she asked, "Sure of what?"

"Are ye sure they no' be wantin' to be more than just brothers to ye?"

She was shocked at such a notion. "Nay!" she said. Silly man she thought to herself. Perhaps he had become over-heated during his sparring and he wasn't thinking clearly.

"Why ye be thinkin' that, lass?"

She smiled at him as if he were a fool. "I am a plain woman, Richard. The lads are after Bree's affections that way, not mine!"

He turned and looked at her with a most serious expression. "Aishlinn, ye no' be plain."

She studied him for a moment. First Duncan, then the others and now Black Richard. While she appreciated their kind intentions she believed not one of them. Shaking her head she said, "'Tis kind of you to say that Black Richard. But ye needn't do so." She was trying not to be rude. She simply knew better.

Black Richard took in a deep breath of air before letting it out slowly. "Aishlinn, I be tellin' the truth. Ye be not plain. Ye be a fine, beautiful woman."

Aishlinn was taken aback and felt her skin blush. These Highlanders certainly were fond of saying whatever was on their minds. "Richard, please do not say that which isn't true!"

"I speak no lies, lass," he said softly. She truly did not know just how beautiful she was.

Aishlinn wished he would simply go away. "Nay. Isobel and Bree are beautiful, Black Richard, not I." She could feel her face growing redder and she had to look away from him. "I am plain."

With a raised brow and look of curiosity to his face, he asked, "Now, who here has told ye that lass?"

Aishlinn thought about it for a long moment and could think of not one person here who had said anything even vaguely unkind to her. "Well, none here have." The people here were far too kind to say otherwise.

"Then who be tellin' ye yer plain?" he asked. Aishlinn remained quiet as she stared at the ground. She was growing more uncomfortable with the conversation and wondered if he would think her daft if she suddenly turned and ran away from him.

"Would it be the brothers ye spoke of? Them that was no' kind to ye? Them that mistreated ye?" he asked.

Aishlinn shot him a scathing look that, had he known her better, would have told him that he was walking in unsafe territory. She chose not to respond to his question. She barely knew this man. And although she was certain he was merely trying to be kind to her, she felt his questions a little too personal.

"'Twas them then," he said quietly. "Now, may I ask why ye'd be wantin' to believe mean and unkind brothers who mistreated ye? Do ye no' think, lass, that 'twas them that no' be tellin' ye the truth? 'Twas them that lied to ye when they said ye be plain?"

Honestly, the thought had never entered her mind. All that she had ever heard from her brothers, as well as her father, was that she was plain and ugly. No man could or would ever want her. She would never be as beautiful as her mum. How many times had they told her such things? Now she was here, living in a most grand castle surrounded by good and kind people; decent people who had gone out of their way to make her feel welcomed and safe.

Black Richard could tell she was thinking hard on what he said. Chuckling slightly, he shook his head. "Lass, I be thinkin' that a thousand men could come to ye and tell ye yer beautiful and ye'd no' be believin' a one of 'em!"

She studied him more closely and wondered if she could trust him. Perhaps he was one of those men who said sweet and romantic things to a woman in order to obtain what he wanted. It was the only plausible explanation she could come up with at the moment. And why he would want such things from her she could not understand. She would ask Duncan of it later.

"Aishlinn," Black Richard said with a most sweet and sincere smile. "Would ye do me the most profound honor and allow me to escort ye to the evenin' meal this night?"

She had no idea how to interpret his invitation. Did he mean it in a brotherly fashion or did he have something else upon his mind? Brotherly attentions she could deal with. Anything other than that and she would simply not know what to do.

Black Richard was beginning to like the fact that he could easily read her face. 'Twas true he thought she was a beautiful young woman with a good spirit and heart about her. He had noticed that the first night he had met her. "I assure ye me intentions are entirely honorable, lass!"

She stood utterly dumbstruck and speechless. Did he really want to escort her this night? Was he asking to court her? It simply could not be. There had to be a reasonable explanation but for the life of her she could not figure it out. She knew not what to say.

"Are ye all right, Aishlinn?" he asked. She looked as though she were about to faint. He had asked many a lass for such a privilege but none had looked at him as if he had suddenly sprouted a second head.

She mulled it over in her mind. She had very strong feelings for Duncan but knew he did not feel the same for her in return. Certain she was that Duncan deserved a finer, better and more beautiful woman than she, Aishlinn had pushed any romantic thoughts of him from her mind days ago. At least she had tried to. Was Black Richard sincere in what he said? She wondered if given the chance could he make her stomach tumble and her heart want to leap from her chest as it did when Duncan was near?

Just as she was ready to give Richard her answer Duncan appeared from behind them. Aishlinn was surprised to see him here for she usually saw him only in the morning and when he came to escort her to the evening meal.

"Black Richard! Aishlinn!" he said as he squeezed his tall and muscular body in between the two of them. "How are ye this fine and sunny day?" He asked with a smile upon his face. He gave Black Richard a wink and a pat on his back.

Black Richard rolled his eyes as he took a step away in order to give Duncan some room. He had been wondering for a time now if Duncan held any feelings for Aishlinn. He had been waiting in the background to see if there were any signs that something more might be going on between the two of them. Having not witnessed any overt actions on Duncan's part, Black Richard felt it fine and proper to finally tell the beautiful lass of his intentions. The fact that Duncan showed up at this very moment told him that perhaps he did have some feelings for her.

"Hello, Duncan!" Aishlinn smiled at him. "How was your practice this day?"

"Fine, lass, fine!"

Aishlinn noticed then that he had a quite peculiar smile upon his face as if he were forcing himself to look more cheerful than he might actually be. "Are you all right, Duncan?"

A look of shock came about his face. What on earth, she supposed, was the matter with him?

"Me, lass? Why I be as right as rain!" he answered, perhaps a bit too cheerfully.

She did not think he was telling her the truth. Glad to see him, she decided not to push the matter further.

She had to step around Duncan in order to see Black Richard. To Duncan she said, "Black Richard has asked if he could escort me to the evening meal."

Black Richard cleared his throat and smiled. Duncan stared at him. "He did, did he?"

"Aye, I did," Black Richard told him as he crossed his arms over his chest.

"Do you think that would be all right, Duncan?" Aishlinn asked.

The two men stared at each other like two bulls ready to do battle. "What, lass?" Duncan asked, not really focused on Aishlinn at the moment. His mind was busy coming up with creative ways to take Black Richard's life from him.

"Do you think that it would be all right," she repeated, "for Black Richard to escort me to the evening meal?"

Duncan did not take his eyes off Black Richard. The last thing he wanted was Black Richard, or anyone else for that matter, to woo Aishlinn. Being stuck between the proverbial rock and hard place, he felt he had no choice at the moment but to smile and tell her, "Why, I see no problem with it, lass. Black Richard is above all else a fine man who would treat a young lass such as ye with the utmost respect. Why, he would no' even think to make any overt advances towards an innocent young girl. Isn't that right, Richard?"

"Aye," Black Richard said. "Aishlinn is a fine woman. I'd be treatin' her in a dignified and respectable manner," he said, still smiling.

Aishlinn could not read between the lines of their conversation and did not pick up on the subtle nuances. But each man knew where the other stood.

Black Richard continued, "A fine, beautiful lass such as Aishlinn, deserves nothin' more than the best, wouldn't ye say Duncan?"

"Aye, I would," Duncan said as his jaws clenched.

They were silent for a few moments. Aishlinn felt something was afoot but was not quite certain what it could be. Men often confused her. Deciding she would never be able to make much sense of them she said, "Fine then. Black Richard, I will allow you to escort me this night."

Black Richard smiled wryly at Duncan before walking towards Aishlinn. He lifted her hand and kissed the back of it ever so tenderly. The gesture brought a blush to her cheeks. "Tapadh leat," he said to her.

Aishlinn smiled as she said, "Se do bheatha."

Quite surprised, Duncan turned to look at her. "When did ye learn the Gaelic?"

"Ya should pay closer attention, Duncan," Black Richard said as he walked away. "elst ye might miss out on something special and important." He winked at Duncan, bowed to Aishlinn and bid her good day.

After Black Richard left, Aishlinn shared parts of their conversation with Duncan. She wanted a man's perspective, as she had no experience in matters of the heart or romance. Duncan was, after all, her foster brother. Even though she held more than sisterly feelings for him, she felt he was the best person to go to for such things.

"You're such a good brother to me Duncan," she told him. "I know you'll be honest with me. Do you think it only a brotherly invitation Black Richard gave, or was it something more?"

Duncan knew full well what kind of intentions Black Richard had and being her brother was not one of them. But he did not want to share that with her. Black Richard was a good man, not a ruffian and not one to bed any lass that would have him. That fact made Duncan's current predicament all the more difficult. He wanted Aishlinn to have a rich and full life. But he did not want it to be with anyone other than himself.

He felt quite selfish but did not care at the moment. He knew Black Richard could quite easily sweep Aishlinn off her feet and that was a chance he was not willing to take. "I think it be more of a friendship he be wantin' to have with ye Aishlinn, and nothing more."

She deflated the moment he said it and it brought a twinge of guilt to his heart. Her punctured posture made him wonder if she had more feelings for Black Richard than she would admit to.

"Is something the matter, lass?"

She shook her head. "Nay." She felt like a great fool at the moment. Such a fool she was to think there might be a small chance that Black Richard, or any man for that matter, might be able to see beyond her plainness and want something more than a friendship. She felt stupid for allowing her heart to believe such a thing possible.

He believed her not. "I think mayhap there be somethin' and ye be afraid to say it."

She sighed heavily before looking at him. "Do you promise not to laugh at me?"

"Aye, I do promise," he said as the guilt grew.

She took a deep breath before asking, "Do you think any man might ever be wanting anything other than a friendship with me?"

He felt like a cad and a whoreson. Duncan knew she thought she was plain and deserved little in life. And when a man finally showed some attention towards her, raising her self-esteem for probably the first time in her life, Duncan had broken it. He knew there was a special place in hell for a man like him.

He held her gaze for a long moment. "Aye, lass, I certainly do." He was not certain if she believed him. "I think there be plenty of men here who would very much like to gain yer affections." He could not tell her he was one of them. "But I ask ye to be makin' me a promise, lass."

She did not look up at him, her eyes fixed at the ground at her feet. "What is the promise?"

"That before ye go allowin' all these lads to be escorting ye to dinner and tryin' to win yer affections, ye'll come to me first?"

Duncan could see by the puzzled look on her face that she did not understand why he would make such a request of her. "Ya see, no' all the men here might have good and decent intentions. I know of a few off the top of me head right now who I'd warn ye against." His own name was first on that list.

She thought about it for a moment. Perhaps this was the kind of thing good brothers did for their sisters. "Do you do that for Bree as well?"

"Aye, I do." He knew it was only true to a certain extent. Bree was a good judge of character and had grown up knowing everyone here and Duncan worried not that she might make a mistake. Besides, Bree had her parents to look out for her. He knew he was being selfish but he wanted

Aishlinn for his own.

Having no experience with men or romance, Aishlinn thought perhaps it was a good idea to first confide in Duncan before making a decision on what man she would allow herself to be courted by. If anyone did in fact ever want that privilege. She agreed and made the promise.

Duncan wondered if he'd ever stop acting a fool when it came to this bonny lass. The thought of anyone else attempting to court her made his stomach seize and his heart fill with jealousy. He had no true claim to the lass, but he would like at least to have the opportunity.

Duncan watched very carefully over Aishlinn that evening while keeping a more watchful eye on Black Richard. The first sign of any romantic twinkling in the man's eye and Duncan was ready to intervene. Although he felt quite guilty for lying to her earlier in the day, his jealousy and his need to have Aishlinn as his own far outweighed his guilt.

He noticed that Aishlinn did not look as happy as she had earlier in the day. She was merely going through the motions and it was his fault she was having a miserable time. He knew she felt quite wounded by the lie he had told her.

The usual bright smile was gone from her face and she spoke very little to Black Richard during their meal. Although Black Richard was making a gallant attempt at being kind to her, it mattered not. Aishlinn was convinced he wanted nothing more than a friendship. Not being experienced when it came to men she was not picking up on the subtle cues that Black Richard was giving her. Duncan noticed them, however; for they were the same kinds of things he would have used himself if he weren't such a coward.

When the meal was finally over and it was time for Black Richard to escort Aishlinn back to her room, Duncan followed the two of them. He stayed hidden and quiet in the shadows. He was quite relieved when Black Richard bid her good night without so much as kissing her hand or whispering anything in her ear. Duncan felt like a rat because he knew that had he answered Aishlinn with the truth earlier, her evening with Black Richard would have gone quite differently.

Typically Duncan would have knocked on Aishlinn's door and bid her good sleep. Tonight however, the immense guilt eating away at his heart kept him from doing so. A part of him wanted to go to her, tell her the truth and all the reasons why he had lied to her. The coward in him said nay. Feeling like a weasel, he slunk off to his room.

Sixteen

Aishlinn's nightmares returned with a vengeance. She had woken twice that night, bolting upright, her nightdress soaked in sweat and clinging to her skin. Her chest felt heavy and it was difficult to breathe and the tears refused to quit.

It was the second dream that had been the worst. In it, she was hiding under Castle Gregor. The soldiers had come; they had learned she was there. Hundreds upon hundreds of the king's soldiers had surrounded the castle and more climbed over the walls in search of her.

As they combed the castle they came upon Isobel and demanded she tell them where Aishlinn was. When she refused, a soldier drew a large sword from his scabbard and stuck it deep into Isobel's heart. 'Twas the same with Bree and Duncan and all the others. Soon, everyone she loved and cared for was dead.

Lifeless, cold bodies, drenched in blood were scattered everywhere. Their dead eyes stared up at nothingness. Some had been stabbed while others had had their throats cut. The soldiers had killed everyone, even the bairns and weans! The soldiers had killed them all in order to find her. In the dream she had tried to scream, to call out, but she had no voice and she could not move.

When she woke, 'twas with such great sorrow and dread in her heart, her stomach was churning and threatening to retch. Large tears ran down her cheeks and her body trembled with fear and anguish. The people she loved could not die on her behalf. She simply would not allow it.

Half asleep she climbed from her bed and wandered aimlessly about her room. She was certain the dream 'twas some sort of omen. It warned her that no matter where she hid she would be found. And the people she cared so much for would end up dead.

She wanted not to be alone and afraid. She wanted Duncan. To hear his voice tell her, as he had done when they first had met, that all was well and she was safe now. Perhaps if she went to his room and quietly peered inside, just to see that he was safe and her dream not real, perhaps then she could go back to sleep.

Carefully she opened her door and crept down the dark hallway to

Duncan's room. She stood outside his door and took a deep breath. Somehow she managed to find the courage to open it. She justified her action by remembering that he had told her many times before that if she needed anything he was right next to her. Tonight she truly needed him.

The moon shone in through the tall windows. It cast a soft silvery glow across the room. In the near dark, she could make out his sleeping form as he lay on his back with one arm folded over his face. Her heart pounded relentlessly and she fought the urge to wake him.

She had given no thought to what she would do after she entered his room. She stood shivering and feeling like a fool. She was afraid to move forward and afraid to go back to her room where she would have to fight the nightmares alone. Perhaps she could curl up on the floor in front of the fire. Knowing Duncan was nearby might be enough to calm her mind and keep the bad dreams at bay.

Duncan woke with the sense that someone was in his room. His instincts told him to reach for the dirk he kept under his pillow. He took a slow breath in and listened to the sounds about him. He could hear the soft crackling of the low fire and the soft breeze as it floated in and carried the sounds of night insects and tree frogs with it.

He could also hear someone breathing near his door. He made the decision to reach for the dirk. With great speed, he rolled over onto his knees, slid his hand under the pillow and pulled the dirk out. He held it up, ready to pounce if necessary. "Who goes there?" he demanded. 'Twas then he heard her gasp.

Still in defensive posture, his eyes adjusted to the moonlit room. "Aishlinn, is that ye?"

"Aye," she whispered nervously. She had not meant to startle him or to wake him. "I'm sorry!"

He returned the dirk and wrapped the sheet around his waist before going to her. "What be the matter? Are ye ill?"

The tears returned. "I am sorry. I had a nightmare."

Duncan put his arms around her and pulled her into his chest. She melted into him and held on tightly as her tears fell upon his chest. Soon she was sobbing, her shoulders racking as she cried. He held her closer. "'Tis all right, lass," he whispered as he rested his cheek on the top of her head.

It all came flooding out then. Between great sobs, she told him of the dream. "The soldiers found me. They killed everyone. You. Isobel. Bree. All the bairns, all the women, all the men, everyone was dead. There was blood everywhere! And it was all my fault!"

"There now, lass," he whispered holding her tighter. "'Twas just a bad dream and nothin' more."

Aishlinn was not convinced it was merely a bad dream. "No, I think it was an omen. No matter where I go or where I hide, they'll find me. They'll kill anyone who tries to help me! I cannot let that happen Duncan!"

"Lass," he said softly as he tried to quiet her tears. "The soldiers are no' lookin' for ye, remember? Gowan, Tall Thomas, Richard and Findley scouted for days and found nothin'. They'll no' be coming for ye."

"Do you really think so?" she asked, needing very much at the moment to believe him.

"Aye, I do," he told her as he prayed that he was right.

They held on to one another for a while longer before the tears finally subsided. She wanted not to let him go. He smelled like soap and smoke and sleep. She missed riding with him, sitting upon his lap while she slept with her head against his chest. She missed that feeling of warmth and safety. She had missed him.

"Duncan?" she whispered.

"Aye?"

"May I stay here, in your room this night?"

He swallowed hard for he was not sure he heard her correctly. "What?"

Aishlinn looked up at him and he could see her eyes, swollen from crying, looking to him for something. "I'll not bother you, I promise. I do not want to be alone. May I sleep by the fire?"

He shook his head. "Nay."

Her shoulders slumped and she slowly let out a heavy sigh. "I'm sorry. I will leave you be now."

His bluntness had saddened her. She had known there would come a time when she couldn't run to him every time a dream frightened her. Perhaps Duncan knew it as well and this was that moment. She tried to step away so that she could return to her room but he held on to her.

"Ya may stay Aishlinn, but ye'll no' be sleepin' on the cold hard floor."

Confused she asked, "But where then?"

"Ye may sleep in my bed."

"But where would you sleep?" She didn't feel it right to sleep in his bed while he slept on the floor.

"I'll sleep there, in me bed, as well."

She was horrified at the thought. "Duncan, that wouldn't be proper!" She thought back to the stories Moirra had shared with her so long ago. Perhaps Duncan was one of those Highlander men who liked his women ready and had been hiding that fact from her. Although, if she admitted it to herself, the prospect of being with Duncan in such a manner did not frighten or repulse her. Still, she knew it wasn't proper.

He smiled at her. "What wudna be proper?"

"For us to sleep in the same bed!" she lowered her voice to a low whisper. "We're not married. It wouldn't be proper to do that."

He laughed at her. "Lass, I promise ye that nothin' improper will be takin' place." That is if he could survive the night without touching her.

She remained quiet, still shaking from the fright the dreams had brought.

"Do ye want to go back to yer own room then?" he asked, knowing it would be better if she would go but wanting very much for her to stay.

While she did not like the thought of being alone this night, she was equally bothered with the notion of sharing a bed with Duncan. She shook her head and quietly said no.

"Well if ye want no' to be alone and ye want to be in me room with me, then ye'll be sleepin' in my bed and no' on the floor. I promise, nothin' improper will be takin' place. I'll stay on one side of the bed and ye to the other."

He finally let go and went back to his bed and crawled in. Propping himself up on one elbow, he looked at her. "What will it be, lass?"

It was true she wanted not to be alone. She knew not what she should do. A very large part of her wanted to sleep near him and to feel safe knowing he was there to protect her from whatever bad dreams may come. But she did not know if she could trust herself, for he did look so braw and handsome laying there in his bed with the moonlight caressing his bare skin. She wished for a moment that she could be the moonlight just for a chance to touch his skin.

"Lass, did we no' sleep near each other for many nights? Out in the country by warm fires?"

"Aye, we did."

"And did anything improper take place on those many nights?"

He made a most excellent point. They had spent many nights together, under the stars sleeping very close to one another. Nothing had happened then, so why should she assume something would happen now? Perhaps it was because her feelings for him were growing more toward romantic inclinations as the days had passed.

"Then what be the difference this night?" he asked. "Be it that there is a nice warm bed involved?" Duncan expected the offer would be too much for her and at any moment she would turn around and go back to her own room. He had spent many sleepless nights when his thoughts turned wicked as he dreamt about having her in his bed. This was not quite what he had envisioned.

Aishlinn was certain he did not hold the same romantic thoughts for her as she did for him. She looked first at him and then at the open door behind her. Her mind buzzed as she contemplated what she should do. Deciding she did not want to be alone, she turned, quietly closed the door and walked to his bed. She stood looking down at him, at his bare chest and strong arms. She prayed that she wasn't making a mistake as she climbed in.

Duncan scooted as far to the other side of the bed as he could and was quite surprised that she had decided to stay. "Are you sure this will be all right?" she asked him as she snuggled deep into the bed while Duncan pulled the covers up over her shoulders.

"Aye, lass. 'Twill be fine." That was the second time today he had lied to her.

She had told herself that she would rise early and return to her own room and no one would be the wiser. She felt safe with Duncan and was quite certain he would not offer any physical advances that she might have to fend off. Deep down however, she wished that he would. She silently cursed herself for having thought it. He was her foster brother for heaven's sake! She would stay on her side of the bed and he on his and all would be well.

They lay on their sides facing each other. As she looked at him, with his bare chest and muscular arms, she took a deep, steadying breath. He was such a handsome man! Oh how she wished -- for a moment or two longer than she should have -- that he did have more than a brotherly kindness towards her.

She thought about the conversation they had had earlier in the day as they had stood on the hill. Did he really believe that someday someone might take a fancy to her? Did he really believe that she was not plain? She closed her eyes and listened to the sound of his breathing. I wonder if this is what it is like for a married couple. Do they lie in their beds like this each night listening to each other breathe?

Her mind wandered to what she might like if she were one day blessed with a man in her life who thought her bonny. She would want him to hold her very close each night with his strong arms wrapped around her like a warm blanket. She wondered what it might feel like to lay her head upon his chest and listen to the sound of his beating heart. She wondered as well what it might be like to be kissed with love and passion and tenderness.

Her mind wandered further to things she thought were far from proper. She was glad that Duncan's eyes were closed and the room dark for she did not want him to see the embarrassment on her face.

How many nights had he lain in his bed thinking of her being here with him? Now here she was, lying close enough that he could reach out and touch her, kiss her. But he could not and would not do that to her. She was a fine and proper young lady and fine and proper young ladies do not do those kinds of things unless they were married.

He knew he could not hold himself in forever. Someday he was either going to have to give in and tell her how he truly felt, or he would have allow her to move on. He could not continue to interfere with her life and keep her from the enjoyment of other men. Someday and someday soon he had to make a decision. Tell her or let her be.

He listened to her soft, quiet breaths as she lay there next to him. He chanced taking a peek at her and slowly opened his eyes. He was startled to find her green eyes staring back at him. Not knowing what to say or do at the moment, he asked, "Are ye comfortable, lass?"

Aishlinn nodded her head slowly as a tender smile came to her face. "Thank you, Duncan."

He knew that if he did not close his eyes that moment, he was going to end up doing something he should not do. "For what, lass?" he asked, shutting his eyes quickly.

"For being so good to me," she whispered before a yawn escaped her. "For being such a good brother to me."

He lied to her again for the third time that day. "'Tis my pleasure, Aishlinn."

It was not a pleasure being brotherly toward her. It was a torture and one he was not certain he could bear for much longer. Knowing well that she would die from embarrassment should anyone find them together like this, he promised himself he would wake early to send her back to her own room and no one would be the wiser.

Bree had gone to Aishlinn's room early that morning only to find her bed empty and unmade. Assuming she was already in the kitchens, she went to look for her there but no one had seen her this morning, which was very unusual. She wanted to find Aishlinn to let her know Manghus' wife had delivered a beautiful baby girl in the middle of the night. Perhaps they could go visit and take a peek at the new bairn.

Bree searched out of doors, even the stables and barns but could not find Aishlinn anywhere. Thinking perhaps Duncan might know where she was she went in search of him. After realizing she was searching the same places again and finding neither Duncan nor Aishlinn, she wondered if it possible they were together. Back into the castle and up the stairs she went first to Aishlinn's room. 'Twas still empty and Bree was beginning to grow concerned as Aishlinn was never difficult to find. Perhaps she would find Duncan in his room and he would know where to find Aishlinn.

She walked the short distance to Duncan's room and quietly knocked on his door. Hearing no answer, she opened it and before she could speak his name she saw them there. Duncan and Aishlinn. Together. In his bed. Duncan had his arm wrapped around Aishlinn who had her back nestled into his stomach. A broad smile came to Bree's face for she was glad the two of them had finally realized how they felt about one another. She quietly closed the door and hoped no one else would find them together.

Such a blessing it was, to be married to such a braw, strong man. It was amazing, really, that someone like him would love someone like her. Her husband was beautiful, if such a thing could be said of a man. Remarkably enough, her husband looked very much like Duncan, with the same chestnut colored hair and mesmerizingly blue eyes. Deep, blue eyes that even twinkled like Duncan's!

And muscles? Glorious muscles! Big, strong arms that had no problem holding her close to his chest as they snuggled together in their marital bed. And strong, well-toned legs, as big as tree roots. 'Twas odd though, her husband had three legs, and one was pressing into her lower back and buttocks. It didn't matter if her husband had three legs, or even five, he loved her, loved her dearly and that was all that mattered!

One of the most amazing things about her husband was the fact that he was not blind. Perfect vision. And still, he thought she was beautiful! He had told her so repeatedly throughout the night. And how many times had he whispered in the dark, his hot breath caressing her ear, how many times had he said "I love you"? More than once, she was certain of it.

His hands were so warm, one of which happened to be pressed rather nicely against her stomach. In truth, she wished he would remove her nightdress so that she might know what his skin would feel like against her own. It would be a most magnificent sensation, she was sure of it. Perhaps after he woke, she might be blessed with discovering the wonders of that sensation. For now, she would let him sleep, and would remain content just to be held.

She snuggled closer to him as she let out a quiet sigh of contentment. Who knew love could make one feel this way? Safe, protected, and cherished. These were the things dreams were made of.

Seventeen

As Bree closed the door and turned around with the smile still on her face, she ran straight into her mother.

"Bree, what are ye doin'?" Isobel asked her.

"Nothing!" Bree answered, knowing full well that if Isobel found out what she knew, Duncan and Aishlinn would be in a great deal of trouble. Thinking quickly, she asked, "How are Manghus' wife and bairn doing?"

Isobel seemed distracted as she answered. "They are well. Have ye seen Aishlinn about this morn?"

"Nay, I haven't." 'Twas partially true she told herself for Aishlinn was not actually about. She was sleeping peacefully in Duncan's bed.

"If ye see her, please tell her I wish to speak to her."

Bree nodded, her back still at Duncan's door. She wanted desperately not to be the one who gave away Duncan and Aishlinn's secret.

"Well?" her mother asked. "Don't just stand there, Bree. Be gone with ye!"

Bree took off running down the hallway, hoping and praying that her mother would not find Duncan and Aishlinn together. 'Twould surely be a most frightful thing for both of them if she did.

Isobel stood with her hands on her hips as she watched her daughter run away. What on earth had gotten into that lass lately, she wondered? Shaking her head she prayed the good Lord to please give her patience when it came to her child.

Needing to speak with Duncan and not being able to find him or Aishlinn anywhere this day, she had grown frustrated. She had not meant to be so abrupt with her daughter, but she had been up all night helping Manghus' wife birth her first bairn. It had been a difficult delivery for the lass but finally, after many long hours of hard labor the wee girl bairn was born. Isobel was tired and wanted nothing more than to sleep. But Manghus was quite insistent that he speak with Duncan straight away, about what, she did not know.

Not bothering with knocking, she opened the door to Duncan's room. Not prepared for the sight before her, anger and frustration rose from deep within her belly as her heart sank. This was not good, not good at all.

"Duncan McEwan!" This was the last thing she needed to have happen.

She continued to yell as two half sleeping, disoriented and terrified young people jumped from the bed. A quick tug of war ensued over the sheet, each of them trying to lay claim to it in order to cover themselves. Aishlinn caught a brief glimpse of Duncan's very naked behind and quickly decided he needed it more than she did and immediately gave up her end of it.

"Of all the lasses in the castle?" She could not remember a time she'd been this angry with anyone. "Of all the lasses ye could have bedded ye have to choose Aishlinn?"

Aishlinn stood frozen in the corner with tears welling in her eyes, horrified that they'd been caught together in such a compromising position. The anger in Isobel's eyes sent a chill down her spine.

Duncan was trying desperately to hold on to the sheet while searching for a way out of his current predicament. He was trapped between his bed and a very angry Isobel. He thought of jumping over the bed and out the window, but a very shaken Aishlinn stood between the bed and his only means of escape -- the window.

"She is an innocent young girl! How could ye have taken advantage of her like this!" Angrier than she could ever remember being, Isobel looked about the room for something to either throw at him or beat him with.

"Ya wait until yer uncle returns Duncan! He is going to skelp ye somethin' fierce. That is if I leave him anythin' to skelp!" She truly thought of picking up a chair and hitting him over his foolish head. A more befitting punishment however, would be to leave him in the hands of Angus who would surely be more than angry with him.

Duncan held up a hand to protest, "Now, Isobel," he said.

"Do not 'now Isobel' me young man!" She would not listen to him. "This poor lass comes to us for help and safety and ye do this to her?"

"Nothin' happened!" Duncan roared. He had never raised his voice at Isobel before, for he knew his uncle would have killed him for showing such disrespect. She was jumping to conclusions and he had to explain to her what had happened. If she would only calm down long enough to listen, he would be able to explain that neither of them had done anything wrong. But in Isobel's eyes, the mere fact that they had shared a bed together was bad enough.

Why was she so angry with him, he wondered? He had shared his bed with plenty of young women over the years. While Isobel had been disappointed in him over those dalliances, she had never been as angry as she was at this moment. Perhaps Aishlinn was as special and important to Isobel as she was to Duncan.

Isobel lowered her voice and glared at him. "Do ye really expect me to believe that?"

"Aye, I do! I would never take advantage of Aishlinn!"

Finally finding her voice, Aishlinn spoke up. "'Tis true Isobel!" she said pleadingly. "'Tis not what ye think."

Isobel looked at the tears streaming down Aishlinn's face. Did the lass cry from embarrassment at having been caught? "Go to yer room and wait for me." Isobel tried unsuccessfully to hide the disappointment in her voice. "Go now."

Aishlinn quickly walked around the bed to leave but paused at the doorway. "Isobel, Duncan was truly an honorable man last night. He did nothing improper and neither did I. He is like a brother to me and nothing more." Without waiting for a response she hurried to her room.

Isobel turned to Duncan as she tried to regain some composure. She wanted very much to believe they were telling her the truth. However, the evidence at hand was quite overwhelming. Taking a deep breath while she studied Duncan closely, she asked, "Is what she says true?"

Nodding his head quickly he said, "Aye, 'tis." He wrapped the sheet tighter around his waist. "Nothin' improper happened."

"Then why do I find her in yer bed this day?" she asked with her hands planted firmly on her hips. She was quite ready to skelp him the moment she detected a lie.

Exasperated, he let out a sigh as he ran a hand through his hair. "'Tis the nightmares she has, Isobel. Every night she has them. She worries the soldiers will come here and find her. She worries that if and when they do, they'll kill all of us, the people she has come to love and feel safe with."

Isobel took a deep breath as the anger slowly began to leave her. She had not known the lass suffered so. Why had Aishlinn had not come to her with her troubles?

"I would never do anythin' to hurt her, Isobel." Duncan needed her to know it was God's truth that he spoke. "She is a fine young woman and deserves no' to be taken advantage of. I'd never do that to her." His eyes pleaded with her to believe him.

Isobel studied him closely for a few moments and decided he told the truth. Duncan was a fine young man but she could tell from the way he spoke of Aishlinn, the way he looked at her, that he held very strong feelings for her. Perhaps respect was one of them.

"Have ye shared yer feelings with her?" she asked.

Duncan stood a bit taller before answering. "Nay. I haven't." As much as he would have liked to do just that, for whatever reason, he simply could not tell Aishlinn how he felt about her.

Isobel was quite relieved to hear it for she felt that Aishlinn was probably not ready for anything akin to a romance. "That is best, considerin' all that the lass has gone through."

"Twas my thinkin' as well." Certain Isobel was no longer ready to skin him alive he began to relax. "She needs time to heal," he told her. "Aye, the bruises and welts may be long gone. But there be other wounds that take longer to heal than the body."

Isobel released another heavy sigh as she wondered what to do with the two of them. True love could not be denied. She knew and believed that with all her heart. She could send Aishlinn to the ends of the earth and it would do no good. No amount of distance between two people who were truly in love would cause their feelings to diminish. If anything it would make them grow stronger.

"Please promise me, Duncan, that ye'll give Aishlinn more time. She's been through a hellish ordeal. She knows no' who she is or what she wants from life." Lowering her voice she asked, "Promise me ye'll give her that?"

"Aye, I so promise." It was what he had been trying to do all along.

Isobel took a moment to regain her composure before she entered Aishlinn's room. She found Aishlinn standing near the open windows with a shawl wrapped tightly around her shoulders and she looked positively miserable.

Isobel quietly closed the door and sat on the stool near the fireplace. She had been angrier with Duncan than she had been with Aishlinn, for she understood far too well how being in love with someone often interfered with one's good decision making abilities. Aishlinn had grown up without a mother and Isobel was certain that Broc had offered very little in the way of guidance when it came to matters of the heart.

"Come here lass," she said, holding her arms open wide.

Aishlinn rushed to Isobel's open arms and sank to her knees. She could not hold back the deluge of tears as she rested her head upon Isobel's lap. The thought of Isobel being angry with her was unbearably painful as well as frightening. She would never want to do anything that would cause Isobel to send her away.

"Duncan did nothing wrong, Isobel!" No matter how much she wished that he had. She sobbed as she wiped the tears from her cheeks with the palms of her hands.

Isobel smiled as she stroked Aishlinn's hair. "'Tis all right, lass. I spoke with Duncan and I am sorry for flyin' into such a fierce rage. I have only yer best interests in my heart."

Och! How she wished she could share with her the reasons why she felt so protective. Isobel wondered if she wouldn't lose her mind before Angus returned.

Remaining silent, save for the tears and sniffles, Aishlinn closed her eyes. If her mother had lived, how completely different her life might have been. She would not feel so lost and confused right now and her heart, she was sure, would not be breaking.

"Why dinna ye tell me of the bad dreams, Aishlinn?" Isobel asked quietly.

"I wanted not to bother you. You have so many duties and responsibilities," Aishlinn said. "My problems aren't as important as others."

Isobel lifted Aishlinn's chin and looked into her eyes. "But Aishlinn, yer not a problem or a bother. Yer very important to me, lass." For a fleeting moment she was quite tempted to tell her why.

"I am?" she asked very surprised to hear it.

"Aye, ye are!" Isobel said.

Aishlinn could not fathom it. "But how? I've only been here a short time."

A warm smile came to Isobel's face. "Does a mother need years to know her children in order to love them?" She wiped tears away from Aishlinn's face. "Nay, she loves them the moment they are born or come to her. I loved Duncan, Findley and Richard from the day they came to live with us. I needed not days or months or years to know them. They were lads who had lost their families, just as ye've lost yers. They were good lads who needed to be loved and protected." It had been easy for Isobel to love all the children she and Angus had fostered.

Aishlinn was perplexed. She was not a bairn or a small child. She was nearly a grown woman. Should that not make a difference? It made no sense to her how Isobel could love her so readily and with such ease. "But I be not a bairn nor a child."

"Nay, yer not. But are ye no' lost? Are ye no' orphaned with no family of yer own?"

Indeed, she was.

"It is not difficult for me to love ye as if ye were my own, Aishlinn. Yer a sweet and fine young woman with a good heart and spirit. What is there about ye no' to love?"

"Why then, could not my family, the people who raised me, love me?" she whispered.

Did it all just boil down to the fact that her stepfather and brothers were just mean and cruel people? She had blamed herself all those years. Had she been prettier or better or worked harder then perhaps someday they would love her. Time and again they proved her wrong.

She realized in that quiet moment with Isobel that it had mattered not what she did, how hard she had worked or tried to please the men who had raised her. It never would have been enough. It would not have changed who they truly were -- mean, selfish, angry men. Black Richard had been right. Why should she believe those who were mean and harsh to her over those who were decent and kindhearted?

"I know no' why some people are mean and selfish, Aishlinn. I think some just have poisoned hearts and minds. Unfortunately, ye were surrounded by them for too long a time."

She smoothed Aishlinn's hair with her hand and thought on how she should broach the next topic at hand. "How long have ye had these strong feelings towards Duncan?"

Aishlinn bolted upright, her face burned crimson. Had her feelings for him been that obvious?

"It matters not what my feelings are for him; he thinks of me only as a sister, nothing more." No matter how badly she would have liked it to be otherwise, Aishlinn knew there was no possibility of a future with Duncan.

Isobel tilted her head a bit. "Are ye certain of that, Aishlinn?"

"Aye, I am." The thought of Duncan having any romantic thoughts towards her was as ridiculous as putting trews on a pig. "He truly looks after me as a brother does a sister," she said. "Why, just yesterday he gave me good advice on men."

"Oh, he did, did he?" Isobel found that notion quite amusing. "And what, pray tell, is this advice he gave to ye?"

"He bade me to promise him that before I agree to allow anyone to court me, I'll come to him first. He can tell me if they be good and kind men." She lowered her voice as if to share a well-known secret among women. "And not the kind only after one thing."

Isobel had to bite her bottom lip to keep from laughing. What a rake her Duncan was turning out to be! Isobel knew it would matter not what kind of man might take a fancy to the young lass, for none would be good enough. She knew that Duncan was very much in love with this sweet young lady. It was merely his way of keeping her from falling in love with someone else.

"Is that not what brothers do for sisters?" Aishlinn asked naively.

"I suppose some do," Isobel said. But she knew 'twas also something a brash young man would do to keep a young lady he fancied to himself. She decided it best, for the moment at least, to not explain it further to her.

Isobel put her hands upon Aishlinn's shoulders. "Now, we'll not worry on the matter any longer," she said as she stood. "I think it be time to teach ye some of the finer things a lady ought to know." She studied Aishlinn for a moment. Such a beautiful young woman she was. 'Twas her eyes though, those deep dark green eyes, that Isobel sometimes found painful to look into.

"Do ye ken how to weave, lass?" she asked.

Aishlinn stood and shook her head. "Nay. My mother was very good at it but I never had the chance to learn."

Isobel swallowed hard at the mention of the lass' mother. "Would ye like to learn?"

Aishlinn's eyes grew wide with anticipation. "Oh yes! Very much!"

"Good. I'll teach ye to weave and to sew properly. Come to my chambers after ye've eaten and we'll start straight away."

Aishlinn flung her arms around Isobel and hugged her tightly. "Thank you, Isobel!" she said as she tried hard not to cry again. What few memories she had left of her mother told her she and Isobel were very much alike. Both were kind, dignified and sweet. She wondered for a moment if it would be disrespectful to her mother's memory to think of Isobel in that manner, as a mother figure.

Aishlinn dressed quickly and ran to the kitchens to eat before racing to Isobel's private chambers. Quite excited to begin to learn to weave, she tapped gently on the door before Isobel opened it. Her chin nearly hit the floor when she entered the room for it was filled nearly top to bottom with books!

Aishlinn had only seen one book in her life. It was the Bible the priest read at the funerals. In the lowlands, they were not allowed such things as to own books. It was considered a blasphemy against God, the church and the King to teach girl children to read, and only a very few of the boys were educated beyond spelling their own names. Reading, owning books, that was a right held only by the privileged and powerful English.

Isobel watched Aishlinn closely for a long moment as she watched the young woman's eyes grow wide with awe.

Aishlinn stood frozen as she soaked it all in. A massive fireplace nearly as big as the one in the gathering room took up most of one wall. A shield with two crossed broadswords hung over the dark mantle. A large trestle table flanked by benches stood in the center of the room. Soft and luxurious rugs were scattered across the floor.

And the books! Hundreds of books sat on heavy wooden shelves tucked into nearly every crook and cranny and dozens more sat atop the table. Aishlinn took no notice of the looms that sat in front of the tall windows, for it was the books that captured her attention and heart.

"Aishlinn, what are ye thinking?" Isobel asked curiously.

"You have books," she said breathlessly.

"Aye, we do," Isobel said, realizing the lass could not read. Isobel knew all too well the opinions the English held on educating girls. "Ya dunna read, do ye, lass?" Knowing the answer beforehand.

"Nay!" Aishlinn said, shocked at such a notion. "'Tis considered a blasphemy for a girl to read!"

Disgusted at those people who refused to educate their children, Isobel huffed. "People with power like to keep their people ignorant. They do it only so they may hold more power over them. Heaven forbid a body should have an intelligent, independent thought! Especially a female!"

She was determined to not allow this young woman to be lost any longer. Books would open worlds that Aishlinn could not begin to imagine existed. "We shall rectify that situation at once!" she told Aishlinn. "Ye'll learn to read and to write and to figure sums. 'Tis quite important for a proper lady to know such things, lass!"

Aishlinn stood aghast at the thought. "But 'tis considered an offense against the church and the King," she whispered as if their voices would be carried straight to the king's ears.

Isobel laughed sweetly and shook her head. "Lass. Ye be no longer in the hands of the English. Here, we do teach our children to read. It is considered an offense not to!"

Slowly Aishlinn's lips began to turn upward and she suddenly felt wicked, as if she were doing something very, very wrong. But the idea of actually learning to read was quite appealing as was the thought of becoming a proper lady. If only her brothers could see her now.

Eighteen

Had she known that learning to read and write would be harder on a body than working in the fields or hunting, she might not have been so excited at the prospect of a proper education. But it was exciting. Isobel opened entire new worlds to her and she was enjoying every minute of it, no matter how tired she was.

She would rise each morning and race to work in the kitchens. The moment she finished whatever tasks Mary had given her for the day, she would happily race to Isobel's room. Even after the many days that followed she still could not contain her excitement. It still felt strange each time she was allowed to touch a book or put a quill to parchment to practice writing her letters. But she relished it and each day she thanked God for bringing her here.

When the nightmares came, Aishlinn would go to Isobel rather than Duncan. Some nights she would crawl into Isobel's bed while other nights Isobel would sit near Aishlinn's bed until she fell back to sleep. It was still difficult for Aishlinn to understand how Isobel could love her as her own.

She would read and write and practice sums for a few hours each afternoon before they would turn to learning to weave. Aishlinn loved the scent of the heavy threads and how soft they felt on her fingers. The sound of the shuttles as she passed one over the other was as soothing to her spirits as a lullaby to a new bairn. She could only hope to someday be as skillful at it as her mother had been and Isobel seemed to be.

Isobel was keeping Aishlinn so busy that it made it nearly impossible for Duncan to spend more than a moment or two with her. He was growing quite frustrated with it, but was profoundly glad to see the excitement upon Aishlinn's face as she learned to read and write.

Isobel had also put a stop to them sitting together at the evening meals. She insisted that Aishlinn sit with her and the other ladies under the guise that it would help her to grow as a refined woman. Duncan could tell from Aishlinn's bored expression during those meals that she did not like it any more than he did. Many times he caught her glancing at him from the corner of her eye.

Sleep brought no respite for him, for 'twas there he found her each night, in his dreams. Vivid, sweet, wicked dreams of her nestled in his arms, as she had been that one delightful night when nothing happened between them but sleep. In his dreams, far more than sleep was happening.

Angus was long overdue to arrive home but finally word had arrived in the form of a messenger. He brought with him a letter for Isobel as well as a group of musicians to entertain the clan. The messenger informed Duncan that the talks were not progressing as smoothly as Angus had hoped and he would be delayed for at least another fortnight.

Though Duncan would have preferred Angus return sooner rather than later, he knew his chief was where he was most needed. The safety and future of the clan took precedence over all else. Duncan could tend to the needs of his clan well enough and he only wished Angus had returned so that he could help him sort out the blasted feelings he had for Aishlinn.

Alone in her room, Isobel read the letter from her husband. Tears burned her eyes as she read it. She could almost hear Angus' deep booming voice whispering softly to her through the words written on the parchment. His letter held promises of the many things he desired to do with her upon his return. Some were so detailed they brought not only a smile to her face but a blush of red as well. Even though he had just turned forty, he often behaved like a man half his age when it came to his wife.

He prayed -- and she knew he meant it only in jest -- that another man, perhaps one much younger and more braw than he, had not stolen her heart in his absence. Expressing his never-ending love and gratitude to her and how much he missed being near her, he prayed she be well and safe. He could barely wait to return home and to Isobel.

Holding the letter to her heart for several long moments she fought back tears for she missed her husband very much. She penned her own letter to him professing her own love and devotion and expressed to him that he was greatly missed, not just by her but their many children and clansmen. She also reassured him that there was no other man on the face of the earth who could steal her heart from him. He was the only man she would ever love.

Isobel decided it best not to mention the young Aishlinn for now. There would be plenty of time to sort it all out when he returned. 'Twas news, after all, that must be told face to face.

Leaving her private chamber to give her letter to the messenger, she saw Aishlinn sitting at the long table. The lass had a most serious expression upon her face as she chewed at her bottom lip and studied the letters on the page before her. Isobel could see that dark circles, from the stresses of learning and lack of sleep, had begun to form under the girl's eyes.

Feeling perhaps that she had been pushing the lass much too hard of late, and with her spirits lifted after reading her husband's letter, Isobel made a decision. She would give Aishlinn the remainder of the afternoon to do with as she pleased.

"Aishlinn?" she said, tucking her letter into the pocket of her skirt. "I've decided that ye've been working far too much of late. It is too bonny a day to be stuck in here."

Not sure what Isobel meant, she asked, "Do you wish me to study elsewhere?"

"Nay! I wish ye to close the books and study no more this day. Go. Soak up some fresh air and sunshine. Find Bree and tell her the secrets ye won't tell any other. Find a lad to bat yer eyelashes at!" Isobel laughed aloud as she watched Aishlinn's eyes quickly fill with excitement and relief. "I'll see ye back here on the morrow. Now be gone with ye, before I change me mind!"

She needn't be told twice. With great care she closed her book before running from the room. Not wanting to risk the chance that Isobel would change her mind and call her back to her studies, Aishlinn raced down the hallway and nearly tumbled down the stairs. Freedom for the rest of the day was too grand a thought to waste anywhere but out of doors.

She dashed through the kitchens and out the door, shouting hello and goodbye to those she passed. She paused long enough to take in a deep breath of fresh air and to feel the sunshine on her face. Arching her back and turning her face to the sun, she stood still for a moment, soaking it in, glad that the rest of the glorious day was hers to do with as she pleased.

As she raced past the laundries and rounded the corner at a full run, she ran straight into Duncan. She landed full into him with a thump, nearly falling backwards. Startled, Duncan reached out and caught her before she tumbled and using more force than he intended, he pulled her right back into him.

"Duncan! I'm sorry!" she smiled at him, excited to be free and to be seeing him.

"Where are ye running off to? Did ye escape Isobel's oubliette, be that why yer runnin'?" he laughed, his eyes twinkling in the bright midday sunlight. He was very glad to see her and not ready to let go of her.

A wide smile came to her face. "Nay! She has given me the rest of the day to do with as I please!" she told him excitedly.

That was indeed promising news for Duncan. He was quite happy to hear he might finally have some time to spend alone with her. Knowing there were far too many watchful eyes around the castle, he worried that Isobel might learn that he was speaking with Aishlinn and decide to intervene. He wasn't willing to risk it.

Suddenly, a somewhat dastardly thought came to his mind. He wanted very much to simply be alone with her, to talk with her and learn how she liked her studies. "Aishlinn, would ye like to go fer a ride with me?"

Her smile brightened. Hopefully he would want only one horse. A chance to ride atop his lap, with his arms wrapped around her was a delightful thought, even if he did have only brotherly intentions towards her.

Within a very short time they were mounted on Duncan's bay-colored mare, with Aishlinn blissfully perched upon his lap. They raced from the castle and headed towards the hillside at a full run. Duncan relished having her so near him. Slowly, he took in a long, deep breath. She smelled of lavender. A few moments after breathing her in he realized mayhap they should have taken two horses. Her scent was intoxicating and her rump was a little too close for comfort. He had to force his mind to think of something mundane in order to try to quash his growing excitement.

Aishlinn dared not admit to herself that she had missed him for she knew it would not have mattered anyway. Her feelings for him were quite strong, but she knew he could not return them. She had convinced herself weeks ago that he needed a more mature, worldly and beautiful woman. If he were to be chief of his clan someday he would also need a woman with a higher station in life than her own.

But for now, it did not matter. She was away from the castle, away from her lessons and ready to simply enjoy some time with Duncan.

They had ridden a good distance before he slowed his mare to a walk. Mundane thoughts weren't working, especially with her body in such close proximity to his own.

While Aishlinn enjoyed a view of the lands before her, Duncan was enjoying a view of his own. He noticed that her hair had grown longer and that her dress no longer hung loosely upon her frame. It seemed to him that she was filling it out quite nicely. Her fair skin no longer held the pallor of someone tired and worn. Her cheeks were quite rosy and she had a healthy glow about her.

He did notice the dark circles under her eyes, more likely than not from lack of sleep. He was certain it was the nightmares that took hold of her each night and he wished that she would come back to him for comfort.

"'Tis beautiful, isn't it Duncan," she said looking out at the majesty of the highlands. He had not taken his eyes from her. "Aye, it is." She was the most beautiful woman he had ever seen.

They rode along in silence for a while longer before Duncan stopped the horse. He had to get her off his lap and quickly. "Let's walk for a while, Aishlinn," he said as he dismounted.

He reached up and took hold of her small waist and helped her down from the horse. Just as he had done the day they had arrived at the castle, he did not immediately release her. He held her and looked into her dark green eyes that were sparkling like emeralds in the sunlight. He wanted nothing more at the moment than to kiss her full pink lips and run his hands through her golden hair.

Aishlinn began to feel uncomfortable for she had never seen him look at her in that manner before. While she did not want him to let her go, she worried that if he didn't, she might be tempted to kiss him. It wasn't easy to push those thoughts and feelings aside, especially when his dark blue eyes seemed to be boring into her soul.

"Did you wish to walk, Duncan, or have you changed your mind?" she asked him, swallowing hard. His curious expression was beginning to make her nervous.

He shook the wicked thoughts from his mind and finally put her down. She had an effect upon him that he had never experienced before. It was as confusing as it was exhilarating. How on earth could one wee woman have such an effect on his heart and mind?

Holding onto the reins of his mount he let out a slow breath. He would surely lose his mind before he got his feelings for her sorted out.

"How do yer lessons go, lass? Are ye likin' them?" he asked as they walked through the tall summer grasses. Think pure thoughts. Think pure thoughts. He repeated over and over in his mind.

She told him yes, she was enjoying them, though she was struggling with the Latin. He told her the same thing that Isobel had; once she mastered the Latin, the other languages would be much easier to learn.

They walked at a leisurely pace while they talked about everything and nothing in particular, merely enjoying one another's company. The sun had peaked and begun its late day descent and the gentle breeze had begun to die down.

"Have I told ye lass that Angus sent musicians with the messenger?" he said as he looked to her from the corner of his eye.

"Nay, I had not heard of it."

"There'll be a grand feast this night and a dance after," he told her. He noticed that her gold hair held a slight tint of red to it when the sun shone on it in just the right manner.

"That sounds like much fun," she said before taking in a deep breath of fresh air.

"Perhaps Isobel will allow ye to sit with me this night?"

She would very much like to sit with him again at the evening meals. While she appreciated all that Isobel was doing for her, with teaching her to read and write and to be a refined and dignified lady, she truly missed spending time with Duncan and his men. She hoped Isobel's good mood and generosity would continue through the rest of the day and that she'd allow them to spend time together later. "Perhaps."

"And mayhap," he began, "ye'll save a dance fer me?"

"Dance?" she asked. She had never danced before. There had been little time or opportunity in her life before coming to Castle Gregor for such things.

"Aye, a dance," he said smiling as he enjoyed the thought of being able to hold her close with no one to question why. He studied her for moment, noticing that her face had grown red. "Would ye no' like to dance with me?" he asked.

She would love to do more than dance with him she thought to herself. Had she the courage to say what was really upon her mind she felt certain he would rescind his offer. "Nay, I would enjoy it very much."

Duncan could sense the apprehension in her voice. "Is there a problem with it, Aishlinn?"

She took a deep breath before answering. "I do not know how to dance." She did not like having to admit it.

Duncan stopped and turned to her with a warm smile and a mischievous twinkle in his eyes. "'Tis quite easy, once ye get the gist of it," he told her as he dropped the reins to his horse and took her hands in his. Her eyes flew open wide as he placed her hand upon his shoulder and his own on her hip. Her stomach tightened and her heart began to pound in her chest. She cursed the feelings wishing them to go away and never return for it was heartbreaking to know nothing could ever come of it.

"It be all in feelin' the rhythm of the music. The music be fast, yer feet will move fast," he said. "Now, pay close attention." With a smile and a wink he began counting one, two, three, one, two three.

Soon, they were dancing in the tall grass without the aid of music to guide them. Aishlinn stepped upon his feet a few times, apologizing nervously after each mistake. Duncan was quite patient with her and encouraged her to not worry of it. She could have stepped upon his feet a hundred times and it would have mattered naught to him.

Sweet laughter came from Aishlinn as she lost herself in the moment with Duncan. It didn't matter there was no music for it simply felt glorious to have his hand in hers, his hand upon her hip as he twirled her about the tall grass. She could not remember a time in her life when she felt this gloriously happy. It mattered not that he could not return the feelings she had for him. For the length of that one dance she allowed herself to pretend that he could.

Suddenly Duncan came to a complete stop. Aishlinn's smile slowly faded away to a questioning expression.

Duncan had that peculiar look to him again and for the life of her she could not figure out what it meant. There was something to his smile, to the way his eyes looked that disquieted her. As she studied his face she felt her stomach begin to bounce around again. Taking a deep, slow breath in, she tried to quiet her stomach. It didn't work, for her stomach still twisted and her fingers trembled.

Would it be so wrong to kiss her now, to tell her how I feel? A fierce battle between right and wrong was taking place in his heart. This was the woman he felt certain he wanted to spend the rest of his life with. What could be the harm in simply telling her that? The fear that flashed in her eyes told him why he couldn't.

How much time would the lass need before she felt safe with him, he wondered. His strong sense of honor told him the lass needed more than two months to get over a lifetime of cruelty and one night of sheer terror. Perhaps if he told her how he felt, and that he was willing to wait as long as she needed, that knowledge might help speed up the process of healing her heart.

As he battled with his conscience, he caught sight of a movement out of the corner of his eye. He heard the sound of beating hoofs pounding nearby. He turned his head and reflexively reached for the dagger at his side. He heard Aishlinn gasp when she turned to see what he was looking at. The terror on her face matched what he was feeling in his stomach.

Riders approached and there were many. Far too many for him to battle alone.

Duncan's heart momentarily seized with dread at the sight of so many riders. He cursed himself for bringing Aishlinn so far from the keep. The only weapons he had were his dirk and his sword. Too far from the castle for his war cries to be heard, his only choice was to mount quickly and fly back to Gregor. As soon as he got close enough, he could let loose with a warning cry and signal to his men to ready for battle. He could only pray that he made it to the keep in time to warn his men and that he could keep Aishlinn safe until they were safely behind the castle walls.

As he was about to throw Aishlinn up on the saddle, he took one last look back at the approaching party. The moment he saw the green and red colors of Clan McDunnah waving in the wind, a great sense of relief washed over him. His shoulders sagged and he put his hands on his knees, breathing in deeply. For a moment, he had been certain it was a hundred English soldiers coming for Aishlinn.

Aishlinn put her hand on Duncan's back as he was stooped over, catching his breath.

"Duncan!" her voice was filled with fear. "We must ride back to the castle straight away!" She was certain he was ready to faint, probably from the same fear she felt at seeing so many men and horses coming their way. And for a brief moment, she worried that her brave warrior wasn't as brave as she had originally thought.

"Nay, lass," he told her as he straightened himself and tried to catch his breath. "That be the Clan McDunnah!" He gave her hand a squeeze. "Aric told us they'd be comin'."

Though she was quite relieved to know it was a friendly party approaching, she imagined it would take a sennight to get her heart to quit pounding so fiercely.

Duncan quickly mounted his steed and bent down to take Aishlinn's hand. He pulled her up into his lap and headed out to greet the Clan McDunnah.

The Clan McDunnah was smaller by half, than the Clan MacDougall, but that did not mean they weren't a fierce lot of men and women. They had fought alongside the MacDougalls in many a battle against the English as well as other clans with which they both feuded. They were as loyal to King David as the MacDougalls were and like the MacDougalls they were fiercely loyal to Scotland.

Duncan yelled out a Gaelic greeting to the McDunnahs as he and Aishlinn rode towards the band of mounted men. Caelen, Aric and three other McDunnahs broke away from the pack and met Duncan and Aishlinn.

"Tapadh leat!" Caelen greeted them with a smile as he grasped Duncan's forearm with his own. He did not look at Duncan, but instead focused on Aishlinn. "What a bonny young lass!" he said in Gaelic.

Uneasiness washed over Aishlinn. She understood most of what he said, the rest she was able pick up on from his expressive eyes. He was a fierce looking man, with long black hair and very dark brown eyes, and appeared to be around thirty years old. Braids framed his temples and a long scar ran down from his forehead, trailed along the left side of his face and down his neck before it disappeared under his tunic. Thick, well-muscled bare legs were tucked into leather boots. He had dirks tucked into each of his boots, two more, along with a sword, hung at his waist, and a broadsword was strapped to his back. Lord only knew how many more weapons the man had hidden on his person.

"She speaks only the English," Aric offered to Caelen. The McDunnah raised an eyebrow as a roguish smile formed on his lips. "What a pity," The McDunnah said in the Gaelic.

Aishlinn understood that as well and made no attempt at correcting Aric. She'd let them think she was completely ignorant for now. The longer he stared at her, the more uncomfortable she became. She felt Duncan's arms tighten around her as he pulled her in closer. She cast a glance up at him. His jaws were clenched and his smile had quickly disappeared.

"'Tis good to see ye healed nicely, lass!" Aric said, apparently oblivious to the angry glares being cast between Duncan and the McDunnah.

"'Tis good to see you, Aric." Aishlinn smiled at him. "Are Rebecca and the children with you?"

"Nay, they're no'," he told her. "I'm afraid 'tisn't a social call that brings us here this day, lass."

Aishlinn was disappointed. She hoped that she would see Rebecca and the children again. "Are they well?" she asked.

"Aye, they are, lass." Aric finally took note of Caelen and Duncan staring each other down. "Duncan," Aric began. "Ya wouldn't have a wee nip of the chief's whiskey with ye, would ye lad?"

Duncan finally broke his eyes away from Caelen. "Nay. No' on me. But we've plenty back at Gregor." He spoke in English out of respect for Aishlinn.

He smiled at his friend and turned his horse around. "Angus is still in the far north," he told Aric as the group headed back towards Gregor. "We've just received word that he'll be delayed a bit."

"Aye," Caelen began. "We received word of the delays as well. Me brother Collin is there. He says there be far too much obstinacy among the clans McKee and Bowie to get much done."

Aric chuckled. "Aye, 'tis true. But they'll eventually come around to the right side of things."

They rode in silence for a short time and all the while Duncan held a firm grip around Aishlinn's waist. Caelen rode to their left, Aric to their right, with the rest of their men following behind them. The roguish smile had not left Caelen's face and he frequently cast glances at Aishlinn. Normally she would have paid no attention to such things, but the manner in which he stared at her made her very uncomfortable.

After a few moments Caelen began speaking to Duncan, in the Gaelic again. "Does she belong to ye?" he asked.

Duncan's reply was short and to the point. "Aye."

Aishlinn understood his question and was quite glad for Duncan's answer to it. Not that she thought he meant it in any kind of romantic fashion. She assumed he meant it as a way of protecting her from the McDunnah and she was very grateful. The McDunnah looked at her with the same kind of hungry, lustful expression as the earl had done months ago. It made her feel unclean and nervous.

Aishlinn was quite relieved to be back inside the walls of the keep. Duncan let her down at the kitchen entrance and asked that she let Mary know there would be additional men at the evening meal.

"Thank ye for ridin' with me this day, Aishlinn," he said before he left to see to their new guests. He did not wait for her response before riding off.

Mary was not happy to hear about the very late arrival of at least a hundred men. She cursed in Gaelic at their apparent lack of consideration for not sending a messenger ahead of time to warn of their arrival. The evening meal was just a few short hours away and it meant much more work for her staff. Lucky for the McDunnah that he was not standing within pan-throwing distance of Mary, for Aishlinn had no doubt he would have gotten both an earful of her Gaelic cursing along with something quite heavy crashing against his skull.

Aishlinn left Mary bellowing out orders and Gaelic curses. She was on her way up to her room when Bree and her friend Ellen came rushing up the steps behind her. The girls were beyond themselves with excitement over the musicians' arrival and chattered on about it all the way up the stairs and into Aishlinn's room.

"We've a grand dress for ye!" Bree told her excitedly. "We've much to do this night!" Aishlinn was beginning to realize that this night might be more special than she had earlier anticipated.

"Why are you so excited?" Aishlinn asked with a giggle.

Both girls rolled their eyes as if Aishlinn were daft. "'Tis a dance, Aishlinn!" Bree shook her head when it was apparent that Aishlinn did not understand the importance of it.

"'Tis not often we get musicians here!" she said as a wry grin came to her face. "We'll get to dance with the lads. I'm old enough now that mum won't send me off to my room before all the fun starts!" she told her.

Aishlinn then understood the young girls' excitement. Aishlinn knew there was one young lad in particular that Bree held a strong fondness for. A dance was the opportunity for Bree to be physically close to him without anyone questioning it.

"I see. Then we best make certain you look beautiful this night!" Aishlinn said.

"Aye! And ye as well!" Bree smiled at her.

Bree had requested baths for both of them and soon one was brought to Aishlinn's room and she wasted no time lingering in it. Excitement can often be contagious, spreading faster than the pox or plague, and before Aishlinn realized what was happening, she found herself excited and looking forward to the festivities.

She would not have admitted it to anyone, but she truly did want to look special this night. Even if she did not win Duncan's eye or his affections perhaps there would be someone else who might think her a wee more than just plain.

She had barely finished her bath when Bree and Ellen returned to her room.

"Have you decided who you wish to dance with this night?" Aishlinn asked them. Both girls giggled and smiled. "All of them!" Ellen said as they burst out laughing.

Bree and Ellen were fussing more over how Aishlinn might look than they worried over themselves. They helped to dry her hair and combed it until it was as smooth as silk. Because her hair was so short the girls were puzzled about what to do with it.

"I say leave the bottom loose but pull it back on top," Ellen offered as she stood staring at Aishlinn's hair.

"Nay. That would be far too simple. Lets do a very intricate braid!" Bree said. Apparently Ellen agreed for soon they were both twisting and combing and pulling Aishlinn's hair in all manner of directions. It seemed to take forever before they were finished. Once done, they each took a step back to eye their work. Satisfied with what they had accomplished, Ellen gave Aishlinn the mirror and smiled thoughtfully at her.

Aishlinn had not looked into a mirror since the day she had laid in bed more than a month ago, still covered with bruises and marks. Reluctantly she took the mirror and swallowed hard before looking at her reflection.

She did not recognize the person who stared back from the glass. Her hair looked amazing! Bree and Ellen had somehow managed to weave a very intricate braid that made it appear as though she had far more hair than she really possessed.

"Do ye like it, Aishlinn?" Bree asked breathlessly. "If ye do no', we can change it."

"Nay! It looks beautiful!" Never did she think she would utter those words when she spoke of herself. Tears came to her eyes when she looked at her reflection more closely. I might not be too plain after all. She was very surprised when that thought came whispering into her mind.

Bree and Ellen raced from the room only to return moments later. In Bree's arms was the most magnificent gown Aishlinn had ever seen. It was made from the deepest of purple brocade fabric and it sparkled in the candlelight. There was much intricate needlework around the bodice, neck and sleeves. Beaming, the two young girls held it up for Aishlinn's approval.

"Please Aishlinn, say ye'll wear it! We've worked very hard at it for days for ye," Bree said.

"Days? But we've only just learned of the dance this day." Aishlinn was puzzled.

Bree and Ellen cast conspiratorial smiles at one another. "We've been workin' on many dresses for ye, lass," Bree admitted. Their secret was out.

Ellen added, "This was by far our favorite. We were savin' it for a special occasion. Please say ye'll wear it."

Aishlinn would not need her arm twisted this night. She couldn't imagine another gown that would make her feel as special as she wanted to feel this night. She was touched by the diligent work and thoughtfulness that had gone into the dress. Her dress. Not someone's cast off but a dress made just for her.

"I could live a thousand years and never be able to repay you your kindness," Aishlinn said. "I used to wish for kind brothers. I never thought to wish for sisters!" She wiped a tear away. "But now I have two in the both of you!"

As they hugged each other, their tears combined with laughter, something dawned on Aishlinn. She had a family and it did not matter one bit that they did not share a bloodline. What did matter was the love and kindness that was shared between the three of them.

Bree had decided they were wasting precious time and insisted they begin dressing Aishlinn. They took great care not to mess her braided hair as they lifted the gown over her head. It took a good deal of time to fasten all the buttons that trailed down the back of the gown. When they were finished, they attached a very fine, sheer veil to the back of her hair. It cascaded down her back where it pooled into a fine purple puddle. Aishlinn felt like a queen.

Once Bree and Ellen were satisfied with how she looked, they all went to Bree's room where Aishlinn helped to ready them. Night had fallen by the time they were finished. Giddy with excitement and anticipation, the three young women walked down the torch-lit hallway and stairs to the gathering room. Each of them was lost in her own thoughts of how she wished her night might go.

Nineteen

God's bones, but she was beautiful! The moment Aishlinn stepped into the gathering room Duncan's heart began to pound mercilessly in his chest. He had never seen her look more beautiful and the sight of her took his breath away. His knees knocked and his mouth went dry all the while his hands trembled. He knew in that one singular moment he could not live another night without telling her how he felt.

She walked with a grace and dignity he had not witnessed in her before. He could not take his eyes from her. God's teeth but she was beyond beautiful!

Others in the room had noticed her as well. Black Richard, Tall Thomas, and Daniel with Wee William bringing up the rear, had entered the room from the opposite side. Black Richard took one look at the lovely Aishlinn and came to a dead stop, causing those behind him to come crashing to a halt and bumping into him. When Wee William crashed into Daniel, he nearly sent them all tumbling to the floor.

"What the bloody 'ell!" Wee William said angrily. 'Twas then that he saw her too. Wee William let out a low whistle. "I'll be damned!" he whispered to Daniel. "Be that our young Aishlinn?" he asked.

"Aye," Daniel said breathlessly.

Richard hushed them. "She is a lady, and gentlemen none of ye are!" Not one of them, especially Black Richard, could stop staring at her. Black Richard swallowed hard and headed towards her.

Duncan had caught sight of Black Richard. The way with which the man's eyes seemed to wash over Aishlinn's body caused a fierce surge of jealousy to shoot through him. If anyone's eyes were to look at her that way, they would be Duncan's and no other's. She was his. Duncan swore that no one, especially not Black Richard, would be given the opportunity to woo Aishlinn this night.

Caelen and his men had seen her as well and Duncan could have thrust his dirk deep into the man's heart for the way he looked at Aishlinn. Caelen was already halfway into his cups and far more a threat to Aishlinn than Black Richard could ever think to be. Caelen made no attempt to move from his table and it was a good thing for him that he didn't. Duncan would have no qualms about killing him if he so much as laid a finger on his Aishlinn.

Duncan all but flew across the room to reach Aishlinn. He had to remind himself that there was proper protocol to be followed. It simply would not do to scoop her up in his arms and whisk her away to a quiet and secluded place where he could have her all to himself.

As always, Isobel stood guard over his soon to be betrothed. It mattered not that Aishlinn did not know yet that she would soon be married to him, for he had himself just realized it. He would share that with her later, after he got a little more used to the idea himself.

If he had to beg for a chance to sit with Aishlinn, he would. If begging didn't work, he was not beyond bribery or kidnapping.

"Isobel," Duncan said trying to regain some of his composure. "May Aishlinn please sit with me this night?" He sent a silent prayer up to the Good Lord that Isobel would say yes.

Isobel paused long enough to study the way Duncan and Aishlinn were looking at each other. Knowing she could do little to stop the feelings they so obviously had for each other, she gave a slight nod of her head. But before Duncan led Aishlinn away, she shot him a look that warned him to keep his feelings as well as his hands to himself.

A sweet smile came to Aishlinn's face as Duncan took her hand and led her to one of the large tables in the center of the room. Had he been chief, they would have sat at the high table together. That would have been enough to let every man in the room know she was his and his alone. But as it was, the high table would be filled this night with Isobel and the wives of Angus' counsel.

Duncan touched the hilt of the dagger at his side and scanned the room. There were many men who stared with mouths agape at his Aishlinn. Nay, he wasn't beyond murder if it was necessary to protect the innocence and purity of his betrothed. That was his as well. He pulled a chair out and waited for her to be seated before taking the one to her left.

Black Richard, Tall Thomas, Daniel and Wee William nearly fell over themselves as they rushed to the table to get a seat near Aishlinn. Black Richard took the chair to Aishlinn's right whilst he shot Duncan a wry smile. Duncan returned it with a look of warning that said not to get too close to Aishlinn.

Wee William and Daniel had simultaneously grabbed the chair directly opposite Aishlinn. One glowering look from Wee William was all it took for Daniel to relinquish his hold upon it and for the smile upon his face to disappear quickly. He took the seat next to Wee William.

Aishlinn stared at the group of men, wondering what on earth had gotten into them. It had to be the musicians and dance that was planned for later. The excitement had to have gotten into everyone's blood and made them all daft. She smiled politely as she took her napkin and laid it upon her lap.

She found it quite odd that they were all so quiet and that they continued to stare at her. Usually they were talking loudly and behaving boisterously.

When they continued to stare, she leaned into Duncan and whispered to him. "Have I something upon my face?" she asked. "Your men keep staring at me."

He had been busy staring at her as well. "Aye, ye do," he told her.

A look of dread washed over her. "I do? What is it?" She was aghast as she lifted her napkin to remove whatever offending thing might be upon her face.

Duncan's lips curved upward and his eyes twinkled. "'Tis yer beauty," he said as he brushed an imaginary hair from her forehead.

He had done it only for a chance to feel her skin against his own. Clearing his throat he turned and glared at his men. "Lads, ye've all seen lovely lasses before," he warned them.

"Aye, we have," Wee William said. "But none as bonny as our young Aishlinn is this night!" He slapped Daniel hard upon his back, nearly knocking him into the table. Wee William laughed loudly as he looked to his friends. "Am I right, men?" His deep voice seemed to shake the entire room.

Aishlinn felt all the color drain from her skin only to be replaced with deep red. She wondered if perhaps they had not been into the chief's whiskey for it was the only plausible explanation. Men were such confusing beasts! She supposed for a moment that men were God's attempt at humor.

Each of the men, save for Black Richard, nodded their heads in agreement. Black Richard spoke quietly. "Forgive the hellions, Aishlinn. They apparently do no' get out of the barracks often enough."

He took a long drink of ale before gently setting the tankard down. "They are no' used to being in the presence of such a beautiful young woman as ye."

Stunned, Aishlinn knew not how to respond to him. She knew she had turned red with embarrassment again and wished she did not do that so readily. She stared at the trencher in front of her and wished she knew how to properly respond to such a compliment. Isobel had been busy teaching her to read and write and weave. Perhaps they should have a discussion of men, and soon, before she lost her mind completely.

Wee William took a long pull of his ale, though not as graciously as Black Richard. He slammed the empty tankard down and cleared his throat loudly. "Young Aishlinn! Would ye do me the honor of the first dance?" He asked as he winked at her. Soon, the other men were asking her for a dance as well.

She wondered if there would be any point in the evening where she would not be turning red. She looked to Duncan for help, but he was staring at her with a daft and somewhat confusing expression. Perhaps he was bilious, or constipated, or worse yet, drunk. It was hard for her to discern between the expressions at the moment.

As graciously as she could she told them yes, she would dance with them. Duncan had to have put them all up to this, she was certain of it. They were all simply being kind and brotherly. "But can we please eat first?" she asked.

Growing quite uncomfortable at the continued stares she was receiving, she let out an exasperated sigh. "And for heaven's sake! Would you all quit staring at me as if you were starving men looking at a piece of roast venison!" She was as surprised as anyone at the words that had just left her mouth.

But none was more surprised than Duncan. He was glad to see that she felt comfortable enough to put them in their places. But in case she hadn't been, his hand was ready to grab his dagger and plunge it into the gut of any man who tried to take advantage of her innocence.

Rapidly, the men diverted their eyes and began to focus on the fine meal before them. Duncan found he had little appetite and that his jaw was beginning to ache from clenching it. He did not like how closely Black Richard sat to Aishlinn, nor the blasted smile that was upon the bastard's face. 'Twere it any other woman who's attention they wanted to garner, Duncan would have merely looked upon it as a challenge. Not this night and not with this woman. She was his.

Throughout the meal, he watched Black Richard closely. Was Duncan imagining things, or was the man's chair moving even closer to Aishlinn's? And the way he spoke to her, as if they had been friends all their lives! He had to remind himself that he had no official holds on Aishlinn and she none on him. Yet. But that knowledge did nothing to quell the growing anger and jealousy that boiled in his stomach every time Black Richard smiled at Aishlinn.

Black Richard had asked how her lessons went. When Aishlinn told of her struggles with Latin, Black Richard, in Latin nonetheless, offered to help her should she need it! And the way the man would gently place his hand on Aishlinn's arm when he wanted her attention? He swore to himself that if Black Richard did not stop, he would knock him on his arse!

At one point in the meal Duncan draped his arm around Aishlinn's shoulders. That should have been enough of a signal to the idiot on her left that she was spoken for. But nay, Black Richard was not smart enough to come to that conclusion. The man was either blind or stupid. Duncan was not sure which.

When they were nearly finished eating, Manghus appeared at their table. "Good evening, hellions!" he said to the men. "Aishlinn," he said with a nod to her. "Have ye taken the time to stop and see the most beautiful bairn in all this great earth?" He motioned his head towards the table where his wife sat with their newborn daughter.

Wee William jumped to his feet quite excited to learn the magnificent Catherine and her bairn were here. "Where?" Wee William boomed.

Manghus laughed along with everyone else. "Settle down there, William! Ye'll make my daughter cry with that ugly face and deep voice of yers!"

Wee William went red. 'Twas no secret to anyone he had a great fondness toward all children and bairns. Aishlinn thought he would make a good father someday. That is if he could find a woman not frightened to death by his enormous size and gravely voice.

Within moments Duncan, Aishlinn and the rest of their tablemates were surrounding Catherine and her wee daughter. Aishlinn's heart swelled with awe at the sight of the tiny baby, all wrapped in a fine plaid.

Thick dark hair surrounded the tiniest face she had ever seen. Her long, thick black eyelashes were closed as she slept quite peacefully in her mother's arms.

Her proud father beamed as he introduced his firstborn to his friends. Whispering, he said, "Lads. Aishlinn. This is me daughter, Aileen."

Manghus touched the baby's cheek ever so gently with the back of his finger. He looked at her with so much love and adoration that it brought tears to Aishlinn's eyes.

She wondered if her real father had lived if he would have looked at her in the same manner? The thought made her heart ache; she had to wrap her arms around herself to keep from crying. She waited for the moment to pass before she told Manghus and Catherine what a beautiful daughter they had.

"Would ye like to hold her, Aishlinn?" Catherine asked, smiling up from her chair. Aishlinn's eyes grew wide but Catherine gave her no time to answer. "I need to step away for a few moments. Would ye take her for me?" Catherine stood and placed the precious bundle in her arms.

"I've never held one before, Catherine! I know not what to do!" Aishlinn protested as fear washed over her. The others looked to her, stunned.

A very appalled Wee William boomed, "What do ye mean ye've never held a bairn before?" He was astounded. Duncan's face hardened into a look that forced the larger man to cower.

"Ye'll be fine lass," Catherine said as she walked away from the table.

"What if I drop her?" Aishlinn asked, nearly shaking as she held the baby in her arms.

They all laughed at her. Tall Thomas said, "No worries lass! We'll catch her!"

Duncan pulled a chair up for Aishlinn to take. Carefully, as if she were holding fine spun glass, she sat down, unable to take her eyes from the baby.

Daniel whispered, "See there lass! Ye ken what to do!"

The baby pulled at her heart. She was so wee and precious! Aishlinn felt an even stronger tug when the little one let out a soft sigh. Aishlinn knew that chances were she would never have a bairn of her own, but she felt that she could be content perhaps, by holding other women's bairns. The feelings rushing through her at that moment might be good enough.

Wee William crouched down to one knee as he looked at the bairn and then to Aishlinn. Even on one knee he was still a formidable sight. "Young Aishlinn, ye do look beautiful holdin' that bairn!"

"All women look beautiful when they have a bairn in their arms, Wee William!" Aishlinn said as she smiled at him.

"Aye, but none as beautiful as ye this night!" he whispered to her. "Now, do ye mind if I have a go at the wee one?" His smile was broad with anticipation for he was quite anxious to hold the baby.

Aishlinn looked to Manghus for his approval before handing his daughter over to the giant before her.

Manghus smiled, "Aye, 'tis all right lass. Ye better do it soon before that big eejit explodes from anticipation!"

Wee William stood straight and smiled as Duncan helped Aishlinn to her feet. With more grace and gentleness than Aishlinn could have imagined, Wee William bent and took the baby. As he did, a great sense of longing washed over her, but seeing that tiny baby being held by a man as big as Wee William brought great joy to her heart as well.

William began to hum softly to the baby in his arms. Aishlinn felt a sense of recognition to the tune but could not quite place it. She looked about at these braw men with sheer amazement. Each of them, warriors who would fight to the death to defend their families and homeland, were reduced to near quivering fools at the sight of a bairn.

There was more love in this one room, in this one moment than Aishlinn had ever experienced or witnessed in her entire life. She knew then that she never wanted to leave this place or these people. She was home.

'Twas not long after that the evening meal ended and the tables were cleared and moved to make way for the musicians. There was much excitement and anticipation in the air as people of all ages stood chattering away with one another. Aishlinn spied Bree across the room as she stood with Tall Thomas. Bree smiled sweetly as she looked up into the young man's eyes. Aishlinn could see how the two felt for one another.

Aishlinn felt momentarily jealous of the two of them. What she wouldn't give to have someone look at her the way Tall Thomas looked at Bree. Pushing the thought aside she waited alone near the entrance of the gathering room.

It did not take long for the musicians to begin playing a quite lively tune. Soon, the floor was filled with people dancing happily about. Wee William had returned the baby safely to her mother's arms and now stood before Aishlinn. He bowed, winked devilishly at her and in one swift movement spun her onto the dance floor.

For a man as large as Wee William, he certainly possessed a great amount of grace! He swept Aishlinn away into the sea of other dancers and she was quite surprised at how well she was doing. She paid close attention to the others in order to copy their steps. A few faulting moments here and there, but it did not matter. Everyone was having a grand time!

As soon as one song ended, another began and Aishlinn found she was dancing with one man or lad after another. Such a wonderful time she was having as she laughed and twirled and scooped along with each of the partners she had. Her cheeks were beginning to ache from smiling so much and not one of the men she danced with complained when she stepped upon his feet.

Black Richard came to her and asked her for the next dance and she graciously accepted. She was out of breath and would have liked instead to take a rest, but she did not want to say no, for she was having so much fun. The next song was a bit slower than the earlier ones and she was glad for the chance to catch her breath.

As she tried to concentrate on the steps, Black Richard smiled said, "Ya dance very well, lass."

Aishlinn thanked him and tried not to step on his feet. He did dance rather well and she was glad he did not make fun of her when she took a misstep and stepped on his boot. "I'm sorry!" she said, "'tis my first time dancing."

"I think a lass as lovely as ye will have many opportunities to dance again," he said. There was something in the way that he looked at her that made her blush.

"Thank you, Black Richard," she said as she looked to concentrate on where to put her feet. "That is very kind of you to say."

The song soon ended and as she attempted to step away, he held on to her hand. "I'd like another, if that is all right with ye, Aishlinn." His smile held hope.

Before she could answer Duncan appeared beside them. "The lass has promised me the next dance, haven't ye Aishlinn?" he said as he stared down at Black Richard. Aishlinn could see Duncan's jaw clenching and knew he often did that when he was upset or angry about something. She had no idea why he would be upset this night, for they were all having such a delightful time.

Wanting very much to dance with him, she looked at Black Richard. "Thank you Richard! But I did promise Duncan a dance." Duncan swept her away, leaving Black Richard standing alone.

"Are ye having a good time this night?" Duncan asked her once they were on the dance floor and away from Black Richard.

"Oh yes! I am! Thank you." She smiled at him, truly enjoying the way his hand felt upon her waist. "Are you?" she asked.

"I am now," he said, as he winked at her and twirled her about the room.

She felt herself go warm inside and had to remind herself to breathe. Proud and honored she was to be dancing with Duncan, she hoped the dance would last a very long time; perhaps a year or two would be sufficient.

He looked so handsome this night in his white tunic that showed off his broad chest and muscular arms. He wore his dark blue and green plaids that draped nicely over his tightly muscled legs. 'Twas all she could do to keep her heart from pounding its way from her chest. The thoughts she was having she was certain were not at all proper.

"Aishlinn," Duncan said, his voice low and smooth. "Ye do look beautiful this night."

Another wave of crimson came to her cheeks. That puzzling smile had returned to his face. Oh how she wished he had more than brotherly feelings towards her!

"Ya blush easily, lass. Why is that?" Duncan asked, sounding quite serious. Aishlinn blushed again and thought that perhaps she should just permanently dye her skin red then no one would be the wiser. She could not find the words to answer him so she remained quiet.

"Is it because ye dunna believe me?" he asked.

She was beginning to grow quite flustered for she truly did not want to blatantly accuse him of lying. "Exaggerating perhaps?" she asked hoping her answer did not insult him. His eyes twinkled when he smiled.

"Nay. I told ye long ago that Highlanders dunna lie, dinna I?"

"Aye, you did. But you also said you might stretch the truth on occasions when it was necessary," she pointed out to him.

His brow creased. "I did, dinna I?"

"You did, Laird McEwan." She was trying not to smile at him for he had a scowl upon his face and she was not certain if he was perturbed with her or not. "So you can see how I might come to that conclusion. That you may not be actually lying, just merely stretching the truth." She took a deep breath, hoping he would not become angry with her for saying what she truly thought.

"I see. Well, there are other things that a Highlander never does."

Aishlinn swallowed hard and tried to sound far less flustered than she actually was. "What is that?"

"We never lie about a woman's true beauty."

Aishlinn's heart skipped a few beats as chill bumps began to cover her skin. What she would not give for Duncan to think of her as more than a younger sister.

Disappointingly, the song ended far too soon. Black Richard appeared by her side again, asking for yet another dance. Aishlinn truly did not want to insult him, but she had been dancing for quite some time and if she could not dance again with Duncan, she would very much like a cup of ale.

As she stood between Black Richard and Duncan another much younger lad came to her and asked her to dance. Feeling a bit overwhelmed at the moment, she politely declined his invitation but was soon approached by another.

She looked to Duncan for help but he was busy clenching his teeth and chest-to-chest with Black Richard. They scowled at each other as if they were ready to come to blows. She had no idea what had happened to anger either of them. She did not want the night ruined by two daft men so she quickly stepped in between them.

"Duncan, could you please take me to a table so that I might sit down to cool for a moment?" Her voice was pleading.

"Aye!" he nearly shouted as he grabbed her by the arm and took her from the dance floor. He walked quickly, bypassing the tables and chairs, pulling Aishlinn along by her hand. As they raced past a group of young men, one shouted out a request for a dance with her. Duncan turned and glowered at the group of lads. He said nothing for the look he gave them was enough to cause them to back down and away.

Aishlinn was confused by Duncan's sudden change in mood. She had to practically run to keep up with him as he pulled her into the dark kitchens. They were empty as everyone was in the gathering room enjoying the dance.

They stopped near a table and as Duncan was about to say something, a lad walked through the door. "Aishlinn!" he shouted with a hopeful smile. "Will ye have a dance with me?"

Duncan growled. The lad's smile faded instantly and he fled the room. "Duncan!" Aishlinn said, "What in heaven's name is the matter with you?"

He let out a heavy sigh before he took her hand again and pulled her outside. He needed to be alone with her and was growing quite weary with the interruptions. He pulled her around the castle and up several flights of stairs until they stood near one of the guard towers.

By the time they stopped, Aishlinn was completely out of breath. She was glad for the cool night air but was genuinely confused by Duncan's behavior and why he had brought her to the towers. Perhaps she had done or said something wrong and he was ready to give her a brotherly chastisement.

Not knowing what to say at the moment and feeling very uneasy, Aishlinn smiled at him. "Thank you Duncan, for a very grand night." She took in a deep breath of air and prayed for her stomach to settle and her heart to quit pounding. A cup of ale would have been good at this moment for her mouth had suddenly gone quite dry.

Standing in silence, Duncan watched her closely. God's teeth she was beautiful beyond all measure. He desperately wanted to tell her how he felt about her and for a chance to kiss those sweet full lips of hers.

"Thank you as well, for having all the men dance with me. 'Twas very kind of you to do that."

His brow furrowed with irritation. "Aishlinn, I did no' do that."

She cast him a disbelieving look. "Of course you did! Why else would they have all danced with me?" She rolled her eyes at him, not believing him for a moment. He needn't be so polite she thought.

"Did ye ever stop to think it's because of how beautiful ye look this night?" he asked, exasperated with her naiveté.

She had assumed they all danced with her at Duncan's request. "Nay! I thought they only danced with me because you asked them too."

To think for even a moment that it had been for any other reason was something that neither her heart nor her mind could grasp. "I thought you did it to be brotherly to me."

Duncan let out a very deep and heavy sigh and ran his hand through his hair. He could not hold himself in any longer.

"Aishlinn, I dinna ask any of them to dance with ye!" He began pacing around the small area in which they stood. "They danced with ye because yer a beautiful woman, no' because I put them up to it!" He hadn't meant to raise his voice and he was very glad to see that she did not cower in fear, as she would have done not too long ago.

He continued to pace. "If 'twere up to me, ye'd no' have danced with any of them!"

Certain she was that it was just his brotherly affections for her that made him want to protect her, she walked to him and placed her hand upon his arm.

"Duncan, 'tis nothing to worry over." She tried to get him to look at her. "Such an overly protective brother you are!"

His fierce blue eyes pinned her in place as he let out a very slow breath. "Aishlinn, I can assure ye my thoughts and feelings for ye are far from brotherly." His jaw ached from clenching it. "They're down right sinful."

She was completely astounded by his remark and she knew not how to respond to it. Certainly he had consumed far too much ale. Her heart warned her against thinking anything else.

"Aishlinn, if I were to kiss ye right now ye'd know it no' to be a brotherly kiss, but one filled with great passion and want of ye."

Such a strange look he had upon his face. As she stood frozen, too flummoxed even to blush, she tried to make sense of what he was saying but her mind was unable to focus. Certainly he could not be serious that he wanted to kiss her.

'Twas then that he did the most remarkable thing. He took her face into his hands. He paused long enough to look into her eyes for just a moment before he bent and touched her lips with his own.

Good Lord above she could not breathe! 'Twas the most tender and gentle of kisses. Her knees buckled, her heart stopped beating and for the life of her she still could not breathe!

She melted into him them, returning his kiss as she wrapped her arms around his waist. Certainly it was instinct that kicked in, helping her to respond to his touch, for she had no experience to guide her. It seemed her heart was having a fierce battle with her stomach to see which could jump from her body first.

The kiss deepened becoming more passionate as the moments passed. He slid a hand around her neck and drew her in closer. He did not want this moment, the kiss or the way he felt to ever end. He wanted her more than he had ever wanted any woman or any thing in his life. His heart pounded ferociously when he felt her melt into his arms. It was nearly all he could do to keep from taking her then and there on the rooftop.

When she felt she was about to faint from lack of air she pushed herself away. She wondered how long it would be before she would regain the feeling in her legs. Her mind swirled with excitement, shock and wonder. Many a time in the past, she had wondered what her first kiss would be like. What the earl had done to her, as far as she was concerned, did not count. Duncan's kiss was the kiss dreams were made of.

Standing there in the dark she looked at him, still quite surprised at what he had said and what they had just done. It took a moment or two before she found her voice.

"Why?" It was the only word she could find the strength to utter.

"Why what, Aishlinn?" he said as he smiled at her, wanting to take her in his arms again and to kiss her for the next fifty years or so. He, too, thought it a most splendid feeling when his lips touched hers. It was something he was quite anxious to feel again.

"Why did you kiss me?"

Duncan smiled as he pulled her back to him and looked deep into her eyes. "There are many reasons, Aishlinn," he told her.

"'Tis yer beauty. 'Tis the way yer dark green eyes get a fire in them when yer sore at me. 'Tis the way ye walk and talk and the way ye laugh. 'Tis the way ye treat everyone so kindly. 'Tis everything about ye, Aishlinn."

She could not have been more stunned had he sprouted a second head. "But certainly you would want a more buxom woman, someone worldly, someone who would set your soul on fire. I am not that kind of woman Duncan! Look at me! I'm --"

He kissed her again before she could say anything else. Her mind raced in a thousand different directions at once. She had wished for this moment, had prayed for it. But she had convinced herself weeks ago that such a thing could not be. As their kiss deepened, she felt all those disinclined thoughts begin to fade away.

She was melting into a pool of something unrecognizable. She wrapped her arms around his neck, unable to think of anything but this kiss. Playfully he nibbled at her bottom lip with his teeth and as she opened her mouth to gasp, his tongue began to search for hers.

Unbelievable sensations began to come over her. Certainly it was not a proper and ladylike thing to do, to allow a man to touch her tongue with his own! She tossed that notion aside. She cared not if it were proper for it brought the most magnificent sensation to her body. She grew quite warm and her knees grew weaker the longer they kissed.

It was as if a deep fire of want and passion had been set aflame in his belly. 'Twas more than just a physical desire to be with her, to lift her skirts and take her then and there. Nay, it was so much more than that. His soul ached for her to be his, for her to love him with the same intensity that he loved her. He wanted her heart.

He had not lied to her; it had been everything about her that made him mad with want and desire. His heart melted like the wax of a candle when he felt her return his kiss again. Knowing well that she had not ever been with a man made him want her all the more. It was more than her beauty and her heart, 'twas her innocence that made him love her.

Aishlinn felt that if she did not come up for air soon she most assuredly would faint. Knowing it would probably not impress Duncan much, to have her drop to the ground from lack of air, she finally pushed herself away.

"I must come up for air, Duncan!" she whispered to him, afraid to let go of his arms for fear she would fall. She fought to take air into her lungs and her body seemed to have lost all control of itself.

"Now," he asked smiling at her, "do ye believe me when I say that yer beautiful?"

She shook her head, unable to think clearly, unable to find her voice. "I think so," she said, her legs still quaking.

"Did ye like that kiss?" he asked her.

"Aye," she said taking in deep breaths. It took several moments before she could finally look into his eyes. She knew not how to describe the intensity of it, the way her body quivered. She decided she needed to say something for fear of appearing a fool. "It was quite nice."

Her face burned when he laughed at her. "Quite nice?" he asked as he bent down and kissed her upon her neck, in that tender spot right behind her ear. She had to remind herself to breathe again.

"Did it make yer legs quiver?" he asked playfully.

Her eyes were closed and she could not answer for his lips made it impossible to say anything. She could not even respond by nodding her head. She'd been reduced to a quivering pool of jelly, unable to think let alone form any type of coherent sentence. Who knew such power could exist in a kiss or a touch?

"Did it make yer heart feel as though it would leap from yer chest?" He asked as he ran the very tip of his tongue along the whole length of her slender neck. She wondered how he knew it as chill bumps came to her skin. 'Twas an exquisite sensation.

He finally put his lips upon hers to kiss her, to taste her, to let her know through that kiss that he wanted her, needed her, and that he loved her. He traced the outline of her arms with one hand while the other clung to her waist.

He wished he could feel her bare skin against his own as he traced his fingers along her arm up to her shoulder before gently moving down her back. A passion swelled in him, a passion that ran deeper than any ocean as he felt his manhood begin to swell.

Fervent want, a desperate need to have her skin against his, to feel her naked and warm against his own body, the thought of taking her then and there became too much. No matter how badly he wanted it, he could not do that to her. Aishlinn was special, sweet and innocent. She was everything he never knew he would want in a woman.

Though he could no longer hide his feelings for her, he could give her the respect she deserved. He would take his time to court her before he would ask for her hand in marriage. A few months ago he would have laughed at such the notion of marriage, of settling down. Now it was all he could think of. How long, he wondered was a proper courtship? If he had not worried she would run from him in terror, he would have summoned a priest immediately.

Excitement began to swell in parts of her body that she had not known she even possessed until he had kissed her. She found herself aching, wanting and needing him with a hunger she had never experienced before. It was all so very new and very exciting yet it terrified her at the same time. How could he want her? Would she sorely disappoint him?

Duncan could stand it no more and knew well that if he did not end the kiss that he could not be held responsible for the actions that would most assuredly follow. Gently, he pulled her away. "Aishlinn, I fear we must stop now."

Disappointed, she gasped, "Why?"

A broad smile came to his face. "I fear if we do not stop now, I'll do all manner of quite sinful and wicked things to ye."

Aishlinn took a deep breath, certain she knew what he meant. She was tempted to tell him that he could do anything he wanted to her as long as he continued to kiss her.

He rested his chin upon her forehead as he tried to steady his own breathing. He was glad that he had finally succumbed to the need if not to directly tell her, then to show her how he felt about her. His only hope was that he could be patient with her during the proper courting process.

When she felt her heartbeat begin to slow, she could not resist the urge to hug him. There were so many questions she had, questions she was terrified to ask. Did he want her as he would a wife, or would she be nothing more than a conquest? Not having the courage to ask it outright, she whispered into his chest, "What now, Duncan?"

He kissed her tenderly upon her forehead and smiled. "I would verra much like yer permission to court ye properly, lass." He closed his eyes and prayed she would say yes. "If that is something ye would like as well."

As she hugged him again, he could feel a sense of relief wash over her. "I would like that very much," she said softly. "But I must warn you, I've never been courted."

Duncan chuckled at her. "'Tis all right, lass. I'll help ye through it."

She could hear the mischievousness in his voice and found she rather liked it. She held on to him, wanting never to let go. She smiled when she thought of this tall, handsome Highlander who not long ago terrified her and now whose arms were the only place she felt truly safe. He wanted to court her. 'Twas delightful indeed.

Twenty

Too much whiskey consumed over the past few months had turned his eyes yellow and glassy. His skin hung loosely on his face and it held the gray pallor of someone much older than his true years. It gave one the impression that death was probably not far off. When death finally came for him there would be no one to mourn the loss.

He lay there in his dirty bed, propped up against dingy pillows. Attacked by a fit of coughing that brought large wads of phlegm to his mouth, he spat across the room. He wiped his sweaty face and phlegm-covered mouth onto the sleeve of his stained nightshirt. His lungs begged for fresh air but he was far too ill to leave his room.

It wasn't a disease that had attacked him; it was his own mind. He tried yelling for the chambermaid but he was too weak to yell loud enough to be heard. Angry that he had been like this for far too long, he picked up the mug from beside his bed and threw it against the wall. Moments later, a very frightened chambermaid came rushing into his room to see what was the matter.

"Where is Edward?" His attempt at shouting sounded more like a harsh whisper. "I need Edward now!" The yelling brought about another coughing fit. The frightened young chambermaid curtsied and left quickly without saying a word.

"Once I'm well again," he said to the closed door, "You'll not be looking at me that way, ye whore!"

He lay there for a long while before his champion, Edward, came into the room. Trying to hide the pity and disgust he held for the sickly man, Edward said, "What is it you need, sire?"

"Have you found the whore yet?" he demanded to know, needed to know. Death might be nearer than he wanted to admit to, but he refused to die until the wench was returned to Penrith and he had killed her with his bare hands.

"As I told you earlier sire, we are still looking for her." Edward had returned just that morning from searching the lands north of Castle Firth. There was no sign of the one the earl referred to simply as "the whore".

Their search had begun not more than a month ago, days after the earl had been found stabbed and near death. Days had passed while he lay unconscious and unable to communicate to anyone what had happened. The list of suspects who might want to see the earl dead was quite long. It included nearly everyone in the castle. Truth be told, Edward's own name was very high on that list.

When death had decided to leave the earl be, he awoke several days after the event. Delirious with fever and infection, it had taken several more days after that before he was able to confide in Edward what had taken place.

The earl would have nothing short of killing the young maiden with his own hands.

Some three weeks after the stabbing, the horse the maiden had stolen in order to flee had returned. The gray mare had come galloping in from a northerly direction and they had assumed that must be the direction in which she fled.

They had ridden as far north as they possibly could with no visible sign of her. Of course the many spring rains had washed away any trail she might have left behind. It was pure conjecture on their part in which direction she had gone.

Edward was convinced that either the maiden was dead or she had fled east and was now living quietly in London. He had tried sharing his thoughts with the earl but he could not convince him of it, therefore the search continued. The earl was possessed, consumed with finding her, and that made the ill man unable to think clearly.

Quite frankly, Edward had grown weary of searching for the maiden. He had no desire to return her to the earl if he did find her. He was simply doing what he must until the bastard finally succumbed to his own madness or whatever disease seemed to be attacking his body. Edward told himself that if he ever did run across the maiden, he would probably thank her, if not for actually killing the disgusting man, then for at least speeding up the process.

"Have you men been searching the south?" he demanded.

"Yes sire, we have." Edward had answered that same question many times before. He hoped the earl did not see the distaste he held for him. It was true that the earl was too sick at the moment to fend off anyone, let alone to bring any type of physical pain to a person. But unfortunately, he was still the Earl of Penrith and certain customs must be maintained.

"Then go west, into the Highlands," he said fighting back the urge to cough again. "I want that whore found and returned to me. Do you understand Edward? I want to feel her body grow cold as I take the life from it!"

"And what if we find she is dead, sire?" Edward asked.

"Then bring me her bones. I'll grind them into a fine powder!"

Edward was convinced the earl had gone completely mad. He had even shared his thoughts with the king just days ago. But the king would not make a decision on who should replace the earl; instead the king chose to wait until death finally claimed the man.

"I want every village, every cottage and every castle from here to Ireland searched for her. I want her found and returned to me, do you understand that Edward? And if you come back again, without the whore -- dead or alive -- then I shall hang you myself."

Twenty-One

The official courting between Duncan and Aishlinn began at sunup the next morning. Duncan had met with Aishlinn outside her bedchamber holding a bouquet of tiny yellow flowers that he had himself picked. He had risen early in order that he might pick them without the scrutiny of his men. The needling and taunting would have been endless. When he gave them to her, she smiled sweetly before turning red. Casting her eyes to the floor she said, "Thank you, Laird McEwan."

Shaking his head and rolling his eyes be pulled her to him and kissed her. Aishlinn felt as though she were a willow bending in the wind when his lips touched hers. She could not stop the shudder that flooded over her and it took several long moments before she could breathe again.

"That," he told her as he kissed her forehead, "is the proper way to thank me."

Aishlinn did not think she would ever have the courage to be so bold as to take a kiss from him. Although she enjoyed receiving his and felt he could kiss her nearly anytime the desire came to him, she was not certain she could ever be the instigator.

He took her hand and placed it upon his arm as he escorted her to the kitchens. "I would like nothin' more than to spend the day with ye, Aishlinn, but I've much work to do this day," he told her as he gave her hand a slight squeeze. "I trust however that ye'll not allow anyone else to court ye before I've finished my duties," he said.

She had not realized he was being playful with her. "Duncan! How can you even suggest such a thing?" She asked, horrified that he would even let the thought cross his mind.

Shaking his head and rolling his eyes again, he kissed her sweetly. "Mo chuisle," he whispered in her ear. She had no idea what he had just said, only knowing that whatever it was, it sounded beautiful coming from his lips. Smiling, she turned from him and stepped into the kitchen to begin her day.

Her smile rarely left her face that morning as she peeled vegetables, washed dishes and swept. Each time she thought of Duncan, her smile would grow broader and when she thought of the kisses they had shared, she'd often turned crimson.

Before the morning was half through Mary had caught on that something was definitely different with Aishlinn. "A stoirin, what has gotten into ye?" she asked with a knowing smile. "I've never seen ye smile so much!"

Aishlinn blushed and said nothing, clamping her lips closed as she peeled more vegetables. She wasn't sure if it was proper yet to let anyone know that Duncan was courting her. Mary studied her closely for a moment. "'Tis someone yer in love with, isn't it lass?" Mary said, winking at her. "Love be the only thing that can put a smile like that on a girl's face. I'll wager I ken who it is that put it there too!" she said, tossing leeks into a bowl.

Laren, one of the other kitchen workers, had overheard the conversation and came to them, anxious to find out more. "Love ye say, Mary?" She looked Aishlinn up and down before pulling a chair to join them. "I think yer right, Mary! Look how the lass smiles so." She elbowed Mary. "Have ye kissed him yet?" she asked, winking at Mary.

Another flush of red came to Aishlinn, but she was resolved to remain quiet on the matter. Mary and Laren exchanged glances with each other before leaning in closer to Aishlinn. "Ya have kissed him!" Mary exclaimed. "How was it, lass?"

Aishlinn shook her head but could not contain the smile. The kiss was beyond anything she could have imagined but she would not share that thought with anyone. "Och!" Mary said, looking to Laren. "I think Aishlinn be one not to kiss and tell Laren!" The women giggled at each other.

"Who be it lass? Tell us!" Laren asked anxiously. Aishlinn shook her head and tried to concentrate on the task before her. Although it was rather difficult and she really wished she could shout to the world that Duncan was the one who had put the smile on her face, she remained quiet.

"Now, Laren!" Mary said, chastising her. "It's apparent the lass dunna want to tell us, although I've a good suspicion as to who the beasty is," she said leaning in to her friend and winking at her. She righted herself and looked back at the leeks. "Black Richard be a good man."

"Nay!" Aishlinn said loudly as she shook her head. She leaned in and whispered, "It isn't Black Richard!"

Mary knew full well it was Duncan. She was merely having fun pulling the secret from the young woman. "Nay?" she feigned surprise. "But he be such a fine, braw man!" she said, trying to look disappointed.

Aishlinn shook her head again and leaned closer to the women. "It is not Black Richard, Mary." She looked to the two women unsure if she should trust them with her secret. "I'm not sure if it is proper to say who it is."

Laren laughed at her. "Lass, whether ye tell us or not, everyone's bound to figure it out sooner or later. Besides, Mary and I have our suspicions."

"Yes and your suspicion was wrong when you guessed Black Richard."

Mary chuckled. "Lass, we know it be Duncan."

"How did you know?" Aishlinn asked bewildered.

Shaking her head, Mary said, "Och, lass! Everyone be seein' the way he looks at ye, and ye him." She raised an eyebrow. "Ya haven't bedded him yet have ye?"

She blushed at such a notion. "Nay!" Aishlinn said rather offended by the question. "Duncan has been quite honorable in that regard." Finished with peeling another carrot, she tossed it into the bowl before her. "He wants to court me first."

"He wants to court ye? Did he tell ye that?" Laren said suspiciously.

"Aye. He asked me if he could."

Mary looked quite shocked at the news. "My Duncan said he wants to court ye?" Aishlinn nodded her head and wondered why Mary looked so surprised.

"Duncan's never courted a lass before," Laren said breathlessly. "Though he has bed many of 'em in his day!" she laughed.

Mary shushed her when she saw the embarrassment in Aishlinn's face. "Ye'll be scarin' the poor thing, Laren! But ye be right, he has bed many and not a one did he court. Must be love he has in his heart for her."

Aishlinn increased the pace and energy with which she worked so that she might flee this room and these women quickly. The more the women talked the more she worried that there might be only one thing Duncan had in mind and she was not certain she could take it. Could it be he was only going through a courting ritual in order to obtain that which he wanted? Doubt began to creep into her heart with regard to Duncan's attentions.

Mary read the doubt on Aishlinn's face. "Lass! Don't look so forlorn. 'Tis a good thing, him wantin' to court ye."

"Aye," Laren said. "If Duncan's wantin' to be takin' his time to court ye, then it won't be long before he's a proposin'."

"'Tis true." Mary smiled. "I know me Duncan. Just this winter past I asked him when he was goanna to quit beddin' lasses and marry one of 'em and settle down." She smiled across the table at Aishlinn. "He told me, 'Mary, if ever ye find me a courtin' one, then ye'll know she be the one whose stolen me heart. Ye can plan on preparing a marriage feast within a fortnight or two after that'." She nodded her head to Aishlinn.

Of course, Mary left out the part where Duncan adamantly told her twould never happen for why should he settle for one woman the rest of his life when he can have as many as he wanted. There were far too many young women willing to share his bed, married to him or not. Mary had worried for a long time that the lad would never settle down.

"I knew it would take a very special lass to settle that lad down!" Mary said with a smile. She looked to Laren. "So I suppose this means we have at least a fortnight or two to plan a marriage feast."

Aishlinn sat in stunned silence. She had not dared let herself to think, even for the briefest of moments, of the future. He had thrown her completely with his kisses last evening and again this morning, making her knees buckle and her stomach ached with want for him. "Marriage?" she murmured.

"Aye," said Mary as she eyed Aishlinn. The girl had paled at the thought. "Ye'd marry him if he asked, wouldn't ye?"

She had been so caught up in the fact that he had kissed her, had told her he wanted her and had wicked thoughts of her. He said nothing of a future.

"Well would ye?" Mary began to wonder if the lass was becoming ill at the notion of marrying Duncan. Perhaps marriage was not on the lass' mind.

"I don't know," Aishlinn whispered. "I had not thought of it." The truth was she had not allowed herself to think it.

"Och!" Laren said. "Of course she would, Mary!"

Mary studied Aishlinn for a moment. "Maybe it not be the weddin' of him she's worried after, that causes her to go pale, but it be the beddin' him part!" Both women looked at each other before they burst out with more laughter.

Aishlinn's mouth fell open, embarrassed and shocked that these women would say such a thing. Mary was old enough to be Aishlinn's grandmother! While Laren was not nearly as old, she had been married for many years and had three children. Aishlinn thought that a mother would know better than to speak of such things.

"Aye, that be it!" Laren said, laughing again when she saw the look of horror on Aishlinn's face. "She be innocent, ye can see that, can't ye Mary?"

"Ye've not bed a man before, have ye lass?" Mary smiled.

Aishlinn bristled. "I do not see where that is any of your concern, ladies." She was appalled to think of speaking of such things in a room filled with so many people. She couldn't imagine discussing it in private either.

"'Tis as I thought." Mary glanced at Laren before turning back to a very red Aishlinn. "That be what worries ye, aye lass?"

Isobel's voice came from the doorway of the kitchen. "What worries her?" she asked.

The three women sat upright as a look of dread came to Aishlinn's face.

"It be nothin' important, Isobel," Mary said as she winked at Aishlinn.

Aishlinn prayed the women would not share the conversation they'd just had over Duncan with Isobel.

"Just a matter of the heart," Laren offered as she bit her bottom lip. Aishlinn sank into the chair.

"Ah. I see," said Isobel. "And whose heart are we discussing?" she asked, looking straight at Aishlinn. "Duncan's?" Aishlinn wanted to slide of out of the chair and crawl away.

"'Tis all right, Aishlinn," Isobel said smiling. "Everyone can see how he feels about ye."

Aishlinn sighed. "Then why didn't I know of it?" She was frustrated. It seemed everyone else had seen it coming but her. She suddenly felt quite immature and far too inexperienced.

Isobel laughed along with Mary and Laren. "Because ye didn't think such a thing could happen," Isobel offered. "Ya still be thinking yer plain and no' worthy of a man's affections, am I right?"

She had her there. Until Duncan had kissed her for the first time last night, she never would have thought such a thing could have happened to her. Aye, she may have wished it and dreamed of it, but to think it could actually happen, that was where her heart had failed her.

"You're right," Aishlinn said, sitting straighter in her chair. It was as if a bolt of lightening had suddenly hit her. The awareness that she had let four selfish, mean and ugly men who did not love her rule her life, even now when she was no longer anywhere near them, gnawed at her.

"My brothers, my step-father, they were just mean, selfish twits." She stood and took the vegetables to the sink. "I am not plain and I am not stupid." Looking at Isobel she said, "I may not be as beautiful as you are Isobel, but I be not a pigling either!"

The more she thought of all the harsh things her father and brothers had ever said to her, the angrier she became.

"I may not be very educated yet, but I will be soon enough." Stewing silently for a moment, she thought of her life thus far while Isobel, Mary and Laren looked at her with proud smiles on their faces.

"I promise you this, you'll not hear me say I be plain or I am not good enough ever again." She put her hands upon her hips as a scowl came to her face. "It be them, my brothers and my stepfather who are ugly, mindless fools and I promise you this as well, I'll never let another man say or do those things to me again."

She walked out of the room, uncertain from where her newfound courage came. Resolved to take a firm hold of her life, she left behind three women who could not be more proud of her than they were at that very moment.

"God's bones, it's about time!" Isobel said. "I wondered how long it would take the lass to figure it out."

"Aye," said Mary. "I pity the fool that crosses her! He might come away missing something dear to his heart!" The other women agreed as they laughed themselves silly over it.

There had been very little time to meet privately with the McDunnah the day before. At first Duncan had been glad for the arrival of Caelen and his men, but once he'd seen the way Caelen looked at Aishlinn, all good feelings were flung out the window.

After having time to think on it, Duncan realized he could not hold the McDunnah's behavior against him forever. He needed to keep the good relations between his clan and theirs for a multitude of reasons. Every Scot loyal to King David would be needed in order to free him from the hands of the English. It would do no good for the clans to waste precious resources fighting amongst each other. They needed their strength to fight against the English.

There was still a good chance that the English would seek out justice for the murder of the Earl of Penrith. The Clan MacDougall had given refuge to the person responsible for the earl's death and he knew the English would use that fact against not only his clan but all of Scotland. The English would use the earl's death as a means of seeking retribution against them. It was just the excuse the English needed to attack and invade.

Duncan would need every able-bodied man he could get his hands on to help defend against the English. He knew the McDunnah was loyal to King David and hated the English as much as Duncan's own clan did. What he did not know, however, was whether or not the McDunnah would fight in order to defend Aishlinn's honor and life.

While the McDunnah was loyal to King David and to Scotland, he was also a very shrewd man. There was a very strong possibility that he would chose not to waste his clan's precious resources if there weren't something in it for him. Had Aishlinn been a nobleman's daughter the situation would be much different. A nobleman might be more willing to pay for the protection of a daughter. But as it was, Aishlinn was a peasant, a scullery maid and an orphan. To date, the only value ever given her was the two sheep her brothers had traded her for.

After leaving Aishlinn at the kitchens, Duncan headed off to meet with the McDunnah. The only thing Duncan had going for him at the moment, was the fact that the McDunnah liked to fight. Caelen McDunnah it seemed had been born for it. Duncan had personally witnessed a time or two where the man had picked a fight just to say he'd fought it and won. Hopefully Duncan could appeal to that side of the man for help if or when the English might come for his Aishlinn.

With her newfound strength and determination Aishlinn tackled her studies that afternoon with the fierceness of a Highland warrior. Smart enough to know she could not learn everything she wanted to in a day, she was determined to succeed and cared not how long it might take.

Bree and Ellen joined her in the study room to help her in any way that they could. Aishlinn decided that while weaving was indeed a wonderful thing to learn she would put that on hold while she turned her entire focus to learning to read and write, as well as speak the Gaelic.

That evening when Duncan came to her room to escort her to the evening meal, he noted that there was something different in her demeanor. She did not look at the floor while she walked; instead she held her head high, her shoulders back, walking with the grace and dignity of a nobleman's daughter.

Although she was quite determined to have a new opinion of herself, not one of conceit but merely one of realizing she was more than she had ever been allowed to be, she was still quite nervous around Duncan. She blushed red when Duncan told her she looked beautiful in the new green gown that Bree and Ellen had made for her. You can't change everything in one night she told herself.

After they had eaten, Duncan asked "Would ye like to take a walk around the loch with me, Aishlinn?"

"Aye. That would be very nice," she said as he took her hand and led her out of the castle and through the gates towards the loch. With no breeze and a nearly full moon, the loch stood gleaming in the darkness like a giant silver platter. Night insects and creatures called to one another, their sounds carried through the warm night air.

As they walked hand in hand Duncan broke the quietness of the night by saying, "There is something different about ye this night, Aishlinn."

"How do you mean?" she asked.

He took a moment before answering. "Ye have a new presence about ye, as if yer stronger, in yer heart." He gave her hand a gentle squeeze. "I wonder, was it my kisses that brought this new presence to ye?"

From the corner of her eye she caught his wry smile. "Perhaps."

She was not sure if she should share her morning conversation and awareness with him. Had he not kissed her and she not had the smile on her face, the conversation with Mary and Laren would never have taken place. She felt it right then to give him most of the credit. "I think it had much to do with it."

"But not all?" he asked playfully.

"It was a realization I came to this morning, with the help of Isobel, Mary and Laren," she said.

"And what was that realization?"

She let out a sigh, wanting very much not to sound full of herself. "That I am not as plain as I might have once thought. Nor am I as unintelligent as people in my past might have wanted me to believe."

Duncan stopped and turned to her. "Well it's about time," he said before pulling her to him. "I've been telling ye that for sennights now."

Were it possible for a man to be considered beautiful, Duncan McEwan would be that man. The moon cast silver bands across his twinkling indigo eyes. When he had pulled her to him for the first time last evening Aishlinn was certain his muscles had been chiseled from stone. His arms had felt so hard and strong yet they gave her a sense of safety.

All she could think of at this moment, however, was how badly she wanted to kiss him. Although she had a new inner strength, she did not think she had the tenacity to reach up and kiss him.

He gave her no time to think of it. Before she could get up the courage, he leaned into her, his lips feeling like a whisper, lingering just on the precipice until she could stand it no more. Putting her hands around his neck she pulled him to her, deepening the kiss and surprising herself with her own courage.

His large hands swallowed her waist as he drew her nearer. He felt her teeth as they began to nibble upon his lips, just as he had done to her the evening before. Duncan found himself growing more excited at her boldness. He wondered only briefly from where this new strength, this new confidence of hers came. Briefly only because he was swept away as she searched for his tongue with her own.

Their breathing came faster as they caressed one another. Her hands caressed his face, then his neck before spreading down his shoulders to his arms.

He wanted, needed and hungered for more of her as he pulled her even closer. There was a passion in her kiss, one he had not expected, had not prepared himself for.

Slowly he slid his hands up and down her back, resting only briefly again at her waist before traveling back up her sides. A gasp came from her as he touched the sides of her breasts before winding his way up to her neck.

Aishlinn had never felt this way before, so desperate for a touch, a kiss. She loved the way his mouth felt on hers, warm and moist. It was as if they searched for a deep secret. And when his hands touched her breasts, she thought she would most certainly faint from the sheer pleasure as well as the improperness of it.

The more he kissed her, the less she cared for what might be proper and what not. She only cared that he would kiss her this way again and again. As her breaths grew faster her body grew warmer, as if she had been stuffed into the ovens.

Duncan could have taken her in that moment, there, on the ground in front of the loch and not cared who might stumble upon them. He wanted to feel her skin on his. He wanted to know what she might look like with her naked skin bathed in the light of the moon. And from the way she was returning his kisses, his touches, he thought she might not object.

Before they could do something they might later regret, he pushed her from him. He could go no farther than this, not here, not now. His heart told him he wanted to do this properly, to court her as a she deserved.

Aishlinn looked at him with a look of exasperation upon her face. "Why did you stop?"

Duncan laughed at her. "Lass, I had to or I'd have stripped ye naked and taken ye here and now. I think ye be deservin' a little more respect than that."

He kissed her lightly on her forehead while she took deep, slow breaths in an attempt to calm herself.

"I don't think ye be wantin' me to do that on our first day of courtin'."

As much as she hated admitting it, she knew he was probably right. Even with her new sense of worthiness and confidence, she did not want the first time she laid with a man to be out of doors, on the ground where anyone might happen upon them.

She almost asked him how long he would court her before he would lay with her, but bit her tongue. Thinking she might go mad before it happened, she could only thank him for respecting her. Inwardly, she wished he would behave like the devil she knew he could be. She prayed that the courting process would not take long for she didn't know if she had the strength to hold onto her own self respect and dignity.

For the next few days their routine remained relatively the same. Duncan would meet her outside her bedchamber each morning with little tokens such as a ribbon for her hair or a bit of dried heather or more flowers. He would escort her to the kitchens before heading off to either train or see to his duties as acting chief.

It was not easy to study in the afternoons, what with her stomach tied in knots with anticipation of him escorting her to the evening meal. After the evening meal, they would enjoy a walk around the loch where they would share stolen kisses that were becoming more and more intense.

A light rain had come to Castle Gregor this day, casting dark gray shadows across the loch and lands. The castle felt oddly quiet as if its moods matched the weather around them.

Aishlinn was finding it more difficult to study for her mind kept turning to Duncan's kisses. Bree and Ellen were with her, giggling more over lads than they were concentrating on their studies. Aishlinn shushed them more than once, reminding them that if Isobel overheard their giggling she would be most displeased.

There was a knock upon the study door and Bree jumped up to see who it was. She returned moments later, an impish grin on her face as she clutched a bit of parchment in her hands. Quickly she scrambled back to her seat next to Aishlinn.

"What is it?" Ellen asked. "Who was at the door?"

Aishlinn was trying to ignore them but it was nearly impossible.

"'Twas a messenger," Bree said. "For Aishlinn."

Aishlinn spun to face her. "A messenger? For me?" she was very surprised over it. It was then that she saw that Bree was clutching something to her chest. "Is that for me?"

Bree nodded. "'Tis from Duncan!" She giggled before handing it over. Aishlinn's hands shook with excitement as she carefully unfolded the parchment. Her smile was instantly replaced with a look of disappointment. "'Tis written in the Gaelic!" she said.

"I'll read it!" Bree said excitedly as she grabbed the parchment. Aishlinn was not sure what the message might say and she was worried it would hold some very improper message. Before she could take it back, Bree began to read it aloud.

"Mo Chuisle," she began.

"In English!" Aishlinn pleaded.

"My pulse, my heart." Bree couldn't help but giggle when she saw Aishlinn turn as red as a beet. "My pulse, my heart. Ye are beautiful and I am finding it quite difficult to concentrate on my duties this day. Meet me near the stables as soon as ye read this. Duncan." Bree clutched the note to her chest as she and Ellen giggled again.

"Och! 'Tis so romantic!" Ellen said excitedly.

Aishlinn took the note and folded it as neatly as her trembling fingers would allow. She tucked it into her apron before going back to her studies.

Bree and Ellen looked at her curiously. "Are ye no' going to meet him?" Bree asked.

"Aye, I will," Aishlinn said staring at the pages before her. It was impossible to focus on any of the words.

"But he said as soon as ye read it to meet him," Ellen said, wondering why Aishlinn didn't rush from the room.

"Aye, it did," Aishlinn said, trying to keep her voice calm.

Bree and Ellen exchanged puzzled glances. "Aishlinn?" Bree said, "Why are ye not goin' to him?"

"I don't want to appear too anxious to see him." She finally smiled at the two girls. "I'll go to see him, but when I'm ready, not merely because he says come woman!" she explained. "'Tis not always a bad idea, ladies, to make a man wait on occasion." She wondered how she knew such a thing. Perhaps it was some more of her natural instincts that were kicking in.

Bree and Ellen were stunned at Aishlinn's reticence. "If it were me," Ellen said, "and 'twere me affections Duncan wanted, I'd not make him wait!" she giggled. "I'd have flown to meet him!"

As much as Aishlinn wished she could have sprouted wings and flown as Ellen suggested, she also did not want to appear that she was too ready and willing to drop everything to be at his beck and call. It was nearly all she could do to keep her feet firmly planted and not go rushing to meet him. Aishlinn knew that by making him wait, just a few moments longer, his want of her would grow even more intense and make the kisses even more passionate.

When she felt sufficient time had passed, she finally closed her books. She bid Bree and Ellen a good day and left them giggling in the study room.

She had to will her feet to move at a steady and deliberate pace. Had she not, she would have run at a great speed and it would not do to go to him covered in sweat and out of breath. As she walked toward the stables she could see him pacing back and forth, running his hands through his hair. He appeared more frustrated than she had anticipated and she suddenly felt guilty for making him wait.

He looked up to see her coming towards him and a scowl came to his face. "Aishlinn!" he shouted causing her to walk just a bit faster. "Where have ye been? I sent the message long ago! Did ye no' read it?"

"I received it and it was written in the Gaelic. I did not know all the words, Laird McEwan. Bree had to read it to me." She could not understand why he was angry with her for she had only made him wait but a few minutes.

God's teeth he hated it when she called him Laird McEwan. He took a deep breath and let it out very slowly.

"When I summon ye, it is very important that ye come to me immediately, Aishlinn." He would be made chief one day and it would not do for him to appear weak by being made to wait by his wife, if only for a few minutes.

She raised an eyebrow. "Summon me? That isn't the way your message to me read, Laird McEwan. It professed that you missed me and wished to see me as soon as possible. Had I known it was official business that you summoned me for, I would have come straight away."

His scowl deepened as his voice began to take on a note of anger. "So if I summon ye, ye shall hurry. But if it be a romantic moment alone with ye that I want, ye make me wait?"

She cupped her hands in front of her. "Perhaps, Laird McEwan, you would like me to follow you around like a pup, waiting for your commands to retrieve for you? Or perhaps like a concubine, to be there to serve your needs whenever they arise?" Outwardly she remained calm, or at least hoped for the appearance of it. Inside she was frightened as well as angry with him.

He saw the flame of anger rise in those deep green eyes of hers, "That is no' what I meant, Aishlinn."

He came and towered over her. "I have many duties to tend to and my time is no' my own to do with whatever I please." It was true that he had only but a little while to spend with her. Could she not see or understand that any free moment he had he wished only to spend it with her?

"I do apologize most sincerely, Laird McEwan." There was coolness to her voice as the flame of anger intensified. "So which is it you want me to be this day? Pup or concubine?" She would not shrink, would not cower and would not bend to him. "Is there something you wish me to fetch for you? Or should I lift my skirts and let you take me here and now, m'laird?"

It wasn't just anger he saw in her eyes, there was hurt there as well. He'd been yelling at her as though she were a possession or one of his men, not the woman that he loved with every fiber of his being. "Did ye make me wait fer ye on purpose?" he asked.

"Aye, I did. But only for a few minutes."

"Why?" he asked as the scowl began to soften.

She swallowed hard, not wanting to admit why. "Because I am not a pup nor a concubine nor one of your soldiers nor your mistress." She looked into those piercing blue eyes and truly wanted nothing more than to have him kiss her, but she would not admit to it.

He sensed there was more. "And?"

She took a deep breath. "Sometimes the kisses are better when you are made to wait a moment longer to receive them."

She worried that he would become so incensed with her that he would be done with her, would send her away, either to her room or from the clan altogether.

But he didn't. With no warning he pulled her to him and began to kiss her hard on the mouth, his tongue forcing her lips open as he wickedly searched for hers. As much as she wished to not respond she could not help it. Grabbing his shoulders she pulled him closer as his hands held her waist with a firm grip and she felt his excitement growing against her. The passion was so intense in the kiss that she would have stripped herself bare had he asked her.

As she melted into him, her body weak, her heart pounding, she knew she wanted to be with him for all their days. She wanted to know what it would be like to lay with him each night, and to feel his hands upon her bare skin.

As quickly as the kiss began, it ended when he pulled away from her. A wry smile had come to his face as she stood trying to catch her breath. "Is that what ye meant by better, lass?"

The slightest breeze could have knocked her over as she stood with quaking knees and shuddering body. "Aye," she said breathlessly, wishing he would kiss her that way again and damning herself for wanting him to.

"Well then, I shall no' be so angry with ye the next time ye make me wait."

Twenty-Two

God's bones, this woman was going to drive him completely mad! "Because I said nay," he gritted, arms crossed over his chest. "And I'll hear no more of it."

Aishlinn was standing before him with her hands on her hips and a fierce look of determination set in her eyes. Over the past days she had changed. It wasn't necessarily a new Aishlinn that stood before him. This was the Aishlinn he had been determined to set free, the one he had been sure had lay hidden just under the surface by the many years of abuse and harsh treatment. A small voice inside his head told him he had gotten what he had wished for and he had no one to blame but himself.

It seemed to Duncan that the more kisses he bestowed upon her, the stronger and more determined she became. He was wondering if perhaps he should not hold back on the kisses for a bit. But as he looked at her now with the fire in her eyes and the willful determination to have him hear her out, he knew he could not. She looked absolutely beautiful in the early morning light with the sun casting streaks of red through her hair. He was angrier with himself more than he was with her. 'Twas all he could do not to drag her across the field to the trees and ravish every inch of her body.

"Laird McEwan," she said, trying to hold her anger in. "Would you prefer then, that when we are ever attacked in the future, that the woman go screaming about in a panic, unable to defend themselves?"

"The women can defend themselves, Aishlinn, and they be quite good at it."

He was beginning to miss the days when all he had to do was scowl at her in order to tame her temper. As far as the women she spoke of, they were good with knives. And there were a few he would put his money on in any wager against any man in either contest or battle.

"Aye, but with knives and pots and pans and nothing more. If you would but at least allow them to learn to use a bow--"

Duncan cut her off with a raise of his hands. Although he was glad to see her becoming a beautiful, determined young woman there were limits to how he would allow her to behave in front of his men. She was quickly approaching a line he could not let her cross.

He was silently cursing Isobel for teaching the lass to read, as well as Bree for reading to her the book where she got this cursed notion of hers. A book about a woman who could outshoot any man with a bow and arrow and who had defended her land, her people and her castle to her death. He'd have to talk with Bree later about what stories she'd be allowed to share with his betrothed.

"Nay," he said firmly. They had been arguing back and forth for at least a quarter hour and were standing near the field where the archers practiced. Wee William and Black Richard had come to listen to the argument Duncan was having with Aishlinn. They stood on either side of Duncan with crossed arms, creased brows and firm expressions to show they gave Duncan their support on the idea that women should not be taught to use the bow and arrow.

Aishlinn was trying very hard to not let her temper get the better of her but it was not easy as these three men stood in front of her. Any one of them was big enough to crush her with their hands, but she was not going to allow them to intimidate them with their size. Well, Wee William perhaps, for one couldn't help but be intimated by a man as large and tall as he.

"Laird McEwan," she said, "I can shoot, and quite well, and I see no reason why we," she stopped when the men snickered. The sweet smile she'd been trying to maintain quickly evaporated.

"Do you not believe me when I say that I can shoot, or that I can shoot quite well?" she asked them. Why must men be so thick headed, she wondered?

"Now lass," Duncan began. "It isn't that we don't believe ye." This was quickly getting out of hand and he needed to put a stop to it.

The patronization in his voice was enough to send Aishlinn over the edge of reason. If neither he nor his men would listen to a good and valid argument, then by God, she would show them. She turned on her heal and headed down the slight incline towards the archers, mumbling under her breath as she stomped along. "Stupid, stupid men!"

"This is why the Sassenach do no' teach their women to read!" Wee William said to Duncan as they watched Aishlinn stomp angrily towards the archers.

Duncan was calling after her, but she ignored him. As she neared the archers, she heard Wee William boom out an order for the archers to hold. Some twenty-five men immediately stopped shooting, lowered their weapons and looked towards him.

Aishlinn approached the first archer and without asking, yanked his bow from his hands and pulled an arrow from the quiver that sat at his feet. The poor archer seemed uncertain as to what he should do. If she were any woman other than Duncan's, he would have reclaimed his weapon and given her a lecture as well as a smack or two against her rump. The archer knew that Duncan would have killed him in the blink of an eye for doing just that, so he stood flummoxed and looked to Duncan who was fast approaching.

"Put that down before ye hurt someone!" Duncan boomed. She had just crossed the line.

Aishlinn continued to pretend she could neither see nor hear him and took aim towards the targets the men had been using. The large bales of straw draped with cloth banners stood at different intervals, some at seventy-five yards, others at one hundred, and others yet at one hundred fifty. She decided against a simple target -- even though she was dealing with simple-minded men. If she were going to impress them, she might as well go all out.

She cared not how angry Duncan was at the moment, for she was determined to prove to him that women can defend themselves and could be quite useful in the event of an attack. They only need be taught properly. It was the principal of the matter.

Holding the bow firmly, taking only a moment to choose her target, Aishlinn took a steady breath as Duncan had stopped just steps away from her.

"Do. No'. Release. That. Arrow." He seethed as he pointed his finger at her.

She did not take his words as a command, but as a challenge. Looking away from her intended target she stared right into Duncan's eyes, paused long enough to cast him a look that told him she'd not be treated like a weak minded fool, then let the arrow loose.

The arrow flew over the field, across the bales of straw and landed dead center of a tall pine tree that was a good fifty yards beyond the furthest target. She turned to see if her aim had been true.

"Ha!" Duncan called out as he saw the arrow had missed the large straw targets the archers had been using. "Ya missed!" he said wagging his finger at her and looking as though he had just won a very large wager against a very wee young woman. His delight was short lived however, when he saw the triumphant gleam in her green eyes and a twitch of a smile on her lips.

"Did I hit the tree behind your men's furthest targets?" she asked calmly as she lowered the bow to her side.

Duncan looked confused, for the tree where her arrow landed, was a good fifty yards beyond the furthest targets.

"Wee William!" Aishlinn said. "Please check the arrow. I believe you will find it firmly imbedded into a bit of purple cloth that hangs on the tree." While Wee William ran to the tree, Aishlinn and Duncan continued to glare at one another.

Wee William was utterly astonished to see the arrow had indeed pierced a bit of faded purple cloth, a remnant of an old target the archers had used months ago. The cloth clung to the tip of the arrow when he yanked it from the tree.

He rushed back to Duncan and Aishlinn, shaking his head in amazement at Aishlinn's shooting abilities. "She be right, Duncan!" Wee William smiled as he handed the arrow to Duncan.

"See, there be a bit of purple cloth there on the tip!" he sounded rather impressed, and it was not easy to impress Wee William. "Never seen anythin' like it!" He stopped talking the moment he noticed Duncan's hard-set jaw, furrowed brow and piercing eyes.

Duncan could see that his men were impressed with Aishlinn's shooting skills. He had done enough to wake the fierceness in her. The last thing he needed was his men's encouragement fanning the flames of her independence. While he would have loved to admit that she was good, quite good in fact, he had given her an order that she blatantly ignored. And she had ignored it in front of his men.

Duncan yanked the bow from her hand and gave it to the stunned archer before grabbing Aishlinn by her arm. His face was purple with an anger he had not thought he could ever feel towards her as he pulled her up the incline and towards the castle. While he might enjoy the fact that she was maturing and turning into a fine woman, he could not have her openly defying him in front of his men.

He said not a word until he was near the kitchens where he paused momentarily and yanked her around to face him, not once releasing the hold on her arm. "Do no' ever defy me in front of me men again." He was beyond anger and his face had twisted into a fury she had never seen in him before and it frightened her.

She refused however, to allow him to see how his anger was affecting her and willed her arms and legs to not quake. "I merely wanted-" she began before he cut her off.

"I care no' what yer intentions were, Aishlinn! Ye openly defied me in front of me men and ye'll never do that again." His voice resembled a low growl.

He pulled her to the kitchens, threw open the door and nearly tossed her inside. He took one step inside and searched for Mary who stood motionless near the basins, surprised by the commotion and the look upon Duncan's face.

"Mary!" Duncan boomed. "Take Aishlinn to her room immediately." He refused to look at the subject of his wrath, who stood just a few steps from him.

"Do no' allow her out. She's to stay there until I say otherwise! Is that understood?" Everyone in the kitchens stopped dead in their tracks as he yelled his command.

Mary could only nod her head yes, for she had never seen Duncan as angry as he was at that moment. Duncan turned his scowl to Aishlinn for only the briefest of moments and without a word he left and slammed the door closed behind him.

Aishlinn had been holding her breath while he was barking his orders and did not let it out until the door slammed behind him. She nearly collapsed to the floor as she released it. She stood shaking as Mary and Laren rushed to her side.

"Lass!" Mary said. "What on earth have ye done?"

Aishlinn could not speak, unsure if she was angrier or more frightened. She lifted her skirts and headed out of the kitchens to go to her room, which she had no intentions of leaving, whether he bid her to or not. Mary and Laren followed after her.

"Lass, tell us, what have ye done to anger Duncan so?" Mary was as shocked as anyone to have seen Duncan that furious.

"I merely wanted to prove him wrong, to show him that I could use a bow and arrow. But he would not listen, the stubborn fool!" Aishlinn said as she climbed the stairs. "I only wanted him to listen to me, to listen to my idea, to hear me out, but he would not," she said, holding a firm grip on her skirts as she tried not to fall down for her legs were still shaking.

"He told me not to shoot the arrow, but I did it anyway."

"Ya mean ye shot it after he said no' to?" Laren asked breathlessly, surprised at the young woman's audacity.

"Aye, I did," Aishlinn said trying to regain some of her resolve.

Mary whistled. "No wonder he's so mad at ye!" shaking her head as they walked down the hallway towards Aishlinn's room. "Were there men about when ye did it?"

"Aye," Aishlinn said, pushing her shoulders back.

Laren opened the door to Aishlinn's room and led them in. "Why would ye do such a thing, lass?"

"He would not listen to me!" Exasperated by the entire incident, she sank down onto the stool near her fireplace.

Mary and Laren stood smiling at her and shaking their heads. "Lass," Mary began. "There be better ways of getting' what ye want from a man. Better n' makin' him so mad he locks ye away in yer room."

Laren nodded her head in agreement. "A lot more fun for the both of ye too!"

Aishlinn stared at them blankly for she had no idea on earth what they were talking about. "What do you mean?" she asked, growing more frustrated as each moment passed. How dare he think he can order me around as if I were one of his men?

"Ya leave him satisfied with ye." Mary winked at her.

"Aye. A man will give ye anything yer heart desires if ye've just left him feeling," she searched for the right word. "Fulfilled."

Mary and Laren giggled but Aishlinn was too angry to make sense of it. The women caught note of her confusion.

"Lass, it'll do ye good to know, for future reference, that ye have more power over a man than ye realize." She looked to Laren who nodded her confirmation. "When ye've laid with yer husband, or yer man, and ye've just knocked the wind from him with a good bout of lovin', that's the time to ask fer what ye want."

Aishlinn cocked her head and suddenly realized what the women meant. Horrified, she said, "I've not done that with Duncan!"

How on earth could they even suggest such a thing? Especially right now. The last thing she wanted at the moment was advice on the delicate intimacies between a man and a woman. What she wanted was a large club with which to pound on Duncan's skull.

They laughed at her. "Lass, we ken ye haven't!" Laren said. "'Tis probably why Duncan be so frustrated of late!" She and Mary burst out laughing again.

"Aye!" Mary agreed. "Nothin' can make a man more frustrated than not havin' those physical needs met!"

Laren smiled broadly. "Aye! Me Rupert? If he goes more than just a few days without me attentions, he gets to be a beasty!"

Aishlinn was appalled. "Do you mean to suggest that I," she paused for she couldn't say it aloud. Foolish auld women. They think everything can be solved with a kiss or a tumble under the sheets.

Mary shook her head. "Nay, lass. We mean only to explain to ye one of the reasons Duncan might be a wee frustrated of late."

"But ye must know too, lass, that ye canna defy him in front of his men," Laren offered. "Such a thing makes him look weak and he canna lead his men into battle if they dunna believe in him. If a woman's able to make him daft and weak in the knees and be allowed to walk all over him, well then, what of the enemy?"

Mary agreed. "'Tis true. He has to, at all times, appear strong and firm in their eyes. They must believe that he can lead not only them, but his clan as well."

Mary came and put her hand on Aishlinn's shoulder. "Lass, we ken ye might not understand it all, but it be good advice we're givin' ye." She patted her shoulder. "When yer with Duncan and his men be around, ye do as he says without question."

"But when yer alone, just the two of ye, and there be somethin' ye want, 'tis then that ye use yer feminine charms and beauty," Laren explained.

Knowing these women were older and had been married many years, she could only believe that they knew more than she, not only on how to deal with a man, but how to please one as well. There were countless questions she would have loved to have asked them, but didn't have the courage. And she was still far too angry at the moment to think of a romantic interlude with Duncan.

"Now," Mary said, taking Laren by the arm and heading towards the door, "ya let him calm himself a bit lass. And when he comes to ye, ye apologize for yer behavior."

Aishlinn began to protest as Mary held a hand to stop her. "Lass, I ken ye think ye've done nothin' wrong and maybe ye haven't. But listen to me on this. Ye apologize, beg forgiveness and make a promise to him that ye'll never argue in front of his men again. That will help smooth things over. There's no sense in fightin' over it, for ye'll be the one to lose in the end." She smiled at her.

"Ask yerself this: do ye want to be right, and take a grand risk at losin' him forever because ye be just as stubborn as he is? Or do ye swallow a wee bit of pride and keep him, and get to love him for the rest of yer days?"

Laren nodded her head in agreement and the two women left Aishlinn alone to ponder the advice they had offered. Days ago she had sworn to herself that she would not bend, would not cower to any man ever again.

She stood and began to pace. Her mind told her that she should not back down nor should she allow Duncan, or any man for that matter, to see her fear. For too many years she had allowed men to belittle her and frighten her into succumbing to whatever demands they might make of her and she refused to live that way again.

'Twas her heart however, that told her that Mary and Laren were right on a few points. And she knew deep down that Duncan's intention had not been to be cruel or belittling towards her.

She did not want to risk losing Duncan, for she truly loved him. She was certain that she could have searched the world over a hundred times and would never have met anyone like him. There would never be another man who could make her heart pound with excitement at the mere mention of his name. There would be no other who could take her breath away with a simple kiss or a touch of his hand. And there would never be another who would make her feel as safe, protected and as cherished as she felt when she was with him. Save for when he was sorely angered with her.

More than likely as well, there would not be another that would drive her to anger with his obstinacy and stubbornness. But no matter how angry she might be with him, she still loved him with all that she was. Her heart truly belonged to him now, and perhaps that made it worth swallowing a bit of her pride.

Twenty-Three

Harry came rushing into the castle at a full run. The guards had sent the young lad in to announce that Angus was home! The boy went crashing through the kitchens shouting the news at the top of his lungs. "Angus be home! Angus be home!"

By the time the boy reached the third floor of the castle, he was covered in sweat and out of breath. He pounded a fist upon Isobel's door, shifting his weight from one foot to the other as he waited anxiously for the door to open.

Isobel had answered her door with a look of concern that was quickly replaced with a bright, beaming smile when Harry told her the news. Excitement swelled over her for she had not expected Angus to return for another sennight. She missed her husband terribly and was glad for his return. But when her thoughts turned to Aishlinn, a momentary dread washed over her. The time for truth telling was near. She sent a silent prayer up to the Good Lord to keep Angus from having apoplexy.

Isobel raced to Aishlinn's room, where she had been sitting since the early morning. Duncan had not yet sent word that she was free to leave for he was still quite upset with her.

Isobel bounded into Aishlinn's room with the news. "Aishlinn! Angus is home!" She said, breathless with excitement as she stood in the doorway.

Aishlinn's heart skipped several beats before she was able to stand. Fear enveloped her for her entire future would be decided this day. Would he send her back to the English? Both Duncan and Isobel had done their best to convince her that would not happen. But until she heard it from the chief's own mouth, she could not shake the fear from her heart.

"Please stay here, in yer room until I come for ye. Do not leave, not even if someone comes to tell ye that Duncan has released ye. Do ye understand?" Aishlinn could sense apprehension in Isobel's voice and it frightened her.

"Aye," she said as her hands began to shake. Her stomach lurched at the thought that Angus would find her family straight away and send her to them. She could not bear being sent away, not now, not ever.

Isobel saw the fear in Aishlinn's eyes and came to hug her. "All will be well, Aishlinn," she smiled at her. "There is no need to worry, lass. Ye'll not be sent away, I promise ye that." She gave her another hug before leaving the very frightened and doubtful Aishlinn standing alone in the middle of her room.

Aishlinn's thoughts immediately turned to Duncan. Tears blurred her vision and a large lump formed in her throat. She loved him, more than she could have imagined was possible. She wrapped her arms around her chest and wished it were Duncan's arms holding her now.

She needed to hear his voice, needed to hear him tell her that all was well. He had been her protector since the moment he had pulled her from the freezing water months ago, a lifetime ago. Kneeling at the end of her bed, she prayed that he still loved her, even after the morning's events. She prayed as well that she'd not be sent away.

It was a striking sight to behold as more than forty horses came pounding through the castle walls, thirty riders in all these tall, strong-muscled men of the Clan MacDougall. Some were shirtless; some wore trews, while others wore the plaids. All were covered with grit and grime from the many days they had traveled to return home. A good number of them appeared to be in their thirties and forties, still well-muscled and sound-bodied when one considered their ages.

The sound of all those hoofs clopping against the cobblestone courtyard, saddle gear jingling, and the people shouting out their welcome homes was nearly deafening. Aishlinn stood in awe as she witnessed the return of Angus McKenna and his men.

Even from where she stood at the tall windows of her bedchamber, she could tell the man on the grey-speckled stallion, surrounded by his men, was Angus. Tall, well-muscled, his golden hair in braids at his temples, he sat tall and proud in his saddle. There was no doubt in her mind for there was only one whose strength seemed to radiate from somewhere within him, casting an aura of strength, honor and nobility.

A sea of very happy people, glad for the return of their men, soon engulfed them. Wives and children came to greet their husbands and fathers and sons with tears in their eyes, relieved they had all returned safely home.

Her assumption that the man leading the group was Angus was clarified when she caught sight of Isobel and Bree rushing to embrace him. He was taller even than Duncan and looked as though he could well hold his own in any battle. He wore a dark blue tunic and blue and green plaids similar to those Duncan wore. Dusty, travel-worn leather boots fit snuggly over massive legs. He was indeed a sight to behold.

It took a long while for the excitement to die down and the people allowed the men to pass. She lost sight of Angus and the others when they entered the castle.

With all the commotion that was taking place, Aishlinn was certain it would be many hours before Isobel would send for her. Her heart ached with dread for her entire future lay in the hands of a man she had never met.

When Isobel and Angus were finally alone in their room, he carefully removed his broadsword and strap and laid them upon a table. Exhausted from riding hard for days, he slowly sat down on the edge of his bed and stretched his legs. Before he could remove his boots, Isobel sat down on the floor and began tugging them off.

"Woman! I've told ye countless times I'm perfectly capable of takin' off me own boots!" Isobel smiled at him and said nothing as she tugged a few times before the first boot came free.

"But ye dunna listen to me, do ye?" There was a twinkle to his green eyes, and a loving smile upon his face. He knew not what he would ever do if anything happened to his wife. She was his entire life and without her, he was nothing.

Isobel had to tug harder at the second boot, and when it finally relented, she lost her balance and fell backwards. "Isobel!" he shouted as he tried to grab her before she fell, but missed.

She lay on her back, laughing as she tossed the boot away. He smiled when he realized she was fine and he slithered from the bed and straddled her, gently holding her wrists to the floor. "Just where I've been wantin' ye for weeks now," he said with a wink.

"Ya need a bath husband, and fresh clothes and a hot meal," she said. "There will be time for that later. Ye've much to tend to."

He had missed his wife far too much to worry about anything but spending a few precious moments with her. "Aye, but ye are the first thing that I wish to tend to, my love."

He bent and kissed her sweetly, his lips pressing tenderly against hers. Wrapping her arms around his neck, she returned his kiss, blissfully glad that he was home. She tried telling herself that it would only be a few simple kisses she would give him before insisting that he bathe, eat and tend to very important business.

Soon the kiss deepened, the passion swelling from deep within them both. Angus' breathing began to quicken and his heart pounded ferociously against his chest. Married these many years now, he still held a fiery want and need of his wife. Too many nights spent apart of late had left each of them with a deep longing and need of the other.

They began to pull and tug at each other's clothing, desperate to feel the other's skin pressed against their own. Eager hands searching, touching, and needing the other to know how much they had been missed.

Before either realized it, they were lost in a frenzied session of lovemaking that would quench the desire that had been building for sennights. But it would quench it only for a short while. They had many weeks of being apart to make up for.

Afterwards, they lay upon the floor tangled up in one another's arms with sweat covered brows and gasping for air. They both knew the satisfaction they felt at the moment was only temporary. Later they would take their time at it and might be locked away in their room for a day or two.

"Now will ye bathe and eat, husband?" Isobel giggled as she laid her head upon Angus' chest.

"Aye. But only if ye promise to bathe with me," he said as he caressed her cheek with his thumb. The image of his wife sharing a tub with him floated in his mind and brought a smile to his face.

Isobel shook her head, smiled and sat up. "Yer nearly as insatiable now as ye were when ye were younger!"

"'Tis only because ye've grown even more beautiful!" 'Twas true, he thought. She had grown even more beautiful over the years.

When he tried to pull her to him again, she resisted the temptation. "As much as I would like nothing more than to join with ye again and again for the next sennight or two, there are important things ye do need to see to, Angus." She bent and kissed him on his forehead. "Tend to those things and I promise, we'll not leave our room for the next few days if that is what ye wish."

Knowing well that she would make good on her promise, he jumped to his feet as he helped her up. "Verra well then. But let's get these matters dealt with quickly," he said as a wry smile came to his face. "I've much more I want to do with ye."

Isobel had decided to have Duncan speak with her husband first. She felt it best that he give his account of how they had come upon Aishlinn and why they had brought her here. She would have time to talk with her husband afterwards.

Isobel's hands began to shake at thinking of what would be taking place in a very short time. As she stood alone in her bedchamber, she poured herself a dram of Angus' best whiskey in hopes that it would calm her nerves. It helped to only temporarily quell her worry. She thought of partaking another dram but knew she'd be no use to anyone if she got too far into her cups. Very soon Angus was going to need her strength and she his.

Duncan waited for his uncle to bathe, don fresh clothes and eat before speaking with him. Angus' private room seemed far too small for such a large man, but still it seemed to suit him. The room had tall windows, much like the other rooms in the castle. Heavy blue drapes were pulled back and let in an ample amount of sunlight. A low fire burned steadily and crackled in the huge stone fireplace. Heavy shelves lined the walls and were filled with books and maps and mementos. A massive desk sat in front of the windows and that is where Duncan found Angus sitting when he entered the room.

"Duncan, my boy!" Angus said, glad to see him. He remained seated, tired and worn from the many days mounted upon a horse. "Isobel tells me ye've something important to discuss with me." His deep voice resonated through the room like thunder.

Duncan took a seat opposite his uncle and let out a long sigh. "I'm not sure where to begin, Uncle."

"I find it usually best to begin at the beginning." Angus studied him for a moment. He could tell there was much on Duncan's mind.

Duncan agreed. He began with the search for the stolen cattle, telling how he and his men had gone looking for the reivers and how they had come upon Aishlinn. Duncan went on to tell him the lass' story of stabbing the earl.

"We could no' leave her alone in the forests uncle, so badly beaten she was. We were certain she would die."

"I wudna expect ye to leave a lass stranded out in the middle of nowhere in such a state!" Angus reassured him and bade him to continue.

Angus' face had turned to a deep scowl by the time Duncan had finished. "Are ye sure the earl be dead then?" Angus asked.

"I've no reason to think otherwise," Duncan replied.

"Well, there is some good to come of it all then." Though glad to hear of the death of the earl, he was still troubled with the fact the young woman was still there. "Have ye no' found her own clan?" he asked.

"Nay," Duncan told him, growing slightly nervous for he knew where the story went and was not sure how Angus would take it.

"Why no'? Let her be their problem when the English come looking for her." The safety and well being of his clan was Angus' first concern. They needed not to battle with the English at this particular time.

"She does no' ken who her clan might be," Duncan told him. "And Isobel thought it best she stay with us while she healed and rested. I agreed with her."

Suspecting his foster son was holding something back Angus studied him closely for a few moments. When Duncan kept averting his eyes, looking about the room at anything but Angus, his suspicions were confirmed.

It suddenly dawned on Angus then, why Duncan was behaving as he was. His eyes flew open and he slammed his hand down hard upon his desk. "Damn it, Duncan! Ye've gone and fallen in love with her, haven't ye?" His face had turned red as he yelled at him.

Remaining calm, Duncan sat straighter in the chair. "Aye. I have."

Angus shot up and began pacing. The last thing he needed at the moment was trouble with the English.

"We've got the clans Keith and MacPhearson ready to attack because they want our land. And now ye add the English into the mix?" The clans Keith and MacPhearson were the main reasons he had spent more time than he wanted to in the far north. 'Twasn't just to help the northern clans to settle their own disputes; he was there to shore up allies for a fight he was certain would be coming from the west. Running his hands through his hair, he continued pacing.

"I sent out scouts, uncle. They searched for days and found no English, no soldiers, no one searching for her. I think the guard who helped her to escape, may have done more to ensure her safety, but what, I dunna ken."

He could only hope that whatever the guard had done or said would continue to keep the English from searching for Aishlinn. He'd feel better about it though if he knew for certain what had happened, what had taken place after Aishlinn escaped.

"We've the support of the McDunnah on our side, should the English come for her," Duncan offered, hoping that would help Angus feel better about the situation.

"The McDunnah?" Angus asked, rather leery.

"Aye. He is here, with a hundred of his men. They arrived a few days ago. They're having troubles with the Buchannans."

The Buchannans were a greedy and lecherous lot of men. Their allegiance was not with Scotland, nor with the English; it went to the side with the most coin with which to purchase it. Unfortunately, their numbers were rising of late and they were fast becoming a rather large thorn in the side of the McDunnah, as well as his own.

Angus took a deep breath. "How bad is it, lad?" he asked.

"I love her. I wish to marry her."

It wasn't the answer he wanted to hear. "Do ye love her enough to die for her?"

"Aye," Duncan said clenching his jaw. He would die for her, a thousand deaths if he had to. He had been angry with her earlier in the day, so angry that he had sent her to her room for her own protection for fear he would say something that he knew in his heart he would later regret. Though he admired her tenacity and stubbornness, there was a time and place for it. Standing on the archery field and openly defying him was not it.

"Well ye may just get yer wish lad, if the English show up here, for we've no guarantee they won't!" Angus said rather impatiently. "Do ye expect the clan to defend her to their deaths as well?"

"They would, without even asking," Duncan said with great certainty. He knew how the rest of the men and the clan felt for her. "They love her as well."

Sighing heavily, Angus shook his head and returned to his desk and sat. "She must be something very special then," he said as he looked at Duncan, understanding fully how the young man felt, for he held the same love and devotion towards Isobel. He would die for her, as would his clan. He could only hope that the need would not arise for such a sacrifice.

Twenty-Four

Isobel had finally come to fetch Aishlinn to take her to Angus. "He may seem a rough man, but in truth, he is no'. Dunna let his size and deep voice fool ye either. Underneath it all is a man with a heart as big as the world, lass. Just tell him what ye've told me, leaving nothing out," she explained to Aishlinn as they stood outside the door to Angus' private room.

"Be not afraid. Tell him everything, Aishlinn." And with that, she gave the frightened lass a hug before she opened the door to send her in. "I'll be right outside the door if ye need me."

Aishlinn paused a moment before entering and Isobel shut the door behind her. She stood on trembling legs for her entire future lay in Angus McKenna's hands. He held the power to allow her to stay or to send her away.

Angus stood behind his desk with one massive arm resting on the wall as he stared out his window. "Be that the lass I've heard so much of?" He said without looking at her.

"Aye," she whispered, too frightened to step forward. He was even more imposing a figure in person than he was when she saw him first from her bedroom window. He was tall with very broad shoulders and arms the size of tree trunks.

Angus remained lost in thought, his gaze frozen as he looked out at his lands. He was trying to make sense of what Duncan had just told him and he felt an overwhelming sense of uneasiness over it.

When he finally turned towards her, a most bewildered look instantly came to his face. His eyes grew wide as he stood in stunned silence, his mouth opened but no sound came from it, and his face had suddenly paled. Aishlinn grew fearful for she had no idea why he looked at her that way and thought perhaps he had suddenly grown ill.

"Laiden," he finally whispered.

Aishlinn was quite surprised to hear him call her by her mother's name. "Nay. I am Aishlinn," she said, wondering if perhaps Duncan had told him of her mother and Angus was confusing their names.

Angus gripped the edge of his desk with both hands. If he let go, he would certainly fall over from the shocking image that now stood before him.

It canna be possible he told himself as utter disbelief took hold of him. He began to wonder if he had not completely lost his mind. A sea of old memories came crashing through his heart and mind and he felt he might drown in them.

"Aishlinn?" he finally asked. His voice was husky for his mouth had gone completely dry. "That was me mother's name."

She had never known another Aishlinn before and wondered then why Isobel had not shared that with her. She was growing nearly as confused as Angus looked to be.

"It canna be," he said, breathless from the shock his system was taking. His face had grown paler. "It can no' be."

"Shall I get Isobel for you, m'laird?" she asked, convinced he had become ill and might need the healers.

He shook his head and straightened himself. Not taking his eyes from her, he quickly came around the desk. He towered over her, his face awash in confusion and pain. Aishlinn grew more nervous and frightened.

"Forgive me, but ye look just like a lass I knew a long time ago," he said with a pained smile. "Laiden be her name."

Aishlinn cocked her head slightly. "You knew my mother?" she asked, bewilderedly.

He knew her mother. A sense of dread then came to her next, for if he knew her mother then he knew what clan she belonged to. The possibility of being sent away flooded her eyes with tears.

Angus had known the moment he saw her that she was Laiden's daughter. There was no doubt for she was nearly an exact replica. 'Twas as if Laiden herself stood before him, a ghost from his past; the sight of the lass before him had taken his breath away.

Angus put his unsteady hands upon her shoulders, unsure if he should believe his eyes and ears. He touched her just to see if she was real. When she did not disappear into a cloud of mist, he gave her shoulders a light squeeze. "Aye, I did."

He guided her to the chair in front of his desk and sat her down. Bewildered and excited, he could not take his eyes from her. He kept shaking his head, muttering under his breath that he simply could not believe she was really here.

When he realized the look on her face had changed from one of curiosity to that of fear, he apologized. "I'm sorry to stare lass, but ye look just like yer mum."

"I do?" Her mother had died so long ago that all Aishlinn had left were memories of things and small moments about her. She had long ago forgotten what her mother looked like, or the sound of her voice. And no one who had known Laiden had ever told her before that she resembled her. It had always been the exact opposite.

"Och! Aye!" Angus said. "All ye have to do is glance in a mirror lass, and ye'll see yer mum!" Angus ran his hands through his hair, shaking his head again. His mind whirled as he tried to make sense of it all. "Duncan said ye be an orphan."

Too afraid to speak, Aishlinn could only nod her head yes. Everyone had told her that Angus was kind, strong, fierce and brave. Unfortunately, no one had mentioned to her that he was daft. Perhaps it was the result of too many battles and wounds to his head.

Angus jumped to his feet and began pacing back and forth. Occasionally he would stop, look at her and shake his head. Aishlinn stayed frozen in her chair completely baffled by his behavior.

After pacing back and forth for a long time, he went and stood before the window, and stared out at the lands before him. For a time he was quiet, as if he were entranced by something that lay beyond the room, beyond the windows. When he finally spoke again, his voice was low and he suddenly sounded quite tired.

"He came to me," Angus began. "Twenty years ago he came to me, with her dress, drenched in blood. Said a band of thieves had killed her as she traveled to see her father."

The pain was as fresh in his heart as the day he had learned she was dead. The same intense anger and guilt returned with those memories.

"She had gone there to see her father -- her father was an Englishman, ye ken." He shook his head as he closed his eyes.

"She said she had to see her father one more time. I begged her not to go, to wait until I returned, but she was a strong-headed woman!" Laiden had been that and so much more. Sweet, bonny and kind, yes, but what a temper the lass had!

"She was beautiful, like ye are. And more strong-headed than anyone I had ever ken. Or have kent since." He let out a long heavy sigh.

"I believed him. He had her dress and it was covered in blood." He took a deep breath and righted himself before turning to look at her. "I should no' have believed the lying bastard!"

He was growing angry at the realization he had been lied to. "I should have insisted he take me to her, show me where she was buried. I was so devastated that I fell into the bottle for months before comin' out again."

Aishlinn listened silently. She had no idea whom he spoke of and was afraid to ask.

"When did yer mum die, lass?" He stood still at the windows his jaw clenched as his hands began to shake with a burning anger.

"'Twas winter. I had just turned five years," she answered him quietly.

"Who raised ye, after yer mum passed?"

"My step-father," she answered, sensing the anger building in him.

"His name, lass!" Angus shouted. "What was his name?"

Aishlinn sank in her chair, growing more and more frightened. "Broc," she managed to whisper. She wished Duncan were here to offer his support and strength, for it appeared the man before her was quickly losing his mind.

A blank stare came to his face. He tilted his head back and a deep, guttural howl of anger came from some unfathomable part of his soul. He sounded like a wounded animal in an unparalleled amount of pain and anguish. Aishlinn sank still deeper into her chair and prayed that Duncan or Isobel would hear him and come to see what was the matter.

When he was finished, out of breath and with so much anger upon his face that Aishlinn was certain he was going to lash out at her, tears burned her eyes. As he came around the desk, his face contorted into an expression she had never seen before on any human, she threw her arms over her head, afraid that he was coming to beat her. Though she had developed an inner strength and resolve over the past fortnights, the instinct to protect herself kicked in.

He knelt before her, taking her hands in his. "Aishlinn. Do no' be frightened of me!" he pleaded. "'Tis no' ye I be mad at lass! I swear it!"

She was not certain if she should believe him. "Do ye no' understand what I've just told ye lass?" he asked, lowering his voice.

"Nay, I do not," she whispered. She could not stop the flow of tears that trailed down her cheeks.

"'Twas Broc who lied to me, lass, lied to me about yer mum. He was the one who told me the thieves had killed her." His eyes pleaded with her for understanding.

Why would Broc have lied to Angus? How had they known each other? "I don't understand." Her mind reeled, trying to make sense of it all.

He took a deep breath. "Aishlinn. I was in love with yer mum. I loved her more than anythin' in this world. Broc loved her as well, but she loved him naught. He wanted to possess her, to break her spirit. 'Twas me she was to marry, no' that son of a whore!"

My mother was to marry Angus? Her head swirled and she was certain she would faint at any moment. Her mother was to marry Angus, but she married Broc instead. Why would she have done that? Why would Broc tell Angus that Laiden was dead? To keep her to himself? And where in this story did Aishlinn fit? Her mind was swimming with a hundred questions she had no answers to. It was becoming increasingly more difficult to breath.

"Yer mother and I were to marry. She went to talk to her father, to tell him the news, Aishlinn, that we were to be married. I was off fighting a clan to the south of us, gone nearly a fortnight I was. I begged her not to go, but she was gone when I returned. Broc came to me, not but two days after I returned, and he told me that she was dead. He had her dress, covered in blood and told me that thieves had killed her."

Her mouth and eyes flew open as the most intense feeling of anger began to boil in her stomach. For a moment she thought she would retch and had to take deep breaths to settle her stomach. Broc had lied. He had lied to keep Laiden to himself. Hatred, even more than what she had felt toward the earl or toward her brothers, swelled. How many other lies had the bastard told?

Angus could see that it was all beginning to make sense to her. He could see the anger as it flashed in her eyes. "Broc had to have lied to Laiden as well, or she certainly would have returned to me."

"I never knew!" Aishlinn said. "I did not learn of it, until the day we buried her, that he was not my real father." The tears burned at her cheeks.

"Moirra was begging him to let me live with her and he refused! He would not allow it!" She wiped tears on the sleeve of her dress. "He said he owed it to Laiden to raise me. All the while I was growing up, he would say that, he owed it to Laiden to raise me."

It made sense to her then, that it wasn't out of loyalty to Laiden he had raised her, 'twas out of guilt or a sick madness in the man's mind and heart.

Angus stood again, anger and rage coursing through his veins. "He may have said that, but that wasn't the real reason why he did it."

Aishlinn lifted her head to look at him. "Why then?"

"Because he hated me more than he loved yer mother. He did it to keep ye from me." With clenched jaws, he tried to maintain his composure. Had she not been there in the room he might very well have torn the entire castle apart with his bare hands, for the anger in him was so intense.

"Keep me from you?" she asked as she wiped more tears from her cheeks. For so many years, she had longed for answers, longed for her mother to be alive and tell her why she had married Broc. Now, as she learned more pieces of the story of her mother's life, she was not certain if she could bear more of it.

"Why? What am I to you?" She was not sure she wanted to know the answer.

Angus' heart melted when he looked into those dark green eyes. A tender smile came to his face as he tried to fight back his own tears, his own agony. He put his hands on her shoulders, his voice cracking from the pain in his heart. "Because yer me daughter."

Aishlinn sat in stony silence for a long while as anger, fury and heartache built inside her. Angus was her father. How many years had she wondered? How many nights had she laid awake wondering and dreaming that she would someday learn the truth? Nothing she could have imagined could have prepared her heart for this moment.

Finally finding her voice, she began to mutter aloud as she paced. She clenched her hands into fists and wished for something to hit. Her voice rose as her anger simmered like grease in a fiery hot skillet.

"He lied. All those years he lied to me. He lied to everyone." What lie might he have told Laiden that would have convinced her to marry him?

"He had to have told her you were dead," she said. "'Tis the only explanation as to why she married him. Pregnant, young, alone and thinking she had no other choice."

Angus sat upon the corner of his desk watching Aishlinn as she paced and swore and cursed Broc.

"That evil, lying, cheating whoreson!" she yelled. "'Tis a good thing he is dead now, or I would travel back to Penrith and kill him with my bare hands!"

Angus had to squash a smile of admiration.

"I would crawl through the bowels and fires of hell on my belly at this moment for a chance to kill him!"

With that temper flaring and those deep green eyes of hers burning with anger, 'twas no doubt of it, she was Laiden's daughter.

How differently his life would have been had he not been lied to. So in love with Laiden he was. He would have gone to the ends of the earth and back for her had she asked him to.

His thoughts turned then to Isobel. How she must be hurting! He loved his wife immeasurably. She and Bree were everything in this world to him. She must have known the truth the moment she laid eyes upon Aishlinn. How her heart must have ached with the knowledge. He felt guilty now, for not being here for her when she first learned of Aishlinn's existence.

He needed to go to Isobel, to hold her close and offer her comfort. Together they would help heal each other's hearts, just as they had done some twenty years ago. They had found a comfort in each other then, as they had both grieved the loss of Laiden.

Angus had not ever expected to love again after losing Laiden, so convinced he was that his heart was broken beyond repair. But somehow, gradually over the following year, he had realized he had fallen in love with Isobel. He had felt a great deal of guilt over it. But he knew in his heart that Laiden would not have wanted him to suffer and grieve all his life for her. She would have wanted him to be happy and to move on without her. He married Isobel nearly two years after Laiden's death. They were blessed with Bree less than a year after.

Aishlinn's voice, still seething with anger, brought him back to the here and now.

"My whole life he told me I be plain, not beautiful, not smart, and not anything like my mother! He'd not let me play like lasses play, with dolls and such. He'd not let me have friends! He kept me busy in the fields and hunting and building things! Treating me as a boy, working me 'til my fingers bled and my body and mind so worn I could not think!"

Angus spoke softly to her then. "Lass, I swear I thought her dead. Had I known, had I known Laiden was still alive, I would have come for ye both." He let out a heavy sigh.

"Had I known ye lived lass, I would have come for ye." Angus needed her to understand that he had thought she had perished along with her mother.

"'Tis not you I am mad at!" she shouted at him. "'Tis Broc and his three sons!"

Isobel had quietly entered the room and gone to her husband. Her eyes filled with tears. Angus pulled her into his arms and held onto her tightly; more for his own comfort and need for strength at that moment, than anything else.

"Why, Isobel, did ye no' send for me sooner?" he asked, kissing the top of her head and breathing in her scent.

"The talks were important, Angus," she said, wiping away tears with the end of her shawl. "But had ye not returned when ye did, I would have sent for ye!"

Aishlinn eyed Isobel curiously. "You knew?"

Isobel nodded her head. "Aye. From the first moment I laid eyes upon ye, I ken it."

"But how?" Aishlinn was not certain she wanted to know the answer and began to wonder how many others might have known and said nothing.

Isobel smiled as she went to Aishlinn and wrapped her arms around her. "Because, Laiden was my sister."

Aishlinn pulled away from Isobel's embrace, shocked and confused. "Why did you not tell me?" she asked.

Isobel took a deep breath. "I felt it best it come from yer father, Aishlinn."

My father? To hear the words aloud, to hear Angus referred to in that manner brought more tears to her eyes. She choked them back, struggling to maintain what little composure she had left. She could not be mad at Isobel for keeping it secret and Aishlinn knew it must have been painful for her to not share it.

"Who else knows?" Aishlinn finally found the courage to ask.

Isobel shook her head. "No one."

Aishlinn slumped back into the chair, her mind racing with even more unanswered questions. Angus was her father and he had apparently loved her mother enough to want to marry her. But why, why did she end up marrying Broc? How had she even known Broc?

Isobel came and sat across from her. "I ken ye have many questions Aishlinn. Some we'll have answers to, others not. I'm afraid the answers ye seek the most are buried with yer mother and with Broc."

She gently squeezed Aishlinn's hands in her own. "Yer mum and I were half-blooded sisters. Her father was an Englishman, but mine a Highlander -- a true Scotsman. My father died when I was but a bairn. Our mum married the Englishman when I was three. He had promised we would stay in the highlands, but soon he changed his mind and forced us to move to the lowlands. We hated it there."

Isobel turned and smiled at her husband. "Our grandmother was the cook here, long before Mary, and we would visit every summer. Our mother had decided to move us here for we all missed the highlands, especially yer mother. We met Angus the summer yer mother turned ten and five." She turned back to Aishlinn who sat stoically before her.

Aishlinn could see the pain in Isobel's face as she spoke. "I was in Inverness when I learned of Laiden's death. I moved back here, to Dunshire immediately." A tear escaped her eye. "I came back to help my mum and grandmother. Laiden's death nearly killed us all, but none more so than Angus."

Both women turned to look at Angus who had been standing very quietly near the fireplace. The pain of the memories could be seen etched across his face.

"Angus had fallen into the bottle for a very long time, so great was his anguish over losing ye both," Isobel said, turning her attention back to Aishlinn. "We all believed the lie Broc had told, Aishlinn. Had any of us even an inkling that what he said was not true, we would have come for ye both."

Aishlinn did not doubt it for a moment. How differently all their lives would have been had they not believed the lies.

"I believe that you would have," Aishlinn said softly as she gave Isobel's hand a light squeeze. She could not blame anyone in this room for anything Broc had done.

"'Twas a year after her death, or what we thought was her death, before Angus and I realized we were in love. We were married and less than a year later we were blessed with Bree," Isobel said.

"My guilt, after seeing ye for the first time Aishlinn, was immeasurable!" she told Aishlinn. "I felt like I had betrayed yer mother, my sister." More tears flowed and she was powerless to stop them.

"Isobel, none of this is your fault, or Angus'," she told her. "This is all Broc's doing. The blame is his, and his alone. You did not betray my mother. Broc did. He betrayed us all."

Aishlinn's heart ached for Isobel and Angus. She knew they must feel a tremendous amount of guilt for believing Broc. They had built a life together, Angus and Isobel. Now, all these many years later, here comes Aishlinn, a ghost from their past, to show them their life had been built on the lie told by a man with a sick heart and a sick mind.

It made sense to Aishlinn now, why Broc had not allowed her to leave his home after Laiden had succumbed to the fevers. Had he allowed Aishlinn to leave him, there was a chance his lie would have been discovered. She wondered if Moirra had known the truth or at least enough of it that she would have seen to it that Aishlinn was returned to Angus. Perhaps that was why Broc kept her: to save his own life.

Angus let out a long sigh. "Aishlinn, I am truly sorry for all that was done to ye." His shoulders sagged with guilt and sadness over the life his daughter had been forced to live.

Aishlinn stood, pushed her shoulders back and her lifted head high. "I'll not have either of you feeling guilty over the lies told by a mad man," she said firmly. "What's done is done and we cannot change it. Broc had control over us for twenty years and I'll not allow him to keep it!" She put her hands upon her hips. "He was a sick man and we all know it. There'll be no more guilt, no more what ifs."

Angus chuckled slightly and shook his head. "Ya do have yer mother's temperament."

A smile came to Aishlinn's face. "I'll take that as a compliment and thank you for it." Too many years she had heard she was nothing like her mother, not in looks or spirit or heart. Her heart swelled with pride to learn those were simply more of Broc's lies.

Isobel went to her husband and hugged him tightly. She whispered something into his ear. Whatever she had said caused him to raise his eyebrows and his lips to curve up rather devilishly. He chuckled at Isobel before turning his attention back to Aishlinn. "I believe we have another matter to discuss," he said.

Aishlinn eyed him curiously and wondered if perhaps there were more secrets to unfold this day. "What matter?" she asked nervously, doubting she had the strength to take any more secrets.

"The matter of Duncan," Angus said. His eyes twinkled when he saw her face burn with embarrassment. "It seems he's fallen in love with me daughter!"

Slowly Aishlinn sat back in the chair. It felt utterly strange, for one, to have Angus so readily refer to her as his daughter. Even more embarrassing was the prospect of discussing her feelings for Duncan with him. She sighed heavily for she doubted Duncan still cared for her, not after what she had done to him earlier in the day.

"It matters not," she said. "He was so angry with me earlier, that I do not think he still holds good feelings towards me."

A scowl came to Angus' face. "Angry with ye? Over what?"

Isobel recounted the incident on the archery field for him. "I see," he said, running his hand along his chin as his face beamed with pride. "Me daughter can shoot that well, aye?"

More embarrassment flooded over Aishlinn. "It matters not that I can shoot well. What matters is that I was rude to him in front of his men." She clasped her hands together to hide the fact that they were shaking.

"I doubt it will be something he can get over easily. I am certain he no longer cares for me as he did."

Angus let out a huge laugh. "Ya think that do ye?"

It was impossible to look at either of them, for fear her true feelings would be readily seen in her face. She loved Duncan, loved him more than anything. But she knew that she had made a terrible mistake by openly disrespecting him in front of his men and she was certain that he would not be able to forgive her. Slowly she nodded her head and whispered, "Aye."

"Well ye better be tellin' Duncan that he no longer cares for ye, because

I dunna think he kens it!" Angus chuckled.

Aishlinn looked at him, quite puzzled. "What do you mean?"

His smile was broad as he put his hand upon her shoulder. "Because right before ye came to see me, he told me that he loved ye."

"He did?" Her heart began to pound and her palms grew moist. Aishlinn knew he had cared for her, but he had not yet told her that he loved her. Certainly Angus must have misunderstood the words Duncan had used to describe his feelings for Aishlinn. "He told you that?"

"Aye, he did." Angus squeezed her shoulder slightly. "Go. Talk to the lad, Aishlinn."

She stood quickly before realizing she could not go to Duncan. "I can't!" she said.

"Why not?" Isobel asked.

"He has not released me from my room yet! He said I was not to leave until he gave his permission." She felt silly saying it aloud. She had disrespected him earlier and wished not to that again.

Angus laughed more boisterously. "Lass, ye go find him. And if he grows angry with ye over it, ye tell him to haud his wheesht or ye'll tell yer father of it!"

Aishlinn smiled and flung her arms around Angus' neck. Her father, she thought. My father. Tears filled her eyes at the thought of knowing that she did in fact have a father and one who was able to care for her, to claim her as his own in the blink of an eye. It mattered not to him that twenty years of lies had separated them and had kept them apart. She was his daughter and that was all that seemed to matter. Tears raced down her cheeks as she sobbed, her head resting on his chest.

Angus patted her back and tears filled in his own eyes. "Lass, don't be cryin' now." He looked to Isobel for help. "I canna stand it when a woman cries!" he said. Isobel came to them both and wrapped her arms around them.

"I haven't met a highlander yet who could!"

After speaking with her father, Aishlinn left him and Isobel and went immediately to seek out Duncan. She wanted to first apologize for being disrespectful to him earlier that morning. She could only hope that he would accept her apology. Secondly, she wanted bring him back to Angus and Isobel and together, they would tell him that she had indeed found her real family.

She was not certain where he might be so she stopped in the kitchens to ask if Mary had seen him. "Aye, a while ago lass. Has he given ye permission to leave yer room?" Mary asked as she stirred a pot of stew that hung in the fireplace.

Without a clue how to explain the last hour of her life, Aishlinn fibbed. "Aye. He has."

"He said he needed some fresh air," Mary said as she cocked her head towards the door. "Ye'll probably find him out of doors. Check the training fields, he likes to go there sometimes to think." Aishlinn was out the door before Mary had time to bid her good day.

Black Richard had spotted her as she exited the kitchens. He ran to catch up with her. "How be ye this fine day, Aishlinn?" he asked as he walked alongside her.

"Fine, and you?" She was on a mission to find Duncan and wanted not to waste time with idle conversation, therefore she did not slow her pace.

"I am well," he said, wishing she would stop for a moment to talk with him. He caught a glimpse of the determined expression upon her face. "Ya seem to be in a bit of a hurry this day," he said.

Aishlinn stopped rather abruptly and put her hands on her hips. "Aye, I am. Is there something you need?" she asked and hoped that she did not sound as perturbed as she felt. She needed to speak with Duncan straight away.

Black Richard reviewed her for a moment. He had been carrying around some strong feelings for her for quite a time now. He decided to throw all caution to the wind, swallowed hard and felt as though he were leaping into an unknown abyss.

"Only the company of the most beautiful woman in the clan." He hoped she would see and hear his sincerity.

She hadn't a clue that Black Richard held any romantic feelings towards her. Had she not been so focused on finding Duncan she would have realized more readily what he was saying. Instead, she was distracted and wanted only to find Duncan.

"Who might that be, Richard? I'll help you find her as soon as I'm done."

He sighed heavily as his shoulders sunk. "I be lookin' at her right now." He wasn't ready to give up the pursuit just yet.

Aishlinn shook her head, anxious to be done with him. "Black Richard, I've really no time at the moment," she said as she resumed walking.

"I can see that, lass," he said resuming his pace beside her. "I wish it were me ye were in such a hurry to find," he blurted out. "And not Duncan."

She stopped, quite perplexed by his statement. Again, men were such confusing beasts. "What do you mean?"

A blind man could see how Aishlinn and Duncan felt about one another. What was not quite so apparent however, was whether or not they had acted upon those feelings.

"Aishlinn, I ken ye have feelings for Duncan, and he ye." He paused for a moment to focus at his feet. "If however, it does not go well with Duncan, the way ye wish," he looked into her face then, into those bonny green eyes of hers and felt a tug at his heart. "I would hope ye would keep me in mind."

Aishlinn was quite confused and not at all certain what the man was getting at. "In mind? In mind for what?"

He could not resist the urge to move a bit of loose hair from her cheek and tuck it behind her ear. 'Twas a very intimate gesture to be sure and one he probably should not have succumbed to the desire to take. He cared not, for he was certain it would be the one and only chance he would ever have to feel the softness of her skin. "As a suitor, Aishlinn."

His statement flabbergasted her, for not long ago, Duncan had told her that Black Richard held nothing more than a friendship toward her. She supposed she should be quite angry with him right now, but could not find it in her heart to be. Duncan had lied, she was sure of it, but he had lied only because he wanted to keep her to himself. Black Richard, although quite a braw and handsome man, did not make her stomach jump or her heart race rapidly whenever he was near the way Duncan's presence did.

Not long ago she would have turned red with embarrassment and not had a clue what to do or how to respond to such a statement. Flattered by his words, she smiled at him sweetly as she laid her hand upon his cheek ever so gently. "Thank you, Richard."

"But?" he was certain he knew what she would say to him next. 'Twould be something along the lines of thank you but no thank you and he felt his heart sink at the thought of it. Regardless of what she would say next, he felt relieved in letting her know he was quite interested in more than a friendship with her.

"But my heart," she said as she pulled her hand away, "belongs to Duncan."

Black Richard nodded his head, disheartened that her hand left his face far too soon. He had known all along but had decided to take a chance anyway. At least they both knew for certain where the other stood.

As he was beginning to bid her good luck with Duncan, from out of nowhere he heard a low, guttural growl right before being knocked completely on his arse.

Seeing Aishlinn and Black Richard together had been more than he could take. Duncan had been standing with Wee William, Tall Thomas, and Rowan when he had caught sight of the two of them, walking along as if they had not a care in the world. White-hot anger burst before his eyes when he saw Black Richard touching Aishlinn's face. White turned to red the moment he saw Aishlinn return the touch with one of her own as she smiled ever so sweetly at him.

All went black from there and the next thing he knew, he was growling as he ran towards Black Richard, grabbing him about the waist and knocking him to the ground with a loud thump.

Having been caught off guard, Black Richard was temporarily stunned with the wind knocked from him. As he was rolled over onto his back, he saw Duncan's face, twisted in anger, staring down at him. Black Richard's years of warrior training and battle experience kicked in. Gaining his wits, he took a deep breath as he arched his back, grabbed Duncan by the arms and threw him off, sending him tumbling over his head where he landed on his back.

Duncan immediately got to his feet, crouching in a defensive stance. His anger kept him focused only on the man before him, and not Aishlinn as she stood nearby yelling at them both to stop. The two men paused only long enough for each to size up his opponent. Duncan took a deep breath as he lunged again at Black Richard, grabbing him by his bare arms as he quickly knocked him off balance by thrusting an ankle behind Richard's calf, bringing him hard to the ground.

Duncan pounced upon Black Richard, pinning him to the ground with the weight of his knees and sheer brute strength. Duncan was momentarily caught off guard by the fact that Black Richard was smiling up at him.

"So ye do have feelings for the lass after all, aye, Duncan?" Black Richard was goading Duncan and it was working for more white-hot anger surged through him, and gave Black Richard the break he needed.

He lunged his legs upwards and kicked Duncan at the tender spot on his lower back with his knee. Duncan loosened his grip as he was forced to suck in air. Black Richard used the opportunity to his advantage and twisted Duncan off him and pinned him on his back.

They paid no attention to the people who had gathered around them, least of all to the woman they fought over. As the two of them fought, Aishlinn shouted at three boys who were standing together watching the two grown men make complete fools of themselves.

"You!" she shouted at them, "Fetch me buckets of water straight away!" The boys were too startled to object and scurried away to do as they were told.

Aishlinn stomped angrily up to Wee William who was cheering the fight on. "Wee William!" she yelled at him. "Give me your sword and scabbard!" she demanded.

Wee William looked at her as if she were a fool and said "Nay. Let the lads fight it out, lass." He was enjoying the pummeling going on before him.

Aishlinn huffed as she swiftly reached toward Wee William's waist and in one deft move unbuckled the belt that held his scabbard. She let the belt fall away as she stormed back to Duncan, who now had Black Richard pinned underneath him again. Taking the heavy scabbard into both her hands, she lifted it high into the air before bringing it down hard against Duncan's skull. She didn't really have the strength to actually wield it in any professional manner. She let the weight of it do the work for her.

Duncan had not expected an attack from the rear. Quite shocked and in a good deal of pain, he released his grip on Black Richard and brought his hands to the back of his head.

"What the bloody hell!" he yelled as he rolled over to his back and saw his Aishlinn standing over him. She was glowing from the tiny twinkling sparks that floated in front of his eyes from the hit he had taken. She looked downright furious.

Quickly and with great precision, Aishlinn pulled the sword from the scabbard with her right hand and held the tip of it just inches from Duncan's chest. With her left, she thrust the scabbard down hard against Black Richard's sternum, pinning him to the ground.

"Do not either of ye move!" she said angrily. "I've had enough of this nonsense and it will stop now!"

For a brief moment, Duncan was not sure if she wouldn't thrust the sword deep into his heart. He quickly dismissed the thought, but when he made a move to stand, Aishlinn edged the sword closer to his chest.

"You think I'm good with a bow? You should see me with a sword, Duncan," she seethed at him.

He decided perhaps it best not to take the chance at the moment as he could see the intense fury within her eyes.

Of course Aishlinn had been stretching the truth a bit with tempting him to think she could actually do anything with a sword other than swing it. She felt Duncan needed not to know that at the moment. She was attempting only to get this ridiculous situation under control. If it took a lie to do it, then so be it.

"Are you two quite done?" she asked, scowling at the men who lay before her, each of them thunderstruck at the way in which she held the sword and scabbard. The fury could be seen in her eyes and warned them not to tempt her.

The two men cast furtive glances at one another before they nodded their heads. "Aye." They spoke in unison before casting disdainful looks at one another.

Aishlinn studied them very carefully for a moment and decided they would indeed settle down. She carefully returned the sword to the scabbard and walked back to Wee William, who stood with his mouth agape.

'Twasn't very often you saw a young lass settle two men with both a sword and a scabbard. Wee William, though disappointed the fight had ended too soon for his liking, was growing more proud of Aishlinn as the days passed.

Aishlinn turned to face the men who had been fighting over her. They had remained firmly planted upon the ground, breathing heavily as they attempted to wipe the sweat from their brows with the backs of their hands. It was more than utter disappointment she felt in each of them, she was furious with their behavior.

"I cannot believe that two grown men would behave in such a manner!" She began pacing back and forth as Duncan and Black Richard stared at her.

"Of all the pig-headed and foolish ways for ye to behave. Fighting like two mangy cur dogs over a piece of fresh meat!"

Both men began to protest and Aishlinn stopped them both with an angry scowl. "I'll hear not a thing from either of ye at this moment!"

She continued to pace and yell at them that they be daft, eejit men. She came and stood over Duncan, with her hands on her hips. "Do you, Duncan, intend on beating every man who ever might say good day to me?" she fumed at him.

"Aye. I do," he said.

"I think the correct answer is 'nay' ye daft fool!" she yelled at him.

"Nay. I meant what I said," he said, trying to catch his breath.

Aishlinn stood over him, her hands on her hips, severely disappointed in him. "Why? Why would you do such a thing?" she asked angrily

"Because yer mine," he said with a broad smile.

Aishlinn was determined not to let his beaming smile and twinkling blue eyes get the better of her. She did love him, but she wasn't about to let him behave in such a beastly manner any time any man might say good day to her. She'd simply not allow it.

"I am not a possession Duncan! I'm not a trinket nor a trophy," she seethed at him and resumed her angry pacing.

She was speaking more to herself at this point than to anyone else. "Of all the stupid. I just canna believe. It is just downright. I am just. Appalling behavior." Complete sentences were simply too much work at the moment. "What exactly were the two of you fighting about?" she asked them.

Neither man could put into precise words just what had happened. Duncan knew it was a fierce jealousy that had overcome him when he had seen the two of them together. Black Richard had fought merely to get Duncan's goat, jealous over the fact that he had won Aishlinn's heart.

"That's what I thought! You don't even know," she said. "Or you won't even admit it."

She went back to pacing and talking to herself, turning on occasion to chastise them again. As she rambled on, Duncan watched his soon-to-be betrothed with great admiration. He loved the fire that came to her eyes when she was perturbed. He thought those eyes might be able to melt iron this day, for she was completely furious with him.

"Damn, but she is beautiful when she is angry!" Duncan and Black Richard spoke at the same time. They turned and looked at each briefly. The scowl had returned along with the jealousy.

Black Richard smiled at him and he raised his eyebrows. "'Tis true!"

Duncan saw red again and he tackled Black Richard back to the ground. Wrestling and tossing each other about, Black Richard could not help but egg Duncan on.

"Have ye asked her to marry ye yet?" he said, as he flipped Duncan over to his back. He could see the rage as it burned in Duncan's eyes.

"For if ye haven't, I was thinkin' of askin' her meself!" Black Richard had to stifle a laugh for he knew that even if he had the courage to ask such a question, Aishlinn would undoubtedly turn him down. Black Richard knew her heart belonged to Duncan, but at the moment, he was deriving too much pleasure in infuriating the man.

Duncan growled as he knocked Black Richard backwards. Rolling around in the dirt and grass, he cared not why Black Richard was intentionally attempting to anger him. If anyone were to propose marriage to Aishlinn, it would be Duncan and no other.

They had all but forgotten Aishlinn's rage as they rolled and tumbled upon the ground. But she soon reminded them. Suddenly they felt a deluge of icy cold water as it hit them hard and gushed over their bodies. Barely a moment passed before they were hit with another.

"What the bloody hell!" Duncan yelled.

Aishlinn tossed an empty bucket to the ground as she grabbed a third and flung its icy cold contents at them. So angry she was at the moment, she could have beat them both senseless with the empties.

The two men held their hands up in surrender. "We're done lass! We're done!" they shouted at her.

"Are you certain?" she asked as she cocked her head to one side. She still had a firm grip on another full bucket of water.

"Aye!" they told her. The history over the past minutes told her not to believe them. She flung the contents of the other bucket at the two of them for good measure.

Duncan let out a string of blasphemies as the cold water crashed over his body. He was ready to jump up, grab his soon-to-be betrothed and fling her over his shoulder and paddle her arse soundly. Well, perhaps he would lavish her with passionate kisses first.

Aishlinn stood, out of breath and overwhelmed with anger. As she was about to give them another tongue lashing, Harry came racing towards them shouting Duncan's name. He fell to his knees in front of Duncan, fighting for breath.

"What is it, lad?" Wee William's voice boomed from behind Aishlinn. It startled her nearly witless and it seemed even the birds had decided it was now best to remain quiet. Now he decides to use his voice?

"Tall Thomas sends for ye, Duncan!" the boy said, gulping for air. "He says for ye to come straight away!" The lad sounded serious and fearful.

"Did he say why?" Duncan asked and jumped to his feet before helping the boy up to his own.

Harry shook his head. "He said to fetch ye, to tell ye 'twas important and to not say anything in front of-" he stopped and cast a look at Aishlinn.

"In front of who?" Duncan's face had turned hard and sober.

The boy pulled on Duncan's tunic to whisper in his ear. Duncan bent down and listened. The color drained from his face before he straightened himself. He turned and stared deep into Aishlinn's eyes. She was certain she saw black clouds of worry and rage flash over them.

"What is it?" she asked uncertain she truly wanted to know the answer.

His worked his jaw back and forth as he walked towards her. He could see the fear rise in her eyes as she figured it out.

"What is it?" Aishlinn asked as Duncan took her by the arm and led her towards the castle. Panic turned in her stomach when he would not answer.

Wee William and Black Richard followed close behind, their faces belying the fact that they were just as concerned as Duncan as to what was taking place. The two men had managed to glean from Harry what Tall Thomas' message had been.

Duncan led her through the kitchen door. "I need ye to go to yer room, Aishlinn, and stay there. I'll come for ye soon, I promise," he said as they walked through the gathering room. Richard, Gowan, Manghus and Findley stood huddled near a table. Rowan and Angus were racing down the stairs.

Without stopping, Angus boomed, "Aishlinn, go to yer room and wait. Do no' come out until we send for ye."

It did not take long for her father to start acting fatherly. She nearly shook out of her slippers when he boomed his order. Under different circumstance she would have protested vociferously. But with feeling as though the wind had just been knocked from her sails she did not have the strength or the courage to test him.

Duncan tugged at her arm. "It's the English isn't it?" she asked, the fear in her voice quite evident.

No one had to say a word for the looks upon each of their faces was enough to confirm her fears. Duncan led her up the stairs and to her room. "Lass, 'twill be all right. Do no' worry. Just stay here and I'll send Bree to ye." He left quickly without uttering another word. She promptly went to her private privy and retched.

Duncan could tell from the serious expressions upon his men's faces that nothing they were about to say would be good news. Rowan was waiting for him in the gathering room.

"What in the name of God is going on?" Duncan demanded as he barreled through the halls towards the private meeting room.

"I dunna ken, Duncan. All Richard and Findley would say was that they had word on the English and Aishlinn."

Duncan flung the door open to the war room and saw his men huddled near the end of the large table. The McDunnah sat at one end of the table to Angus' left. Several of the McDunnah's men stood behind him, arms crossed, curious expressions upon their faces.

"What's happened?" Duncan asked. He was not afraid of the English, he was afraid for Aishlinn.

Richard came to stand beside him. "I've word on the English," he said. "And Aishlinn."

"Tell me!" Duncan shouted.

"Duncan!" Angus boomed. "Calm yerself lad or I'll have ye removed."

Duncan took a deep breath and nodded his head, first to Angus then to Richard. He did not doubt for a moment that Angus wouldn't make good on his promise.

"Findley and I went to Dunblane for supplies," Richard began. "We were in a tavern having an ale when some English soldiers came in. Findley and I got close enough to listen." He paused for a moment knowing that what he was about to tell Duncan was not good news. "They be looking for Aishlinn."

Duncan's heart went cold. "Yer certain?" he asked calmly.

"Aye," Findley said. "Green-eyed beauty with blonde hair cut short."

"How many men?" Angus asked as his face paled.

"There were only a few in the tavern. We left immediately. Did not even bother to get the supplies. As we traveled back, we caught sight of several campfires." Richard recounted the event while he watched Duncan closely.

"We got as close as we could. There looked to be at least a hundred."

Duncan's jaw clenched as his hands balled into fists. A hundred English soldiers sent to look for one young woman? It made no sense they would send that many. His mind raced as he thought of Aishlinn and what Angus would do. It felt as if the earth was giving way under his feet. Slowly he sat down in the nearest chair.

"Duncan," Findley said. "They be a day and a half away."

He could not speak for his mind was racing with how quickly he could get Aishlinn to safety. There was not a cowardly bone in his body. He was not running from the fight. Once he got Aishlinn to a safe place, he could then concentrate on the fight. If he had to worry over her, he would be no use to anyone.

"Duncan," Richard said. "There be more."

Angus and Duncan looked to him. "In the tavern, the English were speaking of a troth."

A deep crease came to Duncan's forehead. "A troth?" he asked perplexedly.

"The soldiers said the earl had given a troth to her family but she had run away." He paused to let the words sink in. "The earl be no' dead Duncan."

Duncan shot up from his chair. "What do ye mean, the earl be no' dead?"

His chest tightened. Intense white-hot anger burned spots in front of his eyes and his palms began to sweat. Duncan did not doubt that Aishlinn had stabbed the earl as she said she had. But she had been wrong to believe he had died from his wounds.

Findley walked to him. "He evidently survived the stabbin', Duncan. They're sayin' the earl has given a troth for her hand. They're saying he misses her dearly and wants his beloved returned as soon as possible." He paused for a moment. "He's offerin' a reward to anyone who returns the lass to him."

Duncan's mind whirled. His first thought was of Aishlinn and how she would respond to the news. Aye, she had become stronger over the past sennights, blossoming into a fine, strong woman. But that strength had been built partly on the premise that the earl was dead and no one had been looking for her to punish her for the crime of killing him. Would learning that the whoreson wasn't dead and the English were in fact looking for her be enough to destroy the woman she had become?

The earl was alive and had given a troth for Aishlinn's hand in marriage? There could be no truth to it. The troth was merely a ruse, a lie told to either convince or entice those who did not know the whole truth to aid in finding her. He would kill the bastard before he would allow Aishlinn to be returned to him.

His thoughts then turned to the three brothers. They had traded her to work at Firth without her knowledge or consent. It was quite feasible that they would have entered into a marriage arrangement without her knowing or consenting to that as well. He would kill the earl first, then the three brothers.

A buzzing sensation began to build in his ears. He could not lose her now.

"Well now, this changes things a bit, don' it?" Caelen McDunnah offered. A curious smile had come to the man's face and Duncan was not quite sure what to make of it.

"What do ye mean, Caelen?" Angus asked, turning to face him.

The McDunnah tilted his head. "If the Buchannans get wind of this, they'll be after the lass fer certain. They'll want to ransom her back to the earl. There probably would be no amount of coin the earl wudna pay to get her back." He paused for a moment before continuing. "There'll be no safe place fer the lass to go."

Every man in the room thought on that for a moment. This did not bode well for any of them. One of the McDunnah's men, a stocky man with a bald, tattooed head and a full, long red beard spoke up. "Why should we be goin' up agin the English or the Buchannans for this lass?" he asked bluntly, looking at the MacDougall men who stood across the table from him.

Caelen McDunnah threw his head back and laughed boisterously for a long moment. "God's bones, man! Have ye seen the lass?" He shook his head and whistled.

"She be a damned beautiful young thing! Beautiful enough she could make a grown man cry with wantin' her. 'Tis probably why the earl wants her so." He shot a wicked glance towards Duncan who was slowly making his way around the table.

The logical thinking part of Duncan's mind told him it would do no good to start a battle with the McDunnah. But his heart beckoned him to defend Aishlinn's honor against anyone who would defile it or speak out of turn regarding her, even a supposed ally.

"If the lass weren't already taken, I wouldn't mind a go at her meself! A lass as beautiful as that makes a man's bones ache with want! And it be the quiet ones that fool ye. They be the ones full of hidden passions that can set a man's teeth on edge!" He was laughing again, apparently enjoying the effect he was having on Duncan.

There was very little time for Duncan to act. He had taken no more than a half a step towards the McDunnah when Angus bolted upright out of his chair, took a firm hold of the man's throat with his right hand, lifted him off his chair, and pinned him against the wall.

He had moved so quickly that no one had seen him pull his dirk until they saw it firmly pressed against the McDunnah's throat. It had taken only a moment or two however before every man in the room had pulled a dirk or a sword, one side pointing their weapons at the other.

"That be me daughter ye speak of Caelen McDunnah!" Angus growled through gritted teeth. The sunlight blazing in through the window glinted off the blade of the dirk. "I'll thank ye kindly to watch yer filthy tongue when ye speak of her."

A flash of surprise, blended with a pinch of insanity Duncan supposed, flashed across the McDunnah's eyes. He caught also a glimpse of fear, for Caelen McDunnah, while always eager to fight, was not quite crazy enough to take on Angus McKenna.

Caelen let out as much of a laugh as he could considering the firm grip Angus had on his throat. "Aye." He gasped for air.

Duncan was surprised at Angus' words. He knew that Angus had met with Aishlinn earlier. Duncan had been certain that Angus would have eventually accepted Aishlinn as his foster daughter, especially once he had the opportunity to get to know her. However, he had not expected for Angus to accept her so quickly, or so readily. His behavior confused Duncan.

Angus took his time letting the man down. Caelen coughed and sputtered and gulped for air. It took a few moments before he could speak.

Between coughs, the McDunnah attempted to apologize to Angus. "I was told she be an orphan," he coughed again.

Angus stared at the man for a moment before turning his attention to the rest of the room. "Aishlinn is in fact me daughter. Me blood daughter." He looked at Duncan, whose eyes had grown wide with surprise. "I've just learned of her return to me this day. I thought her dead but by God's grace, she has been returned to me."

Duncan could not have been more surprised had Angus donned a dress and gone skipping about the room claiming to be a faerie. His next thought was of Aishlinn and how she must be taking the news and why she did not tell him. Then he remembered the fight between himself and Black Richard less than a half an hour ago and felt like a fool for not being there for her when she needed him most.

Caelen's voice broke through the silence of the room. "She be a chief's daughter then?" he asked no one in particular. He was merely thinking out loud.

"That would give the Buchannans even more reason to come for her. They'll be wantin' to sell her to the man with the most coin. And," he held his hand up defensively towards Angus who was beginning to scowl at him again. "Dunna take this the wrong way, Angus. But they would. And the English have far more coin than ye do. Ye'll need to be protectin' the lass, 'tis certain. But I tell ye this," he took a deep breath, "if the Buchannans get wind of yer daughter, Angus, they'll most certainly be comin' fer her."

Rowan interjected. "Angus, the McDunnah speaks the truth." He glanced at Duncan who was working his jaw back and forth.

"We ken it. We've got the English after her and soon, the Buchannans. We must do everythin' we can to keep Aishlinn safe from all of them. But what?"

The room fell deathly quiet for a long moment. 'Twas the McDunnah who finally spoke. He bore a wry grin on his lips and the twinkle of insanity had returned to his eyes. "There be only one way to break a troth." He eyed Angus carefully.

It took only a moment for it to dawn on Angus where Caelen was headed. "With another troth," he murmured.

"Aye," Caelen said as he crossed his arms over his chest. "I'd be more than willin' to make the sacrifice for ye, my friend. I'll marry yer daughter. And I promise, to me dyin' breath, I'll protect her. I'll let not one Sassenach --nor a Buchannan -- anywhere near her. I swear it."

Angus nodded his head thoughtfully for a moment. "'Tis true. Ye can break a troth with another. Or if the lass in question marries and the marriage is consummated." He ran his hand through his hair.

While Duncan knew every word that Angus spoke was the truth, he felt comfortable with the fact that Angus knew how Duncan felt about Aishlinn. He also knew how Angus felt about Caelen and arranged marriages. He was certain there would be no way Angus would agree to his daughter marrying Caelen McDunnah.

The next words out of Angus' mouth nearly knocked Duncan to the floor.

"My daughter shall marry then."

Duncan swallowed hard. It would be only over his dead body that he would allow any man to marry his Aishlinn. No matter that the reasons behind it were meant only to keep her safe. She was his. If he had to kidnap her and flee to the farthest reaches of the earth in order to protect her and keep her as his own, then so be it. They could call him a coward if they wanted, for running and hiding, but he did not care at the moment. He could not let any harm come to Aishlinn and he could not let any other man claim her as his own.

Before anyone could speak further, Duncan rose and raced from the room. He bounded the stairs two at a time, raced down the hallway and flung open the door to her room.

She was sitting on her bed, huddled between Bree and Ellen, each of them with an arm wrapped around her as if they were holding her together. Her eyes were red and swollen from crying and the look of dread and fear on her face caused his heart to seize.

His strong and fiery Aishlinn, the one he had helped to set free, was gone. Before him sat the frightened and terrified lass he had rescued from a freezing stream not long ago. 'Twould only get worse once she learned the earl was not dead and the lie of the troth came to light. He wondered how she would respond once she also learned that below stairs her father sat with Caelen McDunnah and planned a marriage between them.

"Bree. Ellen. Leave us," he said, not taking his eyes from Aishlinn. The girls did not argue and left immediately. Duncan locked the door after them. He knew he had but a minute before Angus and the others would be there. Knowing Angus, he'd bust down the door if he had to.

"Aishlinn." His heart was pounding in his chest and his hands trembled. He was never this afraid on the battlefield. She stared at him, waiting and frightened. He had to pull himself together before it was too late.

"We've no' much time," he began. "The English are looking for ye."

She could not hold back the tears. "I'm sorry," she blurted out. "I meant not-" She choked on the tears as she scrambled from her bed. "I'll leave, straight away."

She would rather live her life without him knowing he was safe, than to stay and have harm come to him, her family, or anyone else.

For a moment, he could not move. Countless thoughts bombarded his mind and heart as he watched her rifle through her trunk. A hard lump had formed in his throat that made it impossible to speak. He had been right earlier; if she stayed he would be no good to anyone for all he'd be able to think of was her safety.

Aishlinn stood at the end of her bed, holding a few of her dresses against her chest. All she could think of was stopping the battle that would most assuredly ensue if the English found her here. They would show no mercy toward anyone who had given her refuge. The only way to stop it would be to leave. She searched the room with her eyes, wondering what she should put her things in for she had no satchels or bags.

As Aishlinn tried to figure out how to leave and where to go, Duncan remained motionless for only a moment longer. She was mumbling something when he went to her. He took the dresses from her arms and tossed them onto the bed.

"Aishlinn. Listen to me, lass," he whispered and wondered where to begin. She looked up at him, her eyes filled with tears and fear.

"The English be no' here. Yet." He grabbed her arms to gain her attention. "We've no' much time," he repeated. "I need ye to listen. The earl be no' dead."

He wished he had had time to choose his words more carefully, but chances were that Angus was headed up the stairs ready to give Aishlinn the news that she had been trothed for. Again.

"Not dead?" she repeated. "But I stabbed him. Twice!" She found it impossible to believe the man had not died.

"Aye, I ken it!" Duncan needed her to stay focused and to listen. "He lived. His soldiers search for ye, lass. They say the earl gave a troth for ye."

The floor seemed to have disappeared and her legs turned to jelly. If Duncan hadn't been holding on to her she would have fallen over. "That's impossible," she whispered before it hit her like a bolt of lightening.

Her brothers had to have accepted the troth. Or else it was an outright lie. Would the earl troth for her in order that he might legally take that which she would not give him? Would he kill her after he had? Certainly neither the church nor the king would recognize their marriage -- if it ever took place. She was not royalty, had no title or dowry. She didn't have a drop of "privileged" English blood in her veins. She was a peasant. It was a lie, a ruse and nothing more.

The knock at her door brought her back to the here and now.

Duncan gently squeezed her arms. "Aishlinn. Angus and Caelen have a plan." He was not sure if he could get the rest of the words out. "The only way to break a troth is to have ye marry someone else."

For the first time in hours, she felt hope. Was Duncan proposing? Even if he was and they did marry, it still wouldn't solve the problem of the impending English invasion. She searched his eyes, looking for something to tell her more. There was another knock at the door, much louder this time. She thought she heard Angus' voice on the other side.

"Aishlinn, if ye marry another then ye canna be forced to marry the earl."

She could only nod her head as she waited to hear him say the words. But there was something in his eyes that told her there was more bad news.

"They want ye to marry Caelen McDunnah." He nearly choked on the words.

Her eyes grew wide and her mouth fell open. Thunderstruck and aghast at the notion of marrying anyone but Duncan, she could not get her mouth to form words, until there was another, louder knock at her door. It was definitely Angus on the other side and he did not sound pleased.

"Nay!" She nearly yelled it. "I'll not marry Caelen McDunnah!" She pulled from Duncan's grasp and searched her trunk for her leather boots. "I'll no marry anyone but-" She stopped herself short.

She wouldn't marry anyone but Duncan. But since he didn't appear to want that responsibility at the moment, she decided that jumping from her window and running away was her only option.

"Marry me," Duncan finally managed to say.

She had been tugging on a boot when he said it. She stopped mid-pull and looked at him.

Duncan admonished himself for acting like such an idiot when it came to her. He had been letting fear guide him these past months. He'd been afraid of pushing her, hurting her, or rushing into something serious. Today he had been afraid of what the English would do once they found her. Now he was afraid that either Caelen or the earl would take her as wife. He was done with being afraid. He would not let fear guide him any longer.

"I love ye," he said. "Marry me."

The pounding was louder and Angus voice could clearly be heard from the other side of the door. "Aishlinn!" He was booming. "Open this door at once!"

She couldn't move. Duncan had said he loved her. While she wished the circumstances had been different, a wee bit more romantic perhaps, he had still said it.

"I'll bust this door down, lassie!" came Angus' muffled voice from the other side of the door. "Duncan! I ken yer in there!"

"I love ye," Duncan repeated. "I want to marry ye."

Aishlinn nodded her head. "I love ye as well." She sat motionless on the edge of the bed, her boot still only half on.

How could a heart be filled with untold joy and utter dread at the same time? Had the circumstances been different, she would have leapt into his arms and covered his face with endless kisses. But as it were, there was an impending invasion of English soldiers to deal with.

Even if she married Duncan, it would solve nothing. The earl was still alive and apparently had lost what little mind he had left for he had given a troth for her hand. The hand that had stabbed him twice.

"I want to have yer bairns," Duncan blurted. When he realized the words had gotten jumbled inside his head he turned red with embarrassment. For the first time this day, he saw a smile come to his future wife's face. "I meant-"

Aishlinn giggled. "I know what you meant!" It felt good to laugh, if even for a moment.

"Ye'll marry me then?" He cocked a hopeful eyebrow at her.

"Aye," she said, still smiling from her perch on the bed. "And ye can have as many of my bairns as ye want," she said in a mock Scottish brogue.

Just as he was headed towards her, the door to her room came crashing in. Angus stood breathless in the doorway, his face contorted in anger. "What the bloody hell are ye doin'?" he demanded.

Aishlinn leapt to her feet and tumbled into Duncan, for she had forgotten she had only one boot half way on. Duncan had caught her, wrapped his arms around her and looked at Angus.

"Uncle!" he began.

"Shut the bloody hell up!" Angus roared at him. "I want no' to hear yer voice at the moment, lad!"

He turned to look at his daughter. He counted to ten before he spoke again. "I trust young Duncan here has told ye what has happened?" he asked her.

She held on to Duncan, as much to keep her balance as she did for protection. She'd only just learned that Angus was her father. With no history between the two of them, she knew not what he might do if angry enough. "Aye," she said with a nod of her head.

"I trust the eejit also told ye of the earl's troth?"

Another curt nod of her head was all she could manage.

"I also trust he told ye of Caelen's offer to marry ye?"

She found her voice. "Aye, he did. And I'll not marry the McDunnah." She hoped her voice sounded firm and unyielding, and not like the quivering mess she felt like inside.

Angus shook his head and looked at Duncan. "Lad. There was a reason I chose ye out of all others to be me successor."

Duncan swallowed hard, preparing himself mentally for whatever Angus would say next.

"I chose ye, because of yer ability to keep yer head level. I chose ye because of yer skills on the battlefield." Angus drew his hands behind his back and clasped them together. "But this day, ye make me question that decision."

Duncan could not fault the man for doubting him. He had proven over the past few hours that he was far from level headed when it came to Aishlinn.

"It seems me daughter has an effect on ye that makes ye act like a fool." Angus raised an eyebrow at Duncan. When he saw no argument coming from Duncan he continued.

"I canna say that I blame ye fer it. Good women sometimes have that effect on a man." He cast a smile at his daughter. "Yer mum had that very effect on me, lass."

He turned back to Duncan. "Do ye plan on gettin' yer wits about ye anytime soon, lad?"

Duncan stood a bit taller and looked Angus in the eye. "Aye. I do." He had decided just minutes ago that he was through with letting his worries and fears over Aishlinn's safety drive him any further. Realizing he would be no use to her if he could not keep a level head, he had made the firm decision to take charge of the situation and their fate. He would no longer leave anything to fear.

"Good." Angus accepted his answer. "Now, about the matter of the McDunnah's offer."

Aishlinn began to protest until Angus shot her a warning look. "Lassie, I'll thank ye kindly to remain quiet," he told her as he crossed his arms over his chest and stepped over the splintered door that lay on the floor. "While it was kind of the McDunnah to make such an offer, I refused it."

Aishlinn nearly collapsed with relief. Duncan eyed him curiously, not certain where Angus might be leading them.

"While the McDunnah is a good ally and is loyal to King David, as well as a fierce warrior, I canna have me daughter marry him."

Duncan could not resist the urge to ask him why he had turned the McDunnah's offer down.

"Because I love me daughter," Angus said as he smiled warmly at Aishlinn.

It wasn't just his smile that warmed her heart it was his words as well. Twice in one day, two men had expressed their love for her. Whilst one was romantic in nature and the other fatherly, she doubted she could ask for much more.

"She's just been returned to me this day. And I hate arranged marriages." He waved his hand and looked as though he'd just tasted something quite sour. "Women are not possessions, nor are they chattel and I hate how they're often used as such." He shook his head in disgust.

"I'll not be usin' me daughters in such a manner. They'll marry who they love." He paused before quickly adding a condition. "As long as he be a good man, and one that I can trust would bring her no harm or heartache. While I'll always take me daughters' feelings into consideration, I'll not let either of them marry some eejit who can't keep his wits or offer her much by way of a good life." His lips curved into a wry smile as he turned once again to Duncan. "Can ye keep yer wits about yerself now, lad?"

Duncan nodded his head rapidly.

"And by way of a life, what can ye offer me daughter?" Angus asked, looking quite serious.

A rather loud laugh escaped Aishlinn before Duncan could answer. He looked at her, quite puzzled. "He wants to have me bairns!" She could not control her laughter.

For a moment, their roles had been reversed, as Duncan burned crimson from head to toe. "Lass!" he said firmly as he scowled at her. "I'll thank ye kindly to keep our private conversations private!"

Aishlinn pulled her lips in and bit down to keep from laughing further. She nodded her head and tried to look innocent and demure. It was rather difficult at the moment, especially when she saw the look of consternation on her future husband's face.

Angus shook his head, not wanting to know what his daughter was talking about. "Now!" he said as he clapped his hands and began rubbing his rough palms together. "We've the matter of a weddin' to discuss. I've sent fer the priest. He'll be here in an hour's time."

For a moment Aishlinn allowed herself to be swept away in a sea of blissful happiness. She'd be marrying Duncan, apparently far sooner than she was prepared for.

While she had sometimes daydreamed of her wedding day, as girls are oft want to do, this was not what she had planned. Part of her dream was coming true, for a handsome young man who loved her dearly was sweeping her off her feet. However, she had always envisioned a beautiful gown and a church filled with flowers and friends. Not that she had had any friends growing up. That was part of her dream as well. And there would have been a grand feast afterwards and much dancing would have taken place.

But as things were happening so quickly, there would be no large church wedding, no beautiful silver gown, no flowers and no grand feast. She supposed in the grand scheme of things, the wedding itself did not matter as much as the marriage. She'd be marrying Duncan, a man she loved more than life itself.

'Twas then that it hit her, with as much force as if she'd been hit in the back of the head with a mace. What of their life after the wedding? The English soldiers were looking for her at this very moment. While a marriage to Duncan would keep her from having to marry the earl, it would do nothing to keep the English from attacking the castle or her family. The marriage could not stop the English from finding her and taking her back to Penrith for her crime.

She paid no attention to the conversation that was taking place between her father and Duncan. The nightmares were coming true. Her mind was replaying them over and over as she stood quietly, still being held in Duncan's arms. They had not been just vivid dreams; they were omens. The future had been foretold in them and it was undeniable.

The English would find her. And when they did, they'd kill anyone who stood in their path or had offered refuge to her. It was as simple as that and there was only one thing she could think of to keep that from happening.

Twenty-Five

She had decided to wear the purple gown, the one she had worn when Duncan had kissed her the very first time. While most lasses might have preferred to wear a more cheery or brighter color, the purple was Duncan's favorite. Over her gown she proudly wore the dark blue and green plaid of the Clan MacDougall.

It was a very quiet ceremony held in the gathering room just as the sun had begun to set. The room had been filled near to capacity with their fellow clansman as well as the McDunnah men. While nearly everyone in attendance was glad to see the two young people marry, apprehension over the impending arrival of the English hung in the room like a thick, worrisome fog.

After the priest pronounced them married, Duncan kissed her sweetly, almost chastely as the people surrounding them cheered on. Aishlinn blushed and though her heart ached with knowing what she would do come morning, she wanted to enjoy what little time they had together.

Guilt tugged at her for not sharing with Duncan her plan to save them, but she knew that had she told him, he would have locked her in her room for the rest of her life.

There was no time for congratulatory celebration for the newlyweds. Duncan took her hand and leaned in to whisper to her. "'Tis not the wedding I'm sure ye imagined, nor the one ye be deservin', lass. I promise we'll have a better celebration after we be done with the English."

Aishlinn thought his smile could light up the darkest of rooms and nearly burst into tears. She knew that after tonight, her eyes and heart would never again be blessed with seeing it.

They went to Duncan's room, for hers had lost its door and could no longer afford them any privacy. Someone had put fresh linens on the bed and a single white rose lay atop the pillows. A low fire burned in the fireplace and candles had been lit and placed about the room.

When her eyes fell back to the bed, a great sense of nervousness enveloped her. They'd be consummating their marriage soon and she hadn't a clue what to do.

Duncan saw the look of apprehension in her eyes and it brought a smile to his face. "Are ye frightened, lass?" he asked.

"Aye," she whispered. Terrified was a more apt description. "I know not what to do," she murmured softly.

Duncan let out a chuckle. "No worries, lass. I'll help ye through it."

He bent to kiss her and the moment his lips touched hers, everything else in the world seemed to slip away. She wrapped her hands around his neck, twisting her fingers through his thick hair as she stood on her toes to reach him. Until just a sennight or two ago, had someone told her not only would she be married someday, but married to a man who made her heart pound, her palms sweat, and her stomach twist and flip at his mere touch, she would have laughed herself silly over it.

Desperate to feel his skin against hers, Duncan undid the broach holding her plaid together and tossed it on the table beside his bed. Carefully he removed her plaid and laid it upon the chair near the table. He was trying to not appear as desperate for her as he felt.

Within a moment, he wrapped his arms around her and began to fumble with the buttons on her gown. He did not want to stop kissing her, but he felt he might explode from want if he didn't remove the gown quickly enough. A moan escaped him as he tried to concentrate on the buttons. But her tongue, her kisses, her rapid breathing made it nearly impossible for him to think of anything but the kisses.

"How many buttons are on this gown?" he asked as he put his lips to the nape of her neck.

"I know not. Bree and Ellen have to help me into it," she said breathlessly. Her skin was covered in chill bumps and her knees were beginning to knock together.

"How fond are ye of this dress?" he asked her, his need for her was rising quickly.

Aishlinn was lost in her own thoughts, wanting to feel his lips on hers again. "'Tis the dress I received my first kiss from you in," she whispered, wishing he would hurry with it.

"My first kiss ever, really." She felt a smile come to her face when she thought of that night and how impossible it had all seemed then.

Duncan growled, trying to hold himself in. Had he not been an honorable man, he would have simply lifted her skirts and taken her there on the floor.

"I'm afraid lass, that if I don't get these many buttons undone soon, I'll die from want of ye."

Aishlinn giggled slightly, as she remembered Mary and Laren explaining to her the control a woman had over a man. She realized then what they had been speaking of. She turned around quickly and lifted her hair so that he could undo the buttons. Her hands trembled while her stomach felt as though someone were tickling it from the inside.

Duncan would have preferred to just rip the damn thing from her, but fought that urge. He'd been around enough women to know the importance they sometimes put to things. Knowing the dress held special memories for her, he couldn't allow himself to do it.

He groaned as he his fingers seemed to not go nearly as fast as he would have liked. He would have a talk with Bree later about the number of buttons that would be acceptable on any future gowns she might make for his wife.

His wife. The realization of it sent pleasant shivers down his spine. She was his. Forever his. As he undid the last button, the candlelight flickered across her back, giving him a glimpse of the scars left by an evil bastard of a man. He held his breath and remained still. Silently he vowed that come the morrow he would personally kill the man responsible, even if he had to ride across English lands to do it.

It took only a moment for Aishlinn to realize why he had paused. Perhaps he had changed his mind when he caught sight of the scars. Bree and Ellen had insisted they were not hideously disfiguring and barely noticeable. But Aishlinn had serious doubts and was certain they lied only to protect her.

"I cannot blame you if you've changed your mind, Duncan," she whispered. Her heart fell to her toes when he did not immediately answer.

He turned her around so that he could look at her beautiful face. God's teeth, but she was beautiful.

"Nay, I haven't changed me mind," he whispered as he brushed his lips tenderly over hers. "Mayhap ye'll change yer mind when ye see me battle scars," he teased.

He could have a thousand scars covering him from head to toe and it would not have mattered one wit to her. It was his heart and how he felt about her that mattered.

Duncan took in a deep breath before he began kissing her again. He would never spend another lonely night alone in his bed mad with lust and want of her. She would be there every night with him. Och! There would be much lust, much need of her, but he wouldn't have to throw himself into the cold loch to fight it. He would be able to reach out for her and she would be there.

"I love ye, Aishlinn."

Her eyes filled with tears. She knew he meant the words he spoke. "I love you, Duncan," she whispered.

She had to kiss him then to keep the tears from spilling forth. Instantly, a strange and new sensation fluttered through her body. It was rather reminiscent of being extremely hungry, a need of something but what that something was she had no clue.

She wiggled out of her dress, letting it drop to the floor, and stood before him in only her shift. A most serious expression of determination appeared on his face right before he began to ply her again with warm, passionate kisses.

A burning need filled her to the marrow and she wanted to see him, all of him. She undid the broach clipped to his plaid, not certain what to do with it. Duncan took it from her and tossed it over his shoulder where it landed with a plink somewhere near the door. His plaid fell away and he pulled his tunic over his head and tossed it to the floor as well.

She sucked in air deeply as she looked at his well-muscled and toned arms and chest. His skin had been kissed by the sun and seemed to ripple in the candlelight. There were scars upon his shoulders as well as his tight, wavy stomach, scars he wore with pride for he had earned every one of them in battle. Her eyes moved downward and when she caught sight of his manhood, she closed them quickly, embarrassed for having looked there.

Duncan chuckled at her crimson face as he grasped her neck and pulled her to him. He lifted her in his arms, kissed the soft spot at the base of her neck whilst he gently laid her down upon the bed. Her eyes were still closed, her fingers holding onto the sheets tightly as if she were bracing herself for the unknown.

He chuckled again as he lay beside her and began to kiss her lips, her cheeks and eyelids. She finally let go her hold on the sheets and wrapped her arms around his neck.

"I'll be gentle lass, I swear it," he told her, kissing the nape of her neck. As much as he wanted to simply plunge himself into her, he wanted for her to enjoy their first time together. It was important for her to feel the pleasures he could give her.

"Tell me if I do anythin' that hurts," he whispered as he kissed her bare shoulders. "Tell me if I do anythin' ye dunna like."

Aishlinn could not imagine him doing anything to her that would be at all unpleasant. Excitement coursed through her as she pulled him closer, desperately needing to feel his lips against her own. "Kiss me," she said breathlessly.

He honored her request. Her mouth was hungry for his and his for hers. She felt his hand as he touched her thigh every so gently with just the tips of his fingers. More chill bumps covered her body and she thought she might faint from the sheer exhilaration he brought to her with his touch.

His feather soft touches, as he slowly ran his fingers across her skin, brought forth more chill bumps. Ever so carefully and slowly he pushed her shift up exposing her skin, her secret places. It left her feeling nearly intoxicated.

When he kissed her belly button she thought for certain she would lose her mind for it seemed so inappropriate! She stopped breathing altogether when he touched her breasts, for she didn't think that was proper either. He stopped only long enough to lift the shift over her head before tossing it to the floor.

She had not been prepared for this, for laying completely naked and exposing herself in such a fashion! She had imagined she would have only needed to expose the places necessary for consummation, not every square inch of her body!

"Breathe lass, or ye'll swoon on me," he chuckled as he began to kiss her again.

She forced herself to breathe for the last thing she wanted was to swoon and miss out on what might happen next. Running her hands along his arms then his back, she could hear him moan with pleasure. She was surprised to find that when she heard his soft moans, they brought an intense and thrilling excitement to the pit of her stomach.

Before she realized it, Duncan was on top of her and his kisses were growing more penetrating and passionate. The powerful, urgent need boiled within her like liquid heat. It was as exhilarating as it was confusing. Exhilarating because she had never before felt so alive and blissfully happy all the while feeling very alarmed and anxious.

'Twas confusing because she knew not what the vibrant, pulsing need was, only that it made her feel there was more to this joining of husband and wife than just deep, ardent kisses, heavy, anxious breathing, and feverish, unrestrained touches. There had to be more to it.

'Twas then that she felt something rather large as it lingered near the entrance to her womanly nether regions. She gasped when she realized just what "it" was and what he planned on doing with it.

Before she could even ask "are you quite serious that you mean to do what I think you mean to do," he did just what she thought he intended to do.

"Ow!" she said, taking in a deep breath and holding it until she nearly swooned from fright and shock and the pain.

Duncan paused, lifted his head from her neck and looked at her with a fearful and frustrated expression. "Do ye wish me to stop?" he asked.

She was certain that what he truly meant to say was, "Please, I beg you do not ask me to stop now." Or to hear her say "Nay, husband, please continue at your leisure."

For a moment she could not speak. She could only hold her breath and retain her deathlike grip on the sheets near her hips. After several agonizingly long moments, the pain began to subside and she was finally able to find her voice, or a close likeness to it, for she wasn't sure she recognized the sound that came from her own mouth. "Nay," she told him.

She was frightened for his wellbeing and health for there were many times over the last sennight that he had told her he was ready to explode with want and desire for her. The image of her husband exploding into a thousands pieces of flesh all over the marital bed kept her from saying nay. How would she begin to explain it to anyone?

She fought the urge to laugh a moment later when she heard his deep sigh of relief at her answer. Somehow his frustration made her feel a bit better about the entire situation and for the life of her she could not figure out why. Perhaps it made him seem more human and less God-like, more real and less perfect, even though he was as close to perfection as any man could possibly get, at least in her way of thinking.

Not a moment had passed before he began to slowly move within her, kissing her tenderly as he caressed any part of her body that was naked and exposed. As he moved, she realized that "this" was the deep need she had been craving. He whispered to her in Gaelic, a few of the words she recognized, others not.

As his pace quickened she began to feel very odd, tingly sensations as she began to meet his movements with her hips. It was all beginning to make sense, this joining of a man and a woman. It did not take very long after that for her to realize what Mary and Laren had been talking about when they discussed the pleasures joining brought to both man and woman when it was done correctly.

"Mo Chuisle," Duncan whispered. "Is tu no ghra," Aishlinn knew what those words meant. More excitement rushed over her when he used the Gaelic to say he loved her.

When she thought the feelings of joining with her husband could not possibly get any better, something unfamiliar began to spread over her body. It began from somewhere deep within her and rapidly rose before exploding to every inch of her body. Her toes curled, her fingers dug into her husband's back, and her eyes rolled back into their sockets.

She was horribly frightened by it, not at all certain what it was that was happening to her. Perhaps it was apoplexy and the thought of dying now, in this moment nearly scared her to death. "Duncan, what is happening?" she whispered quite desperately.

She heard him chuckle slightly and then nothing else as the explosion grew to great waves that plunged her into an unbelievable sea of what could only be described as a maddening yet blissful, inconceivable ecstasy. For a moment she thought her soul had left her body as she dove her fingers even deeper into Duncan's back. She shuddered involuntarily and felt the need to scream for…her mind went blank for she couldn't think of what to scream for other than for him to not stop.

If I die now, then so be it. I will die feeling the grandest of pleasures. Aishlinn had not realized she had said the words aloud until she heard Duncan's light laughter before he said, "Ye're welcome." For once she did not turn red.

The feeling subsided, yet lingered just on the edge and she was certain she would go mad if he did not stop, to let her catch her breath. He began to kiss her again and within moments all thoughts of stopping disappeared.

All she could think of was that joining with her husband had turned out to be far more pleasurable than her mind could ever have imagined. Her heart swelled with love for this man and she knew he loved her and would do anything for her. Aishlinn hoped that he was enjoying himself as much as she was and she took the chance to open her eyes. He looked to be in a good deal of pain. "Are you all right?" she asked him.

"Aye," he whispered, moving slowly as he kissed her again. It was not long after that she felt the tides of passion return and soon they were both lost, thundering along in that intense and unbelievably joyous wave.

She felt Duncan begin to shake against her as he moved faster, calling out her name, expressing his love to her once again. Aishlinn realized the pleasure she brought to him was just as intense and exquisite as what he had brought to her. She smiled just before the explosion overtook her again.

When it was over, he lay soaked in sweat atop her, his face buried in the pillow, trying to catch his breath. As she hugged him, tears came to her eyes. There were too many reasons to count as to why she felt like crying at the moment.

He began speaking to her, his voice muffled and she could not make out the words.

"Are you all right?" she asked him again.

He slowly lifted his head and there was a very broad smile on his face.

"Aye. I am now." He kissed her lips, her forehead, her cheeks and her eyes. "I love ye, Mo Chuisle."

She found she rather liked the way his words made her stomach flutter and her heart race madly. Her heart began to seize momentarily, for the thought of morning time came to her mind. She would miss him but she knew she would be able to carry this one night with her throughout eternity.

Duncan rolled to his back and he pulled her near. She rested her head upon his chest, just as she had imagined doing many times over the past weeks. It was just as pleasant as she thought it would be. She could hear his heart pounding against his chest, like a big Scottish drum.

As they lay there with their legs intertwined and trying to come back down from the celestial territories they'd just explored together, Duncan gently caressed her arm with the back of his hand.

He imagined the smile on his face to be permanently sealed there for all eternity. He had been with many a woman in his life, far more than his fair share he supposed. But none had brought forth the passion or the intensity to lovemaking that Aishlinn had. He would have sworn on his family's graves that she had touched his very soul.

He felt hot tears as they landed on his chest. He hoped they were tears of joy and not sorrow or regret over marrying him. He also hoped he had not caused her any great amount of pain. "Lass, why do ye cry?" he whispered, his voice laced with concern.

"I'm happy." It wasn't a complete lie, for she was happy beyond all human comprehension. Intermingled with that however, was the sorrow for what she would do when he fell asleep.

Duncan patted her arm gently, giving her a slight hug. "No regrets?"

"Only that I had not met you long ago." Which was the truth. Had she grown up here, had her life been different, then her heart would not be now disintegrating into ashes.

"We've our whole lives to make up fer it," he said sweetly.

Aishlinn could only nod her head. She wanted not to utter any lies to him. Lies, it seemed, had been what her entire life had been based upon. Wanting only to leave him with a night of very happy memories, she remained silent.

Twenty-Six

Aishlinn had accidentally discovered the secret passages below the castle by chance one day when she had first begun working in the kitchens. Back then she had still been quite frightened and unsure of herself and the people who had opened their home to her. She had tucked the knowledge securely away in the event she should ever need to flee.

She waited for Duncan to fall asleep after they had joined together a third time before quietly pulling on her shift and slipping to her own room. She found that her legs had the consistency of fresh porridge and walking was quite difficult.

Moving quietly in the dark of her room, she prayed she'd not make any sounds that would carry through her broken door. She slipped into a plain brown dress and tugged on her leather boots. She pulled a wimple over her head and grabbed a plaid from her table.

She wanted to leave something behind for Duncan, something other than just memories of last night. Taking the chance, she quickly took a few things from her trunk and slipped back into his room where she left them on the pillow next to his beautiful face. Tears threatened and her throat felt swollen when she looked at him for the last time. She prayed over him that God would keep him safe and that he would understand that what she was doing was for the good of the entire clan.

She made her way down the stairs and to the kitchen unseen, grabbing a lighted torch along the way. Though she would have preferred to leave on horseback, she could not take the chance of walking across the courtyard to the stables.

Quietly, she slipped down the stairs into the larder where the secret door to safety lay hidden behind a set of heavy wooden shelves. She rested the torch on the wall while she pulled at the shelves. The door moaned and creaked its opposition and she sent up another fervent prayer that no one in the castle had heard it.

Not wanting to take the chance at the door voicing another loud objection at being closed, she left it open as she retrieved the torch and fled. Her mind went back to a night not long ago when she had fled through the secret corridors and passages of Castle Firth. That night Baltair had helped her flee to freedom and had blessedly saved her.

This night however, she did not flee in fear to save her own life. She fled to save the lives of others.

She wound her way through the damp corridors, her heart pounding with the fear that Duncan would wake too soon and thus foil her attempts to save his life. She knew he wouldn't understand her motives or her reason.

Her husband was stubborn that way and she supposed she rather liked that about him. Her stomach tightened when she thought of him as her husband and all that could have been had her life not been built around the lies of one mad man that had been traded for the lies of another.

Heavenly Father but she would miss Duncan! Choking back tears and the urge to turn around just to see him one last time.

The hidden corridors wound this way and that under the castle walls a great distance before ending at a set of stairs that led up. A heavy wooden door lay concealed under a tall oak tree and it took several attempts at pushing it with her shoulder before it finally relented. The hinges, rusted from lack of use, creaked ominously and she hoped it was far enough away from the castle that the guards would not hear.

She took a chance and stuck her head above ground so that she could see the watchtowers of Castle Gregor far in the distance. She worried that the guards might see the light of her torch, even across this expanse of land. Tossing the torch to the floor, she watched as it sizzled and hissed before relinquishing its flame. She took a deep breath and climbed up, pausing only long enough to cast one last look at Castle Gregor. Her heart sank for the hundredth time in less than a day and the tears returned. She knew this would be the last time she would ever lay eyes on her home.

Duncan woke to early morning sunlight shining upon his face. He was feeling quite content and happy until he reached out for his wife and found the spot where she should have been empty and cold.

He bolted upright when he saw the dried flowers, heather, and parchment lying on her pillow. His heart seized in his chest as he grabbed the parchment and opened it and saw that it was the note he had written her not long ago.

He let loose with a low, angry growl as he flung himself from the bed and dressed quickly. He tucked the heather inside his tunic and strapped his broadsword to his back before grabbing his scabbard, mace and dirks.

Tucking his weapons into his boots and belt he rushed from the room and yelled for Angus.

Angus was opening his door as Duncan stomped down the hallway. "What the bloody hell?" Angus boomed and tried to focus his bleary eyes. When he saw the look on Duncan's face he knew it could not be anything good.

"Aishlinn be gone!" he yelled as he approached him.

"What the hell do ye mean she be gone?" Angus bellowed his question.

"She left! Sometime in the night."

They stood staring at one another, angry expressions painted on their faces. Within moments the hallway had filled with people wondering what the yelling was about.

Angus fists clenched into balls and his knuckles turned white. "Do ye think…" his voice trailed off for he could not bear to speak his thoughts out loud.

Duncan nodded his head. "Aye, I do!"

Angus rushed back into his room to dress while Duncan gave an order to a lad who stood in the hallway.

"Get all the men in the gathering room at once! Every last man in this castle is to assemble immediately. Have the warnings blown!"

The lad left at a full run, understanding the importance of Duncan's order.

"What has happened?" Isobel asked worriedly as she wrapped a plaid around her shoulders.

Angus was livid. "Me foolish daughter has left! And I suspect she's gone to turn herself over to the damned English!"

His voice boomed as he strapped his broadsword to his back and hurriedly tucked a dirk into each of his boots.

Horror washed over Isobel's face. "Why? Why would she do such a thing?" She could make no sense of it.

"Because she believes if she turns herself over to the English, there'll be no battle!" Angus roared. "She thinks she's saving the clan by doing it!" His hands shook as he shoved a dirk into his belt and strapped his sword around his waist.

Isobel covered her mouth with her hand. "How could she have left unseen?" she asked.

Duncan's eyes grew wide. "The passages," he said, turning on his heals and running as fast as he could to the kitchens.

"Mary!" he called. "Have ye been to the larder yet this morn?"

"I have," Laren said from her place by the fire, her voice quivering at

Duncan's scowl and angry voice.

"Could ye tell if the passage door had been moved?" he demanded.

She nodded her head. "It was standing wide open when I went down this morn. I thought it was the lads! They sometimes like to sneak down there to drink ale when no one is looking!"

Duncan let loose a tirade of blasphemies as he left the kitchens and headed back to the gathering room. Men were pouring in from all directions, some fully dressed and strapping on weapons, while others came barefooted or bare-chested or both.

"Aishlinn has gone," he said, as Richard and Findley entered the room with Black Richard and Wee William.

"Gone?" Wee William asked looking perplexed. "Gone where?"

Duncan ran a hand through his hair as anger flashed within him. "We think she's gone to turn herself over to the English."

Black Richard stood aghast at the idea. "Why in God's name would she do that?"

Angus entered the room in time to answer his question. "She thinks if she turns herself over to the English, there'll be no bloodshed in her name." His voice boomed, silencing each man in the room.

"She left through the passages, Angus," Duncan told him. "But I've no idea how long ago."

When he got his wife back he would tie her to their bed each night before he'd allow her another opportunity to do something so foolish.

Angus began giving orders. "I want fifty, nay seventy-five of my best men on horseback within the next five minutes." He yelled at Richard who quickly left the room with Wee William and Rowan following in close pursuit.

Angus looked at Duncan. "With any luck, she be wanderin' aimlessly about and has not yet run into the English bastards."

The two men looked at each other for a moment. Duncan shook his head. "Ya've no' yet been blessed with seein' yer daughter's persistence and stubbornness first hand," he told him. "She's either holdin' them all prisoner at the end of a bow, or she's surrendered and is halfway to England!"

Angus pursed his lips. She was definitely Laiden's daughter. No child of his would be so foolish.

Aishlinn was not certain how long she had been walking for she had no idea what time she had left the castle. Her feet and legs told her that it had been quite some time for they were beginning to ache. Of course the exercising of marital rights and consummation that she had partaken of not once, not twice, but three times last night did not help her current physical state much.

She had no real idea where she was going and could only pray that she would catch up to the English before Duncan woke and found her gone. She prayed as well that if Duncan and Angus set out for her, they would not find her.

Perspiration had broken out on her forehead from the great distance of land she had covered. The sun had risen long ago and was very high in the eastern sky. She was walking through a dense thicket of woods, heading in a northeasterly direction. With no real idea as to where the English might have been, she resolved herself to the fact that she might have to walk all the way back to Penrith in order to save the lives of her clan. It was a sacrifice she was willing to make, however, and she could only pray that she would not starve to death or fall and break her neck in the process

As she walked along she kept her eyes firmly planted on the ground for she had already tripped three times. Lost in her thoughts and prayers, she was shaken back to the present by the twitter and snort of a horse. When she looked up to find the source, she was staring into the eyes of a very frightening looking man. Within moments three more equally terrifying men presented themselves, each on horseback. Each wore the bright red coats of King Edwards's army.

"Well, good day to you!" the soldier said. "What's a pretty thing like you doing out here all alone?" he asked as he dismounted his steed and walked towards her, smiling as if she were a long lost friend. His teeth were just a few shades darker than stone and his eyes held a hopeful glare.

Aishlinn swallowed hard for she was quite afraid, but her pride would not allow her to let him see her fear. "I am Aishlinn," she said firmly. "I am the one your earl seeks."

The soldier stared at her. "Show me your hair." He demanded disbelievingly. Aishlinn removed her wimple and he could see that, in fact, she did have short blonde hair.

"I see why the earl wants you. You are a pretty thing."

The way his eyes washed over her made her skin crawl but she stood firm and resolute. "Where is your camp?" she asked, lifting her chin in an attempt to look far more confident than she truly felt. "Take me to your sergeant," she demanded of him.

The soldier drew his hand back and slapped her hard across her face, the force of it knocking her to the ground. She tasted blood as anger roiled in her belly.

The soldier bent over and glared angrily at her. "You'll not be giving me orders!" he spat at her then stood. He motioned to one of the other soldiers and told him to bind her hands.

"Take the wench to Andrew," he ordered.

Before she could stand, her hands were bound with leather ties and she was tossed over the front of horse. The front of the saddle dug into her belly and sent a surge of pain clear to her toes as she tried to adjust herself. The soldier mounted and slapped her hard on her rump. He had a disgusting laugh, rather nasally in its intonation.

"Settle down there woman! You'll see yer earl soon enough."

They rode hard and fast and by the time they reached the English encampment Aishlinn was ready to vomit from the hard ride and the saddle that dug into her stomach.

The soldiers stopped in front of a tent where she was unceremoniously tossed from the horse and landed hard on her rump. She wished momentarily that she had a sword, or a dirk that she could plunge into the bastard's belly. Quashing her anger, she knew it would do her no good to fight. After all, she had willingly turned herself over to them. What had she expected? The same kindness and compassion her clan had shown her?

A very tall man with dark hair, wearing the bright red coat of the English military exited the tent at hearing the commotion. His coat however, was embroidered with gold braids at the shoulders and cuffs and signified his command position. He stared down at her with dull brown eyes. He held an irritated expression to his face, as if he had just become aware that he had stepped in manure. "What is this?"

"She says she is the one we seek, Andrew." The soldier who had slapped her face walked towards him. "She does have green eyes and short hair."

The man they called Andrew continued looking aggravated. "How did her lip come to be cut?"

"She fell," the soldier offered nonchalantly.

Aishlinn shot him a look that told anyone who might be paying any close attention that the man lied. Andrew asked her, "Is this true?"

She hadn't a clue how to answer and decided honesty might be the route best taken at the moment. She shook her head but remained quiet.

"Which of them hit you?" he asked calmly.

Aishlinn looked at the soldier standing next to Andrew who followed her gaze. "Go to your quarters and stay there," he ordered him. Before he stomped away indignantly, the soldier shot Aishlinn a look that warned she might want to watch her back in the future.

Andrew bent and grabbed Aishlinn by her elbow and helped her to stand. "I am deeply sorry for the deplorable actions of my men," he said as he guided her into the tent. No matter how nicely he attempted to speak, her instincts warned her not to trust the kindness he was displaying.

He sat her upon a chair and untied her bindings. He studied the burn marks the binds had left and shook his head. She did look a mess, with leaves in her hair and the cut lip, but he imagined she would clean up nicely and be presentable to the earl soon enough.

"Tell me your name," he said as he walked to a table and poured a tankard of ale. She declined his offer with a shake of her head.

"I am Aishlinn," she told him.

"What is your last name?" he asked, pulling up a chair and sitting directly across from her.

"I am a bastard child. I have no last name." She would not give up her family name no matter what torture they chose to put her through.

Andrew raised a curious brow. "Where have you been kept all these many months?" he asked quietly as he crossed one leg over the other and rested his hands upon his knee.

"With a family several miles from here."

"Who are they?" he asked.

"I lied to them," she began. "They knew not from where I came. They kindly took me in. I helped the lady wife around her home and with her bairns."

"I asked for a name," he said.

"Please, I tell you the truth. They know nothing of the earl and how I came to be here. They are truly innocent." She swallowed hard, hoping she would not trip in her own lie.

"When a visitor came to their home and told of the soldiers that were near and that they looked for a lass with cut hair and green eyes, I knew it was me they searched for. I knew I had to leave for I wanted no harm to come to them. I snuck away in the night to turn myself over to you." Her voice cracked as she fought back tears. Parts of what she told him were true and she prayed that he would accept her story.

Andrew eyed her for a moment. "So in order to save the lives of the family that took you in, you readily turned yourself over to us?" he asked calmly. Aishlinn could detect a hint of disbelief in his voice.

"Aye," she said.

He stood then and walked about the room, his hands clasped at his back. He paused and looked to her. "Do you really expect me to believe that?"

"'Tis the truth. I swear it!" Aishlinn said, sending prayers up to God to make this man believe her.

He strode so quickly to her that she had no time to brace herself before he slapped her across the face. The force of it brought stars to her eyes as she fell to the floor. Her cheek burned and she felt the welt rise almost instantly. He picked her up by her arms and shook her.

"Do not lie to me again!" he said squeezing her arms with so much force she thought they might snap in two.

"I speak the truth!" she pleaded with him. "I swear it! They were so kind to me. I knew your soldiers would not take kindly to anyone who helped me!" Her voice rose, thick with fear as she pleaded with him. "I want no harm to come to them. Please, I beg you!" Tears began to stream down her face.

"I do not believe you," he seethed. "If you do not tell me the truth, I shall let my men have their way with you. Each and every one of them." Aishlinn's mind raced as she prayed for the right words to convince him she told the truth as well as a way to prohibit him from keeping his promise. "But the earl, he has trothed for me," she said desperately through her tears.

"Yes, he has," Andrew said, his voice cool. "We have been told to bring you back, dead or alive. Though the earl would very much rather have you alive, it matters not to me." He squeezed her arms tighter causing Aishlinn to wince. "I believe you have been sent here as a trap," he told her.

Aishlinn was confused. "A trap?"

Andrew let go long enough to slap her again. Aishlinn looked at him, stunned for she didn't know what he was talking about. "We know the Scots do not hold us in high regard. They'll use any excuse to attack us. You've been sent here, have you not, to keep us busy while the ignorant Scots surround us?"

She shook her head vigorously. "Nay! I swear 'tis not true!"

Andrew studied her for a moment and he could see the fear in her eyes. He rather enjoyed that look upon her. Carefully, he sat her back in the chair and began to pace. Aishlinn rubbed her face where he had hit her. She was suddenly beginning to wish she had not come, had not turned herself over to them. It had all seemed so hopeless last night, as if she had no other alternatives. She wondered if this was how her mother had felt all those years ago, desperate and with very little, if any, choices at her disposal.

"We leave immediately," Andrew told her. "The earl waits not far from here." A smile came to his face as he saw terror flash in her eyes. "Though he is not well, he does very much wish to see you again before you die."

Aishlinn choked on the bile that formed in her belly and raced up her throat. It really was over for her then. But that had been her intent all along, to give herself up, to accept the punishment for stabbing the man who had tried to rape her. She had done it to save her people. A sense of calm came to her then. She could only hope that death would come quickly and that God would forgive her and allow her through the gates of heaven to be with her mother.

Twenty-Seven

It had not taken them long to assemble the men and set out in search of Aishlinn. Her tracks were easy to follow as Duncan, Angus and more than a hundred warriors, including those belonging to the Clan McDunnah, headed northeast in search of her. The tracks they followed appeared fresh and they estimated they weren't more than three hours behind her. She was on foot so the chance of reaching her quickly brought a twinge of hope to Duncan's heavy heart.

He was angry with her for leaving, angry with her for acting so foolishly with no apparent regard for her own safety. He was angry with himself as well for not thinking, even for a moment that she would be crazy enough to pull such a stunt.

If they were lucky enough to find her alive and well, he would be quite tempted to lock her in the oubliette for a fortnight! Well, maybe not an entire fortnight, maybe only a few days. Or mayhap only a few hours. Just long enough to get her attention and show her that she could not just take matters into her own hands and leave without thinking the entire situation through. How could she do this to his heart?

They followed her trail across the glen and into a dense thicket of woods. Duncan growled when they were forced to slow their pace when the tracks became more difficult to see in the forest. A few men dismounted to get a better look. After what seemed an eternity, they picked up her trail again and traveled on.

His mind wandered to hellish thoughts; thoughts that they might not find her alive or well. She could very well be in the hands of the English at this moment and God only knew what they were doing to her. Breathing in deeply to settle the growing queasiness, he pushed his horse faster. He had to find her. He had to bring her home.

He made a deal with God that if He would allow him to find his wife alive and unharmed, he would forever serve Him in whatever capacity the Lord wanted him to. He would give all his worldly possessions to the church. He would attend mass on a regular basis and would never take the Lord's name in vain again. There wasn't a bargain he was not willing to make in order to see her safely back in his arms. He'd not lock her in the oubliette. Instead, he would climb back into bed with her where he would hold her and not ever let her go.

They had been in the dense thicket for quite awhile when one of the men spotted something white lying on the ground ahead. He jumped from his horse and retrieved the wimple and brought it to Duncan. Aishlinn seldom wore one. His blood grew cold when he found a few short, golden blonde hairs stuck to the cloth.

"Duncan, there be tracks here as well. Looks like four horses," the man said as he walked along following the tracks for a distance.

His blood froze when he realized his wife had gotten her wish. She was now in the hands of the English.

Aishlinn drew into herself as she sat with her hands bound in front of her riding atop a dark gray horse. A soldier rode on either side of her, one of which had the reins of her horse tied to his saddle. They were riding fast and she was barely aware they were heading due east. She paid no attention to what was taking place around her. She was lost in a deep part of herself where the world around her could not enter.

She thought of Duncan, hoping that he would understand her decision and that he would not be too angry with her. Hopefully, she told herself, he would move on with his life and find someone new to love. She prayed that the good Lord would give him a new life, like the one He had given Isobel and Angus.

It would not be long before she would be presented to the earl and her life would again be in his hands. She fought back the urge to retch at thinking of what he would do to her. It would be nothing like the love and tenderness Duncan had showed her last night. She would withdraw her mind from it, accept whatever deplorable thing he wanted to do as long as it meant no harm would come to her people.

Clouds that threatened rain had formed by the time they reached a small clearing. A heavy mist hung in the air, chilling her to the bone.

Several grand coaches and more soldiers took up nearly the entire clearing. A large tent, with the flag of England flying high atop it sat in the rear of it all and smaller tents were scattered about the encampment. The earl was more likely than not within the large tent. She fought back the urge to wretch, swallowed hard and forced herself to look away.

Several soldiers stood near open fires and seemed uninterested at the troop that bounded into the encampment. Aishlinn's soldiers stopped not far from the main tent and helped her down. Her legs were weak and wobbly, but the soldier caught her before she collapsed to the ground.

Leaning against the horse for support she rested her head against the beast's neck as they waited for direction. Andrew soon appeared and led her to one of the smaller tents.

"I shall inform the earl that you are here," he said as he took her inside and sat her in a chair.

"Please, do not even think of escape for I'll not hesitate to cut your throat if you should try," his voice was hard and cold. Giving her a slight bow, he left her alone.

A cold, dreadful chill ran down her spine. It would not be long before she would be taken to the earl. She wished that she had been afforded time to pen a letter to Duncan. She would have liked to thank him for the new life he had given her -- albeit not long enough for her liking. She would have tried to explain that it was her love for him that helped her make this decision.

She would have written a letter to Isobel and Angus as well. She would have thanked Isobel for the kindness she had shown her and told Angus how proud she had been to be his daughter, even if it were for but a day.

Not much time had passed before Andrew returned. The stern and unhappy expression his face held increased her sense of dread.

"The healer gave the earl a sleeping tea," he said. "Lucky for you. You will get to live a while longer." He folded his hands behind his back as he studied her.

"I think we should take advantage of the earl's slumber and get you into a more presentable state," he said before leaving the tent. He returned after a brief time with a basin of water, soap and linens.

"Clean yourself. I'll return shortly to help you further."

Her unease intensified for she was quite certain that he did not mean to offer any kind of help that she would want. She hung her head in her hands and prayed.

After having a good cry, Aishlinn stood and washed her face and hands. The cold water chilled her, but not nearly as much as the thoughts of what the earl was going to do to her. It felt as though the blood in her veins had been replaced with ice.

It was some time later before Andrew returned. This time she readily accepted his offer of a tankard of ale. She took it with the hope of becoming so intoxicated that she would not know what was taking place.

She emptied it quickly before slamming the empty tankard hard on the table.

"Remove your gown," Andrew told her.

She stared at him blankly and steeled herself.

"Remove it now, or I shall remove it for you." His firm tone and cold stare told her that he had no qualms in keeping his word.

She stared him down for a moment before undoing the laces and pulling the dress over her head. Shivering, she clung to her dress in an attempt to cover herself. Her shift did little to hide much of anything.

Andrew grabbed her gown and tossed it to the floor. He stared at her approvingly for several long moments. "I see now why the earl lusts after you so."

"Remove your boots," he directed her. Aishlinn paused for a moment, knowing it would do no good to argue. She sat down in the chair and removed her boots. The earth was damp and cold under her bare feet and it brought more chill bumps to her skin.

"I do believe the earl is ready to see you now." The smile on his face sickened her and she suddenly found herself wishing for something with which to stab him.

He wrapped a linen sheet around her shoulders, letting his fingers linger on her neck. A wicked smile flashed across his face before he grabbed her elbow and led her from the tent. It seemed to have grown colder out of doors. Or perhaps it was fear that made it seem that way. It wouldn't be long now before she was dead.

They paused briefly in front of the earl's tent as Andrew eyed her closely. "I do hope that he does not kill you straight away." He leaned in to whisper his intent. "For I would most definitely like a taste of you when he is done." He breathed heavily into her ear before kissing her lobe.

Revulsion shot through her stomach and she thought of kneeing him in his blasted English groin. Andrew tossed her into the dark tent and closed the flap.

It took a moment for her eyes to adjust to the darkness for there was only one candle burning. As her eyes began to focus, she caught a faint image of someone lying in a bed that stood at the rear. Just like the sick bastard to be waiting for her in bed.

She strained her ears to listen and she thought she could hear a sick rattle of breath coming from him. She forced herself to take a step closer in order to gain a better look at him.

Something gnawed at the back of her mind. There was something about the moment that did not feel at all right. Aye, the entire situation was dire and wrong, but why he had he not pounced on her the moment she entered as he had done that night back at Firth?

Aishlinn soon realized why he hadn't come after her. The earl was not at all well; his face was sallow and gray and his eyes were sunken. Apparently he had not bathed in quite sometime for she could smell his stench from where she stood.

"There you are." His voice was husky and low, weak sounding. She barely recognized him or the sound of his voice.

"Come to me," he said.

She couldn't move.

"If you do not come here this instant, I shall have my men bring you to me. And they'll not be at all kind about it."

She did not doubt him. She inched her way slowly towards him and a sense of relief began to come over her. He was sick and diseased. Gone was the strong and terrifying man. Only a shell of the man who had terrified and beaten her remained.

Hope began to rise; for she knew he could not harm her in the way she feared the most. Kill her? Yes. But there was no way he could take from her what she had denied him months ago.

"I have been looking everywhere for you," he told her, motioning for her to come closer.

"All across the lands, I've had men searching day and night for you." He coughed hard for several long moments before wiping his mouth on his sleeve.

"You've been very good at keeping yourself hidden." He looked at her with yellowed eyes. "Andrew tells me you have turned yourself over willingly?"

Aishlinn did not answer. Her mind was suddenly racing towards thoughts of escape. It would take very little effort on her part to hold a pillow over his face until he took his last breath. She could very well then shimmy under the walls of the tent and run for safety.

"Did you do that? Turn yourself in willingly?" he demanded to know. Aishlinn nodded her head yes as her eyes looked for an opening, a way out.

"Why?" He tried to shout but could not.

"Did you come back to stab me again, you whore?"

Aishlinn could only stare as her mind raced for a means of escape.

"Would you like to know what I'm going to do to you?" he asked. She really didn't think there was much he could do given his current state of health.

"I'm going to ask Andrew to assist me. He's not nearly as nice as I would have been to you, had you simply given in to me that night." He took a ragged breath.

"Andrew's going to come in and strip you bare, you see. Then he is going to do all those nasty yet wonderful things to you that I wanted to. And I'm going to watch with great pleasure. Then I'll have every one of my soldiers come in and do it to you again, and again and again until you bleed from it."

His face lit with a wicked smile. The confidence she felt just moments ago vanished quickly with his threat. The earl might not be able to carry out his wicked desires, but his men were quite capable.

Dismay and fear eroded her reserve while her mind raced for a way out of her current predicament. Perhaps if she begged for mercy, pleaded with him. Perhaps if she promised to be a nurse to him then he might change his mind.

"My lord, I beg you, show mercy. I was but a scared and frightened young girl when last you saw me." She could not believe the words that were coming from her mouth and nearly choked on them.

She rushed and knelt before his bed. "I knew not what I was doing, my lord. I knew not what kind of pleasure a man could bring to a woman." She would most certainly retch all over him, but she had to do something to save herself.

She had been fully prepared to be disemboweled, hung or tortured as a means of death. Being raped repeatedly by countless men had not crossed her mind and that she could not and would not abide. Determination set in. There had to be a way out of this.

The earl's smile broadened. "So. You've learned in your time away the pleasures a man can bring to a woman, have you?" He coughed again and his stench was enough to knock a pig over.

"Aye, I have," she answered, swallowing hard, trying to look pathetic, forlorn, sorry, anything that would get him to change his mind.

"Remove the linen," he told her. She knew she needed to keep him calm. There was no limit to the pain he would inflict if he was angered enough.

Taking a deep breath, she let the linen fall to the floor. Her filmy shift offered little in the way of hiding her bare skin. A disgusting smile formed on his lips when he caught a glimpse of what lay under the transparent fabric.

"Remove your shift."

She simply could not bring herself to do it. While she had given herself over to them willingly in order to stave off a battle between her clan and the

English, she could not suffer the indignantly of assisting him further.

"Please my lord, do not ask me to do that." Her voice squeaked with fear.

He grabbed her by her hair and pulled her to his face. "You'll do what I say whore, and you'll do it now."

Though he was sick and weak, he had enough strength left in him to pull hard on her hair. She had suffered worse, but it was still quite painful. "My lord, you're hurting me," she said as she tried to unfold his fingers from her scalp.

"Andrew!" he shouted. The wave of panic hit her hard. He would not let go. She should have just grabbed the pillow and held it over his head. It was too late now.

The tent flap flew open and Andrew stood smiling at the entrance. "My lord?" he said, looking quite eager to help. Tears flooded her eyes for she knew it was all over then. The earl would make good on his promise.

"Help me, will you? The whore seems unwilling to remove her shift."

Aishlinn pleaded with them to stop as Andrew bounded for her. Andrew grabbed her arms and lifted her to her feet. She saw nothing but sheer evil in the eyes that stared back at her.

"Please! I beg you!" Her cries for mercy fell on deaf ears.

Andrew pulled her hard into his chest as he grabbed the back of her head and forced her mouth to his. Her stomach churned when he stuck his tongue deep inside her mouth. Repulsed and growing more terrified, she tried to fight him off and struggled against the tight hold he had on her.

When she had made the decision to relinquish her freedom and turn herself over to the English, she had prayed for a quick death. She realized now that she should have known better. Now that she was trapped inside the tent with two vile men, her instinct to fight was too strong. They'd have to take that which they wanted and she was not going to let them take it without a fight. She would hold on to her dignity for as long as possible.

Andrew finally broke away from her mouth but maintained his tight grip on her arms. Without taking his eyes from Aishlinn, he said to the earl, "I love it when they fight, don't you my lord?"

Malevolence flashed from his eyes to hers. In that small flash of time, Aishlinn could see what the future held for her.

A blood curdling scream came from somewhere beyond just the pit of her stomach. It came from her very depths of her soul. Though she knew it would do no good, for none here cared what might happen to her, she screamed. There was no one here who cared what these men would do to her; they were merely waiting for their turn at her. She began hitting

Andrew with her fists but her resistance seemed only to please him.

"Fight? You want a fight, Andrew?" she seethed. "I'll give you a fight!" she yelled as she tried to lift her knee to thrust it into his groin. He jumped back, just enough to miss it. His smile rapidly turned to an angry glare.

As he drew back his hand to hit her, Aishlinn heard an odd sound, like a muffled thump. Andrew's expression changed in the blink of an eye. He now looked perplexed, as if he were studying some strange and foreign object. A moment later, his grasp on her loosened and he slowly fell to his knees.

Twenty-Eight

For a moment it felt as though time had slowed to a crawl. Andrew had collapsed to his knees before landing face down on the ground. Dazed and more than slightly confused, Aishlinn watched as he toppled over. A dirk had somehow become firmly imbedded in the middle of Andrew's back. Her breath caught in her throat and she could not move, nor could she take her eyes off the dead man who lay at her feet.

It was the earl's raspy and angry voice that brought her back to the here and now of it. "Who in the hell are you?" The earl shouted as much as his diseased lungs would allow.

Aishlinn looked up and saw Duncan as he stood in the entrance of the tent. His jaws were clenched and his face held a fierce look of anger. Relief washed over her at the sight of him. "Duncan!" she cried, unable to say anything else as she rushed to his open arms. He held her tightly, relieved to see that she was alive but still very angry at the situation she had put herself in. He sent a prayer of thanks up to the Heavens when he felt her collapse into his arms.

A loud commotion began outside the tent as Duncan let loose of Aishlinn and walked to the bed. "Who the hell are ye?" Duncan demanded.

"I'm the Earl of Penrith you insolent fool!" His body shook as he was overcome by a coughing fit.

Duncan looked down at the man in utter incredulity. This was the monster that had killed his family? This was the bastard who had tried not once, but twice to rape his wife? His mind could not wrap around it. This could not be the same man he had envisioned running his blade through for the last ten and seven years.

"Ye? Ye be the Earl of Penrith?" he asked unable to believe the man before him had been the source of countless nightmares and untold anguish.

"Aye, he is Duncan," Aishlinn said from the tent opening. "Quickly, please take me away from here Duncan," she pleaded with him as her body began to shiver.

Duncan could not take his eyes from the man who lay before him. "Ye killed my family," Duncan whispered. "Many years ago, ye slaughtered an entire village. Ye killed innocent people. Ye killed my entire family." Rage began to creep in.

He could not believe this was the man who had destroyed so many lives. Nay. What lay before him was no man, but a sick, demented monster who derived great pleasure in seeing others suffer at his hands. Duncan shook his head. He could not believe he was this close to him.

Duncan battled with his conscience. No matter how desperately he wanted to simply run his broadsword through the man's heart, he could not kill an unarmed man. In the battles that he had played out in his mind over the years, never had he imagined that he would find the whoreson sick and unarmed.

Duncan would leave the man to suffer with his disease. It appeared that death was not too far off into the future for the earl. He'd let the man suffer in agony and waste away into nothing.

Duncan turned away from the earl and bent down to retrieve his dirk from Andrew's back. He wiped the dead man's blood on the earl's blankets.

"Ye'll burn in hell soon enough," Duncan told him. The earl remained silent as he watched Duncan closely.

Duncan went to Aishlinn then and held her for a moment. "Dunna leave me side!" he told her. "Follow me and stay right next to me!"

Aishlinn nodded her head and took hold of his arm. This had not turned out as she had intended. She was supposed to have saved her clan, but instead, it turned out they were saving her.

As she turned back to take one final look at the earl, she saw a dagger in the decrepit man's hands. She shouted a warning to Duncan who had begun to step from the tent. "Dagger!"

The earl's knife barely missed Duncan's head as it bounced off the walls of the tent and landed on the floor. Duncan spun quickly around and flung his dirk across the room. It landed dead center of the earl's chest as it made a revolting sound when it tore through flesh, muscle and bone.

Aishlinn gasped as she saw the blood begin to ooze and drench his nightshirt. An odd expression had come over the earl's face. It wasn't the sweet release of death but something rather wicked and repulsive.

Duncan shook his head and retrieved his dirk from the dead man's chest. When he returned to Aishlinn's side he noticed then that she was standing in just her shift and for a brief moment, he wondered if he had not arrived in time to save her from these sick bastards. "Did they hurt ye?" he asked.

Aishlinn shook her head vigorously. "Nay!"

Duncan quickly removed his tunic, and placed it over Aishlinn's body. He donned his broadsword again and kissed her on her forehead, relieved to find her alive and for the most part unharmed.

"Stay beside me at all times. We've men fightin' out there and I dunna want ye getting' in the way. Do ye understand?" he said. For once, he hoped she would listen.

"Aye. I do," she answered as she grabbed his arm and clung to him with both hands. She wasn't about to let go of him. Not now, not ever.

Complete mayhem was taking place in the clearing outside the earl's tent. Dozens of dead English soldiers lay sprawled across the ground. More stood fighting the countless clansmen who had come to rescue her. She could hear the clash of metal as sword met sword. The sound of skulls cracking and dirks driving deep into bodies made her sick, but she felt terribly relieved that they were there. She prayed that God would protect her clansmen.

Duncan lifted his shield from the ground where he had left it before entering the tent and crouched low. Aishlinn followed suit. They had to climb over dead bodies as they headed towards the line of trees to their right. Duncan had horses and men waiting for her there.

As she crouched behind her husband, the sounds of battle thundered on. As they started for the line of trees an arrow shot through the air and landed in Duncan's left shoulder. Aishlinn screamed as he fell to the ground face first. He rolled over to his side, reached up and pulled her down then threw his body on top of hers, shielding her from the barrage of arrows. Aishlinn heard several distinct whooshes followed by thumps as arrows pierced the ground around them.

"'Tis my fault! I knew this would happen!" she cried. "'Tis all my fault!"

"Haud yer wheesht, lass!" Duncan scolded. "I'm not hurt that badly! Lay still and pretend yer dead," he told her. She might not have to pretend if the onslaught of flying arrows did not cease.

They lay on the ground, unmoving for several long moments before the flying arrows finally stopped. Duncan winced from the pain of the arrow sticking from his shoulder and his face began to pale. It was not long after before she felt him go limp as he lay on top of her. Aishlinn shook with terror and great waves of guilt began to build in her heart. Had she never left, this would not have happened! She had meant to save her people, not throw them into a battle.

She heard Duncan's voice as he lay on top of her and it sounded weak. "Yer cold," he said. "Try not to shake so, lass. When we get home, we'll warm ourselves by the fire, I promise." He closed his eyes and his breathing slowed. "I love ye, Aishlinn," he whispered in her ear.

He was dying; she knew it. He was dying just as he promised he would. Dying for her, fighting for her honor, for her life. She whispered to him how sorry she was that she had gotten them all into this mess. She choked on tears as she repeatedly apologized and professed her love for him.

Duncan did not respond. He lay on top of her, limp and lifeless and she had no one to blame but herself. An anger, unlike anything she had ever experienced before began to consume her. It built in the pit of her stomach and grew quickly, spreading to every part of her body like a fire that had grown out of control. She wanted to slay every last English soldier who might remain standing, like the woman in the book Bree had read to her.

She was angry with herself and with the English bastard that now lay dead in his tent. No matter how hard she tried, she could not tamp the anger down and it kept growing until she felt her skin might glow white hot, like the iron in a blacksmith's forge.

As she lay there with Duncan's lifeless body on top of her, soaked from the rain, mud and her husband's blood, an Englishman fell dead at their side. Not far from where they lay, she heard Angus shouting something in Gaelic and she thought she heard Wee William's voice too.

A violent determination came over her and she decided to act. She would rather die fighting than be slain while she lay on the ground hidden under her dead husband. Vengeance would be hers this day. Vengeance for the lies Broc had told that kept her from knowing her real family and vengeance for her husband's death.

She squirmed and managed to wriggle herself from under Duncan's body. A dead English soldier was an arm's length away. She rolled over to her stomach, reached out and grabbed the dead man's sword and stood. A bloodlust rose in her as she began violently swinging at any soldier who came near her.

Months ago, she would not have been able to act in such a manner. Now she swung and thrust her sword at anyone who dared come near her. Three came at her from different directions and she took hold of her weapon with both hands as she swung full circle. She sliced each of her enemies at their waists, all the while letting loose with another blood curdling scream. Blood spattered across her face and chest but it mattered not. She was avenging the death of her husband.

She crouched low to get a better grasp of her surroundings. Angus was to her left, fighting off two Englishmen, Wee William had three not far from Angus. Rowan was to her right, Gowan ahead of her, both busy with their own battles.

Not far from where she stood was a mounted soldier. A flash of a very determined smile came to his lips as he dashed towards her. She stood, waiting until the last possible moment before thrusting her sword into the soldier's steed. The horse cried and whinnied before it fell, trapping its rider beneath it. Begging God's mercy for killing such a beautiful animal, she took her sword and thrust downward into the man's chest.

The sword began to grow quite heavy in her hands and she started to tire. She would not however, give up in her pursuit to avenge her husband's death. Nor would she give in to the weight of the sword.

Her clansman surrounded her as they fought the English. There was much grunting and moaning mixed in with the clanging of metal. Blood flowed from dead or dying soldiers. The rain had increased and in the distance she could hear the roar of thunder.

She saw Caelen McDunnah across the clearing fighting sword against sword with an English soldier. For a moment she pondered his presence. Why was he here?

Her eyes searched for a better weapon, for she knew she could not hold the sword much longer. Catching sight of a fallen archer, she raced towards him at a full run, grabbed his quiver and bow and surveyed her surroundings. Her legs felt heavy but she would not give in. She stood and began to take aim at the English soldiers. Within a minute's time she had killed seven of them, emptying the contents of the quiver. Seeing no more arrows within reach, she returned to the sword and began hacking her way through the crowd of battling men.

More English soldiers fell at the hands of her clansmen as she battled her way through the remaining soldiers. Her frenzy intensified as she sought out more of the bastards.

From somewhere to her left Angus bellowed a warning. "Behind ye!" She turned in time to see the soldier as he lunged his sword towards her. She had not moved quickly enough and the tip of his sword sliced through her upper left arm. Consumed with hatred and rage, she ignored the blood as it trailed down her arm.

She used her rage and plunged her sword deep into the English soldier's belly. With her sword lodged firmly in his midsection he felt backwards and landed in a twisted heap. Using her foot as leverage, she wiggled and pulled until the sword finally let loose with a nauseating sucking sound.

She turned to seek out more men to kill. Duncan's tunic and her shift clung to her body soaked in mud, sweat, blood and rain. She fought to raise her sword again as her breath came in great bursts. Using her free hand to wipe the sweat from her eyes she looked about readying herself to kill anyone who came near her.

She noticed that her clansmen were staring at her with wide-eyed bewildered expressions. A deafening silence had filled the air. Angus began to cautiously walk towards her with one hand held out fearful she was so caught up in the moment that she might kill him.

"Aishlinn," he said nervously. "'Tis me, Angus. Yer da." She stared right through him as if he were an apparition made of mist.

"Lay the sword down, lass. They all be dead now," he spoke quietly, trying to reassure her that it was over. He took another step towards her and prayed she would soon acknowledge him. "'Tis all right, Aishlinn. 'Tis over."

She recognized him finally and let loose the sword. It landed with a thud on the ground at her side. The ferocious rage she had felt only moments ago was now replaced with absolute despair and anguish. She fell to her knees, her body racked with guilt, remorse, and grief. She cried not for the lives she had just taken, but for her dead husband whose body lay not far from her. His men had surrounded him, shaking their heads and mumbling words she could hear over the sound of her own sobs.

Angus pulled her into his chest, her fisted hands grasping his bloody tunic to keep from falling completely over. When he spoke, his voice was soft and low. "'Tis all right, lass." His attempts to soothe her did not work.

"No! No it isn't! Duncan is dead and it's all my fault! I might as well have thrust a sword into his heart with my own hands. It's just the same!" she cried out, holding onto her father. The guilt was maddening. She would never forgive herself for her husband's death. He had made good his promise to defend her honor to his death if necessary. Because of her, his death had become necessary. He had sacrificed his own life so that she could live.

Twenty-Nine

A torrent of grief enveloped Aishlinn's heart as she clung to her father. No matter how hard they tried to pull her from him, she could not let go. She heard muffled voices as if they were speaking to her through heavy blankets. She could not see for the tears blurred her vision completely. Her body and her soul were breaking in half and there remained nothing left of her heart.

Finally, she looked up and into her father's eyes. "Please, please plunge your dirk into my heart and kill me now for what I've done!" she begged him between sobs. "I know I'll burn in hell for all eternity, but that would be better than living without him!"

Pain covered Angus face as he watched his daughter suffer in utter agony. He hated when lasses cried for he knew not how to deal with it. "Lass, ye need to calm yerself down!" he shouted at her for he knew not else what he could do or say.

She had to see Duncan, one last time. She had to hold him in her arms and tell him how sorry she was and that she would spend the rest of her days in agony over losing him. Finally, she pulled away from her father and raced to her husband. She pushed through Wee William and Black Richard to get to him. Gowan knelt beside him, his face looking horribly pained.

Aishlinn flung herself on top of her husband as the tears racked her body again. She clung to Duncan, crying uncontrollably as she laid her head upon his shoulder.

"I am so sorry," she choked between sobs. "I would plunge a dagger into my own heart if it would bring you back, if only long enough so that you could hear my words." She shook violently and felt as though the air had been kicked from her lungs.

"Has anyone ever told ye, lass, that ye be horrible at judging if a man be dead?"

For a moment she thought she had imagined hearing his voice. Her eyes flew open as she bolted upright. His eyes were open and he had a slight smile upon his face as he tried to hide the pain. For a moment she could not breath, could not speak.

"You're not dead!" she shouted, stunned and relieved.

Duncan winced. "I told ye to no' to leave my side, lass," he managed through clenched teeth. Gowan had removed the arrow while Aishlinn had been clinging to her father and too overcome with grief at thinking Duncan was dead. "But ye just never listen to me."

She kissed him, every inch of his face she plastered with kisses as she held his face in her hands. "I'm sorry," she said between sobs and kisses. "I never meant for this to happen." She looked up to Gowan. "Will he live?" She couldn't bear the thought of losing him now.

Gowan nodded his head. "Aye, I ken so."

"But only if ye promise to never, ever leave in the night like that again," Duncan told her. "Or I promise I will die, on purpose, just to get even with ye!"

"Never," she told him. "I promise to listen to you always!" She smiled as she kissed him all over again.

Duncan sighed heavily. "I'm not sure I should be believin' ye," he said with a smile.

Aishlinn looked at him, heartbroken that he did not believe her, but really, could she blame him? If it took every day of the rest of her life to regain his trust, then so be it. "I swear it! I will always listen to you," she pleaded with him.

"Aye," came Angus' deep voice from behind them. "She'll listen to the words that leave yer mouth, lad." He smiled as he placed a hand upon Aishlinn's shoulder. "But that doesn't mean she'll mind them!"

Duncan reached out to pull her closer to him. When he touched her arm, Aishlinn winced from the cut. Duncan examined the torn tunic and saw the gash in her arm. "What the bloody hell happened to yer arm?" he demanded.

"One of the soldiers cut me with his sword," she told him.

Duncan was instantly incensed and tried to sit. "Where is the bastard?" he shouted.

"Layin' dead on top of the other two she killed," Angus said, motioning over his shoulder at a heap of fallen soldiers.

The men broke out in laughter. Duncan eyed his wife for a moment. She was a sorry mess, with her hair and clothes plastered in mud and blood. "What the bloody hell happened?" he asked.

Wee William spoke up. "Well, while ye were lyin' on the ground takin' a wee bit of a nap," he began, "yer wife took up arms and slayed at the least a dozen men." He crossed his arms over his chest and smiled proudly.

"Nay," said Black Richard. "'Twas at least ten and five."

"I counted twenty-one!" said Rowan. "Seen it with me own eyes!"

Duncan stared in disbelief at his wife. Aishlinn sank lower, bracing for the wrath she was certain would come forth from her husband at any moment. She tried to muster a sweet smile, but it came out looking more like she was bilious and in pain.

Angus let out an exasperated sigh. He rolled his eyes and looked down at Duncan. "They keep this up and before this day is out, they'll be swearin' she took on the entire regiment single handedly while we all stood shittin' our trews in fear!"

While the men argued over the number of soldiers Aishlinn had slain that day, Duncan reached up and touched Aishlinn's cheek. "Wife!" he said. "Will ye please take me home and nurse me back to health?"

Aishlinn nodded her head. "I'd be glad to, husband." She bent and kissed him full on the lips and when she was done, he smiled back at her deviously.

"I imagine I'll be needin' plenty of rest," he told her. "Bed rest."

"Aye, and that you'll get!" she told him firmly, not picking up his sly inference.

"I'll see to it that you're well cared for. You'll stay in bed a month if you need to."

Duncan smiled at her. "A month ye say?" he winced again as he tried to sit. Aishlinn pushed him gently back. "Stay put!" she scolded.

Duncan motioned for her to come closer. She bent low so that he could whisper in her ear. "Will ye be joinin' me in my bed rest, wife?"

Aishlinn began to protest that now was not the proper time to be thinking of such things. Duncan forced himself to sit. He pulled her to him and kissed her firmly on her mouth. When he let go, he saw that he had left a smile upon her face. "Lass?" he asked.

"Yes?" Aishlinn said, rather breathlessly.

"Haud yer wheesht and love me."

Epilogue

Three months later

"Are ye listenin' to me, wife?"

"Aye, husband. I hear you."

"But are ye listenin' to me words?" he asked. His wife had a habit of hearing the words he spoke, but not always heeding them.

Aishlinn sighed heavily. "Yes!" she told him.

"Yer no' peekin' are ye?" he asked as he glanced down at her.

"Duncan!" She was growing frustrated with him. "How on earth could I peek? You've got me blindfolded and my face stuck to your chest!" She could hear him chuckle wickedly.

"I think we might use this blindfold again," he whispered in her ear.

Aishlinn had learned over the last three months that her husband was quite inventive when it came to new ways of bringing pleasure to her in their marital bed. She was glad for the blindfold and her face being hidden, for he could not see the rush of red that came to her face.

Duncan kissed the top of her head as they rode down a path. She was perched atop his lap, her arms wrapped around his torso tightly. He had a surprise for her, hence the blindfold. Duncan could barely wait to see the expression on her face once the blindfold was removed.

When he pulled the horse to a stop, Aishlinn sat upright. She didn't think they'd ridden very far from the castle and wondered why they had stopped so quickly. Duncan dismounted while Aishlinn strained to listen for any familiar sound that might give a clue as to their surroundings.

"Come here, lass," Duncan said, reaching up for her. Aishlinn leaned over so that he could grab her waist and set her upon the ground. She realized then there wasn't a man on God's earth that she would have trusted to blindfold her. A thrill shot up her spine when his hands lingered for a moment at her waist.

Duncan took her hand and elbow and guided her only a few short steps before stopping. "Do no' move, wife," he told her as he walked away. "I mean it!"

Her anticipation grew but she would not allow herself to peek. She had made a promise that she intended to keep, no matter how long he might force her to stand there. Waiting. For heaven only knew what or how long!

She felt him standing beside her again. Suddenly, he tugged at the blindfold and the sun blinded her momentarily. When her eyes adjusted she saw that it wasn't Duncan who had removed it, but Wee William.

Duncan stood in front of a cottage with his arms spread wide. The sound of people yelling "Surprise!" erupted all around her. Her father and Isobel were there, as well as Bree and Mary. Black Richard stood near them, with Rowan, Manghus and Gowan and countless others.

Her heart pounded in her chest and her lips curved into a very surprised smile.

"Welcome home, Aishlinn," Duncan said as he bowed towards her.

"Home?" she asked.

"Aye," Duncan told her. "This is what I've been doin' with me days of late," he said, walking towards her, smiling brightly. "Building us a home."

She was dumbfounded. She had thought her husband had gone back to training with his men, a notion she had objected to quite vociferously. Aishlinn worried it had been too soon after taking the arrow to his shoulder and nearly dying from it. But he hadn't been training; he had been building them a home.

Tears came to her eyes when she stood before the stone cottage. Duncan scooped her up and carried her across the threshold. His smile never left his face as he sat her down and watched her closely while her eyes searched the room.

It was much bigger than the home she had grown up in. A massive fireplace stood to her right, a large kitchen to her left. A table, much too big she supposed for just the two of them took up a place not far from the kitchen. She caught sight of a heavy curtain covering a doorway next to the fireplace. A ladder led to a loft above it.

"Duncan!" she exclaimed. "It's beautiful!"

He grabbed her hand and led her through the curtain. "This'll be where we'll make all our wee bairns," he whispered to her as she looked about the room. A large bed stood against the wall while stands flanked each side of it. The fireplace stood directly opposite it. There were rugs upon the floor and tapestries on the wall. She recognized them from Duncan's room in the castle.

The house had quickly filled with family and friends, all wishing them good luck. Ale was poured and many toasts were made for them to be blessed with many bairns. Aishlinn could not quit smiling, for she was indeed truly happy. Blessed she was, to finally have a home of her own.

Aishlinn stood near the fireplace, hugging herself, watching the people around her having a grand time. It came to her then, as she looked about the home that Duncan had built for her, that nothing in this home was actually hers. Sadness threatened to creep in at thinking of it. She had nothing of her past, nothing of her mother's, nothing of her own here. She knew she should be happy, but she felt a tug of sadness in her stomach.

Angus and Wee William came to speak with her. "Do ye like the house, young Aishlinn?" Wee William asked smiling. "I helped Duncan ta build it!"

Aishlinn smiled up at the lumbering giant and noticed there was plenty of headroom for him. She imagined he would have to stoop over in order to fit into most cottages. "Aye, I do William!" She gave him a hug about his waist. "I notice we've quite tall ceilings."

"Made sure of it!" Wee William boasted. "I get such a crick in me neck when I visit others." He winked at her.

"And ye'll be noticin' also, the glass in the windows?" Angus asked. "I insisted upon it. Nothing too good for me daughter, ye know." He smiled as he accepted the hug from her.

"Thank you both, so very much," Aishlinn told them. She tried to keep the smile upon her face, but the melancholy in her heart threatened to dampen her spirits. She wanted not to seem an ungrateful person.

Angus picked up on her mood. "What be the matter, lass? Do ye no' like yer new home?" he scowled at her.

"Nay! I love it!" she assured him. "It is more beautiful than I could have imagined." She tried smiling again, but it wasn't working.

"What be the matter, lassie?" Wee William asked. "Is there somethin' ye be wishin' we did different?"

Aishlinn shook her head. "Nay," she told him. "It is quite silly really. Nothing at all for you to be concerned with." She rubbed her father's arm.

"I'll no' be believin' ye, daughter," Angus told her. "Now tell me, what be the matter?"

Knowing well that they would not give up until she confessed what bothered her, she sighed heavily. "When I look about the home, and it is a grand home," she said, pausing to take a deep breath, "there is nothing of mine here. Nothing of my mother's."

She waited to see if they would laugh at her silly notions. When they did not, she continued to explain. "I know I did not have much in the way of an upbringing. And it would be very nice to leave my past behind me. But I've nothing to remind me of my mother. I had to leave her things behind." It seemed a lifetime had passed since that fateful day.

"When my brothers told me I was leaving that day, I hid some of my mother's things in the barn. Up in the loft there was a spot I could hide things in. So I hid her candlesticks and her trinket box, thinking I could come back for them some day. I even hid the bowl she used to make her bread in." She wiped away a tear as Angus and Wee William looked at her. They didn't look at her with pity, just sadness.

"Lass," her father said. "It breaks me heart to see ye so sad. We'll replace those things for ye. I ken it won't be the same."

"Nay," she told him. "Duncan and I will fill this house with our things. I was just sad for a moment. I'll be fine and I don't want you worrying over it." She gave him a big hug as Isobel approached.

"How do ye like it, Aishlinn?" Isobel asked.

"'Tis beautiful!" Aishlinn answered. "I'm certain you helped with it, for I see books and art all about."

Isobel smiled. "Aye, I did. And I've something else I want to show ye." She took Aishlinn's hand and led her into the bedroom. As Aishlinn sat upon the bed, Isobel went to the trunk that sat at the foot of it. She pulled out a basket and sat it between the two of them.

"These are some of yer mother's things," Isobel told her as she opened the lid of the basket. "There isn't much mind ye, but a few things I saved after --" she stopped short and shook the memory from her mind.

Isobel removed a leather necklace with a small seashell fastened to it and carefully handed it to Aishlinn.

"Yer mother made this when she was a little girl. We had gone to the ocean to stay with some of her father's relatives for a time. She was eight, I think, when we were there."

Aishlinn felt her heart swell with joy. She was holding a piece of her mother's past in her hands. Tears welled in her eyes as she draped it around her neck.

Next, Isobel pulled some colorful threads from the basket. "These were some of her favorite colors to weave with," she said, laying the spools in Aishlinn's lap. Dark green, dark blue, crimson and goldenrod colored threads filled her lap. Aishlinn tenderly brushed her fingers across them, knowing these were things her mother had loved and had once held in her own hands. Aishlinn promised herself she would make something from them very soon.

Isobel gently removed a small blanket and handed it to Aishlinn. "This was yer mother's blanket when she was a bairn." Aishlinn noticed that Isobel's eyes were brimming with tears. She was glad for the gifts, but sad that Isobel's memories were so painful.

"Ye can wrap yer own bairns in it," Isobel said, wiping a tear away. "I think she would have liked that."

Aishlinn held the soft blanket to her face, breathing in the scent of heather and lavender. The small blanket soaked up the tears that fell from Aishlinn's eyes.

Not able to stand it any longer, the women embraced, hugging each other tightly as the tears came. Angus had been standing quietly in the doorway. He came to them and knelt on one knee hugging them both tightly.

"I hate it when lasses cry!" he said with a scowl. A tear came to his own eyes then, thinking of Laiden, of his daughter and of what had taken place over the years.

Isobel and Aishlinn laughed at him wiping away tears from each other's faces. "I haven't met a Highlander yet, who could stand the sight of a woman in tears," she told Aishlinn as she hugged her again.

Later that night, long after the guests had left, Duncan held Aishlinn close to him in their bed. She slept peacefully with her arm draped over his chest, her head nestled into his shoulder. He enjoyed the way her breath tickled his skin and how warm she felt next to him.

It had taken weeks for him to be able to sleep soundly without the fear that he would wake and find her gone. Tonight, he lay awake thinking about their future, the bairns he wanted to give her, the life he wanted her to have. He felt blessed, more blessed than he knew he deserved to be. His entire world was under this roof, in this bed, and he didn't think he could ever be happier than he was in this peaceful moment.

"Husband?" Aishlinn whispered sleepily, startling him slightly. "Why are you awake?" she asked, snuggling in even closer.

"Just thinkin', wife," he said as he gently caressed her bare arm.

"Thinking of what?" She yawned, hugging him gently.

Duncan let out a sigh. "How much I love ye. How blessed I am to have ye as me wife." He hugged her; his heart filled with more love than he felt a man ought to have for someone.

Aishlinn lifted her head and looked at him with sleepy eyes. A warm smile came to her face. "I love you as well." She kissed him tenderly, her lips barely touching his, but it was enough to bring desire to his belly. Damnation, he thought. All she had to do was cast him a glance, barely touch him, and he was filled with want and lust of her.

An urgent need, one he thought she had quenched for him just a few hours before, rose once again. Never in his life had he felt so starved or so needy. 'Twas as if the more she fed him, the more he needed. There'd been no other lover he had ever taken that had managed to make him feel this way. Nor had there ever been one to satisfy him with the intensity his wife managed to bring to him.

He rolled her over to her back, his hands desperate and needy, caressing every inch of her soft skin that he could reach. He could feel her desire for him rising with each rapid breath she took, as she tenderly caressed his back and arms, pulling him closer.

As he nuzzled her neck, he whispered in the dark to her. "I want to give ye many bairns, lass." Her neck was soft and smelled of lavender, the scent of her made him nearly delirious.

"You will," she said as she released soft moans of pleasure, pulling him on top of her. She loved the way he felt when he was joined with her, the sweet rhythm that would increase with his desire and need of her. His need to bring her pleasure only intensified the explosions that washed over her each time they joined. Knowing she brought him just as much satisfaction made it all the more wonderful and left her feeling quite proud that she could make him call out her name.

She had been keeping a secret from him for many days now, wanting to wait until the moment was right. As he made love to her now, speaking of the many bairns he so desperately wanted to give her, professing his love of her, she felt was it the perfect time.

"Come spring, the first should be here," she whispered in his ear as she pressed her fingers into his back.

Duncan stopped instantly and looked at her not certain he had heard her correctly. His mind whirled and he forgot for a moment that he was supposed to be making love to his wife. "Aishlinn?" he asked. "What did ye say?"

She smiled up at him. "I said come spring you'd be getting your wish. Our first bairn should be here then."

Stunned, he could only look at her. "Are ye certain?"

"Aye, I am certain." She kissed him, wanting very much for him to return his attentions to loving her.

Duncan doubted his heart could ever be filled with more joy than at that very moment. He was going to be a father come spring. Come spring, their cottage would be filled with the delight of a bairn, the love and laughter that he and his wife had so profoundly wanted to give to each other.

He stopped for a moment to look at the beautiful woman he had married. "Are ye certain 'tis all right to do this? I dunna want to bring you any discomfort."

"The only discomfort you'd bring me is if you stop now," she whispered in his ear as she pressed her fingers into his back, urging him to continue. "Now haud yer wheesht and love me."

Prologue to Findley's Lass

Findley's Lass
The Highlands, Spring of 1344

They were just children. Five boys, ranging in age from eight to ten and two, and not one of them had any sense of direction. But what they lacked in that regard, they certainly made up with fierce determination and tenacity. And rock throwing skills.

At first, Findley was certain the boys were nothing more than a ruse to keep suspicion away from some group of men, cowards more likely than not, who had actually stolen the thirty head of cattle. Who would hang a group of lads that young for stealing cattle? Let the lads take the blame, and mayhap a beating, instead of placing guilt where it should really lie.

But the more Findley, his younger brother, Richard, and their good friend, Gowan, interrogated the thieves, the more Findley believed their story: They had stolen the cattle, not only to feed their people, but also to prove to their mum they were indeed fine warriors. The only thing the lads would admit to was the fact that four of them were orphans who had been adopted by a fine woman named Maggy and that their clan had been wiped out by a pox years before. They refused to divulge much else.

Now Findley and his men were leading the boys and the cattle down the small hill toward their home. Findley shook his head, pitied with the sight before him. One hut made of mud with a thatch roof surrounded by a few tents -- all of which had seen much better days -- sat between a meandering river and a dense forest.

A small garden sat near the edge of the forest to the south of the home. Chickens pecked away at the dirt. Not far off stood a small, fenced area that apparently housed the three plow horses the reivers had managed to use in their theft of Angus McKenna's cattle.

Although the small farm was not nearly as grand as the castle that Findley and his men called home, it was still clean and tidy in appearance.

Several very auld women sat around a long trestle table, chatting away as they appeared to be mending clothing. The smile on the oldest looking woman -- if such a thing were possible as they were all rather ancient looking -- disappeared as she saw the men and boys approaching on horseback. Her wrinkled face, brown from years of exposure to the sun, looked more like a dried apple with tiny eyes attached to it. If looks were arrows, Findley and his men would have died instantly from the glare she shot at them. Within moments, the other women who sat with her, followed suit with glares of their own. Clearly Findley and his men were not welcome here.

The chickens squawked their contempt and displeasure as Findley and his men disturbed their late morning feast. They went scattering about as the group walked their horses through the yard. The boys sat tense and nervous on their mounts, casting each other looks of despair and dread. Findley supposed they were anxious about seeing their mum and owning up to their transgression.

As they drew nearer, one of the auld women left the table and disappeared inside the hut. Moments later the door flew open with a loud bang and the most beautiful auburn-haired lass Findley had ever seen came running out. His mouth suddenly felt quite dry and his heart thrummed rapidly for several long moments.

She stopped dead in her tracks at the sight before her. Three large Highlanders sat atop massive steeds and they had her boys. Her stomach tightened as her emotions bounced from relief at seeing her sons alive to anger that they'd left their home without a word to anyone.

The Highlanders alarmed her. Reflexively, she slowly dropped her hands to her sides to make certain her sgian dubh was still in her pocket. Her first inclination was to demand they let her boys go. If that didn't work, she was not above thrusting her knife into each man's heart.

She eyed Findley and his men suspiciously as she stood motionless some twenty feet away.

"I take it these reivers belong to ye, lass?" Richard asked as he dismounted. He flashed a smile that normally made young lasses giggle and twitter, for he was considered a very handsome man. His smile apparently had no such effect on the woman standing before them. Her face had turned to stone as she continued to stare.

The two youngest boys, each of whom had been riding with an older brother, slipped down from the horses. They went running toward her, happily crying out. "Mum!" as they flung themselves around her waist. She hugged them closely, never once taking her eyes off the men.

"Who are ye?" she asked, her voice catching slightly as she fought back her burgeoning fear. Strange men coming to her home was never a good thing.

"I be Findley McKenna," Findley said, finally finding his voice as he dismounted. "This be me brother, Richard," he said with a nod in Richard's direction. "And that be Gowan," he said with a nod toward his friend. Gowan smiled and bowed slightly at the waist before he, too, dismounted.

The three older boys quietly slid down and stood by their horses. "Mum," said the oldest before realizing he didn't quite know how to explain the chain of events that led to this moment.

"Robert," she said, still clinging to the smaller boys. "Ye are well?"

"Aye, we're well. They've done us no harm," he said, looking first at the men then down at his bare feet. He and his brothers stood side-by-side, hands shaking as they waited for the skelping to begin.

"Collin? Andrew? Does he speak the truth?"

The boys nodded and muttered "Aye."

She took a deep breath before speaking. "Come here," she told them.

Solemnly, as if their feet were encased in stone, the boys went and stood in front of her. She eyed each of them for a moment before opening her arms and pulling them to her. Tears began to stream down her face and she trembled as she held them. The boys' shoulders finally relaxed and they returned her embrace.

After a few moments, she let them loose and wiped the tears from her eyes with the backs of her hands. "I swear if ye ever do that to me again, I'll skin each of ye alive!" she seethed. "What on earth possessed ye to leave in the middle of the night like that?"

Each of the boys took a few steps away as she thrust her hands to her hips and glared at them. "Do ye have any idea the fright ye put me through?" her voice rose, angrier than she could ever remember being with them. "Do ye have any idea how we've all worried over ye? No' knowin' if ye be dead or hurt or kidnapped?"

She began pacing in front of them and the more she yelled, the more the boys' shoulders sagged. They kept their gaze firmly planted on the ground as their mother continued to chastise them.

"Of all the foolish things to do! And for what purpose? Where on earth have ye been and what have ye been doin'?" She aimed her last question at her oldest son, Robert.

He cleared his throat before answering. "We went to get a cow."

Maggy stared at him, quite baffled. "What?"

"We went to get us a cow."

Her brow furrowed into a deep crease. "A cow? And how did ye plan on buyin' a cow when ye've no' a coin to yer name?"

Robert started to speak but thought better of it.

"Speak the truth, Robert, do no' stroll around it," she said bluntly. "Ye went to *steal* a cow."

Robert stood upright, squared his shoulders and looked his mum straight in the eye. "Aye, we did."

Maggy eyed him for a moment, hands once again resting on her hips. "I've taught ye all better than that."

"Aye, ye have, mum. But --"

She wouldn't allow him to finish. "But? There be no *but*. Stealin' is wrong and ye ken it! There be no reason on God's earth to be stealin'!"

Robert found the courage then to speak his mind. "Aye, stealin' is wrong, but 'twas more wrong listenin' to me brothers' and me family's stomachs growl all the time from hunger! I could no longer stand to listen to it!"

"So ye took it upon yerself to go steal a cow?" she demanded. Aye, she understood well enough how he felt, for it angered and saddened her to no end to listen to the hungry stomachs of all those entrusted to her care. But that didn't mean she could allow her sons to steal.

Robert decided it would do him no good to continue to speak on the matter. His mum's mind was made up and there would be no explaining it to her.

Maggy looked at Findley. "If ye plan on hangin' me sons, I'd ask that ye hang me instead."

Her sons gasped and began to protest at her offer to take their places. Findley and his men however, threw their heads back and laughed. "Nay, lass, we do no' plan on hangin' *any* of ye!" Findley said after he got his laughter under some semblance of control.

Maggy was not amused. "Whatever ye plan on doin' to me sons, I ask that ye let me take their places. Whether it be a skelpin' or other form of punishment."

Findley shook his head, unable to to stop smiling at the beautiful young woman, before it finally occurred to him that she was quite serious. Apparently she had dealt with men less kind, less honorable than he. "Lass," he said as he walked toward her. "I'd never beat a child, or a woman, no matter what their transgressions might be."

He could tell from the fear that flashed in her eyes that she did not believe him. He also took note that she had slipped her hand into the pocket of her dress. "I'd have done the same, to feed me own family, if the circumstances were the same." He stopped just a few feet from her and crossed his arms over his chest with his feet spread apart.

One only had to look at the scrawny forms of the boys and the gaunt faces of the auld people around him to sum up the situation. This was a disparate group of poor people, thrown together under less than desirable circumstances. And the beautiful woman standing before him was doing her best to take care of them and teach the lads right from wrong.

"I ask that *ye* show yer lads a bit of compassion, lass, fer they were only trying to take care of their family, like good men do."

Maggy Boyle wasn't sure what to make of his impassioned speech. But there was something in those brown eyes of his that told her he meant what he said. There was something there, in that thoughtful smile of his, that held a promise, an assurance that she hadn't felt in a good number of years. Mayhap this man could be trusted.

Prologue to Wee William's Woman

Book Three of The Clan MacDougall Series

Late Winter 1345

Winter was unrelenting. It held on to the land as fiercely as a Highland warrior grasped his sword, refusing to let loose its grip and allow spring its turn.

The cold night air bit at the men who sat silently atop their steeds. Watching, waiting, looking for any movement, any sign of life that might stir in the cottage that lay below them. Gray smoke rising slowly from the chimney before disappearing into the moonlit night was the only sign of life coming from within the cottage.

Puffs of white mist blew from the horses' nostrils like steam from a boiling kettle. The nine were draped in heavy furs, broadswords strapped to their backs, swords at their sides, and daggers hidden in various places across their bodies. If by chance anyone was awake at this ungodly hour, the sight of these fierce men would bring a chill of fear to even the bravest man.

Each man had been handpicked by his chief for the special qualities he held, whether it was his fealty, his fierceness, or his ability to enter a place unheard and unseen. 'Twas a simple task they'd been given: sneak in under the cloak of darkness and retrieve hidden treasures so they could be returned to their rightful owner.

The first inkling that things might not go as planned came from the fact that the night was not bathed in darkness as had been hoped. A full moon shone brilliantly, casting the earth in shades of blues, whites, and grays. Had they not been delayed two days by a snowstorm of near biblical proportions, they would have arrived two nights ago when it was certain to have been pitch black.

No worries, the leader of the nine had assured his men. The inhabitants of the cottage were more likely than not fast asleep at this hour. They would proceed with their mission, moon or no.

After studying the land and the cottage a while longer, the leader gave a nod of his head. He and his men proceeded toward the little farm, taking their positions around the perimeter. Two of his stealthiest men headed towards the barn where they dismounted and with the grace and silence of a cat, they entered.

The leader stood with two of his men not far from the entrance of the cottage. They waited patiently, keeping a close eye on the barn as well as the cottage. Everything seemed to be going as planned. But the leader of the band of retrievers would not breathe a sigh of relief until they were far away from these God-forsaken English lands. The longer he remained on English soil, the dirtier he felt and the more anxious to return to his homeland he became.

He wished he could break down the door of the cottage and slit the throats of the three bastards inside. His chief had shot that idea down, but not before thinking on it for a long moment. The chief had admitted nothing would have brought him greater pleasure than knowing the bastards would not live to see the light of another day. But he could not allow his men to take the chance of being found and taken to the gallows.

Nay, their mission was simple and if all went well, no blood would be shed this night. In a matter of days, should the weather hold, the treasures would be returned and the men handsomely rewarded for their efforts.

Uneasiness began to creep under the leader's skin. The men in the barn were taking too long. Concern began to well in his belly. If the treasures weren't where they should be, he'd have no problem then in busting down the door to the cottage and killing the men inside. He shuddered when he thought of returning empty handed. 'Twas a possibility he did not enjoy. He swore under his breath he'd tear this farm apart until he found what he had come for.

God's teeth! What was taking them so long? He exchanged a look of concern with the two men who sat on horses beside him. Something was wrong. He could feel it in his bones.

After what seemed like hours, his men appeared from the barn and looked across the yard. They held up empty hands as they shrugged their shoulders. Damnation! This was not good, not good at all. He let out a heavy sigh and hung his head.

'Twasn't exactly how he had planned it, but at least now he had the opportunity to bash in the skulls of the three men inside the cottage. The idea of giving those sons of whores their due brought a pleasant tingling sensation to his belly. The night would not be wasted after all.

Prologue McKenna's Honor

Book Four of The Clan MacDougall Series

An old adage declares there is no honor among thieves. The same can be said of traitors. Traitors often hide in the open, in plain sight. The truth is there for people who choose to see it, for those who are determined to see things as they are and not as they wish them to be.

In reality, traitors are nothing more than pretenders. Master manipulators. Actors in a play in which only they know who is who and what is what.

The people around them are but an audience, often seeing only what they *wish* to see.

When a traitor performs, openly defending the weak, speaking only with highest regard for his king and country and displaying an unequaled façade of honor, well, who would question his fealty? The traitor reveals only what he *wishes* others to see and only what he knows they wish to believe.

All the while the traitor silently laughs at the folly he has created, taking great pleasure in the absurdity of the entire situation.

And if he is extremely careful the world will never know who or what he *truly* is.

However, as is often the case with thieves, traitors, and ne'er-do-wells, fate steps in at the most unexpected times. It rips away the heavy curtain of subterfuge and duplicity, to openly display to the world not what it wishes to see, but what it in fact *must* see.

Such inaugurations to the truth are often painful and traumatic, leaving the newly inaugurated feeling stunned, stupefied and bitter. For some, the only means of survival is outright denial. They shun the truth, cursing it, preferring instead to live in denial. Mayhap because they love the traitor so much, it is easy to justify the traitor's behavior. Or, they may not wish to believe they could have been so easily duped.

But as in all good plays, there are subtle twists and turns. Some are quite obvious, others, not so much. Mayhap the truth isn't always what it seems. Mayhap there is far more to it than anyone realizes.

What then, motivates a man? A man like Angus McKenna who has spent his life defending the defenseless, offering hope to the hopeless, lifting up the weak? Honorable. Honest. Steadfast. A leader of men. A man loyal to king and country. A man above reproach. This is the man Angus McKenna's people see, the man other leaders see, the man the world sees.

Ever since the day he took his oath as chief of the Clan MacDougall and made the promise to uphold and protect his clan above all other things, Angus McKenna put his family and his clan first. Each decision he made since that fateful day in 1331 was made with only one thought in mind: how will it affect his family and his clan?

Nothing mattered but the safety and wellbeing of his people. Not his own comfort, his own desires nor his own needs could be taken into consideration when making decisions that would directly affect his people.

What could have made Angus McKenna don a red and black plaid and turn against his king? His country? How could a man like Angus McKenna do such a thing? What could be of such a value that he would plot to murder his king and to forge a pact with the English? A pact that would cause the fall of his country and put it squarely into the hands of the very people he has spent his entire life fighting against.

Gold? Silver? Power? Something more?

Time and experience reveal that things are not always as they appear.

Prologue Rowan's Lady

Book One of The Clan Graham Series

Scotland 1350

The Black Death did not discriminate.

Like fire from hell, it spread across England, Wales, Italy and France. Untethered, unstoppable.

It cared not if the lives it took were of the noble and wealthy or the lowly born and poor. It showed no preference for age or gender. It took the wicked and the innocent. It took the blasphemers and the righteous.

The Black Death took whomever it damned well pleased.

It took Rowan Graham's wife.

Rowan would not allow his sweet wife to die alone, cold, afraid, and in agony, no matter how much she begged otherwise. He would not allow anyone else to administer the herbs, to apply the poultices, or to even wipe her brow. He was her husband and she, his entire world.

Knowing that the Black Death had finally reached Scotland, Rowan's clan had prepared as best they could. The moment anyone began to show signs of illness, they were immediately taken to the barracks. Seclusion was their only hope at keeping the illness from spreading.

Within a week, the barracks could hold no more of the sick and dying. In the end, the quarantine was all for naught.

By the time Kate showed the first signs of the illness, the Black Death had taken more than thirty of their people. Before it was over, Clan Graham's numbers dwindled to less than seventy members.

At Kate's insistence, their three-month-old daughter was kept in seclusion. It was the last act of motherly love that she could show her child. In the hours just before her death, Kate begged for Rowan's promise on two matters.

"Ye shall never be afraid to speak of me to our daughter. It is important that she know how much I loved her, and how much *we* loved her together." 'Twas an easy promise for Rowan to make, for how could he ever forget Kate?

'Twas the second promise she asked that threatened to tear him apart.

"And ye must promise ye'll let another woman into yer heart. Do not save it long fer me, husband. Yer too good a man to keep yerself to a dead woman."

He swore to her that yes, someday he would allow his heart to love another. Silently however, he knew that day would be in the very distant future, mayhap thirty or forty years. For there could never be a woman who could take Kate's place in his life or his heart.

"I love ye, Kate, more than me next breath," Rowan whispered into her ear just before her chest rose and fell for the last time.

Fires were built to burn the dead. When Rowan's first lieutenant came to remove Kate's body to add it to the funeral pyres, he refused to allow Frederick anywhere near her. Rowan's face turned purple with rage, his chest heaved from the weight of his unconstrained anguish. He unsheathed his sword and pinned Frederick to the wall.

"If ye so much as think of laying a finger to Kate, I shall take yer life," Rowan seethed. Frederick knew it was a promise Rowan meant to keep.

Later, with his vision blurred from tears he could not suppress, Rowan bathed his wife's once beautiful body now ravaged with large black boils. He washed her long, strawberry blonde locks and combed them until they glistened once again. When he was done, he placed a bit of Graham plaid into the palm of her hand before wrapping her cold body in long linen strips.

Alone in the quiet hours before dawn he carried Kate her to final resting place under the tall Wych Elm tree. He stayed next to her grave for three full days.

Frederick finally came to see him late in the afternoon of the third day.

"I ken yer grievin', fer Kate was a fine woman." Frederick said. "Ye've a wee bairn that needs ye, Rowan. She needs ye now, more than Kate does."

Rowan was resting against the elm tree, with his head resting on his knees. In his heart he knew Frederick was right, but that did nothing the help fill the dark void that Kate's death left in his heart.

For a brief moment, Rowan could have sworn he heard his wife's voice agreeing with Frederick. Deciding it best not to argue the point with either of them, Rowan took a deep breath and pulled himself to his feet.

For now, he would focus on the first promise he had made to Kate.

"Ye be right, Frederick," Rowan said as he slapped one hand on his friend's back while wiping away tears with the other. "I need to go tell me daughter all about her beautiful mum."

Suzan lives in the Midwest with her verra handsome husband and the last of their four children. They are currently seeking monetary donations to help feed their 16 year old, 6' 3" built-like-a-linebacker son.

When she isn't working, taking care of her family or spoiling her grandchildren, she writes. Some say it borders on the obsessive. Suzan prefers to think of it as passion.

"There is great joy in writing, but an even greater joy in sharing what you've written."

Suzan Tisdale

Books by Suzan Tisdale

In the Clan MacDougall Series:

Laiden's Daughter

Findley's Lass

Wee William's Woman

McKenna's Honor

In the Clan Graham Series

Rowan's Lady

Frederick's Queen (June 2014)

Email: suzan@suzantisdale.com

Website: www.suzantisdale.com